THE GREGOR DEMARKIAN HOLIDAY SERIES
BY JANE HADDAM

Not a Creature Was Stirring
(*Christmas*)

Precious Blood
(*Easter*)

Quoth the Raven
(*Halloween*)

A Great Day for the Deadly
(*St. Patrick's Day*)

Feast of Murder
(*Thanksgiving*)

A Stillness in Bethlehem
(*Christmas*)

Murder Superior
(*Mother's Day*)

Dear Old Dead
(*Father's Day*)

Festival of Deaths
(*Hanukkah*)

Bleeding Hearts
(*Valentine's Day*)

Fountain of Death
(*New Year's*)

And One to Die On
(*Birthday*)

Baptism in Blood
(*Baptism*)

# Deadly Beloved

## Jane Haddam

BANTAM BOOKS

NEW YORK   TORONTO   LONDON   SYDNEY   AUCKLAND

This edition contains the complete text
of the original hardcover edition.
NOT ONE WORD HAS BEEN OMITTED.

DEADLY BELOVED
A Bantam Book
PUBLISHING HISTORY

Bantam hardcover edition published September 1997
Bantam paperback edition/July 1998

ISBN: 0-553-57200-8
*Published simultaneously in the United States and Canada*

Bantam Books are published by Bantam Books, a division of Bantam Doubleday Dell
Publishing Group, Inc. Its trademark, consisting of the words "Bantam Books" and
the portrayal of a rooster, is Registered in U.S. Patent and Trademark Office
and in other countries. Marca Registrada. Bantam Books, 1540 Broadway, New York,
New York 10036.

PRINTED IN THE UNITED STATES OF AMERICA
OPM   10   9   8   7   6   5   4   3   2   1

*Deadly Beloved*

# PROLOGUE

## *Walking Down the Aisle to the Funeral March*

### 1.

THERE WAS A FOG IN Fox Run Hill that morning, a thick roll of gray and black floating just an inch above the ground, like the mad scientist's dream mist in some ancient horror movie. Patsy MacLaren Willis moved through it much too quickly. There were stones on the driveway that she couldn't see. There were ruts in the gutters where she didn't expect them. It was just on the edge of dawn and still very cold, in spite of its being almost summer. Patsy felt foolish and uncomfortable in her short-sleeved, thin silk blouse. Foolish and uncomfortable, she thought, dumping a load of clothes on hangers into the rear of the dull black Volvo station wagon she had parked halfway down the drive. That was the way Patsy had always felt in Fox Run Hill all the time she had lived there, more than twenty years. It was as if God had touched His finger to her forehead one morning and said, "No matter what you do with your life, you will always be out of step, out of touch, out of place."

The clothes on hangers were her own: navy blue linen dresses from Ann Taylor with round necklines and no collars; Liz Claiborne dress pants with pleats across the front or panels under the waists; Donna Karan wrap skirts with matching cropped jackets. The clothes went with the Volvo in some odd way Patsy couldn't define. The clothes and the Volvo went with the house too—a mock-Tudor seven thousand square feet big, set on a lot of exactly one and three-quarter acres. Fox Run Hill, Patsy thought irritably, looking up at all the other houses facing her winding street. An elegant Victorian reproduction. A massive French Provincial with a curlicue roof and stone quoins. A redbrick Federalist with too many windows. The only thing she couldn't see from here was the fence that surrounded it all, that made Fox Run Hill what it really was. The fence was made of wrought iron and topped with electrified barbed wire. It was supposed to keep them safe. It was also supposed to remain invisible. Years ago— when the fence had just been put up, and the first foundations for the first houses had just been dug on the little circle of lots near the front gate—someone had planted a thick stand of evergreen trees along the line the fence made against the outside world. Now those trees were thick with needles and very tall, blocking out all concrete evidence of the existence of real life.

Patsy checked through the clothes again—dresses, slacks, blouses, skirts, underwear of pink satin in lightly scented bags—and then walked back up the drive and into the garage. She poked against the pins in her salt-and-pepper hair and felt fat wet strands fall against her neck. She shifted the waistband of her skirt against her skin and ended up feeling lumpy and grotesque. Three days before, she had celebrated her forty-eighth birthday with a small dinner party at the Fox Run Hill Country Club. Her husband, Stephen Willis, had reserved the window corner for her. She had been able to look out over the waterfall while she cut her cake. She had been able to look out over the candles at the people she had been closest to in this place. It should have been the perfect moment, the culmination of something important and valuable, the recognition of an achievement and a promise. Instead, the night had been ugly and flat and full of tension, like every other night Patsy could remember—but it was a tension only she had recognized. If she had tried to tell the others about it, they wouldn't have known what she meant.

Nobody here has ever known what I meant, Patsy thought as she came up out of the garage into the mudroom. She kicked off her sandals and left them lying, tumbled together, under the built-in bench along the south wall. She padded across the fieldstone floor in her bare feet and went up the wooden stairs into the kitchen. The house was cavernous. It should have had a dozen children in it, and a dozen servants too. Instead, there was just Stephen and herself, having their dinners on trays in front of the masonry fireplace in the thirty-by-thirty-foot family room, making love in a tangle of sheets in a master bedroom so outsized, the bed in it had had to be custom-made, and all the linens had to be special-ordered from Bloomingdale's. Patsy stopped at one of the two kitchen sinks and got herself a glass of water. Her throat felt scratchy and hard, as if she had just eaten razor blades. I hate this house, she thought. Anybody would hate this house. It was not only too large. It was fake. Even the portraits of ancestors that lined the paneled wall in the gallery were fake. Stephen had bought them at an auction at Sotheby's, the left-over pieces of somebody else's unremembered life.

"I paid only a thousand for the lot," he'd told Patsy when he'd brought them home from New York. "They're just what we've always needed in this place."

Patsy put her used glass into the sink. That was the difference between them, of course. Stephen *did* like the house. He liked everything about it, just the way he liked everything about Fox Run Hill, and the country club, and his job at Dela-cord & Tweed in Philadelphia. Last month he had bought himself a bright red Ferrari Testarosa. This month he had been talking about taking a vacation in the Caribbean, of renting an entire villa on Montego Bay and keeping it for the three long months of the summer.

"The problem with us is that we've never really learned to enjoy our money," he'd said. "We've never understood that there was more that we could do with it than use it to invest in bonds."

Patsy had fished the lemon slice out of the bottom of the glass of Scotch on the rocks she'd just drunk and made an encouraging noise. The family room had a cathedral ceiling and thick, useless beams that had been machine-cut to look as if they had been hand-hewn, then dyed a dark brown to make them look old. Stephen's voice bounced against all the wood and stone and empty spaces.

"Now that I won't be traveling anymore, it'll be better," he had told her, "you'll see. I know that you've been terribly lonely, dumped in this house with nobody to talk to for weeks at a time. I know that you haven't been happy here."

Now the water-spotted glass sat in the sink, looking all wrong. Everything else in the kitchen was clean to the point of being antiseptic. The sinks were all stainless steel and highly polished, as if porcelain had too much of the roadside diner attached to it, too much of the socially marginal and the economically low rent.

"Damn," Patsy said out loud. She walked through glass doors that separated the kitchen and the family room from the foyer and started up the front stairs. The stairs made a circular sweep up a curved bulge in the wall that was lined with curved leaded windows looking out on the drive and the front walk. Outside, the Volvo looked dowdy and dumpy and square—just like Patsy imagined she looked dowdy and dumpy and square everywhere in Fox Run Hill, next to all those women who worked so hard on treadmills and Nautilus machines, who came to parties and ate only crudités and drank only Perrier water. The clock at the top of the stairs said that it was 6:26. Patsy stopped next to it, at the linen closet, and rummaged through the stacks of Porthault sheets until she found the gun.

Patsy turned the gun over in her hands. It was a Smith & Wesson Model 657 41 Magnum with an 8-3/4-inch stainless steel barrel, muzzled by a professional silencer that looked like a blackened can of insect repellent. She had bought it quite openly at a gun shop in central Philadelphia, with no questions asked, in spite of the fact that it was a heavy gun that most women would not want to use and illegal to buy in Pennsylvania.

Most women probably couldn't even lift it, Patsy thought, walking down the carpeted hall. The only real sounds in the house were Stephen's snoring, and the whir of the central air-conditioning, pumping away even in the cold of the morning, set so low that crystals of ice sometimes formed on the edges of the grates.

In the bedroom, Stephen was lying on his back under a pile of quilts and blankets, his mostly bald head lolling off the side of a thick goose-down pillow, a single naked shoulder exposed to the air. When Patsy had first met him, he'd had thick hair all over his body. In the years of their marriage, he seemed to have shed.

Patsy spread her legs apart and raised the gun in both hands. She had fired it only twice before, but she knew how difficult it was. When the bullet exploded in the chamber, the gun kicked back and made her shoulder hurt. She wished she'd thought to wear a set of ear protectors like the ones they'd given her when she went out to practice at the range. Then she remembered the silencer and felt immensely and irredeemably stupid. Could anyone as naive and ignorant as she really do something like this? Why didn't she just turn around and go downstairs and get into the car? Why didn't she just drive through the front gates and keep on going, driving and driving until she came to a place where she could smell the sea?

Stephen's body moved on the bed. He coughed in his sleep, his throat thick with mucus. He was nothing and no-body, Patsy thought, a cog in the machine, an instrument. He was the one who had wanted to live locked up like this, so that he could pretend they were safe. If I don't do something soon, he'll wake up, Patsy thought.

She tried to remember the color of his eyes and couldn't do it. She tried to remember the shape of his hands and couldn't do that either. She had been married to this man for twenty-two years and he had made no impression on her at all.

"I know how unhappy you've been," he had told her—but of course he didn't know, he couldn't know, he would never have the faintest idea.

Stephen shifted in the bed again. A little more of him disappeared under the covers. Patsy aimed a little to the left of the shoulder she could see and took a deep breath and fired. Stephen made a sound like wind and jerked against the quilts. Blankets fell away from him. Patsy changed her aim and fired twice again. He seemed to be dead, as dead as anyone could get, but she couldn't really tell. There were three black holes in the skin near his left nipple but no blood. Then she saw the red, spreading in a thick wash on the sheet underneath the body. The longer she looked at it, the more it seemed to darken, first into maroon, then into black. She let the gun drop and brought her legs together. She suddenly thought that it was so odd—even in this, even in the act of murdering her husband, the first thing a woman had to do was spread her legs.

Patsy walked over to the night table on Stephen's side of the bed and put the gun down on it. The air was full of the smell of cordite and something worse, something foul and rotted and hot. Patsy made herself kneel down at the side of the bed and look Stephen in the face. His eyes were open, deep brown eyes with no intelligence left in them. She grabbed him by the hair and turned his head back and forth. It moved where she wanted it to, flaccid and heavy, unresisting. She let his head drop. His eyes are brown, she told herself, as if that really mattered. Then she walked out of the suite and into the hall, closing the single open bedroom door behind her.

The house was still too large, too empty, too hollow, too

dead. Now it felt as if it no longer belonged to her. Patsy walked down the hall to the front stairs and down the front stairs to the foyer. She went through the foyer to the kitchen and through the kitchen to the mudroom. She walked into the garage and then carefully closed the mudroom door behind her. The Volvo was still packed and waiting on the gravel. The fog was still rolling in puffs just above the ground. No one would come looking for Stephen at all today. Anyone who came looking for her would assume that she had gone into the city to shop.

Patsy got into the Volvo and started the engine. Molly Bracken, who lived in the elegant Victorian, came out onto her front porch, looking for the morning paper. Patsy tooted her horn lightly and waved, making just enough fuss for Molly to look her way. Molly waved too, and Patsy began to drive around the gravel circle and head for the road.

The sun was coming up now, forcing its way through the clouds, eating at the fog. It was going to be a perfect bright day, hot and liquid. There were going to be dozens of people down at the Fox Run Hill Country Club, hanging around the pool. The city was going to be full of teenagers in halter tops and shorts cut high up on their thighs.

I am going to disappear, Patsy told herself, smiling a little, humming the ragged melody of something by Bob Dylan under her breath. I am going to disappear into thin air, and it's going to be as if I'd never been.

## 2.

Evelyn Adder hid her food all over the house, in the attic and the basement as well as on the two main floors, in underwear drawers and empty boxes of Tide detergent and behind the paperback romance novels on the bottom shelf in the alcove off the library, in all the places her husband Henry would never think to look for it. It was Henry who had bought the refrigerator with the lock on it that now took up the west corner of the enormous main floor kitchen that had once been the thing Evelyn liked best about the brick Federalist. The locked refrigerator had all the real food in it—the meat and the butter, the bagels and the cream cheese, the Italian bread and the pieces of leftover lasagna and the slices of Miss Grimble's Chocolate Cheesecake Henry liked to eat with his coffee after dinner. The other refrigerator, big as it was, held only those things Henry thought Evelyn should eat, and only in those amounts he thought suitable for a single day. Every morning Henry would get up and decorate Evelyn's refrigerator with grapefruits sliced in half and lettuce and cucumber salads tossed with balsamic vinegar. Then he would sit down at the kitchen table and explain, patiently, why it was they were doing things this way. Henry had been a college professor when Evelyn first met him. He had, in fact, been Evelyn's own college professor, at Bryn Mawr, in medieval literature. It was only after they were married that he had written the book called *How to Take It Off, Keep It Off, and Never Make Excuses Again*. It was the book that had made him rich enough to buy this house in Fox Run Hill.

"How do you think it looks," he would ask her as he arranged grapefruit halves on plates. "What do you think people think it means, that the most successful diet book author in America has a fat wife?"

In the beginning, of course, it had been Evelyn who was thin and Henry who was fat—although Evelyn's thinness had never been entirely natural. Like most of the other girls she was close to at Bryn Mawr, she tended to binge and purge, except they hadn't called it that then. That was in the days before anybody knew about "eating disorders." Evelyn and her friends would get up in the middle of the night and eat five or six gallons of ice cream apiece. They would shove down whole large pepperoni pizzas and three or four pounds of potato chips and thick chocolate cookies from Hazel's in

Philadelphia by the bag. Then they would rush into the girls' bathrooms, stick their fingers down their throats, and throw it all up. Evelyn got so good at it, she didn't even have to stick her finger down her throat. She could throw up just by thinking about it. She didn't think of herself as "disordered" either. If anything, she imagined she was being "classical," like those Romans her Introduction to Western Civilization professor was always telling them about, the ones who ate and ate at banquets until they were sick, then went out into the courtyard and vomited so that they could start all over again. Evelyn would sit in Main Line restaurants and order only salad, no dressing. She would sit upright over the salad and pick at lettuce leaves and sprigs of parsley. Sometimes on outings like this she was so hungry her stomach felt full of ground glass. She would sit across the damask tablecloths and the matched china, watching Henry eating piece after piece of batter-fried shrimp loaded with tartar sauce, and want to rip his throat out with her teeth.

"You're a real inspiration to me," Henry had said at the time. "I never knew anybody who had so much self-control before."

The food Evelyn kept around the house these days was no more real food than the grapefruit halves and lettuce salads. It was mostly what she could shoplift when she and Henry went to the grocery store together. Henry wouldn't let her go to the grocery store on her own anymore. He had even taken away her car so that she couldn't get there when he wasn't looking. Evelyn had to sneak things into the voluminous pockets of her linen tent dresses or shove them into the hollow between her breasts made by her well-constructed bra. Sometimes she picked up a twelve-pack of Hostess cupcakes in the dessert aisle, took it into the ladies' room at the back of the store, and ate the whole thing, right there. Sometimes, when it was cold enough to wear her good long coat, she could push pastry and candy bars through the slit she had made in the lining and come home with a major haul. One way or the other, she got what she wanted. The brick Federalist was full of food. There were Devil Dogs and Ring-Dings under the winter quilts in the linen closet. There were big bags of Cheez Doodles and smaller ones of pizza-flavored Combos in the decorative curved wood Shaker baskets that made a display in the study. There were Slim Jims and packages of Chips Ahoy cookies in the hollow base of the Indian brass lamp in the formal living room. Evelyn Adder weighed three hundred and eighty-five pounds at five foot five—and there was still not a moment in her life when she was not hungry, hungry hungry hungry, so hungry she felt as if she were being sucked inside out.

"I don't understand how you got this way," Evelyn's mother would say, visiting from Altoona. "Nobody in our family ever got this way."

Evelyn kept chocolate-covered marshmallow pinwheels and long thick sticks of pepperoni and big hunks of blue cheese under the winter jackets in the window seat on the half-landing at the front of the house. Sitting there, she could hear Henry as soon as he started to move around in the master bedroom at the top of the stairs. She could also see out onto Winding Brook Road. She saw Patsy MacLaren Willis pack her Volvo full of clothes and get into it and leave. She saw Molly Bracken come off her porch and go down her walk and get the morning paper from the end of her drive. Evelyn sat there for hours, thinking about all the other women on this street, thinking about herself. Between six o'clock and quarter to eight she finished six and a half pounds of pepperoni, three and a half pounds of blue cheese, and thirty-four chocolate-covered marshmallow pinwheels. She also came to this conclusion: Nice little working-class girls from Altoona should not go to Bryn Mawr, or marry their medieval literature professors, or move into places like Fox Run Hill. They would only end up afraid of their own houses, and so hungry they would never get enough, and so frantic they would never be able to think straight. Like her, they would sit around wondering how long it would be before their husbands decided to hire good lawyers and get themselves divorced.

It was now five minutes to eight. Evelyn had stopped eating ten minutes earlier, when she had heard Henry get out of bed and go to the shower. She had put away all the packages and dusted crumbs off the polished oak of the window seat. Now she heard Henry get out of the shower and pad across the wall-to-wall carpeting to the dressing room. She got up and started to make her way downstairs, slowly and painfully. All movement was painful for her these days. Her feet hurt so much when she stood up on them, she wanted to cry. They had become big too, so large and wide she had trouble finding shoes to fit them. She had started buying expensive men's athletic shoes made of black leather and decorated with brightly dyed stripes meant to look like lightning.

"Your feet will get smaller when you lose the weight," Henry would tell her. "They won't hurt so much either. Believe me. I know."

When Evelyn had first met Henry, he had been massive, impressive, beautiful. Now, thinner, he seemed diminished to her. His mouth was always pinched tight. His flesh hung slackly against his bones no matter how much he exercised. When she saw him with the other men on the stone terrace of the country club, drinking gin and tonic, hefting tennis rackets, Henry was always the one who looked fake, phony, totally out of place.

"Marriage is a crapshoot," Evelyn's mother always said, and: "You have to take men the way you find them."

I would be happy to take Henry the way I found him, Evelyn told herself. I just don't want him the way he is now.

There was a professional doctor's scale in one corner of the breakfast nook. Henry had put it there to check Evelyn's progress every morning. He had also locked up the coffee and the tea and the Perrier water, so that she couldn't drink them before he got up and blame any weight gain on fluid in her system. He made her take off her shoes and stockings and dress and stand in the nook in her underwear, her big breasts spilling down over the rounded swell of her belly, her thighs lumpy and veined and mottled blue and red with fat and age.

"Look at you," he would say as she stood there, a breeze coming through one of the open skylights, feeling cold, feeling stupid, feeling as ugly as she had always known she was inside. "Look at you."

Upstairs in the bedroom there were mirrors now, all along one wall, so that she couldn't escape looking at herself. If she tried to close her eyes, she fell. If she fell, she had a hard time getting up. Henry would have to get up himself and help her. Then the questions would start. What are you doing up and dressed this early in the morning? Where are you going? Where are you hiding the food?

"Look at you," he would say, spinning her around so that she was forced to face the mirrors. He would grab at the front of her dress and tear. The dress would pull away from her body and hang off her shoulders in tatters. In the mirror a grotesque fat woman with bulging eyes and pussy red pimples along the line of her jaw would stare back at her, hateful and angry, as hateful and angry as Henry had gotten to be.

"Look at you," he would say, and one day, provoked beyond endurance, finding a trail of crumbs wound along one of her massive breasts, he had torn at her bra too. He had torn it right off, snapping the elastic painfully on her back, dragging the spike of one bra hook into her flesh until she bled. Her breasts bounced up and down and side to side, and that hurt too. Her nipples and the area around them were as thick and dark and dry as leather. There was a mountain of crumbs in her bra, between her breasts. It popped into fragments as soon as her breasts came free and scattered over the white wall-to-wall carpeting like ashes blown into town from a distant forest fire.

"Look at you," Henry had screamed loud enough so that Evelyn was suddenly glad of all that central air-conditioning, all those sound buffers placed on all the properties, all those illusions of space and grace. Her breasts were shaking, hurting, bouncing. They were so big now that she even wore a bra to bed. Henry's face was so red, she thought he was having a heart attack. His eyes seemed to be coming out of his head. The knuckles on both of his hands were white. Suddenly he reached out and snatched at her underwear. He grabbed the elastic waistband in his fists and pulled with all his might. The elastic tore and the nylon tore after it. A second later Henry had shreds of underwear in his hands and Evelyn was standing naked. The only thing Evelyn remembered after that was that her pubic hair seemed to have disappeared. It was hidden by the curtains of flesh that had draped themselves around her, hanging like an apron from her waist.

*Look at you,* Evelyn thought now, listening to the sound of Henry's footsteps on the staircase. A second later he was in the kitchen, dressed in white chinos and a bright red polo shirt and deck shoes, his hands in his pockets, his hair combed to make maximum use of the fact that it was every bit as thick now as it had been when he was twenty. I really hate this man's face, Evelyn thought as she waited for him. I hate it so much, I would like to boil it off with acid. Then she was just glad that she hadn't been sitting down when he came into the room. More and more lately, she didn't quite fit on a single chair. More and more, Henry tended to notice it.

"Well, Evelyn," he said, sitting down in one of the breakfast nook chairs, "are we going to find any surprises on the scale today?"

Evelyn suddenly thought of Patsy MacLaren Willis, out in her driveway with all those clothes. There had never been a divorce in Fox Run Hill as far as Evelyn knew. It was the kind of place men moved with their second wives. Still, she thought, there was a first time for everything.

## 3.

Molly Bracken would have been divorced years ago if her husband Joey had had anything to say about it, except for the fact that Molly was the one who happened to have all the money. It wasn't serious money, the way money is judged serious in a place like New York—not enough to go into real estate deals with Donald Trump or to try a hostile takeover of IBM. It wasn't old money the way Philadelphia liked old money either. Neither Molly nor her family knew of any ancestors who had come over to America on the *Mayflower*. One of Molly's grandfathers had been a shoemaker and the other had worked in the steel mills in Bethlehem until he'd had an early heart attack at the age of thirty-six. Molly's money came from her father, who was that horror of horrors to progressive people everywhere, a commercial contractor. He had put up tracts of houses in every town on the Main Line and finally he had put up this tract of houses, Fox Run Hill. The elegant Victorian had been Molly's wedding present from him, complete with four round turrets and a wraparound porch big enough to hold a high school graduation on. There was even a tower room in one of the turrets, reached by a hidden staircase, with leaded stained glass in the curved windows. Everything about this house was perfect, exactly the way Molly had imagined it would be, back when she was still in grade school and cutting fantasies out of bridal magazines. These days, Molly had heard, girls weren't allowed to do that kind of thing. They had to be serious about their schoolwork and ambitious for careers. They had to want to be doctors and lawyers and Indian chiefs instead of chatelaines. Molly sometimes wondered what happened to those girls. She was forty-eight years old, and all the women she knew who were doctors and lawyers and Indian chiefs were both drab and divorced, as if the two things went together. They were drab because their clothes always seemed to hang wrong and they never wore enough makeup. They were divorced, Molly thought, because they could never just relax and talk about the weather. They had to discuss stocks and bonds, or the Clinton health care plan, or their feelings.

Molly's feelings ran mostly to self-satisfaction. In the kitchen of the elegant Victorian, in the circle of light cast by the sunroom windows, she finished reading the women's page of the *Philadelphia Inquirer* and put her head up to listen for sounds of Joey getting ready for work. It was ten minutes to nine, but that didn't matter much. Joey worked in the customer service department of a bank on the edge of Philadelphia. He wasn't usually expected in until nine-thirty. Molly smoothed the paper out under her fingers and then reached for the coffee pitcher on the trivet in the middle of the table. On the whole, it was shaping up to be a very good day. The weather was going to be bright and hot, Molly's favorite kind. The newspaper had been full of the kind of news she loved best, what with Princess Di having a new lover and Cher rumored to be hidden away in a plastic surgery clinic somewhere. Even the book section had been a blessing, because the book reviewed there was a novel by Judith Krantz, whom Molly not only read and liked, but understood. Sometimes the book review section caused her trouble because, unlike most of the other women at Fox Run Hill, Molly had never been to college. If the book of the day was something philosophical or historical, Molly would be forced to sit quietly all through lunch at the club, just so she wouldn't say anything stupid that would make them laugh at her.

Molly heard the door of the master bedroom suite opening and closing. She nodded to herself with unconscious satisfaction and patted at her hair. Her hair was the same bright blond it had been when she was in high school. She used the same home dye product now that she had used then. What she was really proud of was her figure, which was still a size six. Part of that was diet. Part of that was exercise. Part of that was abortions. Molly had had her first abortion at fifteen, illegally, at a terrible place in New York that Joey had known about from the cousin of a friend of his. She'd had her latest at a polished steel and bright-tiled clinic in Philadelphia, just two and a half weeks ago. She had had eight abortions in all, and if she had to, she would have eight more. Children could ruin your life. Her mother had told her so. Besides, she could see it, all around her, the way children ate up their parents and never gave anything back. Fathers made out all right. They escaped to their offices and their poker games. Mothers were devoured whole and spit back dead. Molly didn't think she had ever hated anyone as much as she hated her mother.

The French doors to the kitchen swung back and Joey came in, his face looking only half shaved, his neck looking too red where the barber had cut his hair too close to the skin. The face and the neck didn't go with the suit. Razors and haircuts were things Joey was required to buy for himself. He always bought the cheapest kinds available. The suit was something Molly had bought for him. It was a good summer wool, custom-made at Brooks Brothers, and it looked much too good for someone who worked in the customer service department of a bank. When Molly was being critical, she had to admit that Joey *never* looked as if he worked in the customer service department of a bank, or any other department of a bank, and not because he looked too good for it. Joey had been the town hood when Molly first met him, and in some ways he still was. No matter how many times he got his hair cut short, it still wanted to form a ducktail at the nape of his neck. No matter how many times he put on good suits and wing tip shoes, he still walked with the hip-jutting swagger he had learned in tight jeans and shitkicker boots. Molly sometimes thought of that, of the way they were together when they first met, and always surprised herself. She could even remember being happy, in an abstract way that had nothing to do with her emotions. The only emotion she could feel, looking back, was an anger so hot and wild it threatened to drown her. It took in everything: the motorcycles and the cars and the sex and the taste of warm Pabst

Blue Ribbon stolen out of somebody's mother's pantry; the abortion in New York with its mingled scents of sweet anesthetic and sour gin; her wedding with its six bridesmaids in shell-pink gowns; this house; this furniture; these dishes; this silverware; this latest abortion; this life. Anger, Molly always thought, was a traitor and a trick. It could ruin your life faster than children could.

Joey sat down at the table and folded his hands in front of him, like a child waiting for class to begin in a Catholic school. Joey had never gone to Catholic school, although Molly had. Her father had given the biggest contributions to the Parents' Education Drive every year, and Molly had been chosen to play Mary in the Christmas pageant two years in a row. Joey was four years older than Molly was, and his face was lined and pitted, ragged and slack. Some wild boys grow up to be wilder men. They harden and plane down. Their faces take on an individuality wrongly supposed to belong only to the American West. Joey was the other kind. He would have run to fat already if Molly had let him. Even with all the working out she forced him to do, Joey had a pronounced pot on his belly and jowls hanging off the curve of his jaw. He was white and pasty too, as if he never got any sun—as if he never spent his Saturdays on the terrace at the club, dressed in golf shorts and a sun visor, talking to all the other men about sports.

Molly pulled the paper toward her again and folded it one more time. It was now too tightly squashed together.

"Well," she said.

"Well." Joey cleared his throat. Then he rubbed his hands together. His hands were fat and white, just like his belly. Molly had a sudden vision of him as a gigantic jellyfish, slick and slimy, curled up on her bed like a piece of animated ooze. She looked away.

"Well," she said again. "There's a dinner tonight. At the club. A planning committee dinner."

"A planning committee for what?"

"A planning committee for a benefit thing. It's Sarah Lockwood's committee. I told you about it."

"Sarah Lockwood," Joey said.

Molly got out of her chair and went to the sunroom's wall of windows, to look out on the pool in the backyard. Sarah and Kevin Lockwood lived in the French Provincial with the curlicue roof. They were the people in Fox Run Hill whom Joey liked least. He disliked them, in fact, for all the reasons Molly wanted to know them. Before her marriage, Sarah Lockwood had been an Allensbar, a real live member of real live Philadelphia Main Line Very Old Money family. Sarah had come out at the Philadelphia Assemblies and had her picture in the paper with a crowd of other girls, all wearing white dresses and carrying red roses. Kevin Lockwood was the president of his own brokerage firm in Philadelphia, one so small and exclusive, it didn't even advertise. There were rumors all over Fox Run Hill that at least one of his clients was a former United States president, and that another was a member of the English royal house.

"I don't want to go to dinner with Sarah Lockwood," Joey said. "She makes me uncomfortable. She talks down to me."

Molly didn't turn around. "It's only for a couple of hours. And all the other husbands will be there."

"All the other husbands are shits. I don't know why it matters so much to you to hang around with shits."

"Everybody we've met since we've moved here is a shit as far as you're concerned," Molly said. "We couldn't have gone on hanging out with bikers forever."

"We should have had children," Joey told her. "That's what would have made a difference. We should have had some kids you could worry about so you could stop worrying about *them*."

"It isn't my fault we couldn't have children, Joey."

"It isn't my *fault* either. Jesus Christ. I mean, I did the best I could at the time. I did what you asked me."

"I asked you to find me someone safe."

"I found you someone safe. As safe as it got. It was 1962."

"Other people got pregnant in 1962."

"Other people died in 1962, from what I hear," Joey said.

Molly bit her lip. "That was God's judgment," she said primly, her teeth clamped together. "This is God's judgment. We committed a murder and now we're being punished."

Molly heard rather than saw Joey stand up. The legs of the chair squeaked against the tile when he moved. Molly made a hot wet mist on the glass of the window in front of her and traced a curving line through it with her finger.

"I know we committed a murder," Joey said. "You've convinced me we committed a murder. That doesn't mean I have to go to dinner with Sarah Lockwood."

"It's at eight o'clock," Molly told him. "In the Crystal Room at the club."

"The Crystal Room."

"It's just a table, Joey. It's not the whole room. It's just us and the Lockwoods and three other couples."

"And all the women are on this benefit committee."

"That's right."

"Shit."

The chair scraped again. Joey was putting it back under the table. Molly took a deep breath and turned around. The tears were so thick in her eyes, she could barely see. The muscles in her arms were so tense, they felt like wire.

Joey was standing near the French doors, on his way out.

"I'll be back at six," he said.

"You're always back at six," Molly told him.

"I'll go to this damn dinner with you as long as you don't expect me to talk to anybody."

"Maybe if you talked to the people here, you'd learn something," Molly said.

"Maybe if I learned something, I wouldn't talk to the people here. Maybe if I learned something, I wouldn't be married to you."

"Maybe if you learned something, I wouldn't make you stay married to me," Molly said.

Joey hesitated one more second at the doors. Then he turned away from her and walked off. He lumbered like an animal past the domed niches and the long columns of plaster cherubs playing among bunches of plaster grapes. The front door opened and shut again. Molly heard the heavy metallic click of the safety lock snapping home. Joey always left and came in by the front door. It was as if coming in through the garage door would say something about him that he didn't want to hear.

Molly went back to the table and picked up her coffee cup. She brought the cup to the sink and washed it out and put it in the white plastic-coated-wire dish rack. Then she dried her hands off on a dish towel and went through the French doors herself, through the foyer, into the living room.

Now that Joey was gone, she was back to normal. She wasn't angry. She wasn't tense. She didn't feel ready to laugh or cry or kick something. She was just thinking about dinner tonight and Sarah Lockwood and what it would be like to know a debutante. She twirled around a little in front of the fireplace, imagining what she would have looked like in a long white dress, holding a single perfect red rose.

On the coffee table in front of the love seat, there was a stack of antiabortion pamphlets. When Molly saw them, she stopped twirling and picked them up and smiled. Joey got worried sometimes when she talked about abortion. He knew only about the one in New York—he thought that abortion had messed up her insides, making her barren—and he thought she was turning into one of those fanatics, the kind who shot abortion doctors or torched clinics or sat out all night on the Mall in Washington, holding a sign with a black-and-white photograph of a bloody fetus tacked across it.

Molly knew that she was much more likely to torch this house than any abortion clinic. She thought about it often, burning small square pieces of paper in crystal ashtrays, watching the paper blacken and curl, watching the flame twist and rise.

"At least this way you'll be settled," her father had told her all those years ago when she was locked in the bathroom of the Fox Run Hill Country Club on the morning of her wedding, refusing to come out. "It doesn't matter who you're married to as long as you're in control of the situation. It doesn't matter what your husband is if you're the one who has the money."

I should have been smarter about it, she thought now. I should have stayed in that bathroom and reduced my wedding dress to rags. I should have refused to go through with it.

It was a strange thing though, Molly thought. Men—both strong men like her father and weak ones like her husband—always made her feel the same thing. They made her feel that she couldn't ever, ever, ever say no.

## 4.

By nine forty-five that morning, Sarah Lockwood had counted up the numbers seven times, and each time she had come to the same small set of conclusions. In the first place, the debt they owed on credit cards now totaled $115,646.28. In the second place, the monthly bills for those credit cards came to $3550. If she added that to the mortgage on the house ($4500 a month) and the payment on the car ($580 a month) and the utilities ($640 a month) and the association fee for Fox Run Hill ($900 a month), their monthly payments came to $10,170—and that didn't include food or club dues or eating out or any of the other things Sarah considered essential. It didn't include new clothes or gas for the car. It didn't include printing for Kevin's résumés or postage for sending them out. It was the kind of debt that made people disappear into the night and take assumed names in distant states. Sarah imagined them blowing into town in some two-bit burg just outside Cleveland, getting jobs at the local diner, renting a mobile home on the edge of a swamp. Sarah had absolutely

no idea how people lived when they didn't have money. Just
the little things took her breath away. Cooking every night,
no matter how tired you were or how much you wanted Chinese food or how sick you felt with the flu. Waiting three
years to buy a new living room couch, even though the old
one was fraying. Driving used cars. Sarah kept thinking of
Matilda, who had maided for them until they could no longer
pay her. Matilda had come every morning in sprigged-print
dresses so thin they seemed to wear out as you looked at
them. She had walked in thick-soled black leather shoes that
always seemed to have holes in the toes. She had put her hair
up in gold bobby pins that shone in the sun and came apart
whenever she bent over to pick something up from the floor.
There was something else Sarah's calculations hadn't ac-
counted for: twice-weekly visits to the hair salon and the
dues at the Fox Run Hill Health Club. If you didn't take good
care of yourself, things happened to you. Your hair got gray.
Your face got creased with lines. Your body got thick and
lumpy. You got old.

Out in the kitchen, Kevin was washing dishes. Sarah could
hear the clink-clink of glassware going into the wire rack.
Ever since Kevin had lost his job, he had been crazy about
doing the dishes. He hated seeing dirty dishes sitting in the
sink. Sarah couldn't count the number of glasses he had broken already, throwing things around out there. Lalique crystal. Steuben. Royal Doulton bone china. Sarah could still see
herself, going from store to store in downtown Philadelphia,
pulling out her gold MasterCard and her gold Visa card and
all the rest of them. For a few years there she had been very
well known to the people who ran the better jewelry stores
and glassware specialty shops in Philadelphia. She had imagined herself to be the kind of woman she had imagined her
great-grandmother to be. Known everywhere. Exacting in
her standards. Meticulous about detail. A real grande dame of
the real Main Line.

Actually, Sarah thought now, she knew exactly how people

lived when they didn't have any money. She had grown up in a family without any money—just that big house in Bryn Mawr with the portraits on the walls; just the yearly invitation to the Philadelphia Assemblies and the obligatory listing in the Philadelphia *Blue Book*. In the end, they'd had a listing in the *Social Register* too. When you don't have two dimes to rub together, you can't afford to be a snob—although, God only knew, people on the Main Line were snobs about the *Social Register*. Sarah remembered nights sitting at the long table in the formal dining room in her father's house, eating bread and gravy off all that Royal Doulton, because the food money had been spent on horseback-riding lessons for herself and her sister. She remembered sitting in the dark on the second floor in the middle of a heavy snowfall, wishing she had enough light to read—because the money that should have gone to pay the electric bill had gone instead to pay her subscription fees to Philadelphia's most prestigious junior dance. She was only eleven years old that year and she had already figured out what was important. She understood that nothing else mattered as long as you were able to live richly among rich people.

Now she was fifty—*fifty*—and she no longer lived richly among rich people. She lived here, where people had just enough to feel important but not enough to really understand what kind of mess she was in. People from Fox Run Hill saw her at the country club or the health club, a tall woman with ash-blond hair and a deep tan and the kind of body Anglo-Saxons get when they do too much exercise—and they made instant evaluations. Sarah Lockwood the debutante. Sarah Lockwood the Main Line Society lady. If I were a Main Line Society lady, Sarah thought, I would be living on the Main Line and moving in Society. Instead, I am living here, moving among nobodies, a failure. Any minute now I am going to be an even bigger failure. I am going to be a bankrupt.

Kevin was still clinking glasses in the dish rack. Sarah got up and moved through the family room to the kitchen, past the miniature date palm trees in their clay planters, past the Braque etching in its plain blond wood frame, past the broken little statue of Aphrodite on a seashell they had bought that time they took their vacation in Greece. She might be in debt, Sarah thought, but at least she was in debt with good taste. She knew what to buy and how to make it work for her.

Kevin was standing directly in front of the sink, holding up a blue crystal sugar bowl as if he had never seen it before. Like her, he was tall and tan and blondish, overexercised and thin. Like her, he was very, very tense. The difference was that Kevin had always been tense. Sarah could remember the first time she saw him, standing in a navy blue blazer that didn't quite fit, at the samovar end of a long buffet table set up on the lawn of her friend Margaret Delacord's house. He had been brought home from Dartmouth by one of Margaret's brothers and then dressed up for this occasion. She should have married one of the boys from her own circle. She should have married one of the boys whose bank account she knew better than his golf scores. That was what all the bread-and-gravy dinners and lightless winter nights had been about. Old name with no money married much money with new name. A Philadelphia Main Line tradition.

But she really *couldn't* have married anybody else. It didn't matter what Kevin's background was, or what his bank account had been on the day she met him, or what his prospects for employment were now. From the moment she had first seen him, Sarah had felt him as a part of her. Blood and skin and bone, muscle and nerve: Going to bed with Kevin Lockwood was a form of narcissism, an implosion as well as an explosion. Sarah thought of it as reaching a state of perfection, an essence of Sarah, like one of Plato's ideas. Even after all this time she was always on fire for him. She would come awake at four o'clock in the morning and peel back the covers so that she could look unrestrained at the curve of his arm, the knobbed column of his spine. Even now, with her head full of figures and an ache full of fear beginning to grow like a puffball at the back of her head, what she really wanted to do was to run her fingers over all the hair on his body, even the hair that was so carefully hidden between his legs.

Kevin saw her come in and put the blue crystal sugar bowl in the dish rack. He put the plaid terry-cloth dish towel down on the counter next to the sink. The muscles in his shoulders were still powerful, although he was slighter than he had been when Sarah first met him. His eyes were harder too, deep blue and cold.

"Well?" he said.

Sarah shrugged. "I've been over it and over it. It always comes down to the same thing."

"You're sure." It was not a question.

"I don't see how we could ever be sure," Sarah said carefully. "Why don't we just say 'likely.' Nothing else seems 'likely' at the moment. Nothing else seems possible."

"We couldn't borrow any more money."

"Nobody would lend it to us."

"We couldn't hold out a few more months to see if I got another job."

"We've held out for eighteen months as it is. If we don't do something soon, I'm going to have to start missing payments. And you know what that will mean."

"This will be quick enough so that we don't have to miss payments?"

"We have about three weeks. We could do a lot in three weeks."

Kevin nodded. "But we don't just want to make payments," he said. "That wouldn't do us any good. We want to clear out that credit card debt."

"I know."

Sarah put her palms flat on the kitchen counter and pulled herself up until she was sitting on it. She had on a bright white golf skirt and a red short-sleeve jersey polo. She had on no underwear at all. The kitchen was dark and cool and shadowy.

"Jesus," Kevin said.

Sarah kicked off her espadrilles. "We can start tonight at the dinner," she told him. "I can talk to the women and you can talk to the men."

"Some of them may have heard I got fired." Kevin put his hand on Sarah's knee.

"None of them will have heard that you got fired. They don't use words like 'fired' in the circles you move in. They say things like 'left to pursue other interests.' "

"It comes to the same thing." Kevin inched his hand higher, to the flat side of her thigh, sinewy and hard.

"None of them will know it comes to the same thing," Sarah told him. She was beginning to feel what she wanted to feel. She was dizzy as hell. "None of them will know anything. You can tell them anything you want to tell them. All you have to do is tell them what they want to hear."

"That I have a deal for them."

"That we're going to invite them here," Sarah corrected him. "That we're going to give a party and they're going to be allowed to come."

"And you really think that's going to be enough."

Sarah inched forward on the counter and into Kevin's hands. In her mind she could see Molly Bracken's face over the broccoli at the Food Emporium, eyes getting wider and wider, smile getting more and more eager. Even the dark roots of her hair had seemed to pulse, as if an electric generator had gone off inside her head, as if at any minute she would start to glow.

"Yes," Sarah said now. "It will be enough. It will be enough for the women, and they'll make it enough for the men."

"You can be a sexist little bitch," Kevin said.

Sarah twisted herself against him. Her clothes had begun to feel too tight, too hot. Everything was too hot. They had made love for the first time on the first day they had ever met, that day at Margaret Delacord's parents' lawn party— and that was thirty years ago, for God's sake. People didn't do things like that then. People didn't steal magnums of champagne from the open bars at post-deb receptions and get drunk on the floor of four-car garages in a thick envelope of summer heat. People didn't forge weekend permission slips and sneak away from college dormitories to spend night after night in cut-rate motels, making the sheets burn with sweat and cigarette ashes. People didn't stop planning and scheming and hoping and studying just to give themselves over to the moment. At least, people like Sarah didn't.

"Sarah?" Kevin said now.

Sarah got her hand under his shirt and stroked the hair on his chest. She pulled at his shirt buttons until they came undone.

"I love it that you stopped wearing undershirts," she told him.

"Everybody stopped wearing undershirts," he shot back.

The next thing she knew, he had lifted her up off the counter and put her down on the floor. She could feel the cool smoothness of ceramic tiles against her back. Her red jersey polo was gone and she couldn't remember it coming off. The air conditioner was turned up high and she was freezing. She felt pliant and stiff at once, like folded meringue.

"Jesus Christ," Kevin said. "Are we really going to get away with this?"

"Yes," Sarah told him.

Then she pulled off her skirt by herself and threw it over her head.

## 5.

By the time Patsy MacLaren had finished her errands and arrived in West Philadelphia, it was noon. The back of the Volvo was now loaded with packages wrapped in plain brown paper. Patsy's thin silk blouse was damp with sweat across the shoulder blades. Out on the street, people were moving slowly. College students were walking around with their shirts unbuttoned and their blue jeans cut off high on the legs. She was only a few blocks from the University of Pennsylvania. This was not Philadelphia's best neighborhood. She would have gone somewhere else if she had had a choice, but she hadn't. She circled one block and then the next. She found a high-rise parking garage and turned into its entry lane. The man in the little glass booth was half asleep. Patsy had to honk the horn to get his attention.

The man in the little glass booth was used to people just driving through. All you had to do coming in was take a ticket. It was going out you had to talk to somebody about, so that you knew what you owed and you could pay. Patsy waited patiently while the man readjusted himself, shifted from one foot to the other, slid back the little glass window, leaned out. Then she said, "Do I have to get a special ticket for all day? Or do I just settle that when I come out?"

The man in the little glass booth blinked. He was old—so old, Patsy wondered if he was suffering from Alzheimer's disease. She leaned closer to the driver's side door so that he would be sure to see her. She stuck her head out the window so that she could be sure he would hear.

"For an all-day ticket—" she said again.

"You can't have an all-day ticket," the man interrupted her. "It's already noon. You won't have been here all day."

There was a certain logic in this. Patsy counted to ten in her head. "Is that a rule?" she asked him. "To get an all-day ticket you have to come in in the morning?"

"It's not a rule," the man said. "It's just common sense."

"But if it's not a rule, I could buy an all-day ticket now," Patsy pointed out. "There wouldn't be any reason not to."

"Sure there would be a reason not to," the man said. "It wouldn't make any sense."

Patsy tapped the windshield with her fingernail, meaning to point to the sign that hung from the rafters just a little way ahead. "It would be cheaper," she pointed out. "If I'm going to stay here for at least six hours, and I am, it would be cheaper to buy an all-day ticket."

"That doesn't sound right," the man said.

"It is right though," Patsy told him. "It's a dollar fifty an hour, for six hours that's nine dollars. But it's only seven dollars for an all-day ticket. So you see, if I buy an all-day ticket I save—"

"Two dollars," the man said.

"Right," Patsy said.

The man leaned back against the far side of the booth and scratched his ear. He was really an awful man, Patsy thought, filthy and tired. He had deep streaks of black under his fingernails and smudges on his skin everywhere Patsy could see it. The hair on his arms was matted and slick. She could just imagine him sleeping between the garbage cans in the alley out back every night when his work was finished. She had no idea at all how people were chosen to do this kind of work.

He came back to her side of the booth and leaned out the little window again. "All right," he said. "I can sell you an all-day ticket."

"Fine," Patsy told him.

"The thing is, you have to pay for an all-day ticket in advance. The whole seven dollars right this minute."

"No problem at all." Patsy unzipped the top of her thick black Coach bag and pulled out her wallet. It was a Coach wallet too. Stephen had always liked Coach. Patsy took out a five and two ones and handed them over. "Here you are," she said.

The man took the seven dollars and put it in his gray tin lock box. Then he shuffled around among his papers for a moment while he found a stiff piece of oaktag that Patsy presumed was the all-day ticket. He stamped it with a hand stamp and gave it to her.

"There it is," he said.

It was stamped PAID. Patsy put it in the visor over her head.

"Thank you," she told him.

"I guess that's how people get to be rich people like you," the man said. "Playing all the angles."

"Thank you," Patsy said again.

The black-and-white-striped electric arm popped up in front of her car. Patsy got into gear and stepped on the gas and went forward. She bumped over a metal plate on the floor and felt the whole car shudder.

She had to go up to the third level before she found a parking place. People were always talking about how Philadelphia was dying, but you couldn't prove it by the number of parking spaces available on a typical weekday afternoon. Patsy pulled in between a white Toyota Celica and a greenish-blue Saturn and got out. She locked up very carefully and went around to the back of the Volvo. The packages looked like nothing but brown wrapping paper. The clothes were hidden completely. Patsy tried the back door, found it locked too, and left it.

To get out, she had to go down an elevator in a well that let her off right next to the booth with the dirty old man in it. He didn't notice her come through. Patsy went out onto the street and looked around. It was still hot and the people still looked tired. She walked half a block north and turned the corner. On this street there were stores and banks and newsstands. It looked a little more alive than the street with the parking garage on it had. It was still terminal, Patsy thought. Sometimes Philadelphia looked to her as if it were slowly being drained of people.

Patsy walked two more blocks and then stopped at a kiosk for a copy of the paper. It was a copy of today's *Philadelphia Inquirer*, which she had already seen, but she didn't care. She paid with a ten-dollar bill and waited patiently while the woman in the booth made change. She tucked the paper under her arm and walked away. There were more and more people on the street. She was getting closer and closer to the university.

The bank was just a block away from the administration building at Penn. Patsy could raise her head and see the start of the attenuated quads the university called a campus. She had met Stephen on one of those quads. He had been hunched up on a stone bench, studying an accounting textbook.

Patsy went into the bank and stopped at the long counter set aside for making out forms and writing checks. She took out her checkbook and wrote a check for $15,000. Then she turned around and looked at the tellers standing at their windows. The bank was relatively busy at this hour, mostly with young people who looked like students. There was a line at two of the three windows. At the third, a heavyset man in a tan linen suit, rumpled and sweaty, was trying to deposit what looked like thousands of penny rolls. Patsy got into line behind a young man with a backpack.

"Deposit," the young man said when he got to the window, after the girl in front of him, willowy and nervous, had finished her business and wandered off.

Patsy waited patiently. The teller did official-looking things with a computer and a print-out machine. The young man took his deposit slip and wandered off himself. Down at the third booth, the heavyset man was still counting out penny rolls. He had what looked like two more large brown paper grocery bags of them sitting at his feet.

"What can I do for you?" the teller asked Patsy. She was cute and perky and barely eighteen years old. She made Patsy feel faintly nauseated.

Even at eighteen I wasn't that young, Patsy thought. She pushed the check across the counter along with her driver's license and passport. The teller picked it up and went white.

"Oh," she said. "Oh. Well. I don't think I can cash this."

"Of course you can cash it," Patsy said patiently. "There's more than enough money in the account."

"Oh," the teller said again. She was looking very frightened

now, as if Patsy had done something crazy and might do something crazier at any moment, as if she expected to see a gun
pulled out of Patsy's black Coach bag. She tapped at her computer and stared at the screen. She said "oh" one more time
and then, "well, yes, I see."

"I would like as much of it as possible in one-hundred-
dollar bills, please," Patsy said. "I have only this bag to carry
it in."

"Just a minute," the teller said.

The lines at the other windows had begun to get longer.
The heavyset man was taking up all of one of the tellers'
time, and now Patsy was taking up time too. Only the teller
in the middle was doing business as usual. People had begun
to shift and cough and mutter. Patsy's teller had gone around
to the back of the bank to talk to a middle-aged woman at a
desk. That must be the bank manager, Patsy thought, and
went on waiting patiently. After all, she had all the time in the
world.

Patsy's teller left the bank manager at her desk and came
back to her window. "I can't cash a check this large on my
own," she said primly. "You'll have to talk to Mrs. Havoric."

"I have to talk to Mrs. Havoric just to get my own money
out of my own checking account?"

"It's for your own protection," the teller said sourly. She
pushed Patsy's check and driver's license and passport across
the counter. "It's to protect you against possible fraud."

"I do have two pieces of identification," Patsy said gently.

The teller looked past Patsy's right shoulder. "Could I help
somebody, please?" she asked in a larger voice.

Patsy stepped out of line. Mrs. Havoric was standing at the
side of her desk, doing her best to look concerned but mostly
looking nervous. She was a stout woman with thick legs and
gray hair and a suit jacket buttoned all the way up the front,
like a blouse. It was a cheap suit that wrinkled easily and
didn't fit right. Patsy walked over to the desk and handed
over her check and her identification.

"I believe I'm supposed to get these authorized by you," she said. Then she took the chair in front of Mrs. Havoric's desk, pulled it back a little, and sat down. Mrs. Havoric did not look happy.

"Well," she said. "Well. You must understand. This is very unusual."

"People taking money out of their checking accounts is unusual?"

"People taking this much money out of their checking accounts is unusual, yes. Fifteen thousand dollars is a lot of money."

"It's mine."

"Yes. Yes. Well. Your identification does seem to be in order."

"Then I would like this money in hundred-dollar bills, if I could have it," Patsy said. "I really don't want too bulky a package to carry around in the city."

"It's very dangerous to carry cash like that in the city in any kind of package."

"I understand that."

"Do you mind if I ask what it is you want so much money for?"

"Yes," Patsy said. "As a matter of fact, I do mind."

Mrs. Havoric looked nonplussed. "Miss MacLaren. You must realize—"

"Ms.," Patsy said.

"Excuse me?" Mrs. Havoric said.

"Ms.," Patsy repeated. "I'm married now. To a man named Stephen Willis. So I'm not Miss MacLaren. I'm Ms."

"Oh," Mrs. Havoric said.

"I suppose I could get my attorneys to force you to give me my money," Patsy said, "but I don't really see why I should have to do that, since legally you're required to give it to me whenever I want it. This is a demand account."

"I know this is a demand account," Mrs. Havoric said sharply. "I just want to make sure you're not taking this money out to buy an oil well, and then next week you come back here and try to sue us for not trying to stop you."

"I won't come back here next week and try to sue you. Word of honor. There is no oil well."

"What if you walk out the door and get mugged?"

"I don't think I'd have to worry about that if this was done discreetly," Patsy said, "which, quite frankly, up to now it hasn't been. Could I have my money in hundred-dollar bills?"

Mrs. Havoric tapped the top of her desk. She looked more than put out now. She looked angry. She was studying Patsy's face with such concentration, Patsy thought she was trying to memorize it.

"All right," she said finally. "Just a minute please. I'll take care of it myself."

Patsy pushed the Coach bag across the desk. "Put it in here," she said. "That way, nobody has to see me with it."

"Don't you want to count it?"

"I'll count it in a stall in the ladies' room. If you have a ladies' room."

Mrs. Havoric squared her shoulders. "I can make a ladies' room available to you," she said. Then she walked away, strutting a little, like the high school English teacher nobody wanted to have for study hall monitor. Patsy watched her pull the teller away from her window and hold up a whole line of people waiting to do simple transactions.

This, Patsy thought, was what women's lib had gotten them all. These days, the Mrs. Havorics of the world were bank managers instead of high school English teachers and it didn't matter anyway. They still weren't making much money and they still weren't happy. That was what marriage did to you, no matter what anybody said about it. It split you and gutted you and stuffed you full of lemongrass. It made you all bitter.

Mrs. Havoric was coming back across the bank with Patsy's Coach bag in her hands, and Patsy suddenly remembered.

She wasn't married anymore.

She wasn't married anymore.

She had given herself a summary divorce this morning, and now she was free.

## 6.

Karla Parrish almost never thought of herself as a successful woman. "Success," in her mind, meant having a big apartment on a high floor in New York City or a BMW and a Porsche in the driveway of a house in Syosset or a lot of jewelry to wear to parties that had to be locked up in a safe afterward, for insurance reasons. Success, in other words, meant having a lot of things, and Karla had never had much in the way of things. Enough underwear to get through two weeks straight without doing laundry, as much in the way of other clothes as could be stuffed into a double strap pack without making her feel like she was lifting stones when she picked it up—Karla never seemed to need that much from day to day, and she honestly couldn't think of what else she would buy for herself if she got the chance. She wore her long straight hair pulled back these days, instead of falling free to her shoulders, because she thought she had to make some concession to being forty-eight. She didn't want to spend the time or the money to get it fixed up in beauty parlors. Her hips were beginning to spread a little now that she was racing through middle age. She was content to buy her jeans a couple of sizes larger and let it happen. Spending hundreds of dollars on a dress that would disguise the weight gain seemed so stupid, she had no idea why anyone ever did it. The one thing she did spend money on was her equipment—the cameras and the lenses and the tripods and the lights—but that was different. That was work. Karla Parrish understood absolutely why it was important to spend time and money on her work.

What she didn't understand was the attitude of this man behind the registration desk at the George-V. She didn't even understand what she was doing at the George-V. "Book us a hotel room in Paris," she had told Evan when they were about to leave Nairobi—and then she had forgotten all about it, because she was tired and dirty and depressed, and the way things were going she wasn't going to feel any better for weeks. She had just spent four weeks taking pictures in Rwanda, and her head hurt. Her film cases were full of images she didn't want to see again. Every time she came to rest in a hotel room or a restaurant, she got phone calls from New York. She wanted to go someplace where she didn't have to listen to anybody talking at her, but she didn't know where that would be. Home, something in her head kept pounding at her, and that was when it had hit her. Karla Parrish was almost fifty years old and she didn't have a home. She had a pied-à-terre in Manhattan with a lot of second-hand furniture in it. She had her camera equipment and the clothes in her pack and some books she'd picked up in the airport in London on her way out to Africa. She had this succession of hotel rooms that looked as if it was never going to end: Nairobi to Cairo to Lhasa to Athens to Tokyo to God-knows-where. Some of the hotels had electricity twenty-four hours a day. Some of them had electricity only some of the time. All of them had dust and bugs and heat in spite of their air-conditioning systems and their cheaper-than-cheap maid service.

The George-V had a lobby that looked like a stage set for a movie about France during the time of Marie Antoinette. The carpet was so plush, Karla felt as if she were swimming in it. The chandeliers were so large and densely packed with crystals, they sounded like factories full of glassware breaking every time there was a slight breeze. Karla saw a woman in a chinchilla coat down to her ankles and another woman walking five overgroomed dogs on silver lamé leashes. Karla could feel the dust in her pores, caked and hardening. Her hair felt so dirty, she wanted to cut it off instead of get it washed.

The man behind the registration desk was beaming and

bouncing in her direction. He came around the counter to where she was standing and took her hand, talking all the time in a rapid-fire French Karla hadn't a hope in hell of understanding. Karla wouldn't have understood if he'd spoken in slow French. She had never paid much attention to her language classes.

Karla let the man take her hand and bow while she smiled back. Then she turned to Evan at her side and raised her eyebrows. Evan was her new assistant, hired less than ten months ago in a fit of craving for organization. This time, Karla had told herself, she was not going to go off for a year in the hinterlands and let her life unravel in the process. She was going to have somebody who would keep track of the bills and the receipts and the travel arrangements and let her keep her mind on her photography. She had put an ad in the Vassar College alumnae magazine, expecting to get a young woman with an itch for travel—and ended up with Evan instead. Vassar was coed these days. It kept slipping Karla's mind.

Evan was tall and thin and wore wire-rimmed glasses, the way all the preppie boys did these days. He was also very smart and very eager and close to fluent in French.

"Evan," Karla whispered, leaning back so that he could hear her. "What is going on here?"

Evan rubbed his soft hands together and blinked. "Monsieur Gaudet is welcoming the famous Karla Parrish to Paris."

"The *famous* Karla Parrish?"

Evan reached into his shoulder bag and pulled out a magazine. His shoulder bag was an expensive piece from Mark Cross, given to him by his mother when he got this job with Karla. Evan's mother was an oncologist in Grosse Pointe.

The magazine Evan handed to Karla was a copy of *Paris-Match*. The cover photo was a black-and-white of a refugee camp in Zaire. Karla checked it out critically and decided that she had blurred the print a little in the bottom left-hand corner. She hated developing on the road. She never got the effects she wanted unless she had days to work at them.

"They put my photograph on the cover," she said. "That's good."

"Page twelve," Evan said.

Karla opened to page twelve. There was a photograph of her there—a terrible photograph, she thought, taken at the worst possible moment in an airport somewhere, with her hair coming out of its pins and her eyes drooping. She looked down the column of print and found her name in bold-faced type halfway to the bottom of the page. This seemed to be some kind of gossip column. She handed the magazine back to Evan.

"I don't get it," she said.

Evan put the magazine back in his shoulder bag. "You could be bigger than Annie Liebowitz," he said solemnly, "if you paid a little more attention to your image."

"I don't think Annie Liebowitz pays attention to her image."

"Annie Liebowitz lived with the Rolling Stones for a year. You live with refugees in central Africa. It's a different situation."

"It's *my* situation."

The man from behind the desk had summoned a bellhop. The bellhop took Karla's backpack out of her hands with all the seriousness he would have brought to the luggage of the Pope. Karla felt like an idiot.

"It's a question of knowing what to do and where to do it," Evan said judiciously. "I got you in every gossip column in France practically, and I set up an interview with a man from *People* magazine. He'll be here the day after tomorrow. And after that you're going back to the United States for a month."

"Am I really? Evan, for Christ's sake. You can't just re-arrange my life that way."

"You don't have anything else to do for the next six weeks," Evan pointed out. "You were the one who said you wanted to be calm for a while."

"I was thinking of taking a vacation in the south of Spain. I always take my vacations in the south of Spain."

"From what I can figure out looking through your records, you haven't taken a vacation in twelve years. I got you a three-day visiting-artist thing at the University of Pennsylvania. Two lectures. Three seminars. One dinner." Evan pawed through his shoulder bag and came up with a folded piece of paper. He handed it over to her and said, "I tried for Yale and I tried for Brown, but they're going to have to wait. You're going to have to let me work on your reputation for a while."

"My reputation is the best in the business," Karla said automatically, but she was looking over the letter from the University of Pennsylvania, half mesmerized by the engraved college seal at the top of the page. "Ambitious," like "successful," was not a word she would have applied to herself. It evoked images of blue-suited armies marching out the door of the Harvard Business School, each of the women wearing two-and-a-half-inch stack-heeled pumps. What else was this, though, if not ambition? She could see herself, standing at the front of a classroom full of teenagers, talking about a slide she had projected high up on a classroom wall. She felt Evan's eyes on her and looked up to find him staring. She blushed hot red and handed the letter back.

"You'll like doing it," Evan said. "You'll see. You'll be a natural at this kind of thing."

"I expect to like doing it," Karla said truthfully.

"And I thought Philadelphia would be a good place." Evan was going on as if he hadn't heard her. "I thought you said you had friends there once, women you knew at college—"

"Julianne Corbett and Liza Verity," Karla said promptly. "They were in my class. I don't know if they were exactly friends."

"It's even better if they're enemies," Evan said. "You can come back the conquering hero. Heroine. You can come back and show them all what you've done with your life."

"Is that what I want to do?"

"The problem with you is that you've never had any time to organize your life. You've been too busy working. You can't leave things to chance like that these days. You have to go out and work for yourself."

"I work all the time."

"That's different."

"I like what I do."

"I like to think I'm bringing you something nobody else could," Evan said, sounding suddenly passionate, suddenly angry. "I like to think I have something unique to contribute to your life."

The bellhop had brought Karla's backpack and Evan's suitcase to the elevator bank. The main elevator was an ornate thing framed in curling brass, its doors patterned to look as if the metal on them had been quilted. Evan wasn't looking at her. There were two young South American women in the lobby, their hair knotted into elaborate wreaths that ended in high swinging ponytails. The heels on their shoes were much too high. They wobbled and stumbled when they tried to walk. Their pocketbooks were too big and too heavy. They both looked like they were about to tip over.

"Evan?" Karla said.

Evan started walking toward the elevators. "We have to go upstairs," he told her. "I booked us a two-bedroom suite."

"It must have cost a lot of money."

"It cost less than it would have. Because you're the famous Karla Parrish. Because your name is in *Paris-Match*. Because it's an asset to the hotel to have you staying here."

Karla was hurrying to keep up. Usually she thought of Evan as smaller than she was. What she really meant was that he was younger than she was, less experienced, with much less authority. In spite of the fact that he was slight, though, he was actually much taller than she was—at least six feet, while she was barely five five. He had stopped next to the bellhop at the elevator doors. Karla hurried a little faster and caught up with him.

"Evan," she said again.

The elevator doors opened. An American couple came out, sounding very Texas and looking like an ad in *GQ*. The bellhop put their bags in the elevator cage and Evan followed them.

"I'm just trying to be of use around here," he said when Karla came to stand beside him. "Don't you ever feel useless, doing what you do? All those people dying. All those people starving. And you just stand around and take pictures."

"You don't want me to take pictures," Karla said.

"You can take all the pictures you want," Evan said. "It's not the pictures. That's not the point. You're a genius at pictures."

"What is the point?"

"Look at all this scrollwork," Evan said, staring at the ceiling of the elevator cab. "The French are really incredible. Less is more. More is more. More is less."

The elevator bounced to a stop. The doors opened and the bellhop got out, carrying their bags. They were in a long, carpeted hallway with ceilings a dozen feet high. Karla thought Evan was right about the scrollwork.

"Did you always know that you wanted to take pictures?" Evan asked her, looking at the wall above her head. "Even when you were at Vassar?"

"I never had a camera in my hands in my life until I was twenty-four years old," Karla said. "Except for, you know, Brownies and that kind of thing."

"I thought a Brownie was a kind of Girl Scout."

The bellhop had opened the double doors at the end of the corridor. Karla walked through them and found herself in a living room larger than any she had ever been in. Evan shook through his trouser pockets and found a tip.

"*Merci,*" the bellhop said. He was not smiling. In France, Karla had noticed, only the managerial class smiled.

Evan threw himself into a mock Louis XVI chair and stared at the ceiling. Karla saw fat cherubs and even fatter grapes, molded in plaster, frozen in time.

"Jesus," Evan said. "The way this thing is going, I'm never going to get you into bed."

# 7.

As far back as she could remember, even in junior high school, Julianne Corbett had used rouge and foundation and mascara to distract people from what she knew to be the truth about herself: that she was coarse-looking and plain; that she was as common and inessential as any of the other girls who had grown up with her on the outskirts of Bethlehem, Pennsylvania, greaser girls, bimbos, Catholic virgins, and working-class sluts. It was funny the way life worked out, sometimes, for some people. It was possible to go on fooling the world for decades if you worked at it hard enough.

The thing about using makeup to disguise yourself, though, was that nobody recognized you when you went without it. Julianne let herself through the back door of her office and looked around for some signs of life but saw none. It was one-thirty in the afternoon, past the lunch hour but still in the dullest part of the day. Tiffany Shattuck, Julianne's secretary, was probably getting some backup typing done. Julianne went to the door of her office and locked it slowly, quietly, so that if Tiffany was standing right outside, she wouldn't hear it. Then Julianne went to the back of her office again and into her own private powder room. The powder room had been the dealbreaker in her decision to rent these offices. If the management of the building hadn't been willing to install it, Julianne would have found another building somewhere else.

In the long mirror over the sink, a middle-aged woman with bags under her eyes and a wilted white blouse looked ready to collapse. Her skin was gray with dust and dirt. Her hair was matted and flat. Julianne washed her face with Dove and threw too much cold water on it in the process. She hated going out looking like this, but there were times it couldn't be helped. Ever since she had been elected to represent the 28th Congressional District, she had become a public figure. When she had been asked by the Governor to run in the special election after old Congressman Herold had died, she had imagined that the public scrutiny would begin and end with the campaign. It had been inconceivable to her that the Philadelphia newspapers would still be interested in her private life when all the speeches were over.

Maybe it will be better when I get to Washington, Julianne thought now, painting over her eyebrows with thick black liner. It was maddening to have to sneak around like this every time she wanted to go and see a friend. She had a lot of friends of that kind too. She always had had. It was all part of growing up so plain, she might as well have been ugly. Julianne couldn't count the number of years she had gone without any boys or men being interested in her at all. All of high school. Most of college. Most of the five or so years after that, when she and Patsy were traveling in India and the Far East and when she was at graduate school. Of course, boys and men were always interested in Patsy. That was part of the relationship Julianne and Patsy had built ever since they had been assigned to be roommates their freshman year at Vassar. Patsy was the kind of girl—thin, rich, tennis-athletic, pretty—who always got what she wanted when she wanted it, especially if she wanted it from men.

Julianne leaned closer to the mirror. She had to be very careful with the eyeliner. She wore so much of it, put on such thick black lines on both her upper and lower eyelids, even a small slip was a disaster. It didn't take much to make her look as if someone had given her a shiner. She put the eyeliner brush down and got out her blusher. She put streaks of red on each of her flat, undistinguished cheekbones until they began to look high and stuck out. She should be over all this by now, she knew she should. She was forty-eight years old and a highly visible and successful woman. She had a law degree from Penn. She had a doctorate from Penn too, in political science and government. She had just been elected to Congress, and as soon as the short congressional recess was over, in just about a month, she would be in Washington, where she had always wanted to be. The problem was that you never got over it all, not really. You carried what you had started out to be with you forever. It was what you really were instead of what you fooled other people into thinking you were. In the long run it was your destiny. Or maybe it wasn't. Julianne thought about all those "friends" of hers, the afternoon hotel rooms, the need to be with somebody else for the trip over and the trip back, and the long lunch hours where nothing mattered but the fact that she had managed to find American flag condoms in a novelty store in Wilmington, Delaware. I'm too old for this, Julianne told herself—but she didn't feel too old for it. She couldn't stop thinking about what it would be like in Washington, who she would find to be with. She wanted to go back out right that minute and start all over again. Maybe when I finally get caught, I can go on *Oprah* and claim to be a sex addict, Julianne told herself. She drew a line around her lips that made them just a little bit thicker than they really were. She filled that in with bright scarlet lipstick on a brush.

Somebody was trying to open the door to the outer office. Julianne shucked off her blouse and her skirt, grabbed her pink-and-white-striped terry-cloth bathrobe from the hook on the back of the powder room door, and hurried out to let Tiffany in. She hesitated only a moment, wondering if it might be somebody else, and then opened up without calling out. Tiffany was standing there, her hand raised to knock. Her hair hung to her waist and her skirt was cut up at least three quarters of the way to the cleft in her legs. She looked like the cover of the latest *Playboy*-goes-to-college edition, except that she was wearing a crucifix and a miraculous medal that hung into her cleavage from gold chains around her neck.

"Oh, God," she said, seeing Julianne in the bathrobe. "What's wrong? Are you sick?"

"I got splashed by a bus on my way back from the library," Julianne said. "I got mud all over me. I thought it would take less time if I came back here."

"Do you need me to get you something? Clothes from your apartment?"

"I'm fine. I've got everything. Don't I have some kind of appointment at quarter after two?"

"Right." Tiffany scratched her head. "The people from the Steel Council. They gave us a lot of money for the campaign."

"I thought I had some health care people. Pennsylvanians for a Single Payer System. Something like that."

"Pennsylvanians for Health Care Reform," Tiffany said. "That's not until four. You have the Girls Club people before that. About the day-at-the-office thing. The role models."

Julianne went back to the powder room. The skirt and blouse she had shucked off were lying on the floor. She wadded them into a ball and stuffed them into her big canvas bag. Her canvas bags were like Bella Abzug's hats. They had become a media trademark. Tiffany had followed her to the door. Julianne got the bright red dress with its big splotches of flowers off the hanger over the radiator and started to put it on.

"One of the things about not having been particularly attractive as a teenager," Julianne said judiciously, "is that you aren't unduly worried about the depredations of middle age. Did anything exciting happen while I was out?"

"Not exciting, exactly," Tiffany said. "I did the clippings."

"And?"

"There was a paragraph about you in a piece in *The New Yorker* about women being elected to Congress. There was a paragraph about you in a piece in *Boston* magazine too, but it was just a reference, because you did all that work with the

Environmental Jobs Council last year. I think they're trying to start the same kind of thing in Massachusetts."

"That's nice."

"It was a slow day, really. Not like during the election, when you were in the papers every day. I think I kind of miss it."

"I don't."

"Well, I suppose it must have been horrible for you," Tiffany said, "being followed around like that. But for the rest of us, it was neat. It was like being connected to a celebrity. I mean, you *are* a celebrity."

"I'm a congresswoman. It's not the same thing."

"During the election I could go into bars and if I said I worked for you, fifteen guys wanted to take me home. I'm not kidding. I never do that well usually. Most of the time, guys in bars go for the tall types. The model-actress types. They don't want secretaries."

"You could try not going to bars."

"You can't find men if you don't go to bars," Tiffany said. "You don't know what it's like out there. It's terrible, really. There aren't enough men to go around. And all the men there just want to get laid."

There was nothing she could do about her hair, Julianne decided. Usually she wore it up, teased and colored and wrapped until it looked half fake, but today it was limp and colorless and it was going to stay that way. Julianne went through the drawers of the vanity until she found a bright red scarf. She twirled it into a band and tied it around her head. She reminded herself of one of those sweater-girl publicity stills from the forties, except that her face was far too heavy and far too lined. She rummaged in her canvas bag again and came up with a pair of long, dangling earrings. They were turquoise and silver and constructed of hundreds of tiny pieces, each meant to swing and sound in the wind.

"There," Julianne said.

"There was something else," Tiffany told her. "In the clippings. Not about you."

"Not about me?"

"It was about that friend of yours. At least, I think she's a friend of yours. One of those women in that picture you keep on your desk."

"Oh? Which of those women?"

"Karla Parrish."

Julianne left the powder room for the outer office. There was a picture of Karla Parrish on her desk, although Karla hadn't been the point of it. The picture had been taken in one of the living rooms of Jewett House at Vassar College in 1967. All the women in the picture had been juniors then, and only one of them was in the least bit noticeable. That, of course, was Patsy MacLaren. Julianne picked up the picture and then put it down again. She hated looking at it. She had no idea why she still kept it.

"So what about Karla Parrish," she asked Tiffany. "Does she live in Philadelphia?"

"I don't know where she lives. The article didn't say. She's a famous photographer."

"Is she?"

"She takes pictures of war zones and refugees and things like that. She has a photograph on the cover of the Sunday *Times Magazine* this week. New York. *The New York Times,* I mean."

"I'd heard she was taking photographs," Julianne said. "I hadn't realized she was that successful."

"The article made her sound like the greatest thing since Matt Brady. 'Documenting the horrors of the twentieth century.' 'Bearing witness to the atrocities of our age.' 'Arguably responsible for more relief efforts than the UN.' That kind of thing."

"I'm impressed," Julianne said. Actually, she was more than impressed. She would not have expected Karla to get so far. She would have expected her to disappear back into the hinterlands somewhere, playing assistant to the president of the local savings and loan.

Tiffany picked up the photograph and studied it. "Is she the pretty one?" she asked.

"No," Julianne said. "She's the one in the turtleneck."

"Oh. You never can tell, can you? Did the pretty one get famous?"

"No. No, she didn't."

"Well, there you are. It's never the people you expect to get successful that get successful, is it? I'd have thought the pretty one would end up as a movie star, but I don't recognize her and you're a congresswoman and Karla Parrish is a famous photographer. She's coming to Philadelphia, by the way. Karla Parrish, I mean."

"I know you mean Karla Parrish. Why is she coming here?"

"To give some kind of talk at Penn. On photography, you know. That was what the story was about. It was in the *Inquirer* today. Anyway, I thought it would be a good opportunity."

"A good opportunity for what?"

"For a photo op or whatever. You know. You and Karla Parrish. You're old friends. You're both concerned with refugees and relief efforts and that kind of thing. I thought it would get us some good press. If the two of you met up again, you know, in public."

Tiffany had put the photograph down on the desk. Julianne picked it up herself and looked it over. There were six of them in this picture, but only four of them counted: Patsy MacLaren and Karla Parrish and Liza Verity and Julianne herself. Julianne couldn't even remember the names of the other two. She put the picture back down on the desk and rubbed her forehead.

"Well," she said. "A photo op. That's fine, if Karla wants to go along with it."

"I'll contact her people. It'll probably be a good career move for her too."

"Maybe it will be."

"I'll get you the things you need for the health care people," Tiffany said. "There isn't much you need to know. There's nothing you're going to be able to do for them this year anyway."

"Mmm," Julianne said.

Tiffany hurried out of the office and shut the door behind her. Julianne picked up the photograph again. She could remember buying this frame, the urgency she had felt at the time to keep this remembrance pristine, to make sure it didn't tear or fade. She had just come back from India and just started law school. She was living in a fifth-floor walk-up only two blocks from the university and eating Chef Boyardee macaroni cold out of cans at least three times a week because she couldn't afford to use her electricity for cooking. She rubbed the side of her face with her fingertips and thought that she ought to grow her nails long and paint them scarlet. If you were going to transform yourself from nothing into something, you ought to take care to make the transformation complete.

"If you could go back and do your life over again," Tiffany had asked her once, "what would you do that was different?"

"I've got the sheets you need if you want to look at them," Tiffany said now, coming in with a stack of papers. "Do you want to see these people as soon as they come in, or do you want me to make them wait?"

"I'll see them as soon as they come in," Julianne said.

"Are you sure you're all right?" Tiffany asked her. "You look pale."

"I'm fine," Julianne said.

Then she looked down and made herself concentrate on the lists of figures on health insurance premiums, which didn't matter because, like most things in life, they could only get worse.

## 8.

As soon as Liza Verity came in from work she saw the red light blinking on her answering machine. There was something about the way it was blinking that made her not want to hear the message—although, God only knew, even Liza knew, answering machines didn't have moods. Maybe it was just that she wasn't in a very good mood herself. Sometimes Liza didn't really mind the way things had turned out. Life seemed to be a matter of choices, and these were the choices she had made. Other times—now—Liza knew it was all wrong. She had graduated from *Vassar*, for God's sake, and back in the days when it was an all-women's college and just as hard to get into for girls as Harvard and Yale were for boys. Liza Verity, class of '69. Women like her did not end up wearing a nurse's uniform nine hours a day, not even as the heads of ICU wards. They didn't end up saying "yes, doctor" and "no, doctor" to overgrown boys who had barely had the grades to make it into Penn State. They became doctors, or lawyers, or congresswomen, like Julianne. At the very least, they married rich men and lived splendidly somewhere in the Northeast Power Corridor and hired Martha Stewart herself to cater their daughters' graduation parties. Liza threw herself down on her small couch and stretched out her legs. Her white uniform shoes were heavy and awkward. Her white uniform stockings reminded her of the silly things they used to wear when she was first in college, back when miniskirts and being mod were still in vogue. Liza remembered thinking, at the time, that there was no end to possibility. She would just go on and on and on, experiencing everything. She would never have to stop. She would never want to stop. She would never grow up or grow old or find herself in a two-bedroom ranch house on a quarter-acre plot in the worst residential section of Gladwyne, just plain stuck.

I should have done something serious to get myself stuck, Liza thought. I should have had an illegitimate baby or blown up a bank or been in a terrible accident or run through dozens of men.

The red light on the answering machine was still blinking and blinking. Liza stabbed at the play button and threw her head back against the couch, closing her eyes. Her uniform was made of some sort of synthetic material that was always too stiff and too sharp. When she had first been in nursing school, she had gone out of her way to get uniforms in real cotton and not minded the extra expense of having them starched and pressed at a laundry. Then the other women in her class had found out what she was doing and it had been impossible. They had all started out half sure that she was just some stinking rich bitch, coming in from Vassar and thinking she was better than everybody else. After they knew about the uniforms, they wouldn't talk to her at all.

"Liza," a voice said from the answering machine. "This is Courtney Hazelwood. Would you be available to do special duty work next week?"

Courtney Hazelwood was the head of the pediatrics nursing unit on the fourth floor. She was ten years younger than Liza, but she had gotten further faster, probably because she had no attitude problem. When Courtney Hazelwood said that nurses were serious professionals who deserved more money, more responsibility, and more status, she meant it.

"Liza." It was a male voice this time. Pompous. Young. Insufferable. "This is Dr. Martinson. Could you call me as soon as possible about the Brevoric case? You forgot to make some notes on the file."

Liza made a face at the machine. Dr. Martinson was barely thirty. He thought he was the next best thing to God, but he was always screwing up, and that was what this would turn out to be. Liza never forgot to make notes on the file. She was meticulous. Dr. Martinson, though, always forgot to make half the documentation he was supposed to. He was always in trouble with the administration about it, because they all had to be so careful with the legal ramifications of everything these days.

"Liza?"

Liza sat up a little straighter on the couch. The voice belonged to Julianne Corbett. Julianne never called anymore, not since the election. She had gotten to be too damned important to bother with Liza Verity. Of course, before the election, while she was campaigning, Julianne had been behaving like the best friend Liza would ever have in the world. Liza had organized a party so that Julianne could meet all the really important people in the nurses' union.

"Liza, listen," Julianne's voice said. "I just found out something wonderful. Karla Parrish is coming to Philadelphia."

Liza's eyes went automatically to the small oak liquor cabinet on the other side of the room, where she kept all her important photographs in frames. Then she looked away, embarrassed, because of course the picture wasn't there. She had taken it down nearly five years before. It makes us all look silly, she thought now. Like the heroines of one of those women's novels who all thought they were the best and the brightest but who had turned out to have failed lives and second-rate lovers instead.

"Anyway," Julianne was saying, "you should call me, because I've had the best idea. I think we ought to have a party for Karla when she comes, don't you? A kind of Vassar College mini-reunion. She's spent the last ten years or something in Africa and I'm sure she's just dying to catch up, so why don't you give me a call as soon as you have the chance and we can work it all out. My number is—"

Liza reached out and turned off the machine. She knew what Julianne's number was—or at least what her office number was. She didn't have Julianne's home number, which was supposed to be all right because Julianne used call forwarding. It was probably just a way for Julianne to keep her at a distance. So was this business about getting Liza to call Julianne back. Julianne knew perfectly well what Liza's work schedule was. Liza had had the same one for two and a half years.

I wonder what Karla was doing in Africa, Liza thought. Maybe she's been like Julianne and Patsy were that time, all in love with primitive peoples and trying to go back to the land. That hadn't worked out all that well with Julianne and Patsy, had it?

Liza picked up the receiver on her phone. You had to do odd things to the answering machine to make sure it didn't start working right in the middle of your making a phone call, but Liza avoided those by just unplugging the thing. Then she dialed Julianne's office number and waited.

"The office of the Honorable Julianne Corbett," a female voice said.

Liza made a face. "This is Liza Verity," she said. "I would like to talk to Julianne."

"I'm not sure the congresswoman is available at the moment. Is there something I could help you with?"

"I'm a friend of hers from college. She left a message on my machine."

"Just a minute, please."

Music began playing in Liza's ear: "Happy Days Are Here Again." Liza made a face at her feet. Then Julianne's voice came on the line, sounding bright and strained.

"Liza," she said. "How good of you to call. I must have just missed you. It was only minutes ago."

I'm sure it was, Liza thought. "What was Karla doing in Africa?" she asked. "Was she living in tree houses and learning how to make native jewelry?"

"No, no." Julianne sounded impatient. "She's a photographer. Did you see *The New York Times* last Sunday, the magazine? The cover story on the war in Rwanda?"

"As a matter of fact, I did." The hospital had several subscriptions to the *Times*, for doctors and patients. The hospital administration seemed to assume that nurses couldn't read.

"Well," Julianne was saying, "that cover picture, that black-and-white thing of all the boys, that was Karla's. And the rest of the pictures in the article were Karla's too. She's practically famous, I mean it. Like Annie Liebowitz or Mary Ellen Mark."

"I'm impressed."

"So am I." Julianne sounded impressed. Liza heard her take a deep breath. "Anyway. I thought I'd give a party, and we could have all the people from our Vassar class that I could find—there have to be dozens of us. The Main Line has a very active alumnae club. We ought to get a very good crowd. What do you think?"

"I think it sounds wonderful." Actually, Liza thought it sounded terrible. She could just picture it: herself in her nurse's uniform and all the rest of them in their Ralph Lauren and Calvin Klein; herself with nothing to talk about but bedpans and union troubles and the rest of them going on at length about the prospects for a rise in IBM stock in the new year. It would be like starting out at Vassar all over again.

"Good," Julianne said. "Then it's all settled. I'm going to have to go through her agent—can you believe that? It's been so long since any of us has seen Karla, I'll have to go through her agent. Unless you've been in contact with her? Have you?"

"Julianne, I didn't even know what she was doing for a living."

"Oh. Yes. Well. Anyway, I'll have to go through her agent, but I'm sure it can all be arranged. And I was thinking that maybe I'd invite a few members of the press too, you know, because—"

"Ah," Liza said.

"I don't know what you mean by that." Julianne was stiff. "Ah."

"Ah, now I understand what all this fuss is about. Why you want to give this party."

"I want to give this party because Karla is a good friend of mine and I haven't seen her in ages."

"I never thought Karla was that good a friend of yours."

"She was one of my closest. And so were you. We were almost a family, the four of us—"

"Six," Liza said automatically.

"Whatever. We were almost a family, and now you're saying God knows what. Honestly, Liza, that attitude of yours is going to get you in trouble."

"It already has. On several occasions."

"Well, then. You see what I mean."

Liza kicked her right shoe off and listened to it land with a thud on the floor. She began to work her left shoe off with the toes of her right foot, digging at the shoe's heel the way some people used toothpicks to dig at their teeth.

"Don't you wish you could find out what Patsy MacLaren thought about all this?" Liza asked Julianne. "Wouldn't you just love to hear it?"

"I have no idea what you mean."

"Sure you do. Patsy MacLaren, relegated forever to obscurity. Karla Parrish, getting famous as a photographer. Karla Parrish getting famous as anything. Do you remember the things Patsy used to say about Karla?"

"Patsy and Karla were very good friends," Julianne said.

The second shoe was off. The two shoes lay like dead white jellyfish on the carpet.

"Patsy MacLaren was never a friend to anyone," Liza said, "and certainly not to awkward, drab girls who didn't know how to dress."

"Really," Julianne said. "The things you think about to say. And I don't see what good it does obsessing about poor Patsy now. She's not even around for you to take it out on."

"I think it's a very good idea that she's not around."

"Well, I miss her," Julianne said, "and you probably do too, if you're honest about it. And besides, it's hardly her fault that she's—relegated to obscurity, as you put it."

"I've got some work to get done around here," Liza said. "Call me back when you've got some details on this thing."

"Oh, I will. I will."

"Say hello to Karla for me if you get the chance."

"You can say hello to Karla yourself. At the party."

"I've got to go, Julianne."

Julianne said something else that Liza didn't hear. Liza hung up and spent a moment staring at the phone, as if it would tell her things she needed to know, like how she could be almost fifty and still not satisfied with her life. Her parents' generation had made such a point of trying to grow up. Maybe she should have made a point of it too, so that she didn't feel adolescent and geriatric at the same time, staring at white shoes on a blue carpet.

Crap, Liza thought, standing up and heading for the small kitchen at the back.

It really was too bad there was no way of knowing what Patsy MacLaren would have thought about Karla Parrish making a success of herself. It really was too bad that Patsy had sunk out of sight and left not so much as a ripple in the water.

Still, Liza thought, sometimes you had to admit it. Sometimes life really did work out just the way you wanted it to.

## 9.

Forty-seven minutes later, at precisely eighteen minutes after four o'clock, a black Volvo station wagon parked on the second level of a Philadelphia garage began to rock. The noise it made was so distinctive, the man in the glass ticket booth at the garage's entrance began to get disturbed. He was worried that there were vandals in the garage, or teenagers looking to steal something they could sell for serious money. The neighborhood around there had been going to hell for years. The man put out his cigarette on the cement floor of his booth and stepped out into the air. He lit another cigarette and rocked back and forth on his heels. Maybe he ought to go back into the booth and call the cops. Maybe he ought to just walk away from there, take what money he could and leave. He wasn't supposed to be smoking this cigarette. Nobody was supposed to smoke on duty in the garage. He took a deep drag and started up the incline.

The Volvo was parked in one of the spaces that faced that ramp. He saw it as soon as he came up over the rise, bucking and shuddering, as if somebody were having trouble with a standard transmission. For a moment he thought that must be what it was. Somebody was having trouble getting their car started. Then he saw the driver's seat behind the wheel and realized that no one was there. The car was absolutely empty and the locks on the doors closest to him were pushed all the way down.

The woman who wanted the all-day parking ticket, the man thought to himself as he continued climbing up the ramp. Then he heard something like a pained grinding of gears and stepped instinctively back. The stepping-back probably saved his life. A second later there was a scream and a blast. The garage was suddenly so hot, it was like being in a blast furnace. Smoke and fire shot up out of the Volvo and side to side too, hitting the cars on either side of it, starting a chain reaction in a small Toyota that had come in only half an hour before. Smoke and fire was rising up into the concrete. Metal was everywhere, and glass, and what felt like melted rubber still hot enough to burn flesh.

The man began to back down the ramp. Then he turned and started to run. He ran right out of the garage and onto the street. The sidewalks were full of people at a dead stop. Black smoke was billowing out of the garage's third level. Windows were broken on cars half a block away.

"Fire department, fire department," the man started shouting, but no one was listening to him.

They were all standing stock-still in the street, so that when the second large blast came—the biggest one, ripping through cars on either side of the Volvo like a buzz saw through balsa wood and shooting bits of debris into the air like lethal snow—three people had their eardrums shattered and four got bits of powdered glass in their eyes.

# PART ONE

*A Marriage Made in Heaven or Someplace*

# ONE

## 1.

FROM THE MOMENT THAT GREGOR Demarkian had first heard about Donna Moradanyan's wedding, he had wanted to be happy about it. After all, he kept asking himself, what could there possibly be not to be happy about? In all the years Gregor had known her, the one thing she had really needed was a good husband. She was only twenty-two years old and on her own with a small child. The small child's father had disappeared into the mists of studied irresponsibility as soon as he had heard of the impending arrival of the small child. The man she was marrying was a blessing too: Russell Donahue, once a homicide detective with the Philadelphia Police Department, somebody they all knew. Donna was even going to go on living on Cavanaugh Street. Howard Kashinian was fixing up another dilapidated stone house on the northern edge of the neighborhood. Donna's parents were giving her the down payment for a wedding present. Russ was just as happy to live there as anywhere else—happier, in fact, since the neighborhood was safe and he liked most of the people in it.

"Donna can even go on decorating everything," Lida Arkmanian had said, explaining the whole thing to Gregor one afternoon just before Christmas. "It will be like nothing has really changed at all, except that Donna will have Russell and Tommy will have a father."

"It's just like Howard Kashinian to ask for a down payment from Donna of all people," Father Tibor Kasparian had said about a week later. "I don't know what we're going to do about Howard. I don't know if there's anything to be done about Howard."

Gregor Demarkian had known Howard Kashinian all his life. He *knew* there was nothing to be done about the man— but Howard Kashinian wasn't the problem, and thinking about him wasn't going to solve anything. Week after week went by. Winter turned into spring. Donna wrapped the four-story brownstone they all lived in in red and silver foil for Valentine's Day and in green and yellow ribbons for Mother's Day. She wrapped all the streetlamp poles in bright red bolts of satin cloth and strung balloons between them for her son Tommy's birthday. Sometimes Gregor would hear her, pacing back and forth in the apartment above his head, her step light and oddly rhythmic. Sometimes he'd see her out his big front living room window, skateboarding along the sidewalk with her hair flying while Lida or Hannah Krekorian kept Tommy sitting safely on a stoop. Once Gregor had gone downstairs to Bennis Hannaford's place, to see if she would feed him coffee and cheer him up, but it hadn't worked. Bennis was Donna's best friend on Cavanaugh Street, maybe the best friend Donna had in the world, in spite of the fact that Bennis was nearly forty instead of just past twenty and nothing like Donna in background at all. Her apartment was full of bits and pieces of Donna's wedding, strewn about like dust among the debris of her real life: big maps of make-believe places called Zed and Zedalia; papier-mâché models of dragons and trolls. There was a floor-to-ceiling bookshelf built into the wall in Bennis's foyer, filled with editions of the books she had written herself. *The Chronicles of Zed and Zedalia* had a unicorn on the cover and a dragon with a curling tail.

*Zedalia in Winter* had a lady in a conical hat and a lot of veils, riding on a horse. The latest one, *Zedalia Triumphant,* had a plain red background and nothing else at all. Bennis was on the *New York Times* best-seller list. As far as her publisher was concerned, she was now making enough money to be considered a Serious Writer, and Serious Writers did not have the covers of their books cluttered up with garish four-color pictures of rogue trolls.

"They wanted me to go out to the Midwest and tour the week of Donna's wedding," Bennis had said as she let Gregor through her door. He had a key to her apartment, but he never used it. It made him feel odd—somehow—to have it. "But I told them to forget it. I mean, for God's sake. I just got back from England. I'm going up to Canada in four days. It's not like I'm recalcitrant about doing publicity."

"Mmm," Gregor had said.

Bennis led him into her kitchen. Her thick black hair was piled on top of her head. Her legs and feet were bare under her jeans. Her long-fingered hands looked cold. Gregor sat down at her kitchen table and cleared a place for himself. Bennis had pieces of a copyedited manuscript spread out everywhere. Every single page seemed to display a pale yellow Post-it Note with a message in navy blue ink and a plain white Post-it Note with a message in red. *Don't you think you should mention Hitler here?* one of the blue-inked messages read. *This is taking place in 1882, for Christ's sake,* the red-inked message shot back. *Hitler hadn't even been BORN yet.* Gregor wanted to ask what Hitler had to do with Zed and Zedalia, but he didn't. Bennis put a large cup of coffee down in front of him.

"Donna's mother is practically living upstairs these days," Bennis said, turning her back to him and fussing with the pile of dirty dishes in her sink. Bennis never seemed to wash dishes, only to fuss with them—but they got done every once in a while, and put away, so she must have gotten serious or used the dishwasher or hired help when he wasn't looking. Gregor drank coffee and wondered why he was thinking so hard about Bennis Hannaford's dishes.

"Donna's mother is upstairs practically every minute of the time these days," Bennis said, actually rinsing out a glass and putting it in the dish rack. She picked it up again, reinspected it, and put it back in the sink. "Donna's going crazy, as you can imagine, and I'm about to go crazy too, because Donna's mother is a nice woman, but honestly, Gregor, she keeps wanting to change things. Do you remember how I was supposed to wear this sort of claret-colored satin skirt to be maid of honor in?"

"Mmmm," Gregor said.

"Donna's mother thinks red is red and wearing red makes me look like a scarlet woman, which Donna's mother half thinks I am anyway. Do you think that's true, Gregor? That I'm some sort of scarlet woman?"

"Mmmm," Gregor said again.

Bennis turned around and leaned back against the sink. She was wearing a turtleneck and a flannel shirt over her jeans. Her great masses of black hair were straining against their pins, showing a little gray here and there. She looked the way she always looked, Gregor thought—as if she were in costume. There was something about her face, something so Old Money Philadelphia Main Line, that didn't go with this style she had developed and now seemed permanently addicted to. Gregor thought she would look more natural playing Elizabeth I of England in an old movie—except that Elizabeth I had never been this good-looking.

Bennis crossed her arms over her chest. "Do you want to tell me what's bothering you?" she demanded. "I mean, for God's sake, Gregor, you're beginning to remind me of Banquo's ghost."

"Nothing's bothering me," Gregor told her. "I've just been a little tired lately. I've got the right to be a little tired."

"Maybe you should see a doctor. You haven't been doing anything to be tired."

"Thanks a lot."

"Well, I mean it. You've been moping around the neighborhood for weeks now. You haven't been investigating a case—"

"There hasn't been a case for me to investigate."

"John Jackman asked you to help with something three weeks ago. I know. I read the note."

"Now you're reading my mail."

Bennis sighed. "Gregor, seriously. Even Sheila Kashinian's beginning to worry about you, and Sheila wouldn't notice if an atom bomb dropped in the middle of her living room. Unless it messed up her curtains, of course, because she just got new white curtains. Don't listen to me. I'm just trying to get across to you—"

"There's nothing wrong with me," Gregor said stubbornly.

"You're off your food," Bennis told him. "Lida left a plate of stuffed grape leaves for you a week ago and half of them are still in your refrigerator."

"You were looking in my refrigerator?"

"I'm always looking in your refrigerator. Gregor, please—"

"The night my wife died, she screamed," Gregor said, wondering where the words had come from as soon as he'd said them, feeling the words like hailstones floating around his head, clogging up the air. "They wanted to give her this shot, this medicine, that didn't really do any good but it was on their manifest, they were afraid I was going to sue them if they couldn't prove they'd done everything possible, so you see it was my fault. That she screamed. That she was in pain. If they hadn't been so worried about me they would have listened to her."

Bennis Hannaford got out a cigarette and lit up. Gregor hadn't seen her smoke in a week. "Jesus Christ," she said.

"She was so thin at the end, her skin looked like paper,"

Gregor said. "I think I'm going back upstairs to my own apartment. I think I'm going to pour myself a stiff drink."

"You can't possibly think it was really your fault," Bennis said, "that they gave her medication. That she was in pain. You aren't responsible for cancer. Doctors aren't all that easily intimidated. For God's sake. This is crazy."

"I think I'm going back upstairs to my own apartment," Gregor repeated, and he stood up. He spent half his life these days in Bennis Hannaford's kitchen, but at the moment it didn't look familiar. The thin stream of her cigarette smoke was curling like a ribbon through the latticework of the light fixture that hung from her ceiling. Gregor Demarkian was a big man—six foot four and over two hundred fifty pounds—and he felt suddenly bigger than ever, huge and awkward, poured from lead.

"Maybe I'd better go upstairs with you," Bennis said.

Gregor turned away from her without answering. It was a million miles from the kitchen table to the kitchen door. It was three million miles from the kitchen door across the foyer to the door to the hall. He had a sudden vision of himself standing in the cemetery on the other side of Philadelphia, putting Elizabeth to rest in the earth next to his own mother. It was raining and a stiff cold wind was coming out of nowhere. There was a tarpaulin spread across the hole in the ground where they were going to put Elizabeth. Elizabeth's casket was covered with white carnations. The cemetery was empty except for himself and the undertaker's men and the Armenian priest whose name he had picked out of the phone book. He was still with the Federal Bureau of Investigation then and living in Washington. He had lost contact with the people he had known in Philadelphia years before. The cemetery that day had felt as empty as the inside of his head and the hollow of his chest. Elizabeth was gone and there was nothing left of him.

He had no memory of leaving Bennis Hannaford's apartment. He had no idea how he got from her kitchen to her front door, or up the stairway to his own front door, or into his apartment. He came to sitting on the floor in his own bedroom, his hands deep into the bottom drawer of his bureau. Seconds later he came out with what he was looking for: his wedding album and the two thick albums of snapshots Elizabeth had used to keep her pictures of their vacations together. The plastic felt tense and wet and hot under his fingers, like something dangerous and alive. He pressed his forehead against the front of the bureau and closed his eyes. He remembered how, when he had first moved into this apartment, he had thought he could hear Elizabeth talking to him in the kitchen. Her voice would come out to him from the neat stacks of stoneware dishes in his cupboards and the tall bottle of milk in his otherwise empty refrigerator. The sound of her would follow him into his living room and down the hall to his bedroom. When he fell asleep, he would hear her singing lullabies. He didn't remember when she had disappeared, but she had. He had become involved in Cavanaugh Street and the people who lived on it. He had found work to do as a consultant to police departments in homicide cases and books he wanted to read and political candidates he wanted to support and movies he was willing to see on the nights Bennis Hannaford couldn't stand looking at the walls of her living room anymore. He had found a million things to fill up his life with, and now Elizabeth was gone.

Elizabeth died of uterine cancer four and a half years ago, he told himself. It was sticky hot outside, but he was cold. He counted to ten and took a deep breath and counted to ten again. His muscles were twitching just under the surface of his skin. I could sit here forever, he thought—and the thought scared the hell out of him.

The phone rang. He had the ringer in the bedroom turned up loud in case somebody needed to wake him. The shrill, long sound made him jump. He leaned back and took the receiver off the base of the phone, where it lay next to the lamp on his night table. He expected to hear Bennis or someone she had called, worried about what kind of shape he was in. Instead, he got John Henry Newman Jackman, the head of homicide detectives for the Philadelphia Police Department and, according to Bennis and Donna Moradanyan, the single most beautiful male human being on earth.

"Gregor?" John Jackman said. "Have you been watching the news tonight?"

"What time is it?" Gregor asked him.

"Go turn on your television set," Jackman said. "Turn it to ABC. Right away."

Gregor stood up and stretched the muscles in his shoulders. The digital clock on the bedside table said 5:58.

"Just a minute," Gregor told Jackman. "I'm going to have to switch phones. I'm in the bedroom."

"Hurry up."

Gregor put the phone receiver on the night table next to the base and went down the hall. His living room windows looked across Cavanaugh Street to Lida Arkmanian's town house. Lida was sitting at the desk in her bedroom, writing something. Gregor picked up the receiver of the living room phone and the remote control from the television set. He said hello to John Jackman and switched the set to ABC. The first thing he saw was what seemed to be a piece of floating black metal. The next thing he saw was an explosion, the bright flash of red followed by the eruption of thick black smoke, the second flash ripping out and rumbling like thunder. The clock in the bedroom must be slow, he thought stupidly.

"Good God," he said to John Jackman. "What was that?"

"Pipe bomb."

"*Pipe* bomb?"

"In a parking garage in West Philly late this afternoon. There was a smaller explosion first and this guy was going by with his video camera, near the university. Anyway, he'd always wanted to get something on the local news and he figured he had a chance and he rushed in and started filming and then the second explosion went off and he damn near got killed. The parking garage attendant was badly hurt. He got his shot though. The kid, I mean. What do you think of that?"

On the screen the smoke had cleared away. There was a picture of a city street with a parking garage in the background. A tall young woman with blond hair and big teeth was talking solemnly into a microphone. Gregor remembered the days when television people tried to make their microphones as small and unobtrusive as possible, invisible, so as not to break the illusion of being part of real life.

"I take it someone died in the explosion," Gregor said.

"Nope," John Jackman told him. "Lot of cars got messed up. That was it."

"Then what are you doing on it?"

"The guy who died died in bed," Jackman said. "Out at Fox Run Hill. You know the place?"

"One of those gated communities," Gregor said promptly. "Bunch of people locking themselves up so that the bogeymen don't get them. Fox Run Hill's out in one of the suburbs, isn't it? That shouldn't be yours either."

"Man who died out there was named Stephen Willis. His wife put three or four bullets into him with a silenced automatic pistol."

"It's still not yours, John."

"It was the wife's car that blew up in West Philly this afternoon."

"Ahh," Gregor said. "And the wife wasn't in it?"

"No, she wasn't."

"And now you want to know where she is."

There was a long silence on the other end of the line. Across the street, Lida had finished writing her letter and was licking the flap of an envelope to seal it. Gregor was always telling her that he could see everything she did in there, but she only remembered to close her drapes sometimes.

"Listen," John Jackman said, "you've got to come down and see me tomorrow, okay? I can't explain all this over the phone."

"About the pipe bomb and Fox Run Hill."

"That's right."

"Even if things look strange now, John, they won't necessarily look strange in the morning. It's only been, what. A couple of hours?"

"Something like that. Not even that. I'm serious, Gregor. You've got to come down. Will you do it?"

Gregor thought about Elizabeth's voice in his kitchen, about kneeling on the floor of his bedroom with his forehead pressed against the front of the bureau, about saying strange things to Bennis Hannaford and not remembering where he had been.

"Yes," he said. "Yes, of course I will."

"Good. Make it about nine o'clock. I've got a couple of things I have to do."

"You'll probably have the whole thing solved before I ever get there."

"I don't think so."

"If you do, I'm going to make you buy me lunch. I'm not going to go hauling all the way down to police headquarters for nothing."

"It won't be for nothing. Do you know Julianne Corbett?"

"The new congresswoman? I know who she is."

"Good. Be there at nine. I've got to go now."

"But what does Julianne Corbett have to do with it?"

"I've got to go now," John Jackman insisted. "I'm glad you're coming down, Gregor. You've been acting very weird lately. I've been worried."

"Don't be ridiculous," Gregor started to say—but the phone had already gone to dial tone and there was no point. Gregor hung up the phone, got off the couch, and went back into the bedroom. Then he hung up the phone there and sat down on the edge of the bed. His wedding album was lying on the carpet next to the bureau. The other photograph albums were edged back a little under his bed. He picked them all up and put them back into the bureau's bottom drawer. He had a picture of Elizabeth in a frame on top of his bureau. He picked that up and looked at it instead.

## 2.

Half an hour later, feeling stiff and sore and half as if he were coming down with a cold, Gregor Demarkian went back downstairs to Bennis Hannaford's apartment. When he knocked, he heard her voice call to him to come in. He tried her door and found it unlocked. No matter how many times he lectured her, she would not listen. Nobody on Cavanaugh Street would listen. This was their Magic Kingdom. At least one murder had happened there since Gregor was in residence—but it might as well not have. It had merely passed into the folklore of the street.

Gregor found Bennis lying on her back on the living room floor, a cigarette in her hand, a rose crystal ashtray planted firmly in the middle of her admirably flat stomach. She was staring at the moldings on her ceiling and humming something by the Eagles under her breath.

"I thought it was you," she said. "Are you feeling better now?"

"I kept expecting you to show up at my front door. Or to send Tibor or Donna or somebody."

Bennis took a deep drag and blew out a stream of smoke. "We discussed it, Donna and me. We decided we were doing you more harm than good by fussing over you the way we were. I would have come up after a while though. Maybe about an hour. Just to make sure you weren't, you know. Suicidal."

"Is that the way I appear to you? Suicidal?"

Bennis took the ashtray off her stomach and put it down next to her on the floor. She held her cigarette high in the air and turned over on her stomach.

"You seem—odd to me," she said, "and to Donna too. Not like yourself. Not even like the way you usually are when you're sad."

"I miss my wife."

"I know."

"I think I miss her all the time. I just don't notice it usually. I—push it away from me."

"Good old testosterone stoicism."

"More like good old Bureau training. And the army too, during the period I was in the army. Even the Bureau may have changed by now, I suppose."

"I can't imagine being married," Bennis said, tapping ash into the ashtray. "I think about it when I'm with Donna sometimes, and I run right into a wall. Did I ever tell you that my mother loved my father?"

"You've mentioned it."

"She did too," Bennis said. "She loved him more than she ever loved any of us and she always knew what he was. I think I grew up thinking it was a kind of disease. Love, I mean. And marriage was just a place where people tried to kill each other off."

"It can be a place where people are safe," Gregor said. "Where you can be exactly who you are and not have to worry about it."

"My father was always exactly who he was. He didn't need my mother for that."

"Your father was a psychopath."

Bennis put her cigarette out and sat up. Then she reached into her pocket for another cigarette and lit up again. The flame from her lighter made her face look made of shadows and light.

"Sometimes, when I'm upstairs with Donna," she said, "I

think about them making it permanent, Donna and Russ, you know, and then, even though I know them both, I get sick to my stomach, you know, I just start getting crazy. Does that make sense?"

"In a way."

"If I didn't have to stick around for the wedding, I think I'd go off to France for a couple of weeks and get into trouble. Maybe you could come with me."

"I'd put a damper on your party. I'd want to do nothing but sleep and eat cassoulet."

"Gregor, listen. About what you said before. I mean, aren't you safe with me? Can't you be yourself with me?"

"Most of the time."

"Only most of the time? I can always be myself with you."

"No, you can't."

"I should know, Gregor. It's me we're talking about."

"Bennis, in case you haven't noticed, there is something you and I don't do together. And as long as we don't do that together, then, unless you're much less vital a person than I have ever suspected, there will be times when you could not possibly be yourself with—"

"My, my," Bennis said. "What's this conversation starting to be about?"

"I think it had better start to be about dinner," Gregor said. "Go put on something you can wear where the air-conditioning isn't turned up to frigid and I'll buy you dinner at the Ararat."

"I think I'd rather go back to that conversation we were just having."

"I think I wouldn't," Gregor said firmly. "I think we've all been . . . thrown off balance by Donna's getting married and I think we ought to forget all about it. Go get dressed, Bennis."

Sitting cross-legged on the floor like that, Bennis Hannaford looked no more than fourteen years old. Gregor thought she was going to go on insisting, but instead she put her new cigarette out less than half smoked and stood up in a single fluid motion.

"I'll only be a minute," she told him.

Gregor sat down on the arm of the couch and watched her walk off down the hall to her bedroom, her bare feet making gentle slapping noises against the wooden hall floor.

# TWO

## 1.

REGOR DEMARKIAN DIDN'T REALLY BELIEVE in mysteries. In his experience, what the newspapers heralded as a mystery was often a case of simple arrogance. Most human beings are naturally pessimistic about themselves. They believe in their own incapacities more than in their capabilities. What most people call their conscience is only their wordless conviction that if they do anything in the least bit wrong, they will get caught. Gregor had spent twenty years of his life with the Federal Bureau of Investigation. He had spent the second ten of those twenty years as the founder and head of what the Bureau liked to call the Behavioral Science Department, as if it were a group of bright young things in lab coats watching rats run around mazes. What it really was was a collection of hardened veterans who spent their time concentrating on the interstate pursuit of serial killers. Gregor had pushed for its establishment because of his frustration at the ineptitude with which the Bureau was investigating the man who turned out to be Theodore Robert Bundy. When Gregor had left the Bureau on his last leave of absence, to care for Elizabeth that last year of her life, it had been going strong, fueled by what had become to seem an epidemic of serial murder. Men who killed women. Men

who killed little boys. Men who killed little old ladies who
wheeled private shopping carts to their local food co-ops.
Gregor couldn't remember hearing about even one serial
killer in all the years he was growing up. Now the world
seemed to be full of them. The new director of the Behavioral
Science Department had been quoted in *Time* only a week
ago, declaring that the whole thing was the fault of the media. Serial killers killed so that they could get their names in
the paper. Andy Warhol had been right. Everybody wanted to
be famous for fifteen minutes. Gregor thought that theory
was a little bit cracked, but he might be wrong. What he was
sure of was that there was no mystery about any of these
men. When the police found a twisted silver key lying next to
the body of a murdered teenage girl left in a ditch in Tacoma,
Washington, it wasn't because she had the magic treasure
chest that would provide the winning lottery numbers for the
next sixteen games but didn't know it. It was just that her
murderer wanted to leave a calling card (the serial ones all
did that these days; they had all seen the movies about Dah-
mer and Gacey) or that the key had been lying in the grass
and when she had fallen she had turned it up. In the end it
would turn out to be more accident than plot. Gregor was
sure this thing with Patsy MacLaren Willis would work out
that way too. She had decided to kill her husband. She had decided to go out with a bang. Now it was just a question of
finding her. What John Henry Newman Jackman needed him
for, Gregor didn't know.

It was seven o'clock in the morning and Cavanaugh Street
was not quite waking up. Gregor had gone through the *Philadelphia Inquirer* story about Patsy MacLaren Willis twice and
come up with nothing more interesting than technical details. The gun that had been used to kill Stephen Willis had
been a 657 41 Magnum. The house Patsy and Stephen Willis
had lived in at Fox Run Hill was over seven thousand square
feet big. He had also drunk two cups of his own very bad coffee. Now he looked out his broad living room window and

saw that the light was on, across the street and one floor down, in Lida Arkmanian's living room. Down the block, all the lights were on in Sheila and Howard Kashinian's town house. Gregor had grown up on Cavanaugh Street when it was still a very poor and very immigrant ethnic neighborhood. People lived in tenements and did their shopping at markets that seemed to have been lifted whole and intact from Yerevan. Now most of the markets had been replaced by upscale little shops that catered to tourists looking for the "authentic" Armenian artifacts to take home to the suburbs and the tenements had all been converted to town houses and co-ops, where the apartments each took up an entire floor. The people of Cavanaugh Street hadn't gotten rich, but their children and grandchildren had, and the children and grandchildren had provided. Lida Arkmanian's reward for thirty years of scrimping and saving and suffocating in a tiny apartment with a window that looked out on a vacant lot was that town house and another house in Boca Raton and a three-quarter-length chinchilla coat. Of Lida's five children, three were doctors, and two were lawyers with very prestigious Philadelphia firms. Hannah Krekorian's reward for all the years she came to church in gray cloth coats that didn't quite fit that she'd found on the sale tables outside the going-out-of-business stores was a duplex co-op with two Jacuzzis and a kitchen big enough to serve a small restaurant. She'd had another duplex co-op just like it a couple of years earlier, but then someone she knew had been murdered in it and she hadn't felt safe staying there. Her two daughters had chipped in to get her this new place, and to send her to Europe for a month to calm her nerves. Gregor supposed that even he himself was rich, at least as he would have defined the word when he was still a child. He owned this third floor floor-through apartment. He had enough in savings and investments and pensions never to have to work for money again. He bought hardcover books when he wanted them without thinking about what they cost. Now he went all the way up to

the broad plate glass of his window and pressed his face
against it. Standing like this, he could just see the front steps
of Holy Trinity Armenian Christian Church. There was a bus
stop right in front of the steps and a streetlamp meant to
keep the bus stop "safe." There was no way to tell if anyone was awake over at the church or not. Gregor turned back
and looked at his coffee table. His coffee mug was on it, still
half full of his awful coffee. The newspaper was on it too,
folded over and looking smudged. Gregor walked away from
the window. He picked up the newspaper and threw it in the
wastebasket. He stood over the wastebasket, looking at the
paper lying in a nest of crumpled Kleenex and the cellophane
wrapper from a package of Drake's Ring-Dings. He always
kept Ring-Dings in the apartment for Donna Moradanyan's
son Tommy.

"What am I doing, exactly?" he asked himself.

Then he went out into his foyer and took his best navy
blue cardigan sweater off the coatrack next to the door. It
always seemed to be chilly in the mornings on Cavanaugh
Street, except in August, when it was wet and muggy and
hot. Gregor let himself out his front door and locked it carefully behind him. He wouldn't be caught dead treating Cavanaugh Street as if it were a village in the old country, with
nothing to worry about from thieves and junkies. He went
down the stairs to the second floor and looked at Bennis Hannaford's door. If he knew Bennis, she would have stayed up
all night working and reading and be in no shape to go to
breakfast now. He went down another flight of steps to the
front hall and looked at old George Tekemanian's door as if
just looking at it could tell him if the old man was awake or
not. Old George usually was, in spite of the fact that he was
well over eighty. Gregor hesitated only a moment before he
knocked. Old George's voice called out "come in" almost immediately, as if he had been awake in there for hours, just
waiting for somebody to show up.

Old George didn't lock his door either. Gregor opened

it. Old George was sitting in splendor in his bright yellow wing chair, wrapped in a red silk dressing gown, sporting thick socks with bats embroidered on them on his long, thin feet. Old George's grandson Martin was always buying him things to make him look more sophisticated, but making old George look more sophisticated was a lost cause. Old George's grandson Martin's wife was always buying him "healthful" food to snack on, but at the moment old George was eating a Twinkie.

"Krekor," old George said. "Would you like to come in and have a Twinkie?"

Gregor let the Twinkie pass. "I'm going over to get Tibor out of bed," he told the old man. "Want to come with me?"

"You won't get Tibor out of bed," old George said. "He wakes up at four to read."

"Whatever. Maybe we'll go to the Ararat and have some breakfast."

"I don't think so, Krekor. The Ararat these days is not what it used to be. It is too full of wedding things."

"I know what you mean."

"I am very glad Donna is getting married, Krekor, but this is truly crazy. She came down here yesterday with samples of satin ribbon to tie the favors and wanted to know which one I like best. She had two dozen samples, Krekor, and they were all some kind of white."

"That sounds more like Donna's mother than like Donna."

"And then there are these showers," old George went on. "In my day, parties of this kind were for women only. Now they're all having them and they all expect me to come. Lida. Hannah. Sheila Kashinian. Helen. Everybody."

"They expect me to come too. I just don't go."

"You have legitimate excuses. I have nothing. Do you know what they do at these parties?"

"No."

"They play games about sex. That is what they do. They make me blush."

"I'm going to go get Tibor," Gregor said. "Wedding craziness or no wedding craziness, I still have to eat."

"I keep telling myself it will be a very good thing for
Tommy to have a father who is around the house and wants to
take care of him. That is how I get through it all."

"I keep telling myself that if it gets very, very bad, I can always take off for the Caribbean for the duration. You're sure
you don't want to come down with me?"

"Yes, Krekor. I'm sure."

"Say hello to Donna and Bennis when you see them then.
I've got to be downtown for most of the day."

Old George Tekemanian took another large bite of his
Twinkie, and sighed.

## 2.

For years, Father Tibor Kasparian had been like nobody else
on Cavanaugh Street. An immigrant from Soviet Armenia, a
veteran of the gulags and the free-floating religious persecu-
tion of the old Soviet empire, he had been not only an oddity
but an object of awe. That he should have come through All
That and still be as sane and stable as he was seemed like a
miracle to people whose idea of adversity ran to rather fuzzy
memories of the Great Depression. That he should still be so
convinced of the truth of the religion he had been ordained
to serve was more than a miracle. It was, according to Mary
Ohanian's passionate declaration, proof positive of the existence of God. Over the years, though, Tibor had become less
exotic. The Soviet Union had broken up, making Armenia in-
dependent for the first time in almost a century. Refugees
had poured onto Cavanaugh Street, as they had onto the
streets of every Armenian-American neighborhood in the
country. There were other people there now who had been
through the kinds of things Tibor had been through, if not for
the same reasons. Bennis had put it best one night in the

Ararat. The thing about Tibor was not that he had suffered for his faith under the Soviets, it was that he had suffered on purpose. Even now Gregor thought he had never known anybody so determined to get into trouble for his principles.

Tibor lived in an apartment attached to the back of Holy Trinity Church, reached by walking through a cobblestoned courtyard carefully overhung with vines. The apartment had been designed for a priest and his family. Armenian priests, like those in most of the Eastern churches, were usually married, unless they had been tapped by their hierarchies as possible material for promotion to bishop. Bishops were not allowed to marry—a rule that was left over from the days when the Armenian Church had been part of the Catholic Church. There were a lot of those, Gregor supposed, although the Armenian Church didn't like to admit to them except when everybody was talking about ecumenism for the newspapers, at which times it was understood that Christians who looked united also looked good. Tibor had had a wife, named Anna, back in the Soviet Union, but she had been executed years before he escaped to Israel and came to the United States. Even Gregor, who was Tibor's closest friend on Cavanaugh Street, had no idea what Anna had been executed for. Tibor now had this huge apartment, given to the priest of Holy Trinity no matter who he was, owned and maintained by the church, and no people to put in it. Sometimes he took in homeless families and refugees, but mostly he just rattled around by himself. And bought books, Gregor thought, as he leaned hard against the front doorbell. Tibor always bought books.

The sky was gray with clouds but very light. The courtyard in front of Tibor's door was slick with dew, making it treacherous to walk on. Gregor heard shuffling on the other side of the door and stood back. The door opened and Tibor peered out, fully dressed but mentally on another planet.

"Oh," he said. "Krekor. Is it late? I was reading."

Tibor stepped back, and Gregor went into the apartment,

almost colliding with a tall stack of paperbacks that had been shoved against the walls just inside the front door. It was a very tall stack of paperbacks—as high as Gregor's waist, and he was a tall man. Gregor leaned over and checked them out. The three on the top were *Clear and Present Danger* by Tom Clancy, *Love Medicine* by Louise Erdrich, and the new *Catechism of the Catholic Church*. The *Catechism* threatened to destroy the whole pile because, unlike the rest of the books in the stack it was the size of a hardcover book. Gregor saw little pieces of paper sticking out of it, covered with marks from a bright red felt-tip pen. Nobody on earth could read Father Tibor Kasparian's handwriting. Tibor saw where Gregor was looking, and shrugged.

"I have one or two philosophical disagreements with the Catholic Church," he said. "Also, unlike this Pope, I think I like inclusive language, except maybe that I am not ready to call God my mother. Come into the kitchen, Krekor. I was just making coffee."

Tibor's coffee was even worse than Gregor's, but he followed the other man through the wide living room anyway. Tibor looked older than Gregor and moved as if he were nearly ancient, but he was actually almost ten years younger. His living room was even more crowded with books than his foyer was. There were books stacked against the walls, books on chairs, books on tables, books in piles on the floor. Gregor saw Mickey Spillane and Judith Krantz, Aristotle in the original Greek and the Old Testament in the original Hebrew, novels by Hemingway and histories by Toynbee and something called *The Semiotic of Toilet Tissue* by nobody he'd ever heard of. The books made up for the fact that there was not a decoration of any kind in the apartment. Tibor had crosses that he hung on his walls here and there, mostly given to him by other people, but he seemed never to have heard of the idea of putting up pictures to make your rooms look brighter.

The kitchen was just as full of books as the living room

and the foyer. Gregor took a stack of Sue Grafton and Sara Paretsky off a chair and sat down. Then he moved a stack of Stephen Donaldson fantasy novels to give himself a little room at the table. Tibor came over and put a cup of coffee down in front of him. Gregor wondered for the millionth time how Tibor managed to get instant coffee to come out like that.

"So," Tibor said, clearing a chair off for himself too. "What is this about? Do you want to go to the Ararat?"

"I did," Gregor said, "but I've been talking to old George. Does all this business with the wedding sound a little— excessive—to you?"

"No."

"Well," Gregor said dryly, "that answers my question."

Tibor waved his hands dismissively. "You don't understand about weddings," he said. "I'm a priest. I've officiated at hundreds of weddings. It's always like this."

"We've had weddings on Cavanaugh Street before. They never made me afraid to have my breakfast in the Ararat."

"That's because they were the weddings of people you didn't know well," Tibor said. "It's not weddings you're so upset about, it's Donna's wedding. Something finally changes in your life here. Things will never be the same."

"Thank you, Dr. Freud."

"Krekor, please. You should give me more credit than to compare me with Freud. But what I'm telling you is true. It is true for Bennis too. She gets through it by interesting herself in the details, but when she comes up for air she is all upset."

"I'm not upset," Gregor said. "I like Donna. I like Russ. I think they ought to get married."

"I do too," Tibor said. "Everybody thinks they ought to get married."

"And old George is right," Gregor went on, "it's going to be good for Tommy. I don't think Donna could go through another round of him waking up in the middle of the night, crying and hysterical and wanting to know why his father doesn't love him. Did you know about that?"

"I had heard about it, Krekor, yes."

"Tommy's bedroom is right over my head. The first time it happened, I was ready to go up to Boston and open Peter Desarian's head with a meat cleaver. But that wouldn't do any good, would it? He'd still be Peter Desarian. Tommy needs a father, but he sure as hell doesn't need Peter Desarian."

"Donna doesn't need Peter Desarian either," Tibor said. "Yes, yes, Gregor, I know all the arguments. I agree with all the arguments. This marriage is a wonderful thing. It is good for everyone involved. Donna and Russ should definitely go through with it. But I worry."

"About it changing things."

"Of course."

"Do you think we're being illogical here?" Gregor asked. "It all seems so complicated and confused and I don't see why it should. It wasn't this ambiguous when I got married to Elizabeth."

"When you got married to Elizabeth you were twenty-five."

"What about you and Anna?"

Tibor shrugged. "Me and Anna were a long time ago under very different circumstances. We were introduced by the bishop, you know. That was how it was done in that time and place. It was hard for a young man in the seminary to find someone suitable to marry."

"But even if the bishop found Anna, you loved her."

"Oh, yes," Tibor said. "I definitely loved her."

"Well, then." Gregor moved some more books. Tibor had a copy of *How to Have a Perfect Wedding* and also a copy of *The Five Essential Steps to Divorce*. Gregor picked them both up and put them on the seat of the chair behind him, nearly toppling a stack of Harlequin romances.

"That's funny," he told Tibor. "I was thinking about divorce this morning. About how easy it is these days."

"Too easy," Tibor said solemnly.

"Probably," Gregor agreed, "but I was thinking about how it's changed things for homicide. Easy divorce, I mean. Men still kill their wives, of course, and wives still kill their husbands, but the kind of spousal murder you get these days is different than it used to be. I'm putting that badly. You always had all kinds of spousal murder, the drunken-rage kind and the sudden-snap kind and logical-conclusion-to-twenty-years-of-beatings kind, but in the old days almost every big city police department had at least one escape-hatch spousal murder every three years or so. You know what I mean?"

"You mean the men and the women couldn't get a divorce and so they murdered the person they were married to."

"Right," Gregor said. "When you had laws that let one spouse refuse a divorce, you had a certain incidence of people who really did work at committing a murder they were trying to get away with. A murder that they'd planned. There isn't much of that in spousal murder anymore. There was that lawyer up in Boston who shot himself in his stomach after he killed his wife so that he could claim they had been attacked by muggers. That's the kind of thing I used to read in those mystery novels Bennis is always giving me and I'd refuse to believe it. Who would shoot himself in his own stomach? That kind of thing hurts."

"I'm sure it does, Krekor."

"Anyway, there isn't much of that kind of thing anymore. People file for no-fault and they don't even need their spouse's permission."

"That's not a good thing either, Krekor."

"No, I don't think it is. But it makes the situation I've just been drawn into very interesting. Did you know John Jackman called me last night? He has something he wants me to work on."

"How would I know that, Krekor? I haven't talked to you."

"I've talked to Bennis," Gregor said, "and you know how it is around here. Never mind. Did you watch the news last night?"

"Of course."

"There was a pipe bomb that went off in a parking garage in West Philadelphia yesterday—"

"Oh, that one," Tibor said, sounding suddenly animated. "It was really two pipe bombs, I think, Krekor. They made a big mess."

"Yes, they did. And the woman who was supposed to have set them is missing, and she's also supposed to have murdered her husband earlier in the day in this place called Fox Run Hill down in Bucks County."

Tibor looked confused. "The murder took place in Bucks County? Why is John Jackman investigating it?"

"He's investigating this end, with the pipe bombs."

"And he wants you to come in on it."

"I know what you're thinking," Gregor said. "The local police are likely to be not pleased. If they really hate the idea, I'll withdraw."

Tibor looked skeptical. "You never withdraw," he said. "You always have some excuse to keep going. So what is it with this case that you are supposed to do for John Jackman?"

"I don't know yet," Gregor admitted. "He just told me he wanted me to work on it, and then he made me promise to meet him at headquarters this morning at nine. Which I'm going to do. It's just that, in the wake of that phone call, I've been reading and watching everything I can about the case."

"And?"

"And," Gregor said, "as I was saying before, it occurred to me that you can't, with something like this, make the kind of assumptions you would have thirty or forty years ago. Patsy MacLaren Willis didn't kill her husband just because she didn't want to stay married to him anymore. There were easier ways to get that done."

"You can be sure that this was not one of those spur-of-the-moment things you were talking about?"

"I can't be sure about anything until I talk to John," Gregor said, "but from what I've read in the newspaper and seen on television so far, I'd say it wasn't likely. For one thing, there was the silencer."

"Silencer?"

"According to the eleven o'clock news, a gun and a silencer were found in Stephen Willis's bedroom along with Stephen Willis's body. No fingerprints yet, of course, and no lab reports. It might not even be the murder weapon. But I don't believe that."

"I wouldn't believe that either."

"So, there's the silencer. And there's the fact that it's not legal for a gun shop in this state to sell silencers. Which means the silencer must have been acquired especially. And what do you acquire a silencer for except to be able to shoot without being heard?"

"True," Tibor said, "but it might not be this woman who bought the gun and the silencer. The gun and the silencer might have been bought by the husband. Maybe he was intending to kill her."

"Maybe. That's not bad for a psychological explanation. Because the next thing you have to account for is the pipe bombs."

"Bombs do not take long to make," Tibor said reprovingly. "I have made bombs in my life, Krekor."

"Fine, but these bombs were on timers. The newspapers didn't say that, but I have to assume it, because it's the only thing that makes sense. Patsy MacLaren Willis parked her car, walked away, and hours later the bombs blew up. Timers."

"All right."

"The question is, did Patsy MacLaren Willis place the bombs and the timers, or did somebody else, and what for? And where is Patsy MacLaren Willis?"

"She could be out of the country by now," Tibor pointed out.

"I suppose she could be. I suppose John is checking up on it. And the Bucks County people too."

"But you don't think she did these things," Tibor said.

"No," Gregor admitted, "I don't."

"Why not?"

"Well," Gregor said, "think about those pipe bombs. Big pipe bombs that made lots of mess and lots of noise and lots of publicity. Why bother?"

"I don't understand, Krekor."

"Why bother?" Gregor insisted. "Why cause an explosion like that if you've just murdered your husband and you want to make a getaway. Why not just get away?"

"Murderers do strange things," Tibor said.

"Murderers," Gregor said firmly, "are always absolutely logical."

# THREE

## 1.

THE NEWS ABOUT STEPHEN AND Patsy Mac-Laren Willis was all over the neighborhood as soon as it hit the news and, as far as Evelyn Adder could tell, it had been all over the neighborhood ever since, jumping from one house to another like a flu bug in January. The husbands were all worried about Stephen, or about Patsy-and-Stephen, however you wanted to put it. It seemed impossible to them that a woman like Patsy, so bland, so cordial, so *nice*, should want to kill anyone, especially with a silencer, especially when he was asleep in his own bed. The women were just excited. They had discovered it first, of course. It was Molly Bracken who had found Stephen's body, at 5:01, when she went running over to the Tudor from the Victorian and found the garage door unlocked. She had gone inside, called Patsy's name, and then looked carefully around Patsy's big, empty house. Sarah Lockwood, who told Evelyn this story, seemed to think it was completely natural. Maybe, Evelyn had thought at the time, Sarah goes running around to people's houses on a regular basis, and just drops in whenever a door is open, whether she's been invited or not. Evelyn didn't know anything about Molly Bracken, but the whole thing seemed strange to her. She would never have done anything like it, especially if it involved Patsy MacLaren Willis. Patsy was—strange, or that was the word for it, and too quiet, and remote. She had made Evelyn half-crazy for years. Evelyn hated not knowing whether people liked her or not. She was always expecting an ambush, especially from women, especially from women like Patsy, who were sensible about everything from food to clothes. For some reason Evelyn found people like Molly Bracken less intimidating, as if she could see the insecurities that propped up all that makeup, the self-doubt that provided the fuel for all that anxious talk. It was people who thought well of themselves whom Evelyn couldn't stand.

Henry couldn't stand the reports about Patsy and Stephen, but he watched them, right through dinner, with the television blasting in the family room while he ate his steak filets and baked potato at a folding tray set up in front of the set. Evelyn had a tossed green salad with balsamic vinegar and a nonfat banana yogurt with wheat germ sprinkled along the top. She had a folding tray too, which was usually an absolute no-no. According to Henry, she was supposed to be "retraining," and while she was "retraining" she was not allowed to do anything else while she ate her food. She was supposed to sit at the kitchen table and concentrate on her plate, with no distractions. She wasn't allowed to read or watch television or listen to the radio. She wasn't allowed even to think about anything except her food, and what it felt like in her mouth, and what it tasted like, and whether this was what she really wanted or not. She almost never had to ask that last question. She already knew the answer. Of course salad with balsamic vinegar wasn't what she wanted, and neither was non-fat yogurt with wheat germ. She wanted a pair of little steaks just like Henry's and a baked potato with butter and sour cream and chives in it. Henry's baked potato had all those things. Now that he was thin, he was allowed to eat.

"I think it was damned stupid of Molly Bracken to go into

that house just because she found the door open," Henry said when Molly was interviewed on the CBS affiliate. "That door could have been left open for any reason. There could have been a burglar."

"How could there have been a burglar?" Evelyn asked reasonably. "There's the gate. We have security guards."

"France had the Maginot Line," Henry said—cryptically, as far as Evelyn was concerned. "Think about the Gordian knot. Security can be breached."

"I still don't see that Molly should have worried about a burglar. I wouldn't have."

"Would you go into that house just because you found a door open?"

"Of course not."

"There, then."

"But it wouldn't have had anything to do with there being a burglar," Evelyn went on patiently. "It's just that I never really knew Patsy all that well. I wouldn't have wanted to intrude."

"It seems like none of us knew Patsy very well. It seems like the woman was crazy."

"Oh, I don't think so."

"Well, what else would you call it? When a woman kills her husband and then blows up her own car?"

"Maybe she was just angry with him," Evelyn said, pushing a piece of lettuce around the small round bowl that contained it. "Maybe he wasn't nice to her and she just lost it."

"Women don't kill their husbands just because their husbands aren't nice to them. Christ, Evelyn, if women did that, there wouldn't be a husband left alive in America."

Maybe there wouldn't, Evelyn had thought at the time—and now, only hours later, she was thinking it again. It was a quarter to eight in the morning and Henry was up and sitting in front of the television set again. He had woken half an hour early and nearly caught Evelyn at her ritual morning window-seat binge. Then he had gotten Evelyn her half

grapefruit without sugar and her four-ounce glass of juice
from the locked refrigerator, and sat down to watch the news
again.

Evelyn was watching him. Feeling huge. Feeling bulky.
Feeling fat enough to explode into fragments everywhere in
the room, and maybe choke him with them. She wanted his
pancakes so badly, she nearly snatched them out from under
his nose. On the television screen, a young blond reporter
was going over and over what it was the police knew now,
which wasn't much different from what they had known the
night before. The television reporter was as thin as a rail and
arrogant with it.

"I've been thinking about things," Henry said. "About today, I mean. We may have to change the schedule a bit."

"We can't change the schedule," Evelyn said. "We have to
go shopping. We're nearly out of everything."

"I know. But I can't go shopping today. I have some work I
have to get done."

"I have to go shopping." Evelyn tried to keep the panic out
of her voice. "We're low on everything. We hardly have a
thing in the house."

"This is not a good psychological sign," Henry said. "It
shouldn't make you crazy just because we have to post-
pone shopping for a few days. We're not going to starve.
Food shouldn't be that important to you."

Evelyn took a deep breath. The window seat was nearly
empty. Something about the Patsy and Stephen thing must
have gotten to her. She had eaten practically her whole stash
of Hostess cupcakes. She hadn't been able to make herself
stop. She had told herself it didn't matter, because they
would go shopping, she would be able to replace them, she
would find a way to get away from Henry in the store and eat
and eat and eat. Now she rubbed the palms of her hands
against her face and tried to breathe normally. She needed
something to make the fear go away.

"We're almost out of everything," she said, sounding rational even to herself. "It's not the food I eat that we're out of. It's the food *you* eat that we're out of."

"Well, yes. I know that."

"We can't just go without food, Henry. And there are things. Dishwashing detergent. Laundry soap. We run out."

"I know that." Henry sounded patient, the way he used to when really stupid students wanted his attention, or when girl students who were plain and stocky instead of slim and pretty tried to ask him a question. "I know there are things we legitimately need, Evelyn. That's not my point."

"If there are things we legitimately need, we should go and get them."

Henry cut the last big wedge of pancakes still in front of him into bite-sized pieces. In pieces, the pancakes looked to Evelyn like caramelized corn, waiting to pop up and get her.

"Well," Henry said. "I've been thinking about it. Maybe I could trust you just this once to go to the store by yourself."

"By myself," Evelyn repeated.

Henry waved irritably. "I can't go on policing you forever, Evelyn. Eventually, you're going to have to take responsibility for all this yourself. I wish you'd join a support group."

"I don't want to join a support group."

"Anyway." Henry wasn't really listening. The television news was showing a weather report. He wasn't really listening to that either. "You have to go out on your own sooner or later. With this work I'm caught up in, it might as well be now."

"I would need the keys to the car."

"You can have the keys to the car."

"I might do anything if I had the keys to the car," Evelyn said.

Henry turned his face away from the television set.

"For Christ's sake, Evelyn. Don't start sounding like *The Three Faces of Eve.*"

"I might stop at Burger King or Dairy Queen," Evelyn

went on. "I might stop at Taco Bell and buy six ten-packs of hard-shelled tacos and extra sour cream and eat them right there in the parking lot."

Henry stood up quickly and reached into the pocket of his trousers. He came out with his car keys and tossed them to her. Evelyn almost didn't catch them. She was that surprised to see them.

"Here," Henry said. "Take those. Go when you want."

"I don't have any money."

Henry reached into his pocket again and came out with his wallet. He opened it up and took out all the green Evelyn could see.

"Here," he said, handing it all to her, twenties without number, tens and fives and even one fifty-dollar bill. "Take it. Go to the store. I really do have to work today, Evelyn."

Evelyn took the money. "All right," she said.

"I've got to go up to the office," Henry said. "I can't be disturbed today, Evelyn. Not for anything."

"I won't disturb you."

"I'm going to lock the door. I know you don't like it, but I have to. I have to concentrate. I can't have interruptions."

"I won't interrupt you."

"That's fine, then." Henry looked around at the family room and the breakfast room and the kitchen. "That's fine," he said again. "I'll just go up to the office now. Have a good time shopping."

"I will."

"Be careful driving the car. It's been a long time since you've been behind the wheel."

"I'll be careful."

"Try to remember that if you load your cart up with junk food, everybody we know will see it. That ought to help you keep your discipline up. Everybody will see you."

Everybody sees me every day, Evelyn thought. If I cared, I would already be thin again. But she understood what Henry was trying to tell her. She even understood that he was right, in a way. She did care what the rest of them thought about her. She was just careful never to ask them to explain it.

"So," Henry said, rocking back on the heels of his shoes. "I'll be going up."

"Fine," Evelyn said.

"I'll be out of communication most of the day."

"Fine," Evelyn said again.

"Right." Henry put his hands back into his pockets and turned away from her. He hurried out of the room, almost at a run, his shoulders hunched over and his legs moving in an odd, jerky way, as if he had suddenly acquired some kind of nerve disease.

Evelyn looked down at the keys in her hand and shook her head. Keys and money. Keys and money. The car was parked out in the driveway because Henry hadn't bothered to pull it into the garage when he came back from the club with it last night.

I wonder what all this is about, Evelyn asked herself. I wonder what it is he's so afraid of.

Then she waddled over to the counter and put the keys and the money in her purse. She thought of the big display of Entenmann's chocolate cakes down at the Stop 'N Shop and wondered how many she could eat in the car on the way home, eat while driving, eat while stopping for red lights on the road between here and the mall. Maybe I'll have to pull over someplace, she thought, and give myself time to eat.

## 2.

Liza Verity never took night duty unless she had to, but last night she had had to, and now, at quarter to nine in the morning, she was exhausted. It had been one of those nights that no nurse likes to have anything to do with. It had started with a bad traffic accident on one of those brutal overpasses that now seemed to define the Philadelphia skyline and then done a domino number on life in the rest of the hospital. The accident was a five-car pileup on one side and a tractor-trailer truck on the other. One of the cars in the five-car pileup had six people crammed into it. One of the other cars had only one person in it, but that person had had a little semi-automatic pistol and been hyped up on something serious. He was at the back of the pileup. As soon as the crashing and the screeching were over, he got out and started firing randomly, hitting cars passing and people standing around to see what had happened. He seemed to take particular offense at the idea of bystanders. There were always dozens of people who stopped to rubberneck at the side of any highway disaster. The man with the semiautomatic pistol shot up ten of them before a teenage boy from Radnor had the courage and the presence of mind to tackle him from behind. The teenage boy got the semiautomatic pistol away from the shooter but suffered a broken arm in the process. By the time all these people got to the emergency room, it was something worse than a mess. They had called six extra doctors and nearly thirty nurses down to duty. There were police everywhere and ambulance men looking green and paramedics looking tired. Liza had been a little surprised to see so few media people. Usually, the local news crews were all over an accident like this one. It was exactly the kind of thing their viewers loved best.

One of the advantages of having been up all night is that it is nearly impossible to summon the energy to be worked up about anything. Coming upstairs from emergency after she was finally let off, Liza had her ass pinched in the elevator by a third-year medical student on apprenticeship roster. She didn't even turn around and slap his face, which is what she usually did when boys of that sort pulled nonsense on her. In her tiredness, everything about the day-to-day workings of the hospital seemed tacky and absurd. Medical students who had to resort to sexual harassment to have a good day. Doctors who wanted to prove their superiority to God at least once an hour, usually by putting down nurses. Nurses' aides who were always a little insulted when they were asked to make beds or change bedpans. Liza got off the elevator on the fourth floor and headed down the hall to the pediatrics unit. She could have gotten out of going down to emergency last night. She was a pediatrics specialist and already technically off-duty when they started bringing the bodies in. Maybe she was just getting a little stale, bored with the routine, impatient with the politics—God only knew, she was all of that, there was no maybe about it. Maybe it was time for her to quit and find herself another job.

The pediatrics unit had a wing of its own with twenty-six rooms in it and over sixty beds. The nurses' station was a curved counter that was always supposed to have somebody standing behind it. There was nobody there. Liza walked around the counter to the door at the back and stuck her head inside. Sharon Birch and Mia Zhiransky were sitting side by side on the office couch, watching something on television.

"Don't you think you ought to be doing something sensible," Liza asked them, "like listening for patients?"

"We've got the warning system on in here," Mia said. "We were just discussing politics."

"Hospital or government?" Liza asked.

"Race." Sharon Birch was tall and thin and black. If she hadn't had bags under her eyes big enough to pack the Rolling Stones into, she might have been beautiful. "We were talking about the news reports. How did it go with the accident?"

"Awful," Liza said.

"Anyone dead?" Mia asked.

Liza nodded. "At least three people. There's probably going to end up being six or more."

"All black people?" Sharon asked.

Liza had to think. It was honestly not the kind of thing she noticed in the middle of an emergency. "Yes," she said finally, having gone over all the patients in her head. "I think so."

"There," Sharon Birch said.

"I still don't think it's race." Mia Zhiransky was small and blond and perfect, their own hospital china doll. "I think it's money. It's always more exciting when something happens to people with money."

"Why?" Sharon asked.

Liza got a plastic coffee cup from the stack next to the coffee machine and poured herself some coffee. "What are you two talking about? What happened to somebody with money?"

Sharon waved her hand dismissively in the air. "It wasn't somebody with real money, like a rock star or anything. It was one of those people who lives at Fox Run Hill. You know the place I mean."

"I'd call ten thousand square feet of house money," Mia said. "It costs a lot more money than I'm ever going to have."

"Maybe you'll win the lottery," Sharon said.

Liza swallowed half the coffee in the cup at once. "What's this all about?" she asked again. "What happened to somebody at Fox Run Hill? Mugger get in past those security guards or what?"

"This woman killed her husband," Sharon said.

"That's it?" Liza was surprised.

"She had some kind of fancy gun," Mia said, "and then she drove her car into a parking garage in West Philly and blew it up."

"She blew up her car?"

"She wasn't inside it," Sharon explained. "She left some kind of time bomb in it and disappeared."

"A time bomb," Liza repeated. "In a parking garage. Was anybody hurt?"

"There were a few people injured," Sharon said, "but nobody was killed. That's why I was saying what I was saying. That it's race. If it was black people who did all that, nobody would have paid any attention."

"It's been all over the news since last night," Mia explained.

"And what hasn't been all over the news is that accident,"

Sharon said. "I mean, there've been some reports on it, you know, here and there, but no real fuss, and all the while they're going on and on and on about this little murder out in Fox Run Hill. Because the people involved in it are white."

"Because the people involved in it are rich," Mia said.

"Maybe it's both," Liza told them, finishing the rest of her coffee and pouring some more. "What happened to the wife who committed the murder?"

"No one knows," Mia said solemnly.

"The problem with these people in the media," Sharon said, "is they think all black people are animals with nothing on their minds but sex and violence. So a few black people get killed, so who cares? So some black guy takes out a pistol and starts shooting up the landscape, what can you expect? It's race, pure and simple."

"I'm not saying it's not race a lot of the time," Mia said. "I'm just saying that this time the deciding factor was money. That's all."

"Look at O. J. Simpson," Sharon said. "What was the point of all that fuss except to make it clear to every single American of the white persuasion that it doesn't make a damn bit of difference what a black person accomplishes in his life, he's still just a hair trigger away from being a thug?"

"All that fuss could have been about violence against women," Mia said. "I mean, for once the media could have been taking violence against women seriously."

"When Sid Vicious killed his girlfriend, it was a footnote on the eleven o'clock news," Sharon said firmly.

Over on the television screen there was a shot of a still photograph of a woman in middle age. There were lines on the sides of her face and bags under her eyes. Her hair was salt-and-pepper gray. Liza drank more coffee and wished she weren't so tired. The face on the screen looked strangely familiar.

"Here we go again," Sharon was saying. "The mysterious Mrs. Willis and her awful moneyed murder. Have you ever seen anybody with so little style in your life? If I had money like that, I'd look great."

"Maybe she didn't want to look great," Mia said.

Liza walked closer to the screen and squinted at the picture.

"Oh," she said.

"What is it?" Sharon said.

"Police today are desperately searching for clues that will explain the bizarre behavior, and present whereabouts, of Patricia MacLaren Willis," the announcer said.

Liza took a step back. "Who?" she said.

"They called her Patsy," Mia said. "It was in the *Inquirer* this morning."

"But that's impossible," Liza said.

"Did you know her?" Sharon said.

"I keep forgetting that Liza went to Vassar," Mia said. "She must know dozens of people like that."

The coffee in the cup was all gone. The picture on the screen had changed to one of a talking head with a microphone. The talking head was standing in front of a big Tudor house with what seemed to be hundreds of police cars parked in the driveway. Liza rubbed her eyes.

"Police are now saying that we may never know the complete story of why Patricia MacLaren Willis did what she did yesterday," the talking head said, "because as the hours go by, there is less and less hope that when she is found, if she is found, she will be found alive."

"Alive," Liza Verity repeated. And then she shook her head very hard, as if that would clear it. "For Christ's sake."

### 3.

Out in Fox Run Hill, Sarah Lockwood was also saying "for Christ's sake," over and over and over again, under her breath. She was standing at the window at the second floor landing of her French Provincial house, looking out on Patsy Willis's Tudor. She had been standing there for nearly half an hour, while police cars came and went and police detectives spread out across the lawn and half a dozen women from the neighborhood found excuses to do their jogging right in front of the Willises' front door. Sarah didn't think she'd ever been this nervous in her life.

"You can't stay up there all day," Kevin called out to her every once in a while. "You're not going to find anything out mooning over a lot of parked police cars."

Now a new police car was pulling up, a different police car, from Philadelphia instead of from the local force. Sarah watched as a tall black man in a good black suit got out—an astonishing sight, since there were never any black people in Fox Run Hill, unless they were in uniform—and was followed by an even taller white man, older and thicker and running to fat. It took a minute for Sarah to place him. Then she raced from the window, leaned over the stairrail, and called down the well: "Kevin, come quick. Look who's here."

"I'm not going to come quick up those stairs," Kevin replied, "unless you're announcing the Second Coming."

"It's Gregor Demarkian," Sarah said. "Come quickly."

There was a short silence from the lower floor. Then Kevin said "Jesus," and Sarah heard his heavy footsteps beginning to run up the stairs.

"Look," she said when Kevin arrived on the landing. "There he is. Do you think the local police have hired him?"

"I don't think it's possible to hire him. I don't think he works for money."

"Somebody must have brought him in though," Sarah said. "It stands to reason. He doesn't just show up on his own."

"Maybe it's something we ought to worry about," Kevin said. "Under the circumstances. Considering what we're up to."

"I wouldn't worry about it. He isn't going to be interested in us. It's Patsy and Stephen he's going to be worried about."

"Murder investigations are funny things," Kevin said carefully. "They can—spread out."

"I know that."

"Then maybe we ought to worry about it. Maybe we ought to be a little careful over the next few weeks. Just in case."

Down in the Willises' driveway, Gregor Demarkian was huddled in a clutch with a lot of men in suits. Sarah Lockwood bit her lip.

"I think it's exciting," she said softly. "I think it makes everything we're doing much more fun."

"You're nuts."

Sarah turned around and put her hand on the bulge in Stephen's pants. It pulsed under her fingers and made her smile.

"Of course I'm nuts," she said. "That's the point."

# FOUR

## 1.

THE FIRST GATED COMMUNITY GREGOR Demarkian had ever heard of had been in Florida, on the Atlantic coast, exactly one year after Ted Bundy had been arrested for the murder of Kimberly Ann Leach. Logically, Gregor was sure that those two facts did not go together in any meaningful way. The gated community had probably existed long before anyone in Florida had ever heard of Ted Bundy. Still, in his mind the juxtaposition was significant. He had known enough really rich people who lived behind walls and gates and guards and security systems. There was a positive fashion for that sort of thing in the early seventies in Beverly Hills. Gated communities, however, were not for the really rich. They were for the people Gregor had learned in college to call the "upper middle class," meaning really successful doctors and lawyers and businessmen, the top management of the larger corporations, the ruling elites of America's better small towns. Of course, Gregor thought as he got out of John Jackman's commandeered police car, these days the top managements of the larger corporations were counted among the really rich. They had salaries in seven figures and bonus packages that would be the envy of most rock stars. Their job seemed to be to move as much production work as possible out of Pittsburgh and into Southeast Asia. And as for the really successful doctors and lawyers—

Standing in the driveway, Gregor looked around. This was a good neighborhood. There were rubberneckers, but the rubberneckers were discreet. They looked like joggers who weren't much interested in what the police were doing. The lawns were beautifully kept too—but Gregor saw that they had been badly planned. They were all the same size and shape, like the lawns in a tract house development, and when you looked at them long enough, you noticed. The architecture had been badly planned too. Each of the houses was carefully unlike any of the others, but too much unlike. Gregor looked over the Willises' Tudor, and then around at a French Provincial, a brick Federalist, and an elaborately gabled and turreted Victorian. Out on the Main Line, where the really rich people lived, the houses were much more alike, and much larger. These looked oddly like stage sets, studied and self-conscious, uncomfortable.

John Jackman touched his elbow. "So," he said, "what do you think?"

"Expensive," Gregor said.

Jackman nodded. "Oh, it is that. Houses go for about five hundred thousand apiece."

"That was the other thing I was thinking," Gregor said. "That isn't expensive enough."

"I know what you mean. The first thing I thought of the first time I walked in here was Bryn Mawr and that place Bennis Hannaford's family had—do they still have it?"

"It was willed to Yale University after Bennis's mother died," Gregor said.

"Right. But that was really a place, wasn't it? At least forty rooms. All those servants' quarters. The stables. You couldn't have fit it on one of these lots."

"Is this the first of these gated communities you've ever been in?"

"Live and in the flesh, yes," Jackman said. "We don't have a lot of them in Philadelphia proper, as you can imagine. And they're not the kind of places the police tend to get called in."

Gregor shook his head impatiently. "Why do they do it?" he demanded. "What's the point of the gates and the guards and all the rest of it? They can't possibly believe it turns them into successors to the robber barons."

"Of course they don't," Jackman said. "They do it to keep the black people out."

Gregor shot Jackman a look and started to say something, but he didn't have time. They were being approached by a large white man in a leather jacket. If the man hadn't been obviously white-haired and old, he would have been menacing. Gregor caught the patch on the sleeve of his jacket and realized it was some kind of police insignia.

"Dan," Jackman said, holding out his hand. "Good morning. This is Mr. Gregor Demarkian—"

"—the Armenian-American Hercule Poirot," Dan finished.

"I hope not," Gregor said.

"Dan Exter," Jackman finished, "chief of homicide for the Heggerd town police. It says something that a place called Heggerd, Pennsylvania, needs a chief of homicide."

"It's not exactly that impressive," Dan Exter said mildly. "The last murder we had out here was four years ago, and it was an assisted suicide we didn't even prosecute in the end. Couple of old people. If you don't like being called the Armenian-American Hercule Poirot, what do you like to be called?"

"Gregor," Gregor said.

John Jackman rocked back on his heels. In one way, he looked out of place there. He was probably perfectly right about the way the people who lived there felt about black people, and he was so very black. In another way, though, he looked much more like he belonged there than most of the joggers. He was less tentative than they were, more sure of himself, more confident of his authority. John Jackman was a young man, but he had a lot of internal authority. Gregor had met him when he was just a rookie cop, and the quality had been evident even then.

"They've been holding off going around the neighborhood," Jackman said, "because they know what a hassle it's going to be, and I don't blame them. Still, it's going to have to be done."

"I know it's going to have to be done," Dan Exter said patiently, "but it isn't going to help us any and it's going to be a problem. Let's get the important things done first."

"Somebody might have seen her leave," Jackman said.

"The security guard saw her leave," Dan Exter said. "Actually, if you ask me, from what this guy said, the woman made a point of making sure he saw her leave. In fact, from everything I've heard over the last few hours, she seems to have made a point of being noticed wherever she went. Did John tell you about the money?" he asked Gregor.

Gregor shook his head. "I thought there had to be money in it somewhere, but he hasn't said anything in particular."

"She went to a bank in Philadelphia yesterday," Jackman said. "It was a couple of blocks from where she parked the car. She wrote out a check for fifteen thousand dollars and handed it to a teller."

Dan Exter scratched his head. "I don't know about you, Mr. Demarkian, but it's my guess that a woman who lived like this in a place like this would know better than to write a check for that much money and hand it to a teller. She would have known she had to clear it with an officer of the bank. She would have known the bank would have to do some reporting—do you realize that? The Feds make the banks report any cash deposit or cash withdrawal in excess of $9999.99."

"Drugs," Jackman said.

"Drugs and the Internal Revenue," Dan Exter said. "Anyway, when the news hit the airwaves last night, we got a call from the manager of the bank branch where she cashed the check—"

"She did actually cash it?" Gregor put in.

Dan Exter nodded. "According to the bank manager, she did. We haven't really had a chance to go into it. John has one of his people interviewing the woman this morning—"

"Just to go over loose ends," Jackman said.

"—and of course we want to know about the account and why she went to that particular branch and all the rest of that sort of thing."

"The branch was near the parking garage?" Gregor asked.

"That's right," Dan Exter said.

"And the parking garage, from what I understand, is near the university," Gregor went on.

"Exactly," John Jackman told him.

"There might not be much of a reason for her to have chosen that particular branch," Gregor pointed out. "The university isn't in the worst neighborhood in Philadelphia, but it's not in the best one either. I wouldn't think they get middle-aged women walking in off the street wanting to cash checks for fifteen thousand dollars every day."

"They get students who overdraw their checking accounts," Jackman said.

"Go back to the beginning," Gregor told him. "Patricia MacLaren Willis left here yesterday morning—when?"

"Early," Dan Exter said. "It wasn't even eight."

"And then what happened?"

John Jackman shook his head. "We don't know. Not yet. The next time we hear about her, it's when she's parking at that garage, about noon."

"And making herself conspicuous?" Gregor asked.

Jackman nodded. "The guy at the garage I talked to myself. She pulled in there and made him sell her an all-day ticket in spite of the fact that the day was half over. Gave him a complicated financial argument, according to him, which probably means she talked common sense for ten minutes. This is not a rocket scientist we're dealing with here."

"Then she parked her car and left the garage," Gregor said. "Then what?"

"Then she went to the bank," Dan Exter said. "At least, the times are right that she didn't do anything between the parking garage and the bank."

"Where she cashed a check for fifteen thousand," Gregor said. "Then what did she do?"

"She had a big pocketbook," Dan Exter said. "Something called a Coach bag, according to the bank manager—"

"Coach is a brand," John Jackman sighed. "I keep telling him."

"She had the money packed into this Coach bag and left the bank," Dan Exter said, "and that's the last we know until the pipe bombs blew a couple of hours later. Which, by the way, is all I think we're going to know."

"Somebody will have seen her," John Jackman said confidently. "Just wait. Somebody always does."

"Listen." Dan Exter appealed directly to Gregor Demarkian. "This is a plain, ordinary middle-aged lady we're talking about here. Not in spectacular shape. Not unusual in any way. Not dressed to be noticed—"

"No?" Gregor asked.

"She was wearing a thin silk blouse and a skirt that was 'kind of beige,' according to the bank manager," Dan Exter said.

"That's interesting," Gregor said.

"Anyway," Exter went on, "the point is, she wasn't much to look at and she wasn't a memorable kind of woman. We may find her eventually, but I don't think she's going to jump right out and bite us."

Gregor turned around in a small circle, looking at the big house, looking at the driveway, looking at the other big houses up and down the street. He could see a head at a window on the second floor in the brick Federalist, but otherwise the place seemed deserted. Even the joggers had disappeared.

Gregor scratched the back of his neck and wished he hadn't worn a suit—but he always wore a suit, even to the beach, he didn't own anything else to wear. He brushed sweat away from his suit collar and started up the drive, knowing that John Jackman and Dan Exter would follow him.

"We might as well get started," he said. "The longer we hang around, the worse it's going to be."

## 2.

In a routine police investigation—the kind that involves poor people who live in ghettos, and drug deals, and domestic violence—crime scene investigation takes a few hours at best and half a day at worst. The lab people come in and do their dirty work as quickly and efficiently as possible. The police come in and talk to half a dozen people with conflicting stories and another half dozen who want to turn state's evidence. But this was not an ordinary crime scene. In the first place, there were elements here that were honestly mysterious, even though they would probably turn out to be not so mysterious in the end. In the second place—well, Gregor knew the drill. You had to be careful when you were dealing with rich people, even quasi-rich people, like the ones who lived at Fox Run Hill. Rich people had lawyers and—more important—knew when to use them. Rich people knew their rights. They thought they ought to have more rights than the Constitution already allowed.

Gregor walked through the cavernous garage and into the mudroom. He checked out the wooden pegs artfully hammered into one wall and the bench that had been machine-cut to look rough-hewn. There would probably be a lot of that sort of thing in a place like this. He looked under the bench and found three pairs of shoes: Topsiders; Gucci loafers with pennies in them; Nike running shoes. All three pairs were the same size and made for a man. There were no clothes of any kind on the pegs. There were two baseball-style caps on a shelf over the bench. One of the caps had the words CAPITALIST TOOL printed on the crown. The other had the symbol for the New York Mets.

"Fieldstone," Gregor said, kicking at the floor.

"This house is big on fieldstone," Dan Exter told him, "also on beams and dark wood. It's like a signature."

"You ought to check out the shoes," Gregor said. "Just because they're all the same size doesn't necessarily mean they all belong to—what was his name again?"

"Stephen Willis," John Jackman said.

"Mr. Willis."

Gregor walked up the four steps from the mudroom and opened the screen door there.

"That's the kitchen," Dan Exter told him. "Wait'll you see what it's like in there."

Gregor went through the doorway and looked around. What it was like in there was large—too large, like some of the statuary of ancient Egypt, as if sheer size had been the point. There seemed to be two of everything: two sinks, two ovens, two refrigerators, two side-by-side Jenn-Air ranges built into a rounded-corner island. Beyond the island was what looked like an ancient keeping room, complete with an oversized stone fireplace big enough to roast a pig in. Gregor went over there and looked around.

"Can't you just imagine watching the Eagles on the tube in this place?" Dan Exter asked him, pointing to the enormous television set placed discreetly in a dark wood cabinet, set up in front of a group of black leather chairs. "I'd be worried about making an echo every time I coughed."

"It's not exactly homey," Gregor agreed. "Are those trophies over there on that wall?"

Dan Exter shook his head. "Some of them are, but most of them are decorations. They're just supposed to look like trophies."

"What are the real trophies for?"

"Golf," Dan Exter said.

Gregor walked over to the trophies. Then he walked past them and looked at the bookcase built into the paneling. There were half a dozen books on securities law, one or two on the history of the Civil War, and a collection of the complete works of Tom Clancy in hardcover.

"Was Mrs. Willis a Civil War buff?" Gregor asked.

"Mr. Willis was," Dan Exter said. "He's got one of those Civil War chess sets upstairs, you know, where the pieces are soldiers in blue and gray. A really expensive set too."

"How do you know it belonged to Stephen Willis and not his wife?"

"It was in Stephen Willis's private closet."

Gregor looked up at the ceiling. What was above his head right then were dark wooden beams, machine-cut to look hand-hewn. "Is upstairs this way?" he asked, pointing to an archway on his right.

"That's it exactly," John Jackman said.

Gregor went through the archway and looked around. There was a broad front foyer out there, and a staircase that curved in an angular sort of way. There was also a closet. He opened the closet and looked inside. There were six men's coats, including a heavy camel hair and a black cashmere and a leather biking jacket that was much too expensive to have ever belonged to a biker. On the floor were four pairs of rain boots, Wellingtons and fancy galoshes, all men's too.

"The bedroom's up here," John Jackman said, shooing Gregor in the direction of the staircase. "Every house in Fox Run Hill has a formal entry foyer and a grand front staircase."

"That's a direct quote," Dan Exter said, "from the developer who built this place. We talked to him last night."

Gregor stopped on the landing and looked out the window there, at the road and the houses.

"All the houses in Fox Run Hill have one of these landing

things too," Dan Exter said, "at least as far as I can figure. Or the ones right around here do. You can see it when you're outside. The window halfway between the other windows."

Gregor looked out at the big brick house. It had a window just above the entryway, halfway between the windows on the regular floors. "You can hardly tell the police have been here," he said. "The place is so clean."

"The place is antiseptic," John Jackman said. "But you can tell the police have been here when you get upstairs. Just you wait."

Gregor didn't have to wait long. He got to the upstairs hall and looked right and left. To one side, the hall seemed as empty and clean as the rest of the house. The wall-to-wall carpeting looked as if it had been fluffed. The walls looked as if they had been polished. To the other side, however, there was chaos. A set of double doors was propped open by what looked like a pair of cardboard boxes. A large young man in a blue police uniform was standing watch between them. Beyond him, Gregor saw mess and insanity. He walked up to the large young man, nodded a greeting, and walked past him into the bedroom. Since John Jackman and Dan Exter were coming up behind him, the large young man did not protest. Gregor walked through to where the bed was and stood at the end of it. The sheets had been stripped from it, showing the bare mattress, still stained with blood. The bloodstains still looked wet.

"I take it he was sleeping when she shot him," Gregor said to John Jackman and Dan Exter, who had come up behind him.

"Let's just say the body was in bed when we found it," Dan Exter said.

"Shot how many times?"

"Three."

"Any stray bullets?"

"Not that we could find, no," Dan Exter said. "She fired three shots, she hit him three times."

"Good hits?"

"One of them was," Dan Exter said blandly.

"What's a good hit except that it kills the target?" John Jackman asked. "Jesus Christ, Gregor."

Gregor walked around the bed to the night table on the right side. This was obviously Stephen Willis's night table. It had a little brass golf statue next to the lamp. Gregor opened the night-table drawer and found a pack of cards that looked well used and a brown wood pipe with a pouch of cherry tobacco beside it. The pipe was not well used. Stephen Willis, Gregor thought, had been one of those men who wanted to smoke a pipe for the prestige, but who could never get the hang of it.

Gregor walked around the bed to the night table on the other side. There was nothing on this one except the lamp, and nothing in the drawer either, except that sawdusty debris that collects inside wooden drawers after a while. Gregor slid the drawer shut and turned to the line of closets that made up the facing wall.

"Are these all the closets in this suite?" he asked.

"No such luck," Dan Exter said. "These are his closets, from what I've been able to figure out. There are other closets in the dressing room, which is back through there."

Gregor went "back through there." The dressing room was large, but mostly with a lot of wasted space. It held a wall of closets and a stationary bicycle that looked even less used than the pipe.

Gregor opened one of the closets. It was the size of a moderately spacious bathroom, and it was absolutely empty.

"Well," he said.

"You can look at the rest of them if you want," John Jackman said, "but I already have. They're all like that."

"Empty," Gregor said.

"That's right," Dan Exter said.

"She took all her clothes," Gregor said.

John Jackman walked to the other end of the room and looked out the large plate-glass window there. "There were clothes in the parking garage," he said, "lots of them, thrown out by the blast. And a lot of stuff burned, of course. We couldn't prevent that."

"What kind of a car was it?" Gregor wanted to know.

"Volvo station wagon," Jackman said. "There's a lot of room in those station wagons."

"There isn't infinite room in those station wagons," Gregor said. "What did she do? Kill him and then pack?"

"Maybe she packed before she killed him," Dan Exter said. "We're running all kinds of tests. We're trying to find out if he was drugged. We're trying to find out if he was poisoned. God only knows what."

"The thing is that it all had to be deliberate," John Jackman said. "Gregor, no matter how you look at it, it had to be deliberate. It had to be planned. She must have worked it all out beforehand—"

"Assuming she's the one who planted the pipe bombs," Dan Exter said. "Don't let's jump to conclusions."

"Who else would have planted the pipe bombs? Who would want to?" Jackman had started to pace. "There's a record of everybody who comes into this place and out of it. Into Fox Run Hill, I mean. It's not like dropping a little something off in the ash can outside a brownstone in the middle of the city."

"The pipe bombs might not have been planted here," Dan Exter argued. "They might have been planted in the garage. You can't tell me you trust that idiot from the garage to remember who went in and out all afternoon."

"Of course I don't," John Jackman said, "but I don't believe the bombs were planted in the garage either. Somebody would have noticed something. Maybe not the garage attendant, but somebody."

"Maybe somebody did," Dan Exter said. "We haven't even started talking to people yet. Someone could come forward at any moment."

Gregor Demarkian cleared his throat. "Excuse me," he said. "I wonder if you've noticed something."

"Noticed what?" Dan Exter sounded exasperated.

"That it wasn't just her clothes," Gregor said. "It isn't just that clothes are missing from this house. It's that everything connected to a *woman* is missing from this house. At least, it has been so far. No women's shoes in the mudroom downstairs. No women's coats in the closet in the foyer. Nothing at all in the night table next to Mrs. Willis's side of the bed—"

"But not everybody keeps things in their night-table drawers," Dan Exter pointed out. "That doesn't mean anything."

"By itself, of course it doesn't mean anything," Gregor agreed, "but I think you'd better have this house searched from top to bottom, and see if you can find anything at all that would indicate that Patricia MacLaren Willis ever lived here, because so far I can't. And since the impression I got was that she was supposed to have lived here for some time—"

"Round about twenty years," Dan Exter said.

"Well," Gregor said, "you see what I mean. If Patricia Mac-Laren Willis obliterated all trace of twenty years of her life from a house this size, she must have been at it for weeks."

# FIVE

## 1.

GREGOR DEMARKIAN COULDN'T REMEMBER FEELING suffocated in Fox Run Hill—but back on Cavanaugh Street, climbing out of John Jackman's unmarked car in front of the Ararat, he *was* aware of feeling suddenly able to breathe. Cavanaugh Street wasn't even very breathable at the moment. Philadelphia is cold in the winter and hot in the summer, and now it was hot, and sticky, and heavy with humidity. It was also getting not-exactly-dark, the way summer nights did. The horizon would have been a red and purple glow if Gregor could have seen the horizon. All he could see were the tops of brownstone buildings and brick row houses, well kept on Cavanaugh Street itself, crumbling and unsteady on the streets shooting off it. Everybody lives in a gated community these days, he thought grimly. Everybody lives in a fortress surrounded by chaos. John Jackman cranked down the driver's side window of his car and leaned out to look at Gregor's face. Gregor thought idly that they ought to do better by the police. They ought at least to buy them cars with power windows.

"Are you all right?" John Jackman asked. "You look funny."

"I'm fine," Gregor said. "Are you and Bennis talking to each other these days?"

"Not exactly." Jackman looked uncomfortable. "I mean, I am the person who was trying to get a member of her own family executed."

"I thought that wasn't up to you."

"It wasn't. But, Gregor. Seriously. If you want to screw up a love affair, I guarantee it, testifying in favor of the death penalty at the punishment phase hearing of your lover's own sister will definitely do it. Even if it's not a sister she especially liked."

"It's a sister she hated to the bone."

"I know. I know. Even so. What are you trying to do, fix me up with Bennis again?"

"No."

"Well, that's good, you know, Gregor, because no matter what else is going on here, Bennis is not exactly ready to settle down."

"I have noticed."

"I'm not exactly ready to settle down either. Is there some point to this conversation?"

Gregor was looking down a side street called Bullock. In the hours he had been away, Donna Moradanyan had gone to work on Cavanaugh Street. White and gold satin ribbons seemed to be wrapped around everything. The streetlamps had white and gold satin ribbons twisted into spirals that reminded Gregor of old-fashioned barber poles. Gregor's divided-up brownstone and Lida Arkmanian's town house across the street were covered in white and gold bows, without an inch of the original masonry showing on either one. The steps of Holy Trinity Church were lined with white silk flowers in pots covered with white paper and decked out in sprightly gold bows. Next to all of this, Bullock Street looked worse than bare and spare. It looked like a black pit. In the building Gregor could see best, better than halfway down the block, caught in a stray gleam of light from a streetlamp, there was a window broken on the fourth floor.

"Gregor?" John Jackman said again.

Gregor snapped to and shook his head. "Well," he said. "Do you have that list of things I asked you to do?"

"My sergeant has them. They'll be done by tomorrow. Are you sure you don't have a fax machine?"

"Positive."

"Then I'll bring the forensics when I come to see you tomorrow. You really ought to get a fax machine, Gregor."

"I know. You'll set up the interviews."

"I said I would. I will if you tell me to. But, Christ, Gregor, appointments to interrogate witnesses—"

"It will help."

"If you say so. But if you ask me, I think we ought to crash every one of those doors every time one of those idiots refuses to open it. Who the hell do they think they are?"

"It's who they think we are that matters."

"I don't like this gated-community crap. Fortress mentality, that's all it is. And worse. Racism pure and simple."

"Not so pure and not so simple. They would probably be overjoyed if somebody like, say, Clarence Thomas decided to buy a house there."

"Clarence Thomas lives in Virginia. They make me angry, Gregor."

"They make me depressed," Gregor said. "But the chances are good that they're going to be able to tell us where our missing woman is."

"They know that? And they aren't telling us?"

"They don't know they know it. Could you find out something else for me?"

"Maybe."

"We need to know if Mrs. Willis had friends outside Fox Run Hill. You said she didn't have a job."

"Not a job we could find out about, no."

"You checked with the IRS?"

"Definitely."

"All right, then. What about the sort of thing women in

her position like to do? Volunteer work. The museums. The symphony. That kind of thing."

"You can't honestly believe she went back to her volunteer work after she'd blown up her own station wagon."

"No," Gregor said. "I'm just looking for a friend. A very good friend. The best friend she has."

"You mean somebody who might be hiding her."

"Not exactly. Not in the way you mean it." He gestured at the Ararat. "You want to come in and have dinner with me, John? If Bennis still isn't talking to you, she can sit with somebody else. Assuming she's here at all."

"If Bennis is here, she wouldn't want to sit with anybody else," John Jackman said. "She'd want to sit with me and make my life hell. Thanks a lot, Gregor, but I just can't. I've got a pile of work to do back at the office."

"The other thing I want from you is sightings reports. I take it you are getting those?"

"Dozens of them. By the hour. We ought to be glad this Mrs. Willis is just an ordinary middle-aged lady. When we have kids or, God help us, black people—"

"I know. You get dozens by the minute. You're not going to save the world, John."

"I know. But I keep trying. I'll pick you up tomorrow morning at eight."

"I'll be ready."

"Dan Exter said you were as impressive as hell. That's a compliment, Gregor. Only thing Dan Exter is usually impressed with is the Queen of England, and he's not so big on her since Chuck and Di turned out to be such putzes."

"Right," Gregor said. "I like him too."

John Jackman started to roll up his window. "Take care of yourself, Gregor. We need you to make us look good, even if we don't need you for anything else."

Gregor was about to say that they needed him for a lot more, but John Jackman already had his window rolled up

and his car sliding down along the curb. Gregor felt the first
heavy raindrops against his forehead like dollops of mayon-
naise. Half a block up, Hannah Krekorian opened a window
and leaned out of it. She looked as if she were about to take a
dive headfirst onto the pavement. She pulled back at the last
minute and disappeared inside her home again. Gregor noticed that the window had a big white and gold bow on it. If
the neighborhood looked like this now, how would it look on
the day of the actual wedding? Would there be carpets of seed
pearls covering the sidewalks? Would there be tulle and lace
skirts around all the fire hydrants?

Gregor decided not to tell anybody what he'd thought
about the fire hydrants. Donna Moradanyan was far too likely
to take him seriously.

He gave one last look around at the well-lit and overdeco-
rated Cavanaugh Street, and one last look into the black maw
of Bullock, and then went in to the Ararat.

No matter what else was going on in his life, he had to eat.

## 2.

Lately, Gregor Demarkian had been staying out of the Ararat
as much as possible. Since he couldn't cook and didn't much
like either delivery pizza or fast-food hamburgers, this was
not as often as he would have liked—but it was enough to
make it seem as if he had been avoiding the place, and as soon
as he walked in he knew that people on the street had been
speculating about why. Of course, people on Cavanaugh Street
speculated about everything all the time. It was what they had
for a hobby instead of needlepoint or crochet. Even so, it
made him uncomfortable. He opened the door and stepped
in out of the rain and fifty heads turned to look at him and
stayed turned, as if he were a curiosity, as if it were his first
week back in the neighborhood. Gregor had vague memories

of the first few weeks he had been back in Philadelphia after retiring from the FBI. At the time, he had been treated like a cross between an escaped zoo animal and a pet iguana.

He brushed the wrinkles out of his suit, saw Father Tibor Kasparian seated alone in the front booth, and headed in that direction. In the light of morning the Ararat was a diner-like place with bare Formica tabletops and glass and silver sugar cylinders and a menu full of cholesterol and saturated fat encased in a cracking plastic cover. By night, however, the Ararat got exotic. That was because it had been written up in the *Philadelphia Inquirer* on and off as an "authentic ethnic experience"—which, in fact, was what it was in the morning. There was no telling what it ought to be called now, with the big menus with their bright red tassels laid out on every bright red tablecloth; with Linda Melajian dressed up in Gypsy skirts and dangling earrings made of bits of gold-colored tin and black plastic beads. It was a mercy nobody had thought of dressing Linda up as a belly dancer—or maybe they had, and her mother wouldn't allow it. The whole thing gave Gregor a headache. Ever since the collapse of the Soviet Union, the people of Cavanaugh Street had been in continuous contact with the people of Armenia, and they all knew perfectly well that Armenians did not wear Gypsy skirts and beaded earrings. They wore Levi's jeans and rayon flower-print dresses from Sears if they could get them—which, thanks to Lida Arkmanian and Father Tibor Kasparian, they usually could.

Gregor made his way over to Tibor's booth and looked down at the books strewn across the tabletop. Tibor scattered books wherever he went, like Hansel and Gretel scattering bread crumbs. Two of the books on the table were in Greek, so that Gregor couldn't read the titles. The third was *The Client* by John Grisham. Tibor was reading a little paperback called *How to Have a Perfect Wedding*. Gregor sat down.

"Well," he said, pointing to the paperback's cover when Tibor looked up. "How do you have a perfect wedding?"

Tibor made a face. "It is apparently a lot of work. I would have thought it would have been enough if the bride and the groom loved each other, but that is not true. There have to be wedding favors. There have to be three different entrees in case there are guests who are vegetarians allergic to cheese."

"I can't imagine anybody on Cavanaugh Street being allergic to anything edible. Has anybody actually seen Donna today?"

"We all see her, Krekor. We do not talk to her. Her mother is here."

"I know."

"Her mother wants to decorate the iconostasis with flowers, Krekor. It isn't possible. The only time we decorate icons with flowers it is in honor of the Epiphany. Or something like that. I think it has been a mistake to conduct our services in Armenian now that we are in America."

"We've been in America for generations. We've been conducting our services in Armenian for all the generations we've been here."

"I know, Krekor, but not one of these new generations can speak Armenian. They don't know what the liturgies say. They don't know what the religion teaches. They get their ideas about weddings from magazines and their ideas about church services from Martha Stewart. I am going to shout at somebody before this all is finished."

"Probably Donna's mother."

"Probably you. I wouldn't want to offend Donna's mother."

"Gregor!" Linda Melajian rushed up in a jangle of beads and tin and rustly cheap fabric. She was out of breath. "What can I get for you? Did you hear about the tea service Donna's aunt sent from Seattle? Donna's father's sister. It was sterling silver."

Linda was wearing a gold and white ribbon in her hair. It didn't go with her Gypsy outfit. Gregor looked around and realized that all the tables had little gold and white bows on them, placed at the base of the glass candle holders that were supposed to look like kerosene lamps but didn't. Had they ever used kerosene lamps like that in Armenia? Gregor had no idea.

"Could you get me some *yaprak sarma*?" he asked Linda. "And a bottle of Perrier water or whatever. And a salad. Is Donna going to have her reception in here?"

"Donna's going to have her reception catered from here, but we're closing off the whole street. She got permission from the city. Like a block party."

"She sent out three thousand invitations," Tibor said. "Not so many people are going to fit into Holy Trinity Church."

"Oh, they won't all come to the church," Linda said dismissively. "They wouldn't even want to. I mean, these days, a third of them will probably be Buddhists and a third of them will probably be atheists, and nobody will have the time."

"Right," Tibor said.

"Anyway," Linda went on, "we're going to block off the whole street and have tables set up on the sidewalks and Lida and Hannah and Sheila and Helen are all cooking and so is Sophie Oumoudian's great-aunt, you know the one, and somebody is bringing liquor from Armenia. My mother says we shouldn't drink any of it because it's probably going to be moonshine."

"It's probably going to be fatal," Tibor said.

"I think it's going to be the best," Linda said. "Anyway, I'll get you your *yaprak sarma*, Gregor, and your salad and whatever. I mean, we're not all out of it at the moment. Bennis was in here earlier. She had pictures of her dress."

"Dress?" Gregor asked.

"Her maiden of honor dress," Tibor said helpfully. "Under the circumstances, I think for Bennis to be a maiden of honor is possibly incorrect."

"I don't think they take it that literally anymore," Gregor said. "At least, not in the United States."

"Of course they don't," Linda Melajian said. "Really, Gregor, it's going to be wonderful. Donna's picked out the most wonderful bridesmaids' dresses and there's going to be a daisy

chain flown in from California—two, I think, actually, one
for each side of the aisle—and I don't know. I can hardly
wait, can you?"

Gregor was about to say that he most certainly could wait,
he could wait forever. He wanted to see Donna married, but
the wedding was doing something worse than getting to him.
Then there was the sound of thunder all around them, the
rumble of something ominous and immediate, and Gregor
looked up. It would have been all right, except that the thunder didn't sound as if it was coming from the outside. It
sounded as if it had exploded in the middle of the Ararat's
dining room, and now it was sending aftershocks around to
all of the glass-and-candlelit tables. Ass, Gregor told himself.
Thunder doesn't have aftershocks.

The Ararat was always so dark at night, it was difficult to
get a grip on anything, even when it was happening right
next to you. It took Gregor a good half-minute to adjust
his eyesight to the dimness in the middle of the room, and to
begin to pick out familiar figures at the tables there. Lida
Arkmanian was there, having dinner with Hannah Krekorian
and the older Mary Ohanian. Sheila and Howard Kashinian
were there, having dinner together and alone and looking
sour-faced and grim in the conduct of it. Even Bennis Hannaford was there, having dinner with old George Tekemanian's grandson Martin and his prissy daughter-in-law Angela,
who were probably telling her off for letting old George have
food that wasn't on his diet. Martin and Angela Tekemanian
regularly took Bennis Hannaford out to lecture her, and Bennis regularly let them. In her opinion, the reason they really
wanted to take her out was that she had made her debut at a
good ball on the Main Line and at the Philadelphia Assemblies, and that was the kind of thing Angela was impressed by.

At the round table in the very center of the restaurant,
however, was the star of their show: Donna Moradanyan. For
once she had neither her small son Tommy nor her formida-

ble mother with her. She was alone with her beloved, Russ Donahue, once one of John Jackman's best and youngest homicide detectives. Russ was tall and spare and redheaded, a curiosity on Cavanaugh Street, filled with the dark-haired children and grandchildren of Armenian immigrants—but he was sitting down. Donna was standing up, and she was something of an anomaly too. Tall and blond and athletic, Donna was the least Armenian-looking woman Gregor had ever seen, although she was definitely Armenian. All four of her grandparents had come from Yerevan.

Donna was standing next to the table, holding the little glass candleholder in her hand. The candle was still lit, which seemed strange to Gregor. Shouldn't waving it around in the breeze like that have blown the flame out? Donna was waving herself around in the breeze. She was wearing one of those spaghetti-strapped A-line shift things with a T-shirt under it. Gregor had seen them everywhere in Philadelphia that spring. The shift was bright red and the T-shirt was stark white. There was something about the way Donna was standing that made her seem just on the edge of violence.

"Oh, dear," Tibor said in a whisper. "I think there is something very wrong here, Krekor."

Tibor's whisper carried, although Donna didn't seem to hear it. The whole of the Ararat had gone deathly still. Even the tourists were quiet, and tourists, in Gregor's experience, never shut up.

"I don't know what you think you're doing," Donna said in a clipped, angry voice. "I'm not even sure I care anymore. But if you think I'm going to let you get away with this—"

"Donna, for God's sake," Russ said, starting to stand up.

Donna put a hand on Russ's shoulder and pushed him back. Russ wasn't expecting the move. He staggered sideways a little and then dropped back into his chair. If he had gone sideways half an inch more, he would have ended up on the floor. He looked stunned.

"Donna," he said.

"Oh, he shouldn't say it like that," a woman at a nearby table hissed. Gregor thought it was old Miss Belladarian, ninety-five if she was a day and a lifelong member of the Society for the Prevention of Vice. "He sounds so weak."

Old Miss Belladarian was sitting with old Mrs. Vartenian, one of the street's prime harridans. She nodded vigorously now and said, loud enough to be heard in Delaware, "Yes, yes. He should be forceful. He should be a man."

Oh, for God's sake, Gregor thought.

Old Miss Belladarian was sighing. "Men aren't what they were in my day," she said piously. "They've lost their manliness to all this new world feminism."

"Nonsense," old Mrs. Vartenian said. "Men were never anything but a pack of children with less common sense than God gave chickens, but they ought to act like men. They have an obligation."

Gregor's head was beginning to hurt again.

Donna was waving the candle around in its holder. The flame still had not gone out. It was beginning to look like a kind of miracle.

"I've had it with you," Donna said, sounding tremulous. "I really mean it, Russell. I've had it with you."

"Why?" Russ asked desperately. "Donna, what the hell is going on here? All I said was—"

"You don't understand one thing about me," Donna said. "Not a thing. Not after all this time."

"Donna, listen—"

"And I can't trust you. That's the important part. I can't trust you as far as I can throw you."

Russ looked stunned. "Trust me? What does any of this have to do with trusting me? All I said was—"

"Ah," old Mrs. Vartenian said. "I see what all this is about now. This is about sex."

Old Miss Belladarian blushed.

Old Mrs. Vartenian starting talking in rapid-fire Armenian, which made Father Tibor Kasparian blush.

Donna seemed suddenly to become aware of the candle and the candleholder in her hand. She looked at it with an expression that seemed to say that she was looking at a dog turd, then turned around, raised it over Russ Donahue's head, and sent it hurtling to the floor. The floor of the Ararat was hardwood. The thin glass of the candleholder shattered into a thousand shards. The candle rolled, still burning, down the slight slope caused by the warp in the floor toward Gregor Demarkian's table. It came to rest under Sheila and Howard Kashinian's table. The flame began to lap blackly against the hem of their tablecloth.

"Jesus Christ," Howard said, bending over almost double in an attempt to stamp the fire out.

Sheila looked at him in exasperation and put the flame out with her shoe. "Ass," she said.

"You," Donna Moradanyan said to Russ, "are absolutely impossible."

Then she stomped away from him, past Gregor and Tibor, past old Mrs. Vartenian and old Miss Belladarian, past Howard and Sheila, out into the purple night. She left the door to the Ararat open when she went, caught in a heavy dark breeze and groaning slightly under the sound of the wind.

"Jesus Christ," Howard Kashinian said again.

Russ Donahue was still sitting in his chair, looking embarrassed and upset and confused and angry all at once. He was much too aware of the people around him, staring in his direction, talking in whispers that weren't really whispers. Gregor had a crazy urge to go tell old Mrs. Vartenian to get herself a better hearing aid. If the woman wanted to conduct her gossip in full view of the general public, then she ought at least to be able to manage a real whisper.

All of a sudden Linda Melajian rushed forward out of nowhere and snatched the candle out from under Howard and

Sheila's table. The edge of the tablecloth was singed black. Linda began to hurry toward the back.

"Somebody close the door," she called over her shoulder, sounding nothing like a Gypsy at all. She didn't even sound like an Armenian. "Oh, dear," she kept saying. "What are we going to do now?"

Somebody shut the door. Gregor didn't see who it was. Bennis Hannaford stood up at her table in the back and came into the center of the room to where Russ was. Russ was still sitting stunned in his chair, his mouth hanging slightly open, his hair wet with sweat.

"What happened?" he demanded when he saw Bennis. "What's going on here? All I said was that I liked her hair down around her shoulders instead of pinned up. That's all I said."

"It doesn't matter what you said," Bennis Hannaford told him.

Russ rubbed the palms of his hands in front of his face.

Bennis saw Gregor and Tibor, walked over to their booth, and threw herself down on one of the cushions.

"Well," she said. "It finally happened. I've been waiting for it for weeks, and now it's finally happened."

"What's happened?" Gregor demanded. "What are you talking about?"

Bennis took her pack of Benson and Hedges out of the pocket of her skirt, lit up, and blew a stream of smoke at the ceiling. The front booth was the only place in the Ararat where customers were allowed to smoke. Linda Melajian's mother hated smoke, and she thought that if Bennis was made uncomfortable enough, she would stop smoking altogether. Linda Melajian's mother did not know Bennis Hannaford as well as she should have.

Bennis took another drag, released another stream of smoke, and sighed.

"Gregor," she said, "if Donna Moradanyan ever actually

ends up at the altar, it's going to be a miracle. Trust me. It's going to be a very big miracle."

Gregor—who had lived with the preparations for Donna's wedding for so long now that he sometimes found himself thinking it had already happened—felt as if he'd fallen down the rabbit hole.

# SIX

## 1.

THE NEWS ABOUT THE WOMAN they called Mrs. Patricia Willis had been everywhere for so long, the news about the arrival of Karla Parrish had been wiped out of public consciousness. Julianne Corbett knew, because she had been watching. She had been watching the story about Mrs. Willis intently. It isn't every day that one of your constituents kills her husband and blows up her car in a municipal parking garage. The story was beginning to take on that eerie timeless quality of an urban legend. There was also the practical factor. Nobody got into the United States Congress on talent, experience, or good intentions. It took money, and that meant campaign contributions. Tiffany Shattuck had found Mrs. Willis's name on the contributors' list the night the explosion happened—and called Julianne about it, at four o'clock in the morning, as if it had been late-breaking word of a presidential assassination.

"She gave us a lot of money,"Tiffany had informed Julianne as solemnly as she could when she had had no sleep and far too much beer. "Over and over again. She was a very solid supporter of your campaign."

Julianne might have been angry, but she had been restless and agitated and unable to sleep, and when the phone rang she had been sitting up in bed going through all one hundred and twenty-four stations on her cable-ready TV, looking for something to watch that made some sense. American Movie Classics was showing *Take Care of My Little Girl*, a just-after-World-War-II social-conscience film where Jeanne Crain learns the evils of the sorority system from an ex-G.I. who has come to her campus on the G.I. bill. At least four stations were showing infomercials about exercise equipment. (Who bought exercise equipment at four o'clock in the morning?) The rest of the offerings all seemed to be religious. Julianne didn't really mind Mother Angelica, but at four A.M. all the offerings on the Eternal Word Television Network were in Italian. She had been about to hunt through her night table for her crossword puzzle books when Tiffany had started heavy breathing in her ear.

"What if somebody finds out?" Tiffany demanded. "I mean, this is the biggest scandal since I don't know what. The biggest scandal ever in the state of Pennsylvania, I bet."

Maybe that was true. Julianne didn't know much about scandals in the state of Pennsylvania. They hadn't been on the menu when she was going to elementary school. What had been on the menu, as far as she could remember it, was what would now be called sexual harassment. It was as clear to her now as it had been at the time—the day Bobby Brenderbader had copped a feel at the drinking fountain; the day John Valland had snapped her bra strap in class while Mrs. Magdussen was explaining the virtue of the Union side in the Civil War. Julianne shook it all out of her head and brought herself back to the present. A middle-aged balding man whose belt was just a little too tight was going on and on about how Christ led him to understand the importance of complex carbohydrates.

"She couldn't have been a really huge contributor," Julianne said reasonably. "I would have heard about it."

"You did hear about it," Tiffany persisted. "She was on the November list. You must remember."

"I don't remember. Tiffany, for God's sake, there were two hundred people on that list."

"I know, I know."

"Was she at the reception?" Julianne's campaign staff had given a reception for her two hundred largest noncorporate contributors, just to stay in touch.

Tiffany cleared her throat. "No, she wasn't. We sent her an invitation and she didn't answer it. She didn't even RSVP. We followed up on it."

"And?"

"And I suppose she said she couldn't come," Tiffany said irritably. "I don't know. I didn't handle her invitation. We had a whole committee to handle invitations."

"Yes, Tiffany. I remember."

"I still say we ought to take it seriously. In this day and age, I mean. It could come back to haunt us in the next election."

"I don't think so, Tiffany. Didn't Rosalynn Carter have her picture taken with John Wayne Gacey?"

"President Carter didn't get elected again either. Julianne, really. You ought to do something about this."

"What?"

"What do you mean, what? Something."

"Well," Julianne said reasonably. "I can't very well give the money back, can I? The woman is dead. Her husband is dead. I'm probably broke. What am I supposed to do?"

"The woman isn't dead," Tiffany said. "Did you hear that on the news? Did I miss something?"

Julianne reached into her night table for the Tylenol. "No, no," she said reassuringly. "It was just a slip of the tongue. I suppose I've been thinking she must be dead. Since nobody can find her."

"She's probably in Bolivia." Tiffany snorted. "If it was me doing something like that, I'd take a lot more than fifteen thousand dollars. You can't get anywhere on that kind of money these days. Maybe you should issue a press release."

"Saying what?"

"Saying that even though she was a large contributor, you'd never even met her."

Julianne swallowed a Tylenol dry, and then another. "I think that would only call attention to something it's unlikely would be noticed any other way. Don't be silly, Tiffany. It's late. Go back to sleep."

"I can't sleep."

"Work on the Karla Parrish reception, then. It's—what? Soon."

"I can't work on the Parrish reception. I can't think of anything but this. It's the creepiest thing I ever heard of."

Four years before, a young woman living near Pittsburgh had killed both her small children because her new boyfriend had promised to marry her if she did. This was not the creepiest thing Julianne had ever heard of. She shifted a little in bed and stretched.

"Go to bed," she told Tiffany. "Seriously. Or work on something current. Stop worrying about Mrs. Willis."

"Nobody calls her Mrs. Willis on television," Tiffany said. "They always call her Patricia. As if they didn't want you to know she was his wife. Do you think all men are worried that their wives are going to kill them in their sleep?"

"No," Julianne said. "Go to sleep. Get off the phone. Let me go to sleep. It's been a long day."

"I'm going to have another cup of coffee and read the *Inquirer* report again," Tiffany told her. "It's the most complete. Maybe they'll bring in Gregor Demarkian. Then we'd make the national news with this thing, and I could say I was part of it."

"Go to sleep," Julianne had said again—and that had been when? Last night? The night before? Sitting at her desk this morning, with the sun coming up outside the windows, Julianne couldn't remember what she had done when over the last month, or why. What she did know was that she was in the office before seven, with her full war paint on, drinking coffee out of a mug big enough to hold a small lobster. The

computer contributor sheets were spread out across her
green felt desk blotter. The invitations list to the Karla Parrish reception was propped up against her Rolodex. Her new
cat calendar was lying flat against the hardwood next to her
phone. Why was it that people still had green felt desk blot-
ters? she wondered. They didn't blot ink pens anymore. Half
the time they didn't even have pens of any kind anymore. The
offices were full of word processors.

Julianne ran her finger down the contributors' lists again
and frowned. She hadn't realized that these lists were so de-
tailed. There was the name: Patricia (Mrs. Stephen) Willis.
There were the amounts and the dates they had been received: $11,000 on the first of June; $14,500 on the twelfth
of September; $22,000 this past March. Julianne knew that
you had to tell some federal commission or other who your
campaign contributors were and what they had contributed,
but she hadn't realized that that information would be this—
specific. She started to rub the side of her face and then
stopped herself. She didn't want to smear her makeup. She
wished it were time for Tiffany to come into the office. There
were things she needed to talk out. Unfortunately, the rules
were clear. When an employee can call an employer at four
o'clock in the morning, the employer is a saint. When the
employer can get an employee out of bed at six A.M. just to
talk office talk, the employer is a tyrant. Julianne shoved the
contributors' lists away from her and stood up.

She wasn't going to issue a press release. Of course she
wasn't. That would be silly. On the other hand, what might
not be silly was a little damage control. Because Tiffany was
right. You could never tell what would damage you these days.

Julianne looked out the less dirty of her windows and
down to the street. She went back to her desk and picked up
the invitations list for the Karla Parrish reception. She had
been reading about Karla, even in the middle of all this fuss
about the death of Patricia Willis. If it hadn't been for that
death, the reception would have been really big news. That,

Julianne remembered, was the kind of luck Karla always had. Just when she was about to make a big splash, someone else came along and made a bigger one, and Karla's splash was lost in the tidal wave. When they were all in college together, Julianne remembered, the bigger splash had always come from Patsy MacLaren.

Julianne ran her finger down the column of names and found the one she was looking for. She took a pencil out of the caddy on her blotter and underlined both the name and the phone number. Then she pulled the phone closer across the desk and started punching numbers into the phone pad.

The phone was picked up almost immediately. It was answered less immediately, by a husky voice that seemed to belong to someone who did not intend to be in a good mood. Julianne looked at her little digital clock and winced. It was 6:12 A.M.

Julianne sat down and took a deep breath. "Bennis?" she said.

On the other end of the line, Bennis Hannaford made a noise that could have been a death rattle.

Julianne shook out her overteased hair. "Bennis, listen to me, this is important. I want you to get in touch with that friend of yours for me, Gregor Demarkian—"

## 2.

As soon as the news got around that Stephen Willis had died, Molly Bracken knew she would have to find some way to use the information. It was terrible living day after day in this big Victorian house. It was so boring, Molly could hardly stand it sometimes. Joey went to the office every day, playing out this little charade they were involved in, but Molly had no place to go but to shop. She did go to pro-life rallies every once in a while, but they didn't want her there without Joey, and she could feel it. Somebody said the Catholics were different. They were used to women doing things on their own because they were used to nuns. To Molly, the Catholic Church was just the old neighborhood in a fancy building. It meant standing there in the middle of all the old ladies from Italy and Poland, with their sachet and garlic smells, with their moaning over rosaries. Molly had joined the Episcopal Church as soon as she had moved out to Fox Run Hill, and made Joey join it with her. Someday, when she was old, she hoped to get to the point when she couldn't even remember having been ethnic in any way at all.

The first thing Molly had done when she found out how Stephen Willis had died was to make sure she met the detectives who had come to investigate the case. There was a black man from Philadelphia (how had he ever gotten past the guard at the gate?) named John Jackman, who was incredibly good-looking, like Eddie Murphy only better. There was the policeman from the town, who was not good-looking at all. Molly hadn't quite been able to hold on to his name, because he had seemed so negligible. Exeter, she thought. Or Exter. Whatever. What was the point of a man who didn't look good and didn't have any money? The detective Molly had really wanted to meet, though, was Gregor Demarkian. Ever since the rumor had first started going around that he was going to come out there to look into Stephen Willis's murder, Molly had lain in wait for him, ready to pounce, ready to tear off a piece of something famous. That was how anybody got anything in this world, she was sure of it. You found somebody who had it and got hold of some for yourself. You—appropriated it. That was the word. It made Molly squirm when she thought of it, as if it were a word with four letters, something she wasn't supposed to say.

Molly had not been as lucky with her waiting as she had hoped she would be. She had talked to the two policemen, and given them information she was sure would make them want to come back to question her later, but Gregor Demarkian hadn't come up her long curving drive and rung her doorbell. Nobody had come, and Molly had spent the afternoon sitting on her window seat, watching the action and wishing she knew how to get back into it. Mostly, she wished she had spent more time with Patsy MacLaren Willis. Dowdy, dour, unimportant——Patsy had always seemed like the least interesting person having dinner at the Fox Run Hill Country Club on any particular night, and half the time Molly hadn't even gone over to her table to say hello. She could kick herself for that now, she really could. She was going to have to be much more careful in the future. You never knew where people were going to end up.

Ever since Joey had left that morning, Molly had been sitting at her kitchen table, nursing a coffee with milk into frigidity. Out on her patio, the sun was bouncing a wicked glare off the aluminum arms of the patio furniture. She really ought to get painted wrought iron patio furniture, Molly thought, the kind everybody else had——but she didn't like the patio much, and it was hard to remember to buy green and white metal chairs when she had sweaters to look at or eighteen-karat-gold chains to consider. She ought to give a party too, Molly thought. She ought to give one now so that they would all have an excuse to get together and talk about the Willises.

The doorbell rang and Molly stood up. Her kitchen wall clock said it was 9:15. No wonder she was bored. Mornings after Joey left were the worst times of the day. Molly padded out toward the front door and then stopped. The bell had rung again, but it wasn't the front doorbell. She went out into the mudroom and to the door to the garage.

Sarah Lockwood was standing in the garage, wearing a blue linen skirt and a white shirt, carrying a pair of blue canvas espadrilles in one hand. It was hot out there. The heat rose up and hit Molly as soon as she stepped beyond the protection of the air-conditioning. Sarah's hair was damp with sweat and humidity. It looked much darker than it usually did.

"Oh," Sarah said when she realized Molly had opened up. "There you are. Did I get you at a bad time?"

I'm really going to have to get some of those little linen skirts, Molly thought absently. Everybody else has them. Molly was also the only person with a house in Fox Run Hill who owned leggings, but she didn't think of that. She stepped back and waved Sarah inside.

"I wasn't doing anything," she said. "I was just sitting over a cup of coffee and letting it get cold. Sometimes I think I ought to take up volunteer work."

"I did volunteer work for years," Sarah said. "I hated it. I think it's very much nicer to be in control of your own time."

Sarah was going through the mudroom into the house. Molly made a face at her back. The kind of places Molly wanted to volunteer didn't take anybody who walked in the door and wanted to sign up. You had to wait to be asked, and Molly could wait forever, in the present arrangement of things. She closed the door to the garage and followed Sarah inside.

"How pretty you've made everything," Sarah was saying, looking around at the kitchen cabinets and the tiles on the kitchen floor. "I would never have thought of putting terra cotta into a Victorian like this. But of course I'm hopeless at decorating. We had to have somebody come in and do our house so that I didn't ruin it."

Molly had had someone come in and do this house. She couldn't decide if Sarah was being sincere or not. Sarah never seemed sincere.

"I could put some coffee on," Molly said. "And I have Perrier. Could I get you something?"

"A glass of Perrier would be nice." Sarah sat down on one of the breakfast room chairs and looked up at the ceiling. Because a Victorian was supposed to be a formal house, there were no exposed beams here. Sarah dropped her espadrilles on the floor and stretched her bare legs into a long, straight line.

"They're back again this morning," she said, tossing her

head side-ways to indicate the Willises' house. "I saw them come in this morning. You'd think they'd have looked through everything in that house by now."

Molly put a glass of Perrier water down in front of Sarah. "Was Gregor Demarkian there? Do you know who I mean—"

"Of course I know who you mean. Everybody in Philadelphia knows Demarkian. He wasn't there, as far as I could tell."

"The paper said he'd been called in to consult on the case." Molly threw her old coffee away, got a clean cup, and poured herself some hot. "I think that means he's the one investigating it, but I'm not sure. I talked to him yesterday."

"Did you? About what?"

"About Patsy. Doesn't it all seem really strange, now that you look back on it?"

"It seems really strange now," Sarah said. "I mean, people I know don't shoot their husbands to death every day. Although I know a few people who ought to."

"I mean, *they* seem really strange," Molly said, coming back to the table with her new coffee. "Patsy and Steve. I never thought about them before this happened, but they weren't really normal, were they?"

"Of course they were." Sarah was impatient. "They were as normal as anybody. They were dull."

"They were dull enough," Molly agreed, "but they weren't normal. I mean, he was never around, was he? He was gone for weeks at a time."

"There was nothing abnormal about that," Sarah was positive. "He worked for some company that had oil interests or something. I don't remember what it was. He had to travel for work."

"A lot of people have to travel for work. They don't just disappear for a month."

"I'm sure she heard from him, Molly. Really, you know, you shouldn't make this kind of—of inference—"

"I wasn't making any kind of inference."

"—it could be taken the wrong way, especially in circumstances like these. The man is dead, after all. And Patsy . . ." Sarah Lockwood shrugged.

"I think he was a bigamist," Molly said.

Sarah looked startled. "What *are* you talking about? How could Stephen Willis have been a bigamist?"

Molly tried to be careful. She hadn't thought this up on her own. She had read it in *The Star*, in an article about another case entirely, but it seemed so obvious to her that all the same elements were there. She didn't let people in Fox Run Hill know that she read *The Star*, though, or the *National Enquirer* either. She bought them in a supermarket in Philadelphia proper, where nobody knew who she was.

"Listen," she said eagerly. "If you think about it carefully, it all fits. It really does. He would be gone a month at a time and once or twice he was even gone longer—"

"Yes, yes, Molly, but it's like I told you. That was for his work."

"It was also a perfect opportunity. I'll bet he didn't spend any more time here than he spent away. He's probably got another family someplace who thinks he's still on a business trip right now."

Sarah sniffed. "They could hardly think he's still on a business trip. His picture has been all over the newspapers and the television stations for days."

"The family might not be here in Philadelphia."

"I'm sure the story has been reported nationwide, Molly. His name has probably been mentioned on the TV news."

"He might not have been using the same name."

"Oh, Molly."

"No, no. Really. It all fits. He goes away to this other place and he has another wife and another name and she doesn't know about it, but then she finds out and she shoots him. That at least makes sense."

"No, it doesn't."

"Yes, it does," Molly insisted. "And even if his other family is right here in Philadelphia, they might not have seen a picture of him. I mean, there have been a couple on the news, yes, but not half so many as the ones there have been of her. It's like now that he's dead, he doesn't matter anymore."

"I still say this is an absolutely impossible scenario. Seriously. Wives kill their husbands every day."

"There must be some reason they kill their husbands," Molly insisted. "It can't be that they just wake up one morning and go boom. I mean, that's crazy."

"Most people were crazy to get married in the first place," Sarah said. "I think really good marriages are very rare. Most people are simply miserable. Then one day it gets to be too much and——" Sarah shrugged.

"I'd never do something like that to Joey," Molly said. "If I got really mad at him, I'd just divorce him."

"Divorce can be expensive, and it doesn't always solve things. Let's not talk about this anymore. It depresses me. I brought over some pictures of the new house."

"The Florida house?"

Sarah was unpacking Polaroid snapshots from the big patch pockets of her skirt. "Kevin said he talked to Joey about it last night, and Joey said something about wanting to look into buying land in Boca Magra. Really, I don't see how you've gone this long without a winter vacation house. Winters in Philadelphia are so grim."

"Mmmm," Molly said.

Sarah spread her snapshots across the table. "It's a gated community, of course," she said, "because Kevin and I think it's foolish to buy in any other kind. Otherwise, you can't be sure of your investment, can you?"

"Mmmm," Molly said again, but she wasn't really listening. Maybe it was really high rent to think about your winter vacation house while a murder investigation was going on, but Molly hadn't gotten that high rent yet. Her head was still full of speculations about Stephen Willis's secret life and Patsy

MacLaren Willis's secret hatreds. Molly decided that when she saw Gregor Demarkian again, she'd rush right out, introduce herself, and tell him all about it.

"This is what we're doing with the dining room," Sarah Lockwood said firmly, shoving a picture of a white, high-ceilinged room under Molly's nose. "We're very, very, very fond of the Moorish look for Florida."

### 3.

Miles away, in the Sheraton Society Hill hotel in central Philadelphia, Karla Parrish was lying in the middle of a big double bed, trying to make sense of a story in the *Philadelphia Inquirer*. This story said that a woman named Patricia MacLaren Willis was assumed to have shot her husband Stephen to death with a semiautomatic pistol, destroyed her car by fire bomb in a Philadelphia parking garage, and then disappeared. It said this more than once, and it repeated the name in every other paragraph.

Patricia MacLaren Willis.

Patricia MacLaren Willis.

Patricia MacLaren Willis.

It didn't make any sense.

Karla rolled over on her stomach and tried again. No matter how many times she read the story, it still said the same thing. But it couldn't, she was sure of that. It would be far too much of a coincidence.

"Evan?" she called out.

Evan was in the living room of the suite, unpacking her photographic equipment. He stuck his head in through the bedroom door and wagged it.

"Not now," he told her. "I have some work to do."

"Did you ever take drugs?" Karla asked him. "Hallucinogenic drugs?"

"I refuse to answer on the grounds that it may tend to incriminate me."

"Well, I never took any drugs," Karla said. "I never even tried cigarettes. And right now I feel like I'm on some kind of acid trip."

"Nobody says 'acid trip' anymore, Karla. It's passé."

"Whatever. What do you do when you see something that can't possibly be real?"

"I go back to bed. Preferably with company."

"Be serious. Have you ever heard of somebody named Gregor Demarkian?"

"Sure. The world's most famous private detective. Except I don't think he really is a private detective. He's a consultant or something like that."

"Is he good at what he does?"

"He's supposed to be."

"Do you think you could put me in touch with him?"

Evan leaned against the doorjamb, curious. "I could, but I don't really have to. He's been invited to that reception Julianne Corbett is giving for you. I could call and see if he's intending to show up."

"Do that," Karla said positively.

"You want to tell me what this is all about?"

Karla shook her head. "Not yet. I'm probably just having the vapors. You want to get us some breakfast?"

"Sure," Evan said, but he hesitated one more moment in the doorway before he disappeared.

Karla rolled over on her back. She was exhausted. That was the trouble. She was exhausted and jet-lagged, and if she wasn't she wouldn't be having this fantasy.

And she wouldn't be so scared.

# SEVEN

## 1.

DONNA MORADANYAN DIDN'T CHANGE THE ribbons. All the next day, and the day after that, Gregor watched, getting up from his kitchen table every hour or so to look out his window at Cavanaugh Street, going out four different times to get a pot of takeout coffee at the Ararat. His table was covered with forensics reports, background checks, financial tracking schemas, lateral witness interviews. John Jackman was good and the organization he had built the homicide department into was better than Gregor had ever imagined it could be, but most of this, Gregor knew, was confetti. It was impossible to know anything about the woman from reports like these. Preferably, Gregor would have been able to meet her, to hear her talk and see her walk. Since that was impossible at the moment—coming in after the fact on cases did that to you—the next best thing would be to find someone who had heard her and seen her. But that was proving surprisingly difficult. Gregor and John Jackman and Chief Exter had gone out to Fox Run Hill to conduct some interviews, but the only interviewing they had done had been of a woman named Molly Bracken, and they had talked to her before.

"She invents things," Dan Exter had said when the interview was over—and of course it was true. Molly Bracken wanted to be part of a great adventure. She was clearly overjoyed that John Jackman and Dan Exter, who had interviewed her initially on the evening of the day the murder and the explosion happened, had returned with Gregor Demarkian.

"She doesn't know Stephen Willis was involved in bigamy." John Jackman shook his head and sighed. "She has no real reason to believe Stephen Willis was involved in bigamy. She just wants to think Stephen Willis was involved in bigamy."

"She got it out of one of those damn supermarket tabloid newspapers," Dan Exter said. "Trust me."

"Fox Run Hill doesn't look like the kind of place where people read those supermarket tabloid newspapers," John Jackman objected.

Gregor thought John Jackman was right, but he thought Dan Exter was right too. There was something about Molly Bracken that did not quite fit at Fox Run Hill. Gregor believed that in spite of the fact that he had never met any of its other inhabitants, except for the joggers who always seemed to jog especially slowly when the police were in the community. Walk the walk and talk the talk, that was how the slang went. Molly Bracken didn't. Every time she opened her mouth, Gregor expected to see gum.

He tried to explain this to Father Tibor Kasparian when Tibor came by at the end of the afternoon, but he only sounded like a snob doing it.

"I wish you could see this place," he told Tibor. "It's odd. Strange. Like a neighborhood of haunted houses from a 1950s movie."

"I thought you said this Fox Run Hill was well kept." Tibor was rummaging through Gregor's refrigerator. There wasn't much of anything in Gregor's refrigerator, but there was always the hope that Lida or Hannah or one of the other women had left something there. Tibor found a carton of cherry yogurt so old it was growing mold, and threw it out. "I thought you said that this was one of those places where they had groundskeepers and staff and all that kind of person."

"It is."

"Then it doesn't sound to me like haunted houses, Krekor. Haunted houses don't have caretakers."

Actually, Gregor thought, some haunted houses did have caretakers—wasn't Manderley supposed to have had one, even after it burned? That was beside the point.

"It's just that the houses are so big," he told Tibor. "Not as big as the house Bennis grew up in, not like that—"

"That was like an institution." Tibor sniffed. "That could have been a school. I think this Yale University Bennis's father left it to sold it to some people to make a school."

"Yes, exactly. These aren't that big. But they seem emptier. You look at them, I look at them, and imagine big hollow wooden shells, with nothing inside them."

"You don't usually get poetic, Krekor."

"I'm not getting poetic. I don't like this place. In fact, I hate this place."

"Because the buildings seem so big and empty?"

"Because *everything* seems so big and empty," Gregor said. "The houses, the grounds, the people, everything. I have to talk to more of them on a regular basis. From what I've seen so far, they're just not really there. I keep imagining Mrs. Willis being like the women I've met so far at Fox Run Hill, and then the idea that she shot her husband and then blew up her car seems impossible."

"But she did it. People are people, Krekor. Nothing is impossible."

"Granted. But the women I've met so far in that place don't have the emotional energy to kick their dogs."

Tibor left to lead his Bible study group. Gregor went back to looking through reports and making lists: things to check into; people to interview; places to see, as a last resort. Finally he did something he hadn't needed to do since he was an agent in training. He got all the pieces of paper together and wrote a biography of Patricia MacLaren Willis. Actually, this was something he had been taught to do with the victim, usually the victim of a kidnapping. Gregor had worked kidnapping details for years before he had found his niche as director of the Behavioral Science Department. Unit, he reminded himself now. Since he had left the Bureau, they had decided to stop calling their subdivisions departments and to start calling them units. Gregor didn't know why, but he suspected it was the budget. If you didn't spend all the budget Congress gave you, Congress decided you didn't need so much money and reduced your appropriation. It was therefore death for any director of the Federal Bureau of Investigation to save any cash. If he got to the end of the year with money on his hands, he had to find a way to spend what he had. Christmas bonuses and that sort of thing were mostly out. The public had caught on to that one, and they didn't like it. Having to order an entire new set of letterhead stationery, with new terms and new names and all the rest of it, was really beautiful, because nobody would question why the FBI needed paper. Of course they needed paper. They needed a lot of paper. Gregor Demarkian was a Franklin Delano Roosevelt liberal and probably always would be. He believed in Social Security and minimum wages and the federal safety net. Sometimes, though, he thought he could understand why there were so many people out there who thought government didn't work.

By the time Bennis came in at a quarter to six, Gregor was hunched over his computer printouts, writing rapidly on a long sheet of yellow lined legal paper with a pencil so dull his handwriting looked as if it were growing moss. Bennis leaned on his shoulder, looked at his writing, and then shook him.

"Gregor, for God's sake, come on. We're due downtown at a cocktail party at seven. Remember? I told you—"

"I remember," he said. He did too. He just didn't want to. He hated cocktail parties. He hated parties of all kinds, except the ones they gave on Cavanaugh Street, where he was allowed to pile a plate high with food and take it off to sit on the sidelines with Father Tibor.

"Gregor, you'd better get dressed. You'd really better. I was intending to take a cab—"

"Anything, as long as you aren't driving."

"Well, I'll have to drive if you don't get up and hurry. What is all this stuff anyway?"

Gregor got out of his chair and began to wander toward the bedroom. "Has Donna Moradanyan made it up with Russ yet?" he asked. "Is there still going to be a wedding? I notice nobody took the decorations down."

"Donna says the next time she sees Russ, she's going to shoot him," Bennis said.

Gregor turned on the light in his bedroom. When he had first moved into this apartment, years ago, he had kept it very stark. The bare minimum of furniture, the bare minimum of carpeting and kitchen equipment, an absolute absence of the personal. Now he was better. He had a painting in the living room and a nice rug under his bed and his pictures of Elizabeth (before her last illness) on top of his bureau. The bedroom was even messy, so that it looked reasonably lived in. For a while after Elizabeth had died, Gregor had become obsessively, depressingly neat. He had now gotten over it.

He found a gray suit and a blue suit and a whole line of white shirts hanging in his closet, fresh from the dry cleaner's. He found clean socks rolled into a ball and a tie in the top drawer of his dresser. He laid everything out on the unmade bed and started to get dressed.

"What's all this writing about?" Bennis asked him again. She was standing right outside the bedroom door, shouting at the crack.

Gregor put on his socks. "Patricia MacLaren Willis," he said, "except from what I've been able to uncover, nobody called her that. They called her Patsy."

"Patsy Willis. Not bad."

"Not Patsy Willis, Patsy MacLaren." Gregor shrugged his arms into the sleeves of his shirt. "This is paper research you're listening to, don't forget. She was the last surviving member of a fairly well-heeled family from the Main Line, not enormously rich like the Hannafords—"

"Can it."

"—and not social, but with enough money in the bank so that even after both her parents died their estate was able to put her through Vassar without having to resort to scholarships or loans. She graduated with the class of 1969."

"Not a really great year except at places like Berkeley," Bennis said. She'd graduated with the class of '73.

"Whatever. Anyway. Patsy MacLaren graduated, and then she went off to do the Indian meditation thing for a year with her college roommate. It took two years, actually. We have a statement from one of the administrators of her trust at the Morgan Bank—former administrators, to be precise. This isn't the kind of trust you would have approved of, Bennis. Patsy MacLaren was eating capital."

"I'm surprised the administrators let her get away with it."

"They had to. Capital was all there was. I said her parents were well-heeled but not rich. According to the bank, Patsy went through a really heavy period of sixties rebellion, complete with LSD and long hair and even a try at going back to the land, and by the time she got back from India and all those places, she didn't want to have anything to do with what she called 'the ravages of capitalism.' I'm quoting now. The man I talked to was still a little annoyed about it all."

"Check the buttons on your shirt," Bennis said automatically. "You always do them up wrong. What happened to Patsy—what? MacLaren? What happened to her after that?"

Gregor already had his pants on and his belt buckled. He looked at his shirt and discovered he had buttoned it wrong. He undid it and started over again.

"She went to graduate school," Gregor said. "At the University of Pennsylvania. In some kind of liberal arts. I think it was English, but I'm not sure. She went for three years."

"Did she get a degree?"

"Not as far as I've been able to make out."

"What happened then?"

"She ran out of money, and soon after that she got married. There was a notice in the newspaper. That was the only way the administrators at the bank knew anything about it. There wasn't any reason that they should. The trust was folded by then. I still would have thought that simple courtesy would require—"

"Did she know any of these administrators at her bank?" Bennis answered. "She might never have met any of them. She wouldn't have had to. I know people with trust funds in nine figures who've never seen a single one of their trust officers."

"I'll check on that." Gregor got his jacket and pulled open the door. "Anyway, Patsy MacLaren got married to Stephen Willis, who was acknowledged by everyone at the time to be a young man on his way up. A few years later they built the house in Fox Run Hill, and that was that."

"What do you mean, that was that?"

"I mean that was all she ever really did," Gregor replied. "She became a housewife. She bought furniture. She played golf. She didn't even volunteer for things, as far as I can tell. She subscribed to a lot of magazines. She gave money to political candidates, including some to this Julianne Corbett person who's giving this party."

"Did she really?" Bennis started fussing with Gregor's tie. "I don't think that's very surprising, Gregor. Lots of people gave money to Julianne's campaign. She won her seat by a really large margin."

"In this case there are coincidences I'd like to check into though," Gregor said. "Patsy MacLaren's roommate at Vassar was named Julianne Corbett."

Bennis looked startled. "Really? Is it the same Julianne Corbett?"

"I don't know. But here's something else: The roommate Patsy MacLaren went to India with was also named Julianne Corbett."

"I know that Julianne has been to India," Bennis said. "She talks about it sometimes."

"The only reason I'm letting you drag me off to this thing," Gregor said virtuously, "is that I think Congresswoman Julianne Corbett has some answers to some questions that I have about Patsy MacLaren. This is going to be a fact-finding mission."

"This is going to be an ordinary political cocktail party that everyone is going to be pretending isn't a political cocktail party," Bennis said firmly, "and you're not going to get to talk to Julianne beyond a handshake. Not unless you arrive with your checkbook open and a letter from a PAC in your pocket. Your tie's fine now, Gregor. Let's get out of here."

Gregor stood back and looked at Bennis. He didn't really look at her very often anymore. Maybe what he meant was that he didn't look at her for real very often anymore. He was so used to having Bennis around that she was just Bennis, a hovering presence trailing cigarette smoke and dressed in jeans and a flannel shirt. Now she was dressed in a long black thing with beads all over it and her hair was up on top of her head in a way that looked as if it was meant to be there. Bennis often wore her hair on top of her head, but haphazardly, so that it looked windblown.

"You look nice," Gregor said uncertainly. The beads seemed to make the dress cling—oddly?—to Bennis's body. The effect made Gregor feel that he ought to blush.

"You look very, very nice," he went on incoherently. "I mean, I think I like your dress."

"Good." Bennis looked amused. "I think I don't like what time it is here, and I think we'd better be going. Are you going to have any problem with that?"

"No."

"Try to remember that this is supposed to be a party for
Karla Parrish, the photographer," Bennis said. "She went to
Vassar with Julianne Corbett too."

"Ah," Gregor said. "So your Julianne Corbett did go to
Vassar."

Bennis pushed him out of the bedroom. "Go. We're going
to be late. We can talk about all of this later."

### 2.

Of course they couldn't talk about any of this later. Parties
weren't like that, and cocktail parties especially weren't like
that. This one was in a town house in Society Hill, a large
brick structure with electrified carriage lamps on either side
of its front door and bright new white paint on all its window
frames. Gregor remembered investigating a murder in this
part of town, the murder of a once-rich man. Gregor wondered whom the town house belonged to. He supposed it
could belong to Julianne Corbett herself, but he doubted it.
She hadn't been in office long enough to have that kind of
money.

Cabs were three deep in the street. The front doors of the
town house were propped open. Gregor saw a dapper young
man in a high collar and a black dinner jacket bustling back
and forth with a clipboard, looking ridiculously happy.

"Is that young man some kind of assistant to Julianne
Corbett?" Gregor asked Bennis as they stepped out onto the
sidewalk and into the crowd.

Bennis readjusted her beaded evening purse on her shoulder and peered at the young man. "Never saw him before in
my life. I'm sure he's nobody working for Julianne. He has a
starched collar, for God's sake."

"Is that irretrievably passé?"

"It's the kind of thing college boys do when they're working too hard to be elegant. God, what a crush. Do you see Karla Parrish?"

"I wouldn't know Karla Parrish from a Teenaged Mutant Ninja Turtle."

"What about Julianne, then? You know what Julianne looks like."

Gregor did know what Julianne Corbett looked like, but he couldn't see her. He saw only tall women with anxious faces who all seemed to be holding their stomachs in, and taller men with pouchy wine-and-cheese guts who should have been holding their stomachs in but didn't seem to care. The ecstatic young man was the only one wearing a dinner jacket. All the rest were in ordinary suits, but expensive ones. The flashy young men had Giorgio Armani. The older and more sober ones had Brooks Brothers and J. Press. Everybody in the place except Gregor and Bennis seemed to have a Rolex watch. Gregor had a Timex, bought at Sears for $17.95. Bennis didn't wear a watch.

"Come on." Bennis took him by the arm and dragged him up the front steps. The closer they got, the thicker the crowd became. It was like a New York City bus at rush hour, with everybody bottled up near the doors and refusing to budge. Bennis was good at this though. She elbowed him through a knot of people discussing tax shelters (*"You know what it's like with taxes. Every time they raise them on serious money they leave a loophole, and Bill Clinton isn't going to be any different . . ."*) and then through another knot of people discussing therapy. The knot of people discussing therapy seemed to be extremely concerned with something called borderline anxiety syndrome.

"We tried doing grief work with that," one of the women said, "but it didn't really do it. I think we're going to have to go to regression therapy before we really get it worked out."

"What's borderline anxiety syndrome?" Gregor asked Bennis.

"God only knows. It probably has something to do with being afraid of your cat. Look. There's Julianne. Let's go over and say hello."

"Don't these things usually have receiving lines? I think it would have been much more sensible—"

"Come on," Bennis said in exasperation.

It was impossible to miss Julianne Corbett. She was not tall, but she was outrageous, a mass of hair and jewelry and makeup. Her lipstick was crimson. Her eyeshadow was sapphire. Her eyeliner was jet black. She was a mass of intense colors from one side of her face to the other, and she was a mass of colors beneath that too. Gregor didn't think he had ever seen a garment quite like the dress Julianne Corbett was wearing. It reminded him of those stained-glass-window cookies they had made in school when he was a child. It seemed transparent and opaque at once and lit up from inside. Gregor saw magenta and lemon yellow and bright kelly green, and then his head began to hurt.

Julianne Corbett was holding out her hand to him, her face stretched into a wide professional politician's smile.

"Hello, hello," she said. "I'm so glad Bennis brought you. You're just as impressive in person as you are in your photographs."

Gregor didn't think he was impressive in his photographs. He thought he mostly looked like a dork.

"These are the photographs that are impressive," he told her, gesturing to the walls around them, which were hung with huge blowups of black-and-white shots. The photographs were not the kind of black-and-white shots he would have called appropriate for a party like this one. They were of starving children and displaced body parts, of civil war and famine and death. They were enormously powerful, but Gregor didn't understand how people could look at them and go on eating what they were eating. Canapés were passing through the crowd on silver trays. A waiter stopped and offered one to Gregor. Gregor declined.

"The really impressive pieces are in there." Julianne Corbett gestured through a second set of double doors into what was probably the living room. This was the foyer, with its curving marble staircase and its checkerboard marble floor. Half the town houses in Society Hill had checkerboard marble floors. "We saved the really strong shots for the inside room. We didn't want to blast people with them as soon as they walked through the door. Have you been inside yet?"

"We just got here," Bennis said.

"Karla's inside, standing at the punch table," Julianne said. "I think she feels a little awkward. This isn't her usual milieu."

"Is it anybody's?" Bennis said.

"Well," Julianne Corbett said. "You two go inside and look. I've got to do my duty around here for a while. But don't leave without talking to me again. I have something very important I want to ask Mr. Demarkian."

Gregor knew better than to say there was something very important he wanted to ask her. There was no need to alert her to what could be a potential embarrassment. He took Bennis's arm and propelled her toward the inner doors. Through them, he could see a tall woman with flat brown hair, looking uncomfortable in a dress that didn't seem to fit right. Bennis would know why it didn't. Gregor decided that he liked this woman's face.

"Is that Karla Parrish?" he asked Bennis.

Bennis looked in the direction he was pointing and nodded. "Oh, yes, it is. But she needs some advice on wardrobe if she intends to show up at things like this. Although it's very sweet, isn't it? She's like a lamb among the wolves."

"Culture vultures," Gregor agreed solemnly.

He felt a tug on his sleeve and turned around to find the young man in the high starched collar and the dinner jacket at his elbow. The young man was even younger than he had seemed to be at a distance. His face looked as smooth and round as the face of a boy who is just starting to shave.

"Mr. Demarkian?" he said. "You don't know me, but my name is Evan Walsh. I'm Karla Parrish's assistant."

Evan Walsh was wearing wire-rimmed glasses. Gregor thought idly of the sixties, when wire-rims had been the mark of hippies. Now they seemed to be the distinguishing element in the wardrobes of young men in dinner jackets.

"Mr. Demarkian?" Evan Walsh repeated uncertainly.

"I'm sorry," Gregor said. "These parties tend to make me drift off. How do you do?"

"I'm going to go over and introduce myself to Karla Parrish," Bennis said. "I'll catch up with you later."

Gregor watched Bennis begin to wend her way through the sparser knots of people inside to get to the table where Karla Parrish stood. He saw Karla Parrish straighten when she realized that somebody was actually going to talk to her. He smiled to himself and said, "She's not used to this kind of thing, is she? It's very attractive, in a way. Very affecting."

"Yeah," Evan said. "Well, I'll feel a lot better when she is used to this kind of thing. She's too easy to get to, the way things are now. It worries me."

"What do you mean, that she's too easy to get to? Do you think somebody has designs on her money? Were you just talking in general?"

"Well," Evan said. "That's what I wanted to talk to you about. It's about this news story that's in all the papers, this case you're involved in, the one about Patsy MacLaren. Karla wants to talk to you about it. You see——"

Gregor never found out what Evan saw. What happened next happened in slow motion, but it happened in an instant just the same, and there was no time for anything. Gregor had been watching Karla Parrish and Bennis Hannaford all the time he was talking to Evan. He had seen Karla get herself a glass of punch from the bowl and Bennis eat at least three stuffed celery spears. Bennis ate like a horse and kept it off with nervous energy. Then Karla and Bennis walked away from the table and up to one of the walls, where Karla started pointing things out. Gregor wondered what it was they were looking at a photograph of. They seemed very intent.

The next thing Gregor noticed was that the table with the punch bowl on it seemed to rock, which was impossible. An older woman who had been leaning against it jumped and turned around. A young man who had been reaching for the ladle in the punch bowl stepped back in confusion. There was a nervous little titter of laughter, and then it happened.

The explosion was so loud, it made Gregor's ears ring. The flash was so bright, it blinded him. The next thing he saw was fire and smoke. The next thing he heard was screaming.

"Oh, God," somebody was shouting. "Oh, God, oh, God, oh, God."

Gregor should have headed for the nearest phone. He knew he should have. He shouldn't have headed through the double doors into the living room. He had no way of knowing if something else in there was getting ready to explode. He had to go. Bennis was in there. That was all he could think of. Bennis was in there.

And now that the smoke was clearing, he could see the table that had once held the punch bowl.

It had been ripped in half and hacked into splinters by the blast.

# PART TWO

*Bondage in Holy Matrimony
and Otherwise*

# ONE

## 1.

*I*T HADN'T BEEN A VERY big bomb. Gregor knew that as soon as he got through the double doors. The shattered table had looked horrible from a distance. It looked horrible close up. There were one or two people who looked more horrible still. Gregor saw a woman in a bright purple dress he was sure had to be dead. She had pieces of white fluff stuck to her and a pin that read I WEAR FAKE FUR. Gregor saw cuts and bruises everywhere, but not all that much blood. He scanned the faces he could see and came up blank. There was nobody there that he knew. Men and women began to get themselves up from the floor and shake themselves out. Someone was crying.

"Where is she?" someone demanded, grabbing on to his elbow and spinning him around. "Where—is—she?"

For a moment Gregor was certain the "she" referred to was Bennis Hannaford. That was the "she" he was looking for, and that he was beginning to feel increasingly uneasy that he hadn't found. The man clutching his elbow was young Evan Walsh. Walsh looked almost as bad as he might have if he had been in the room at the time of the blast. There were tears running down his sooty face. He must have been the one who was crying, Gregor realized. His hair was a mess. One of the lenses in his glasses was cracked.

"She was right there," he screamed, pointing at the devastation at the center of the room. "She was standing right next to the punch bowl when . . . when the whole thing blew up. She must be under all that wreckage— She—"

"No, she's not," Gregor said firmly. "She'd moved. I saw her. She was with my friend Bennis Hannaford, looking at one of the pictures on the wall right before the blast."

"Then where is she?" Evan demanded shrilly. He looked ready to cry again.

Gregor felt another tug on his elbow and turned this time to find Julianne Corbett, looking terrified.

"What should we do?" she gasped. "Nobody knows what we should do. Was it an assassination attempt?"

Gregor didn't know what it had been, except that it had probably been a pipe bomb—and that gave him ideas he didn't want to bring up at the moment. He took Julianne by the shoulders.

"Call 911," he demanded. "Get ambulances here. And the police. And the bomb squad."

"The bomb squad?" Julianne paled.

"Do you mean to say you think there's another one of those things in here?" Evan shrilled. "We have to get out of here. We have to find Karla. We have to get her out of here—"

"We'll find Karla momentarily," Gregor said. He hoped that they'd find Bennis Hannaford too. It was Bennis he was looking for. It was Bennis his mind was on even as he talked to Julianne and Evan, even as he gave instructions and advice. He pushed Julianne toward the doors again. "Go. Call 911. Do it now. There's a woman over there I think is dead."

"Dead," Julianne said.

Gregor pushed her hard, and she finally went. Evan stayed. Gregor didn't think the young man was going to move until he had his hand in Karla Parrish's.

There were dozens of people who needed help, hundreds of things to do. Enough time had gone by now so that the people on the floor were stirring. The people who had been in the foyer were crowding around the open doors, straining their necks to look in on the chaos. Gregor saw that the tablecloth that had covered the now-shattered table was being eaten up by fire without ever having burst into flame. It was being consumed by a traveling glowing ember. Gregor went over to it, pulled the tablecloth off the wreckage, and began stepping on the glowing ember. It wouldn't make any sense to find Bennis and then be unable to rescue her because they were both trapped in a fire.

The time to have rescued Bennis Hannaford was at least ten minutes gone. Gregor couldn't stop himself from feeling guilty about it, in spite of the fact that he knew he couldn't have done things any differently than he had.

"Mr. Demarkian." Evan Walsh was tugging on his arm again.

Gregor pointed to an enormous blowup of two young girls in ragged, dirty dresses standing next to a bloody body on a dirt road.

"They were looking at that photograph, I think," Gregor said. "At least, from where they were standing the last time I saw them, that seemed to be what they were doing. What's underneath there?"

"Nothing," Evan said a little wildly. "Nothing. A chair."

Gregor had stamped out all of the ember that he could see. The floor was littered with people and debris. There was enough odd stuff under the photograph of the young girls to fill a garbage truck. There was even a person there, although it wasn't Karla Parrish or Bennis. It was a man in a tweed sport coat, and he was crawling on his hands and knees toward the double doors.

"I'm getting out of here," he kept muttering. "I'm getting out of here right now."

Gregor let him go.

One of the things that was on the floor under the photograph was the remains of another photograph, its cardboard frame twisted and broken, the long sheet of photographic paper ripped at the edges but still basically in one piece.

"Help me move this," Gregor ordered Evan. "Pick it up at the edges and lift it straight up. There may be people under there with broken bones or concussions. You don't want to move them unnecessarily."

"I just want to find Karla," Evan said stubbornly. "I'll bet you think I'm a jerk, Mr. Demarkian, but I don't care. I don't care if I'm being responsible or compassionate or any of those things. I just want to find Karla."

"I don't think you're a jerk," Gregor said. "I just want to find Bennis Hannaford."

Gregor grabbed one end of the photographic paper and a piece of broken cardboard from the frame. Evan went around the other side of the pile and grabbed another.

"It was aimed at Karla, I know it," Evan said. "People don't like what she does. The way she exposes the injustice in the world. They'll do anything to stop her."

Underneath the photographic paper there were pieces of cloth and wood and paper, but underneath those there was at least one person, and that person was breathing.

"I don't think the Rwandan revolutionary forces are going to go around setting off bombs at cocktail parties in Philadelphia," Gregor said firmly. "I think it's much more likely here that this was somebody after Julianne Corbett. She is a political figure." The person he could see beneath the wood and cloth and paper did not seem to be wearing Bennis's beautiful beaded dress.

"She's a political figure who doesn't do anything," Evan said. "And what about this thing Karla wanted to talk to you about? This thing about the murder."

"What murder?" Whoever it was was definitely breathing. Gregor kept taking handfuls of garbage and tossing them aside. Evan was standing straight up and looking at the ceiling, doing no work at all.

"The murder," Evan insisted. "That was why she was so anxious to meet you. I told you she was anxious to meet you."

"I think so." Gregor honestly couldn't remember much of anything about what he had been doing five minutes before the blast.

"It was because of this murder," Evan insisted. "This woman named Willis. Or MacLaren. Or there were two women, Willis and MacLaren—"

"There's one woman. Patricia MacLaren Willis."

"Whatever. She saw it in the papers. She was all worked up about it. She wanted me to get in touch with you so she could talk to you about it, but I said you were supposed to be here, you were on the list, and she said she'd wait."

"Do you know what it was she wanted to say?"

"No," Evan admitted. "She just kept laughing and saying that it was impossible. Patsy MacLaren couldn't have murdered anybody. And then I said that anybody could murder somebody. They're always saying that in, like, *Psychology Today* and Agatha Christie novels and all that kind of thing, and then Karla said, but yes, all right, except there are some limits, and Patsy certainly couldn't murder anybody now. And then there were other things we had to do, you know, and we went and did them and do you think that was it? Whoever murdered Patsy MacLaren decided to get rid of Karla because of what she knew?"

"Nobody murdered Patsy MacLaren as far as we can tell. Patsy MacLaren murdered her husband. Stephen Willis."

"Oh. And Karla knows her. Maybe that's it. Karla thinks she's innocent, but she isn't, and Karla knows something about her that could be damaging, so to head her off at the pass—"

It was Evan whom Gregor had to head off at the pass. The breathing person beneath him was now clearly Karla Parrish.

The hollows of her ears were crusted with blood. Her eyes were half open and blank. Evan turned at just that moment and saw her. He jumped three inches into the air and dived toward the rubble, intending to drag her out.

"Don't move her," Gregor commanded. "She's probably got a concussion, for God's sake. You'll make it worse."

"I have to find out if she's alive," Evan insisted. "I have to know. I can't just leave her there."

"You have to leave her there," Gregor insisted. "You can see that she's alive just by looking at her. You can see that she's breathing."

"Look at her eyes," Evan said. "People are dead and still breathing all the time. That's what those right-to-life cases are all about."

"Gregor?" Bennis Hannaford's voice said. "Gregor, can you move her at all? Can you get me out of here?"

Gregor and Evan both looked down at the figure of Karla Parrish. The light was not wonderful in this room, and there was so much confusion. It took Gregor several seconds before he saw the glittering black beads of Bennis's dress.

"I'm under everything," her voice continued desperately. "Gregor, please. I feel like I'm suffocating in here. And I think I've broken my arm."

"You can't move Karla," Evan said. "You told me yourself that could make her worse."

"We can't leave Bennis lying underneath her either," Gregor said. "Would you get control of yourself?"

"I'm in as much control as anybody could be. Don't you think for a minute that you're in any more control than I am. If you touch her, I'm going to beat you up, Mr. Demarkian. I swear to God, I'll beat you up."

Evan Walsh was the kind of person men like Gregor Demarkian never paid very much attention to. Slight of body. Seemingly slight of mind. Frivolous and foppish and dandyish and just a little too feminine in an old-fashioned definition of that word, catlike in the worst sense. The eyes, though, were not the eyes of a frivolous person. Suddenly, Gregor Demarkian didn't like Evan Walsh at all. He didn't even like having to look at him.

"Gregor?" Bennis Hannaford said from under the body of Karla Parrish. "What is that idiot talking about? Can't you get me out of here?"

"Just a minute," Gregor told her.

"I'll break your arm," Evan Walsh told him pleasantly, smiling through his teeth. "Just you try it and see if I don't."

"Gregor," Bennis said again.

They were saved by the paramedics. Julianne Corbett had followed orders. She had dialed 911, and now the emergency services came barreling through the doors like a SWAT team in white coats, and one of them even yelled, "Nobody move!"

## 2.

Karla Parrish had a concussion and had to be rushed to the hospital. Bennis Hannaford had a broken arm and had to be taken to the hospital too. The woman with the fake fur button was dead. A dozen people were hurt. The two uniformed police officers kept wandering around the wreckage of the living room, muttering to themselves. Gregor hung around long enough to let one of them take his name and address, and then left. The one who took his address muttered something about "the Armenian-American Hercule Poirot," but they both had too much on their minds to pursue it, including the possibility that the bomb that had gone off was not the only one that had been planted. After looking Gregor up and down like a prize bull, they both went off to take the names and addresses of other people, and Gregor found himself outside the town house, free to do what he thought best.

Outside on the sidewalk there were more police, and cordons holding back the crowd. The crowd was large and good-natured and unlikely to want to leave anytime soon. They were spiced with camera crews from all the local news shows and reporters with press cards in plastic envelopes on cords around their necks. The reporter from the *Inquirer* recognized Gregor immediately and began to gesture frantically. Gregor walked off in the other direction and had one of the cops let him through the cord and into the crowd. A camera crew from the local NBC affiliate was there, and the reporter leaned a microphone toward him as soon as he came out.

"Mr. Demarkian!" the woman said. "What can you tell us about how it felt to be at the very site of the blast?"

Why did television reporters always want to know how people felt about things? Gregor had grown up in a generation that thought of emotions as private matters, like what went on in the bathroom, and didn't talk about them in public if they could help it. Now even the most respected news shows paraded sobbing widows and orphans in front of their cameras and asked serial killers if they felt any remorse. For Christ's sake. If serial killers felt remorse, they wouldn't be serial killers.

Gregor evaded the microphone and made his way through the crowd. It went a full block without thinning out and then just disappeared. He was on a mostly empty street with small open stores and the amber glow of lights from apartments. He found a pay phone that hadn't been vandalized and put in a call to John Jackman's private number. He got the answering machine.

"Drop whatever you're doing," he told the buzzing tape after the beep. "There's been another bomb. Meet me at St. Elizabeth's Hospital. Bennis broke her arm."

That ought to get him, Gregor thought, hanging up. He kept walking toward the lights, looking for a taxi. He didn't know Philadelphia as well as he should. He had lived so long in Washington, and in the years before that in places as far apart as Encino and Austin. Philadelphia was the home of his childhood, and even then it had been a rather restricted area. Nothing much changes with people, Gregor thought. When he had been growing up the big tensions in Philly had not been between black and white, but between native and "foreign," with the "foreign" including even those people, like Gregor, who had been born in the United States of parents who had not. In those days, too, the greatest point of tension had to do with young men, because young men are always the most dangerous creatures on earth. Or some of them are. Gregor had been bookish and shy and not very aggressive. He had started hard and gone to the University of Pennsylvania in the days when quotas were meant to keep people like him out. That was why he didn't know as much as he should about Philadelphia. Those were the days when leaving your home turf meant getting hassled by the cops or even arrested for something minor, anything so that they could pick you up and throw you back in the direction they figured you belonged. Gregor had known a few places in the city well: Cavanaugh Street and the streets around it; the bus route to the University of Pennsylvania campus; the streets immediately around those parts of the campus that he had to go to. Since he had lived at home, he knew nothing about Penn's dormitories or where they were located. There must be even more of them now, and they could be anywhere. Still, as he walked up the street and looked around, he was fairly certain that they weren't anywhere near there. He would have to get a map, but he thought he could be safe in assuming that if there was any connection between this pipe bomb and the ones that had gone off in Patsy MacLaren Willis's Volvo, it wasn't geographical. Gregor had no idea why it should be. It was just one of those things you had to check out.

Gregor walked one more block—there were a few Spanish stores, including one that seemed to be selling the accoutrements of Santeria—and then began to look seriously for a cab. Sometimes you can go for hours looking for a cab on the streets of Philadelphia at night. This time he was lucky, and a cab pulled up to him less than two minutes after he started looking.

"St. Elizabeth's Hospital," he said, climbing inside.

The cabdriver shrugged. "Sure. I'm going to take a little extra loop on the way. I'll turn the meter off."

"A little extra loop to where?"

"To the bombing," the cabdriver said. "There was another bombing tonight, just like that thing at the garage. It's terrorists, let me tell you. The world is full of terrorists. It's all because of that Saddam Hussein."

"What?"

The cabdriver had swung back into the street with the crowd on it. Gregor could see that the paramedics were still at work, taking people out of the town house and putting them in ambulances. There were a lot more police than there had been a few minutes ago too.

"Saddam Hussein," the cabdriver said again. "It's a conspiracy. It's like, Reagan and Bush, they were paying this guy Saddam Hussein to hassle the Ayatollah, but now he's gotten out of hand, and Mr. Chickenshit Clinton isn't going to do anything about him, and it all ties in with the way those Chinese people keep sneaking into the country. You see what I mean?"

"No."

"Nobody ever does," the cabdriver said glumly. "That's why the country is going down the tubes. You do agree the country is going down the tubes?"

"Sure."

"Good. Good. Talking to some people, it's like they just came from outer space."

## 3.

Walking into St. Elizabeth's Hospital, Gregor thought, fifteen minutes later, was like walking into outer space. Did emergency rooms always look like this? Gregor didn't spend much of his time in them. The only one he could really remember with any detail had belonged to a free clinic called the So-journer Truth Health Center in Harlem, and he didn't think that ought to count. That was supposed to be in a war zone. This emergency room looked like an outpost in a war zone too. So many people seemed to be bleeding, and so many of them seemed to be young. So many people seemed to be waiting, and so many of them seemed to be poor. The patients at the Sojourner Truth Health Center had been almost universally African-American. Here, race was less of a factor than exhaustion. Everybody he saw looked hopeless and tired and halfway dead.

He went up to the woman in the white uniform at the reception window. She had a plate of bulletproof glass in front of her.

"Name?" she said.

"I'm not registering," Gregor told her. "A friend of mine was just brought in here with a broken arm and I think one or two contusions. I'd like to know where she is."

"Are you related to her in any way?"

"Related?"

"Husband? Father? Brother? Uncle?"

"No. We're not related. We were together at this party—"

"You were together at the party but she came to the emergency room by herself?"

"She was brought here by the paramedic team—"

"A paramedic team had to be called to this party?"

Gregor took a deep breath. "Let's take this from the beginning," he said. "My name is Gregor Demarkian."

"Oh, my God!" This was a voice from behind the nurse he was talking to. Gregor couldn't see the speaker.

"This friend of mine, Bennis Hannaford, and I were at a party in Society Hill given by Congresswoman Julianne Corbett—"

"Congresswoman." This was the nurse right behind the glass. She was sitting up very straight in her chair now.

Gregor was glad to have found out what made her move.

"Right," he said. "Congresswoman Corbett. There was some kind of small bomb—"

"I've heard about that. What did you say your name was again?"

"Gregor Demarkian."

"The Armenian-American Hercule Poirot," hissed the voice behind the nurse. "Don't you ever read the papers?"

The nurse ignored the voice. "What was the name of your friend again?"

"Bennis Hannaford."

"Just a moment, please."

"You can't make him sit there and wait," the voice said, sounding scandalized. "He knows the mayor. We'll all be in major trouble."

The nurse Gregor could see went on ignoring the voice. She stood and walked away, leaving nothing but a blank wall behind her. Now Gregor wondered where the other voice was coming from.

He turned around in his chair and looked back out on the waiting room, on all the tired people, on all the pain. Was this a good hospital? He didn't know. He only knew that the waiting room depressed him, the way cities in general had depressed him. He thought of Fox Run Hill with its gates and its guards, and sighed.

The nurse came back and sat down behind the bulletproof glass again. "That will be fine," she told him. "You need to go down this corridor to your left all the way to the end and present this pass at the fire doors. Then you go through the fire doors and to the right until you reach Room E143. Do you understand that?"

"Down here to the left to the fire doors. Present the pass. To the right until Room E143."

"That is correct. Are you carrying any firearms on your person?"

"No."

"Are you carrying anything else that might be used as a weapon?"

"I'm not carrying a knife or anything of that kind, if that's what you mean. I have a comb."

"You will be required to pass through metal detectors at the fire doors," the woman went on, ignoring everything he had said. "The guards there are authorized to confiscate and retain any item you may have that they consider a potential danger to the hospital, its patients, or yourself. Any such item will be returned to you when you leave. Do you understand this?"

"Yes," Gregor said. "Yes, I understand it."

The woman pushed a bright green paper card through the narrow slot under her window and watched carefully while he took it. Then she looked over his shoulder to see who was next in line.

Gregor got up and started walking heavily down the wide corridor toward the fire doors. The corridor was deserted and the fire doors were bright polished metal, hard-surfaced and grim.

He couldn't imagine spending any time here, or trying to get well in this place. He couldn't imagine being able to get well in this place.

He just hoped Bennis was all right, and that she wouldn't have to spend much time here. He wanted to take her home tonight.

# TWO

## 1.

*I*F HENRY HADN'T INSISTED ON going shopping with her again, Evelyn would never have been wearing her sun hat when the big red Lincoln pulled into the driveway of the brick Federalist that morning. She didn't like wearing hats in cars, but she didn't want to take this one off in front of Henry either. It was a hot day and Henry had the Lincoln's air-conditioning turned up full blast. Cold air streamed up under the thin fabric of her cotton dress and around her massive thighs. The dress was beginning to feel a little tight, and that scared her. It was a size thirty-two. How much longer would this go on? Would she just get fatter and fatter and fatter until she could no longer fit through the door of the house? She thought about that woman they had done the piece on on *60 Minutes*, the one who weighed a thousand pounds. Then she felt a sharp stab of hunger in her stomach, and wished Henry away, far away, where he wouldn't be able to see her eating. When people saw her eating, they said things to her. Even if she had the money, she couldn't go into McDonald's or Burger King and sit down and have a hamburger. For one thing, she no longer fit into the seats too well. She didn't fit into the ones that were bolted to the floor at all. For another thing, people passing by her chair said things to her. "No wonder you're so gross," they would say even though they were carrying a couple of Big Macs and a large fries for themselves and she had nothing on her table but a cheeseburger and a Coke. It was as if they thought fat people had no right to eat, ever. It was what Henry thought too.

The car pulled into the driveway of the brick Federalist. Evelyn adjusted her hat, wishing her head didn't hurt so much, wishing she weren't so cold. She had begun to sweat in the way that meant she was going to throw up. She had eaten an entire eight-inch Black Forest cake in the toilet paper aisle while Henry was off at the cold-cut counter, deciding exactly what brand of superlean turkey he wanted to buy. Her hat was a big straw cartwheel that felt tight in just the way her dress did—did your head get bigger when you got fat? Evelyn closed her eyes and prayed to a God she didn't believe in for salvation.

"Look," Henry said, cutting the engine. "They're back. The police and that detective, Demarkian."

Evelyn opened her eyes. She felt a lot better with the air conditioner off.

"He was on the news this morning," she said. "Talking about the bomb last night at that party Julianne Corbett gave. Did you vote for Julianne Corbett?"

"She's not in this district," Henry said. "You should know that."

"Patsy loved Julianne Corbett. She used to point out pictures of her in the newspapers and say what a wonderful woman she was."

"That couldn't have gone on for too long. Corbett's barely been a congresswoman at all. She just got elected, for God's sake."

"She was in politics before she ever got to be a congresswoman. She was very active in Causes. She's a very big feminist."

Henry made a face. "Feminism is a phase. I told you that. What it is you see in those women, I'll never know."

"I was talking about Patsy."

"Maybe that's why you're so fat. Maybe it's feminism. Maybe you've decided that being thin is a form of oppression you're not going to put up with and so you've become gross instead."

"I was talking about Patsy," Evelyn said again.

"Don't talk to the police," Henry said, popping open the driver's side door. "We don't want to get mixed up in that kind of thing."

With the door open, the air from outside rushed in. It was hot and sticky and thick. She opened her own door and got out onto the driveway. From where she stood, she could see Gregor Demarkian and the two policemen. Demarkian was walking up and down the edges of the Willises' long, curving drive.

"It's just like Sherlock Holmes, isn't it?" Evelyn didn't want to move into the house. The house had more air-conditioning in it, even better air-conditioning than the Lincoln. Evelyn liked it out in the heat. "It's just like a detective novel. He ought to have a microscope."

"You mean a magnifying glass, Evelyn. For Christ's sake."

"I'll be back in a minute," Evelyn said.

She could be surprisingly fast when she wanted to be. By the time Henry realized what she was doing, she was almost all the way down the drive, in full view of the three men over in the Willises' driveway. She knew Henry wanted to shout or chase her, but she knew he wouldn't do either. He would be worried about what the detectives would think. She reached the road and walked even faster. Without gravel to fight, she could move more quickly than most people of average weight. She half jogged along the road, listening for the sound of Henry's footsteps behind her. She didn't hear them. He wasn't following her. He was just going to blow up at her when she got home.

In the Willises' driveway, the three men had stopped whatever they were doing and begun watching her. Evelyn carefully blanked out of her mind any speculation as to what they might be thinking—*look at that gross fat ugly horrible woman*—and when she got to the drive itself she came to a stop and climbed carefully up the slope. Slopes were not like straightaways. She sometimes blacked out on slopes.

"Mr. Demarkian?" she said when she got almost to where the three men stood. The older of the two detectives was Dan Exter, who was with the police department here. Evelyn recognized him from the fund-raising drives for the Police Community Contact League. The other one was black, and too good-looking. He was the kind of person who would look Evelyn over and decide that she was too ugly to talk to. But Gregor Demarkian was all right. He could have stood to lose a few pounds himself.

"Mr. Demarkian," Evelyn said, holding out her hand. Then she snatched it back. She couldn't remember if it was the right thing to do. She blushed furiously. "How do you do."

"How do you do," Gregor Demarkian said very politely.

Evelyn had hardly any air in her lungs. The hat on her head hurt her terribly. She looked at the ground.

"I'm sorry for what I saw on the news this morning. About your friend. About Miss Hannaford."

"Thank you. But she's all right, you know. She's just got a broken arm."

"They didn't say on the news. They said some woman tourist from New York was dead."

"Caroline Barrens, yes. She wasn't a tourist though. She was the representative of some kind of PAC. Health care reform. Single payer system. That kind of thing."

"Yes," Evelyn nodded. "Well. I was thinking. That it might make sense, you know. The pipe bomb."

"I wish it made sense to me."

Gregor Demarkian sounded sincere. Evelyn relaxed a little more. She liked this man's face. She liked it a great deal. It was lined and soft and gentle. It was much better than Henry's. Maybe if she left Henry she could marry Gregor Demarkian. Maybe this Bennis Hannaford person wouldn't mind.

"Well," Evelyn said. "The thing is. Patsy was a big supporter of Julianne Corbett's. Did you know that?"

"I know she's on the contributors' lists for Julianne Corbett's campaign," Gregor said. "Those are the public lists, you know, the ones you have to publish by law."

"I didn't know about the money," Evelyn admitted, "but Patsy really admired Julianne Corbett. She had pictures of her all over the house. Did you find the pictures in the house?"

"No." Gregor Demarkian was watching her very carefully now. "No, we didn't."

"Well, Patsy had them. And she was always saying that Julianne Corbett was the woman she would be if only she had made different choices in her life. Julianne Corbett was what she would be if she was only at her best. Does that make sense?"

"I think so."

"I wish it made more sense to me. She was very intense about it. And Sarah Lockwood said she didn't understand it at all, because Julianne Corbett was so low rent, because of all the makeup she wears, you know, and the jewelry and the hats. Does she wear all that stuff in person?"

"She did last night. Except I don't think she was wearing a hat. I don't really remember."

"I thought maybe that that stuff was just for the public, you know, a way of creating a personality people will remember and then when they went to vote you might be the only one they'd heard of. Patsy said it didn't matter to her what Julianne Corbett wore, she was a wonderful woman. And Patsy said that anytime she looked at her, she wanted to change her life. And maybe she did."

"Maybe she did," Gregor Demarkian agreed.

"But I was thinking of something else," Evelyn continued.

"I was thinking that maybe it wasn't Patsy who blew up her car. Maybe it was somebody who hated Patsy and everything about her and they blew her up first and now they've decided to blow up this woman she idolized. Do you see?"

"But there wasn't a body in the Volvo when it blew up," Gregor said. "There was no one in the car."

"Maybe there was supposed to be. Maybe the bomber is just inept. Maybe Patsy is afraid now and she's in hiding."

Gregor Demarkian nodded. "I think she's in hiding. What about her husband? Do you think somebody other than Patsy MacLaren Willis shot her husband?"

Evelyn looked back at the brick Federalist. Henry was no longer in the driveway. The house looked blank. She adjusted the hat on her head again.

"It's funny," she said. "I completely forgot about Stephen. I mean, he was never around, do you know what I mean? He had some job that made him travel for weeks at a time and he was just never here. I'd heard that was going to change though. He was getting promoted or something and he was going to be able to stay put in the Philadelphia office instead of traveling all the time. Had you heard that?"

"Yes. Yes, I had."

"Nobody else could have killed him though." Evelyn felt suddenly depressed. She motioned back at the Federalist. "I live there. I was sitting in my window seat almost all that morning. I saw Patsy leave. With all those clothes, you know."

"She was carrying clothes?"

"She had tons and tons of them loaded into the Volvo. But it was just her. Nobody else came out of the house with her. She left all on her own."

"Did she take anything with her besides the clothes?"

"Nothing that I could see. I don't want you to get the impression that I was spying. I wasn't spying. I sit in my window seat a lot at that time of the morning. Mostly, there isn't anybody at all around except maybe people coming out to get their newspapers. The newspapers are supposed to be delivered right to your doorstep, but they end up on the lawns a lot."

"Did you see Mrs. Willis when she started to pack things into her Volvo?"

"I think so. I saw her when the Volvo was almost empty, and then she began to go back and forth into the house for the clothes, and I thought she was putting together her dry cleaning."

"Weren't there a lot of clothes for dry cleaning?"

Evelyn shrugged. "It's spring. People do that in the spring. Take all their things to have them dry-cleaned, I mean. There wasn't anybody in the whole neighborhood then except Molly Bracken picking up her paper."

"Do you know what time this was?"

"I think so. It was six-thirty or so when Patsy left. I heard my cuckoo clock go off. And I sat there a long time, until my husband woke up at ten minutes to eight, and nobody else came out of the Willis house. Nobody at all."

"That's good to know."

"Yes," Evelyn said, feeling embarrassed again. "Well." The pair of police detectives seemed to be hovering just behind Gregor Demarkian's back. They made Evelyn feel uncomfortable. "Well," she said again, backing up a little. "I have to go now. We just got back from shopping, my husband and I did. I have to unpack the groceries."

"Thank you for coming forward," Gregor Demarkian said.

Evelyn continued to back up. "I'm sorry I couldn't be more help. I really am. I didn't know Patsy all that well. I don't know anybody here all that well. I don't go out much."

"You've given us some very valuable information."

That was supposed to make her feel good about herself. Evelyn knew it. It wasn't working. She backed up faster.

"I've got to go," she said again, and then she was practically running down the drive, jogging back across the road, puffing up her own drive with heavy pumping motions that made her thighs hurt and her feet feel like glass about to break in a thousand pieces. Henry was nowhere to be seen. Evelyn hoped he was hiding out at the back of the house, sulking in privacy.

She made it to the top of her drive and into her garage. She went through her garage and into her mudroom. For most of this last little run she had had to hold her hat on her head. Now she sat down on one of the benches and took the hat off. Underneath it, lying against the top of her skull, she had a twelve-pound pork roast she had shoplifted from the meat bin at the Stop 'N Shop while Henry had been off on his own pawing through the fresh vegetables and lecturing nobody and everybody about the benefits of dietary fiber.

Evelyn put the pork roast in the box she used to keep her slippers in. She put the box under the bench she was sitting on. The pork roast would have to thaw. She could come back for it when Henry was out of the house, and then her only problem would be cooking it and getting rid of the smell of it before Henry caught her.

Evelyn loved pork roast. She loved the thick fat that lined the outside of it. She loved the thick fat that lined the outside of *herself*.

## 2.

If Liza Verity had kept her promise to Congresswoman Julianne Corbett, she would have been at the reception for Karla Parrish when the pipe bomb went off. Instead, she had allowed herself to be bullied into working late for the first night in almost two years. Liza had spent the evening monitoring an EKG machine attached to a six-year-old boy with a rare heart abnormality. The boy was supposed to have open-heart surgery in two days, and he was terrified. This was important work and Liza was happy with herself for doing it, but she was also aware that she wouldn't have done it if she hadn't had to have an excuse that Julianne was sure to accept.

She herself wasn't sure why it had become so important to her not to attend that reception. Maybe it was just that one more Really Successful member of the old Jewett House group was more than she could bear. Maybe it was just that she hadn't wanted to look dowdy and bought-her-dress-at-Sears in the middle of all those people who had paid thousands to look good while they were having cocktails. Maybe it was just that she was sick to death of Julianne.

Whatever it was, Liza had worked all night, gone home at six in the morning for four hours' sleep, and then come back to the hospital to do her regular shift. Now it was noon and she was sitting at a table in the hospital cafeteria, trying to drink enough very strong coffee to keep herself awake. Her uniform felt scratchy and cheap. The coffee tasted horrible. She hadn't eaten in so long, her stomach hurt, but she was much too tired to eat. On the other side of the table, a very young and very new RN named Shirley Bates was reading through the latest edition of the *Philadelphia Inquirer*, exclaiming every second or so about just how horrible all this violence was getting to be.

"Really," Shirley Bates said. "I was warned before I came here, but you never understand until you see it for yourself. That's true, don't you think? I was warned, but the first time I saw a baby come in here with a gunshot wound, I nearly died."

"Mmm," Liza said.

"And now this thing with Congresswoman Corbett. A woman like that. It just goes to show. Nobody is safe anymore."

"Mmm," Liza said again.

"They took all the people at that party to St. Elizabeth's. They should have brought them here. We've got much better facilities here."

"St. Elizabeth's was closer to where they were."

"Closeness isn't everything. Oh, well. There's a woman

who's dead, you know. And this other woman, the one the reception was for, this Miss Paris—"

"Parrish."

"Well, she hardly sounds like somebody who leads a calm life, what with all this going off to war zones and all that, but that's just my point. I mean, she'd just come back from some civil war in Africa and she'd been just fine and she's here for hardly a day and boom. Isn't that ironic?"

"It's certainly something."

"The paper says it's the same kind of bomb in a pipe that blew up that car in the parking lot a couple of days ago. You know the one. Where the woman was supposed to have killed her husband."

"Yes," Liza said. "I know the one."

Shirley Bates let a smug little smile paste itself over her face. Shirley was a plumpish little woman, the kind who always seems to be on a diet to lose just five more pounds. She was one of the least intelligent nurses Liza had ever known.

"You know what I think?" Shirley said. "I don't think that woman killed her husband at all. I don't think she had anything to do with any pipe bombs. No matter what the papers have to say. The papers have all been taken over by liberals anyway."

"What?"

"It will be black gangs, you just watch. That's what it always is these days. No wonder Africa is always in the middle of some kind of war. These are very violent people we're dealing with here."

"What are you talking about?" Liza demanded. "You're not making any sense at all."

"Of course I am," Shirley said. "I'm talking about Negroes. Except we're not supposed to call them Negroes anymore because the liberals won't let you do anything. The liberals suck up to them. But everybody knows the truth anyway. You can't avoid it."

"I don't think I want to continue this discussion," Liza said.

"You don't have to if you don't want to," Shirley said, "but I get tired of pretending that I can't see what's going on right in front of my nose. I mean, just look around this place. Look around down in ER. All that blood. Children coming in battered. Children coming in drugged up. People shot. It's always Them."

I ought to get up out of this chair and move, Liza told herself. I ought to slap this silly woman's face. I ought to do something. But she was too tired. Her legs felt full of lead. Up at the checkout to the cafeteria line, Liza saw Leyla Williams, one of the best nurses in the Peds ICU and as black as the skirt on a witch's dress. She started to wave frantically.

"There's Leyla," she told Shirley Bates. "Maybe she'll come over to join us."

"Leyla?"

Leyla saw them and nodded. Liza started to feel a little better. "Leyla's one of my oldest friends at this hospital."

Shirley turned around, saw Leyla coming toward them, and made a face. "And that's another thing," she said. "They really can't keep this up with the affirmative action. Affirmative action. What a name for it. It just means letting in people who aren't qualified and pretending they can nurse."

"Affirmative action," Liza said. "I get it. That's how you got this job."

"Pardon me?"

"Never mind," Liza said.

Shirley Bates gathered her papers together and got up. "I'm going back to work now. I know I have to live with these people, but I don't have to pretend to like it. You ought to consider these things, Liza. You ought to consider what it means to you to have liberals running the world."

"Right," Liza said.

Shirley Bates said, "You shouldn't let those people fool you. Look what they did to that Congresswoman Corbett, who always made out she was such a big friend of theirs. I mean, most of them are still jungle savages."

"Good-bye," Liza said breathlessly, feeling distinctly dizzy. "Go away."

"I'm certainly going to go away before *she* gets here," Shirley Bates said.

Shirley disappeared just as Leyla came up. Liza leaned across the table and pushed a chair out for Leyla to sit down in.

"I just had the most extraordinary conversation," Liza said. "I can't believe I really heard—"

"We're all still a bunch of savages and we'd still be cannibals, too, except the police put a lid on it," Leyla said equitably. "Haven't you ever talked to Shirley before?"

"Somebody should have warned me."

"Well, now you're warned. Don't worry about it too much. She won't last long. She has an IQ of minus twelve and she's a terrible nurse."

"How did she get the job?"

"She's the niece of the vice president of the board of directors."

Liza giggled. "Affirmative action," she said.

Leyla hooted. "Back when I got hired at this place, the only kind of affirmative action they had was the kind that said people who looked like me couldn't work here. Did you know I got hired as a nurse's aide?"

"You mean you came here before you did your training?"

"When I came here, I had an RN from Penn State and a master's degree in nursing from the Women and Children's Crisis Program at Columbia Presbyterian. Welcome to affirmative action and 1962. What about you? You can't look that awful just because Shirley shocked the shit out of you."

"What? Oh, no. It's not that. I did a night detail last night and then I came back on shift. I haven't had much sleep."

"You shouldn't do things like that. It's no better for the patients than it is for you."

Liza looked down at the table. She had a copy of that day's *Philadelphia Inquirer* too, but it was still folded and unread next to her cafeteria tray. She looked at the black-and-white photograph of the wreckage of Julianne Corbett's party and bit her lip.

"Have you ever, I don't know how to put it, have you ever had information about something important except that the information didn't make any sense?"

"Like what?"

"Well, you know that woman who's supposed to have killed her husband and blown up her own car with a bomb?"

"Sure. Patricia Willis. Today they're saying maybe she tried to blow up Congresswoman Corbett's cocktail party with a bomb."

"I know. The thing is, when I first heard the name—the whole name, Patricia MacLaren Willis—anyway, when I first heard the name I thought it was a coincidence, because I used to know a Patsy MacLaren. And then when I saw the picture, I realized that I did know this Patsy MacLaren. I mean, this Mrs. Willis. Except it's kind of strange. It doesn't really make sense."

"It doesn't make sense how?"

"I don't know how to put it. I look at the picture, and I definitely recognize it, but it doesn't look the way it ought to. I shouldn't be able to recognize it."

"I think you need more sleep," Leyla said solemnly.

"I know I need more sleep," Liza admitted. "It's just—well, what do you know about this Mr. Demarkian?"

"The Armenian-American Hercule Poirot? I know what I read in the papers. I think that if the *Inquirer* doesn't let up on that joke, the man's going to sue them."

"Do you think he'd be, you know, patient about listening to what I had to say? In spite of the fact that it isn't very coherent?"

"I don't know. Do you really want to talk to him?"

"I think I do, yes. I mean, I really don't want to talk to Julianne, I don't know why but I don't—"

"I forgot you knew Julianne Corbett. Vassar."

"That's right. Vassar. I don't know, Leyla, maybe there's too much rivalry there. Too much jealousy. For me. And I don't want to go to the police. That doesn't feel right to me at all. So I thought I'd talk to this Mr. Demarkian and explain what I had to explain and maybe he would listen to me."

"I don't see why not," Leyla said. "Only you'd better be better at explaining it to him than you were at explaining it to me. I still don't have the faintest idea of what you were talking about."

"Maybe I don't have the faintest idea either. It's right there, you know what I'm saying. It's right at the edge of my mind. I can't seem to get ahold of it."

"So go see this Gregor Demarkian. You'll have a story you can tell in the cafeteria for weeks. People around here won't be able to get enough of it."

"Right," Liza said, standing up. "I guess I'd better go now. I told them I'd be only about fifteen minutes and it's been more like half an hour. What an idiot that Shirley Bates is."

"The world is full of jerks," Leyla said.

"Right." Liza picked up her tray. "And my supervisor is one of them. I'll leave the newspaper for you. I didn't have time to read it with Shirley blathering away at me."

"When you meet Gregor Demarkian, find out if he's really sleeping with that Bennis Hannaford woman," Leyla told her. "The newspapers are always so vague. It could make a person crazy."

# THREE

## 1.

GREGOR DEMARKIAN SOMETIMES WONDERED WHY he had ever become involved in law enforcement at all. Unlike a lot of the men he had trained with, all those years ago in J. Edgar Hoover's America, he hadn't grown up listening to radio serials and dreaming about being Eliot Ness. In his last years at the Federal Bureau of Investigation, he had often felt like the housekeeper at a fraternity house. There was just so much mess and it kept coming at you. All you could do was sweep it back and shop for bigger brooms, aware from the start that you were never going to get the place cleaned up so that it would stay clean. In Philadelphia these days, he felt more like he was unraveling wool. Crime was a fabric made of yarns and threads. If you picked at it long enough, it came apart in your hands. That was the kind of thing Tibor was always saying, and Gregor didn't really believe he'd started to think like Tibor. What he was trying to work out was why he felt so much more responsible about it all these days, when he wasn't paid to investigate criminals, when he wasn't sworn to eradicate crime. Sometimes he felt as if the Federal Bureau of Investigation was a machine that had worked well with him and worked just as well without him. Now he was out where there were no machines, and nobody else seemed to be taking care of business.

Gregor certainly felt responsible for what had happened to Bennis Hannaford in spite of the fact that it had been her idea to go to that silly cocktail party. Gregor had received an invitation of his own and ignored it. What kept nagging at him in the aftermath of the explosion was that he had known of the link between Julianne Corbett and Patricia MacLaren Willis, thin though it was. He had known that Patsy Mac-Laren had contributed money to Julianne Corbett's political campaign. Of course, if that was enough of a link to get somebody's cocktail party blown up, the entire Philadelphia Main Line ought to look like a Fourth of July fireworks display every Sunday evening in the summer. What Gregor really felt about the breaking of Bennis Hannaford's arm was scared to death. She hadn't been seriously hurt, but she had been very close to people who were seriously hurt. One woman was dead. Karla Parrish, the woman Bennis had been standing right next to, was in a coma and no one knew how long it would take her to come out of it, if she ever did. There were people with damage to their eyes and their faces. If Bennis hadn't been on her way out to have a cigarette, she could have been—anything. It was the first time Gregor Demarkian had ever been grateful for Bennis Hannaford's nicotine habit.

"The trouble with you," John Jackman said when he dropped Gregor off on Cavanaugh Street after their trip out to Fox Run Hill, "is that you won't admit that for all intents and purposes, you've married again."

"I haven't married again," Gregor said. His voice sounded very fast, made up of rush. "Bennis and I don't—I mean, we've never even contemplated—"

"I know what you don't do," John Jackman said, "but if you think Bennis hasn't at least contemplated it, then you don't know Bennis."

"John, for God's sake."

"You're in each other's laps all the time. She worries about your cholesterol. You worry about her driving. She fusses with your ties. You complain about the way she spends money. People who see you together think that you're married. Or at least living together."

"Living together," Gregor repeated. Today, not only were all of Donna Moradanyan's wedding decorations still up, there were new ones. The entire front of the duplex town house Hannah Krekorian shared with Howard Kashinian's old aunt had been wrapped up in white satin ribbons and decked out in gold satin bows. The town house looked like a gift box of chocolates with radiation poisoning.

"I couldn't imagine just living with someone," Gregor told Jackman. "Especially here. Especially on Cavanaugh Street."

"That kind of thing goes on everywhere these days, Gregor. Even on Cavanaugh Street."

"Maybe it goes on with teenagers, but it doesn't go on with middle-aged men like me."

"Whatever. You've been looking green ever since Bennis got hurt. I'm just saying that if you made this official in some way, people would understand better why it is you're concerned. They'd cut you more slack——"

"I don't need any more slack," Gregor said quickly. "I'm fine."

"Sure you are."

"And it's you she had the affair with," Gregor pointed out. "You said at the time she knew better what she wanted than any woman you'd ever known. I'd think that if Bennis actually wanted the kind of thing with me you're talking about, I'd have heard about it by now."

John Jackman looked disgusted. "Get real," he said. "Women who look like Bennis Hannaford do not make the first move. They don't have to. Women's lib or no women's lib. And besides, she's come close to making the first move with you a dozen times——"

"Don't talk nonsense."

John Jackman had the window next to his elbow rolled all the way down. He was beginning to sweat in the heat and humidity of the evening air. On the corner there was one of those newspaper sales boxes with a copy of the Philadelphia *Star* in its window. The *Star* was running a picture of the woman who had died in the explosion, a posed studio portrait, without the button with its fake fur message.

"Listen," John Jackman said. "I want you to think about what you want to do next. We have to do something next. We can't just sit around waiting for this Karla Parrish person to wake up and tell us what we want to know.

"Not that she's likely to really know anything anyway," Jackman went on when Gregor said nothing. "She was in Somalia or someplace when Mrs. Willis decided to off Mr. Willis."

"Rwanda."

"Wherever. Dan Exter thinks we're all just spinning our wheels."

"We are."

"Well, we have to stop. I'd tell you to say hello to Bennis for me, but she doesn't want to hear it. Does she curse me out when I'm not around?"

"She doesn't talk about you at all."

"It figures," John Jackman said. "I've been thinking lately about getting married, Gregor. I've been thinking it wouldn't be such a bad idea. Even with all the responsibilities."

"Do you have somebody in particular in mind?" Gregor was honestly interested. Bennis was the only woman he had ever seen John Jackman with for longer than a week and a half.

John started to roll up his window. Gregor could hear the car's air-conditioning system grinding away. The engine was rumbling and shuddering under the hood. "I always have somebody in particular in mind," John said. "The problem is, I have a couple of somebodies in mind every month. I'll be down here for breakfast tomorrow at seven, okay?"

"No. I'll meet you uptown. You're sure we have an appointment?"

"As sure as I can be."

"She's put us off twice already."

"I've threatened to give an interview to the *Inquirer* saying she's put us off if she does it again," John said. "Worse, I threatened that *you'd* do it."

"Good."

"You have to be tough with these political people. If you're not, they'll run right over you. Say hello to Bennis for me anyway, Gregor. What the hell."

"Okay."

"It's too bad about breakfast. I like that restaurant you go to." John rolled his window all the way up and pulled out onto the street. There was no traffic coming in either direction and no traffic visible in the distance. It was odd, Gregor thought, the way Philadelphia seemed to be almost deserted at some hours these days. When he was growing up, it had always seemed busy and crowded and funny-dangerous, like a roller coaster whose seats were all crammed full.

On an impulse, Gregor walked to the corner and looked down into the side street. For the first block or so it was all right, marked by some minor examples of Donna Moradanyan's wedding decorations, but after that everything went to hell. It was dark. It was dingy. It was falling to pieces. Gregor couldn't put his finger on it, but there was something about all this, about the way Cavanaugh Street was in the middle of the sea of decaying city around it, that reminded him unpleasantly of Fox Run Hill.

## 2.

Bennis Hannaford was not alone. Her arm was in a cast that reached from her shoulder to her wrist. It had been broken in two places, both above and below the elbow, and she wasn't expected to be able to use it normally again for almost six months. When Gregor came in, she had old George Tekemanian sitting in front of her computer, tapping things out on her keyboard. Donna Moradanyan was sitting on the low embroidered ottoman that Bennis had brought back with her from her trip to Morocco. Gregor didn't suppose that Bennis would be taking any of her infamous trips for the next six months or so either. No waking up on Tuesday to find a note taped to his door saying that Bennis had taken a five A.M. flight to Kathmandu. No getting back from dinner at the Ararat to find a note propped up on the coffeepot in his kitchen saying that Bennis had decided she was going to lose her mind unless she immediately spent a good six days in Marrakech. The cast was stiff and unyielding. It jutted out from her body like a surgically implanted sword.

"So I listened to you and I didn't call off the wedding," Donna said, "but I'm going to have to decide what to do about things and it's just not as easy as you think it is. I mean, he *is* Tommy's father."

Gregor drew up Bennis's wing chair and peered over old George Tekemanian's shoulder at the computer screen. There was a computer graphics picture on it of a nasty-looking little troll, jumping up and down, hopping mad.

"What's all that about?" Gregor asked old George.

"That's my mock-up for the treasure hunt for *Zedalia Triumphant*," Bennis said. "Gregor, listen to this. Peter is back."

"He's not back," Donna said. "He just called me."

"He's coming back," Bennis said.

Donna Moradanyan sighed. Gregor Demarkian had once told someone that she was the least Armenian-looking woman he had ever known, and it was true. Donna was tall and athletic and blond, like some midwestern university's field hockey princess. The Peter involved was Peter Desarian, the boy who had made Donna pregnant with Tommy all those years and years ago and then decided he was much too young to be a father.

"I'm just saying that you have to give it some consideration," Donna said. "The fact that he's Tommy's father, I mean. He is Tommy's father. And Russ isn't anything to Tommy. If you know what I mean."

"Russ has been more of a father to Tommy than Peter ever was," Bennis said. "For God's sake, Donna. What are you trying to do to yourself?"

"I'm trying to do the right thing. That's all. I'm just trying to do the right thing."

"I think you still feel guilty about sleeping with Peter," Bennis said, "so you're trying to punish yourself for it by giving up Russ, and not because you think Peter's going to marry you, because you know as well as I do that as soon as Russ is out of the picture, Peter will be out of the picture too, like a shot—"

"Wait," Gregor said. "What's this? Now Peter wants to marry her?"

"He says he does," Donna said. "He says that if I have to be married, if it's so important to me to have a wedding ring, then he'd rather marry me himself than have Tommy brought up by a stranger."

"Russ isn't a stranger to Tommy," Bennis said firmly. "Peter is a stranger to Tommy."

"This troll is going to have flat feet if this goes on much longer," old George Tekemanian said. "Bennis, you really must come here and do something."

Bennis got up off the couch and went to lean over old George's shoulder. Her encased arm seemed to operate like a ship's boom. Donna got up off the ottoman and started pacing.

"It's what's best for Tommy," she told Gregor. "No matter what it is I'd rather do, I have to do what's best for Tommy."

"Do you really think giving up Russ for Peter would be what was best for Tommy?" Gregor asked. "Even assuming that Peter would keep his word and marry you in the end?"

"Especially if Peter kept his word to marry you in the

end," Bennis said, and then, to old George, "Key in G487-2T and let it run for a couple of minutes."

"Run where?" old George Tekemanian said.

Bennis escorted her arm carefully back to the couch and sat down again. "There's food in the refrigerator, Gregor. Lida came over and brought me a whole bowl of those bulgur-encrusted meatballs you like so much. Donna just needs a shrink."

"I'll get the meatballs," Donna said. "I'll even heat them up in the microwave."

She bolted from the room. Bennis levered her legs up onto the couch, stretched out, and rolled her eyes. She really looked quite well, Gregor decided, although she was a little pale. He wondered what kind of painkillers the doctor had given her and whether she was actually taking them. Bennis didn't like painkillers. She was famous at a hospital in Boston for having been the first person in its 165-year history to have gone off Demerol less than twenty-four hours after having her gallbladder removed. She claimed Demerol made her head fuzzy.

"Anyway," Bennis said, throwing her head back onto the soft arm of the black leather couch, "as you can tell, we're having a crisis. We're going to have a bigger crisis if Russ finds out about Peter, which he hasn't yet."

"I would have thought Donna would have told him first," Gregor said.

Bennis waved a languid hand in the air. "That's part of the reason I know she doesn't really mean it, about Peter. I mean, the real problem here is not that Donna thinks that Peter Desarian's sperm is so important that it ought to override everything the man is—if you can call him a man, I've known twelve-year-olds who were more responsible—"

Donna came back from the kitchen carrying a plate of *kefta* and a fork. She gave the plate and the fork to Gregor and sat down on the ottoman again.

"Whether she wants to believe it or not, I am worried

about the sperm problem," Donna said. Then she blushed. "I don't mean the sperm, exactly. It's just that you read all these things in the magazines, you know, where it's so much worse for the child with a stepparent, especially for boys, they don't relate as well and the stepparent doesn't ever love them the same way a real parent would—"

"How does Peter love Tommy?" Bennis demanded. "Peter never sees Tommy."

"He must love Tommy somewhat, Bennis. Otherwise it wouldn't matter to him so much that Tommy might have a stepfather."

"He's just acting like an adolescent again," Bennis insisted, "and a mean-spirited bastard of an adolescent in the bargain. He doesn't want you and he doesn't want Tommy but life is not all right if the two of you don't want him."

Donna said, "I just don't see how that argument applies here. I mean, this is not a joke, offering to come back to Philadelphia and marry me and give Tommy a real family. I mean, you don't do that kind of thing out of pique."

"Peter would. Or he'd at least promise to do it. And not out of pique. Out of spite."

Gregor finished one of the oversized meatballs and put the fork on the plate and the plate on the floor.

"Just a minute here. Let's see if I have this straight. Peter has found out that you're marrying Russ, but he doesn't like the idea, so he wants you not to marry Russ and to marry him instead."

"What he actually said," Bennis put in, "was that if Donna was so neurotic about her need to be married that she had to go bring some stranger into Tommy's life, Peter would just as soon marry her himself, since that was what she really wanted anyway and it would be better for Tommy. Of course, it isn't what she really wants anyway—"

"Of course it isn't," Donna said. "I even hate talking to him on the phone."

"If you hate talking to him on the phone, you will not like

being married to him," old George Tekemanian said. "This goes without saying."

"It doesn't matter because he won't marry her anyway," Bennis said. "Peter isn't trying to marry her. He's just trying to keep her from marrying Russ."

"I don't believe that," Donna said. "I don't believe that even Peter could be such a—such a—"

"Bastard," old George put in helpfully.

"Let me ask you this," Gregor said. "Have you told your mother about all of this?"

Donna Moradanyan looked at her hands. They were sturdy, bluntfingered hands, with the nails cut short and square. They looked like the hands of someone who had played field hockey too.

"Ah," Gregor said.

Donna Moradanyan blushed. "It's not that I don't get along with my mother. It's just that she—fusses so much all the time. It's hard to think in peace when she fusses like that."

"I'm just pointing out that if this was something you really wanted to do, you probably would have said something to her by now," Gregor said. "And if this isn't something you really want to do—"

"She wouldn't approve of it if I did it," Donna said quickly. "She hates Peter with a passion."

"She absolutely loves Russ," Bennis said.

"I don't see what everybody is making such a big noise about," Donna said. "It's just something that's come up, that's all. It's just something that I have to think through."

"When you have to think through whether or not to jump off a bridge over the Grand Canyon, you need a shrink," Bennis said. "And you ought to call Russ and at least let him know you're talking to him. You're getting married in nine days and you haven't said a word to him in the last twenty-four hours."

Donna got to her feet. "I think I'd better go over to Lida's and pick up Tommy. There isn't anything talking like this is going to get us. I mean, Peter is Peter. We'll see what happens next."

"Get a restraining order so he can't show up at the wedding," Bennis said.

Donna Moradanyan sighed again. She was so tall, she looked like she could have modeled for one of those French statues of Liberty, Equality, and Fraternity. She stretched her arms and legs and shook out her hair.

"I'll see you people later," she said. "I'm going to take Tommy down to McDonald's for dinner."

"Let Russ go with you," Bennis said quickly.

"Russ is working." Donna patted Gregor on the head. "Good night, Gregor. I left a candle decoration in your living room window earlier. It's all wired up and ready to go. All you have to do is plug it in."

One Christmas, Donna Moradanyan had given him a Santa and reindeer for his window and when he had plugged it in it had flashed on and off, on and off, on and off, at the rate of sixty flashes per minute. He hoped this candle would not flash.

"See you later," Donna said again, and then she was gone, first a set of footsteps in Bennis's foyer, then the sound of Bennis's door opening and not quite slamming shut.

Bennis sat up a little on the couch and looked out in the direction Donna had gone.

"It's enough to make any sane person crazy," she said. "She's got a man who loves her to distraction and he also loves her son. He's responsible. He's nice. He's got a decent job. He thinks the earth began on the day she was born. What does she want?"

Gregor picked up his plate of *kefta* again and cracked apart another bulgur-encrusted meatball. The only light on in the room was the light of the flex lamp hanging over the computer terminal where old George Tekemanian sat. Other than that, there was the faint pink glow flowing through the window from the street, and not much of that. It never seemed

to get completely dark in Philadelphia during the summer—
at least, not until three or four in the morning—but it
was never really light out at night either. Gregor disliked the
half-glow of summer evenings more than any other kind of
weather. He found something fake in it, and something de-
ceptive. At times like this he always found himself wishing
that it would soon be fall.

"So," he said to Bennis, "how are you? Does that arm
hurt?"

"All the time," Bennis said, "but it's no big deal. What
about you? Did you find out who murdered that poor woman
yet?"

"I doubt if anybody murdered that poor woman on
purpose. She was from out of town. She wasn't anyone particularly important. There's nothing we can find in her background to link her to Patricia MacLaren Willis. There doesn't
seem to be anybody in her life with any real interest in doing
her in."

"You know all that about her already?" Bennis asked. "How
can you have that kind of information so fast?"

"We can't," Gregor admitted, "but we have preliminary information, and we have some threads to go with. Like the
pipe bomb."

"Which points to Mrs. Willis."

"Well, it would seem to, wouldn't it? Now, we do have
some information on that. It was an almost identical bomb to
the ones that went off in that parking garage. A length of aluminum cylinder packed with mothballs and chlorine bleach.
An electric watch with leads running off it. You could have
gotten the whole thing out of *The Anarchist's Cookbook*."

"Maybe it was a copycat."

"There's more than one recipe for a bomb in *The Anarchist's Cookbook*. It would be too much of a coincidence if Mrs.
Willis and a copycat picked the same recipe."

"Do you think Mrs. Willis planted the bomb?"

"I don't know," Gregor said.

"Do you think the bomb was meant to kill Julianne Corbett?"

"I don't know that either."

"I'm disappointed in you," Bennis said. "Usually by this point you know practically everything. Or else you say you do. Have you heard about Karla Parrish? Is she going to be all right?"

"Karla Parrish is in a coma. Come on, Bennis. Get up and I'll take you to dinner. If you can go out with that thing on your arm."

"I've got a kind of brace for it for walking. I think it's a good thing for Karla Parrish that she was showing me that picture. I think she spent the whole night before that standing right behind the punch bowl at that table. She would have been blown to pieces. I'll bet Mrs. Willis is trying to kill Julianne Corbett. I wonder why."

"Maybe Mrs. Willis thinks Ms. Corbett doesn't keep her campaign promises," Gregor said. "Come on. Get up and get moving."

"I don't move too fast these days," Bennis said. "I hate politics, don't you?"

Actually, Gregor never thought much about politics beyond voting in presidential elections. What he was thinking about was what Bennis had just said about Julianne Corbett and Karla Parrish and Patricia MacLaren Willis, and it suddenly struck him that he hadn't looked at the problem from quite that angle before.

# FOUR

## 1.

GREGOR TOOK A TAXI DOWN to John Jackman's office the next morning. When he had first come back to Philadelphia from Washington, he had liked to take public transportation as often as possible, because it was a way to reacquaint himself with the city, because it was a way to tell himself that this was really home. Washington had never really been home, and couldn't have been. Gregor had had something like the opposite of Potomac fever. All the buildings in the District of Columbia looked too big to him, and too cold, and too gray. Marble and limestone are not good materials to build your city out of when that city is going to be full of working internal combustion engines. Statues and monuments weren't good things to fill your city up with if people wanted to live there. Gregor had never been sure if anybody actually wanted to live in the District. There was Georgetown and Foggy Bottom, of course, and a lot of poor people in tenements, but somehow at 6:45 every evening the entire city of Washington seemed to become uninhabited.

Big patches of the city of Philadelphia seemed to be uninhabited all the time these days, eaten up by soaring concrete highway ramps with no cars on them. Maybe it was just the time of day, after rush hour but before the shoppers came out in earnest. This was why Gregor didn't travel on public transportation anymore. He kept getting caught in places like this. The air-conditioning in his cab was going full blast. He didn't dare roll his window down, even though the morning wasn't hot yet. He pressed his face against the glass and looked at thick concrete abutments and at the blank arc lights that hung over them. Obviously, there was some need to keep this stretch of road lit after dark. Then the cab went too quickly around a curve, throwing Gregor against the back of his seat. By the time he was sitting upright again, Gregor was in another landscape. This was the kind of landscape he could understand. The tenements were in bad shape, but they were full of people. The sidewalks were full of people too. Gregor assumed that a lot of the people he saw were Spanish, because a lot of the signs on the stores were Spanish. The cab pulled up to the curb in the middle of a block and he looked out to see a cluster of dumpy, middle-aged women at a newsstand, poring over a copy of *Bride's* magazine.

"June," Gregor said to no one in particular, getting his wallet out of his back pocket.

"What?" the cabdriver said. He was looking at the women looking at *Bride's* magazine too. "You wonder what it is they're reading there. They don't speak English. I bet not a one of them speaks English."

"Maybe they like looking at the pictures of brides in wedding gowns," Gregor said.

"Why?" the cabdriver demanded. "They can't any one of them be getting married in a white dress anytime soon. They must be forty."

"Maybe it's like fashion magazines. Women look at them even when they can't wear the fashions."

"Maybe. You're that guy in the paper, aren't you? The Lebanese-American Sherlock Holmes."

"Armenian-American. I'm Armenian-American. Except

that isn't true either, because I was born right here in Philadelphia, so I guess I'm just American."

"Whatever."

Gregor decided he had enough change together and got
out of the cab. He handed the money back through the window the driver had left open for him and watched a big Mack
truck rumble toward the nearest stoplight, its side proclaim-
ing it to be the property of Goldman's Kosher Deli. Up the
block a pack of children were playing something marked out
with chalk on the sidewalk. A little way up from that, one of
the stoops was full of slightly older children, all girls, smoking cigarettes and listening to music on a boom box. This was
the city as Gregor remembered the city. He felt better than
he had in days.

"Interesting neighborhood," he told the cabbie.

The cabbie shrugged. "Got a great big police station sitting
right in the middle of it. Even the junkies aren't stupid
enough to pull a drive-by right in front of the police station."

Gregor had heard of plenty of junkies stupid enough to
pull drive-bys right in front of police stations. The people
who pulled drive-bys were not notable for their high practical intelligence. Gregor stepped back on the sidewalk and let
the cab pull away from the curb. The women who had been
looking at *Bride's* were now looking at *Modern Bride*. One of
the storefronts on the other side of the street had a long
white wedding gown in its plate-glass window. It took Gregor a while to realize that this was the St. Vincent de Paul
shop, a charity outlet that sold secondhand clothes. Gregor
wondered who gave her wedding gown to the St. Vincent de
Paul Society. Then he wondered who got her wedding gown
from the St. Vincent de Paul Society. No matter how poor
you were, would you want a gown from a wedding that had
failed to live up to its promise? Or was it the marriage that
would have failed to live up to its promise? And what did
marriage promise? Gregor could remember his marriage to

Elizabeth, what it had felt like to be married, what he had felt it made him obligated to do and be, but it wasn't easy to put that sort of thing in words. Whatever the words were, they would have nothing to do with the cover of the latest *Cosmopolitan*, which also had a bride on it, although a bride with exposed breasts. The white headline to the right of the bride's head read: *Our Exclusive Quiz! Is Your Marriage Destined to Explode?* Underneath that there was another headline that read: *12 Surefire Ways to Make Your Honeymoon Hotter Than Hot!*

Gregor went up the broad stone steps to the police station and through the double bulletproof security doors into the vestibule. The security doors were fitted into a steel frame that had been fitted into the dark wood of the station's interior. Back before the days of drive-by shootings, it had been possible to make an aesthetic statement with a building full of law enforcement officers. Of course, there had been drive-by shootings of a kind even in the twenties; the FBI had committed a few of them itself. Wasn't that the point of what happened to Bonnie and Clyde? Gregor gave his name to the enormous African-American man in the sergeant's uniform behind the desk and asked to see John Jackman.

"Gregor Demarkian," the sergeant repeated. He flipped through a card file on his desk, found something he liked, and nodded. Then he picked up the phone, pressed a button, and said, "Mr. Demarkian to see Mr. Jackman."

He put the phone down again. "You can go right up," he told Gregor. "Through that door and up in the elevator to three. When you get out on three, you will have to submit to a weapons search."

"A weapons search? In a police station?"

"If it was up to me, I'd put a metal detector at the front door, but it isn't up to me. Jackman and Company think metal detectors would inhibit access to the general public."

"I'd think they'd at least do that," Gregor said.

"Of course," the sergeant went on, "that leaves the question of whether you really want this general public to have access, which depends on how you look at it and what you think it is that wants access to here, but I'm not going to bend your ear with it. I think Mr. Jackman is in a hurry."

"Yes," Gregor said.

"They shot a cop," the sergeant said. "A bunch of kids did. Fifteen-year-olds. Shot him right out there on the steps. Right in the head. He was dead before we got to him."

"Oh," Gregor said.

"Soon as I get my twenty," the sergeant said, "I'm moving to Montana."

Gregor turned around and went through the door the sergeant had indicated. He went up in the elevator and got out on three. There was indeed a weapons search station right outside the elevator doors. It was manned by a young woman in uniform and an older man, also in uniform, whose main virtue seemed to be that he was absolutely huge. Gregor wondered where they found regulation blue to fit him. He gave the young woman his Mark Cross pen and spread his legs apart so that she could run the obligatory hand up and down the inside pants legs.

"That's fine," she said after a minute. "You can go on through, Mr. Demarkian. I'm sorry if we've caused you any inconvenience."

"No inconvenience," Gregor said.

"You can go through," the big man said.

The big man was sitting down. Gregor got the impression that he was always sitting down, unless there was trouble, which there probably was very little of. Gregor went down the hall to another desk and gave his name to the clerk there. She was in uniform too, but she wasn't really a cop. Instead of a badge on her chest she had an embroidered patch that read PPD—SUPPORT.

"I've read all about you in the paper," she told Gregor with satisfaction. "And Mr. Jackman talks about you all the time. Mr. Jackman is a really superior police detective, don't you think?"

What Gregor Demarkian thought was that John Jackman was a hell of a lot more than this young woman would be able to handle, but he didn't say so. He grunted a vague, all-purpose assent and wondered why it was that Jackman's support people never seemed to last from one of his visits to the next. Gregor understood the turnover in front-line people—the desk sergeants, the patrolmen. As a rule, Jackman didn't work in wonderful neighborhoods. He didn't have wonderful people coming into his office to visit him. After a while the desk sergeants had to get tired of being shot at and screamed at and the uniformed patrolmen had to wonder if it wouldn't be an easier life working bunco. It was the rapid turnover of clerks and secretaries that bewildered Gregor. Did they all fall in love with Jackman and not get their love returned? Did they all go to bed with him only to realize that fun was all he was interested in? Did he give them too much typing? What?

The door behind the clerk opened and John Jackman came out, his coat thrown over his shoulders like Apollo's cape in the Rocky movies. The clerk glowed at him. The middle-aged woman holding the door for him beamed with motherly affection that didn't quite strike the right maternal note. Gregor had the uncomfortable feeling that given half a chance, maternal instinct could turn into something much hotter with very little effort at all.

"Gregor," John Jackman said.

"Put your coat on," the middle-aged woman told Jackman. "There's going to be a storm out there."

The coat was a raincoat, but even so. It was June. It was going to be hot as a sweatbox any minute now. Gregor raised an eyebrow at John Jackman; John Jackman shrugged.

The clerk at the desk grabbed something from next to her phone file and held it up.

"Look," she told John Jackman. "My sister's wedding pictures came in last night. Didn't I tell you she had the most outrageous dress in the history of creation?"

Wedding dresses did not seem to Gregor to be the kind of

thing John Jackman would be interested in, but watching women around John was like watching men around Bennis, and Gregor found it easier just to ignore the whole thing. He started back toward the metal detectors, sure that John would follow him.

"I'll look at the pictures when we get back," John was telling the clerk. "We've got an appointment with a congresswoman."

## 2.

When Gregor Demarkian was still an active agent with the Federal Bureau of Investigation, he had far and away preferred to interview people in their own homes rather than in their offices or a neutral setting. A home said a lot about state of mind and general psychological makeup. What was more, it was a safe place to most people, which was why it was also a place where people got careless. In the case of Congresswoman Julianne Corbett, unfortunately, they had no choice. According to her secretary, Ms. Corbett kept a residence in her congressional district, but she no longer actually lived there—or she wouldn't, soon, because she was moving to Washington. She also kept an office in the district, but Gregor was under the impression that this wouldn't be her real office for very long either. That one would be on Capitol Hill. What was it about getting elected to public office that made so many people metamorphose into aliens from another planet? Julianne Corbett's constituent office was in one of those blank-faced office buildings with generic elevators that looked like it could turn itself into a warehouse at a moment's notice. All the way down the hall to Suite 323, John Jackman was looking at a scrap of paper in his hand and saying, "Tiffany Shattuck. Her secretary's name is Tiffany Shattuck. Can you believe she has a secretary named Tiffany Shattuck?"

Gregor could have believed she had a secretary named Harry Winston Liebowitz, but that was not a point it seemed useful to make at the moment. He opened the door to Suite 323 and looked inside. There was a bland blue-walled waiting room with a few Danish modern chairs in it and a low coffee table covered with ancient magazines. It looked like the office of a not very well-heeled dentist. At the far end of the room there was a desk. At the desk there was a young blond woman reading a copy of *Modern Bride*. The magazines must have come out today, Gregor thought. That was the only reason he could think of that they would be all over the place like this.

Tiffany Shattuck put her magazine down and blinked at them. "Mr. Demarkian," she said. Then she frowned at John Jackman. "You were at the explosion the other night. You're some kind of policeman."

John Jackman sighed.

Just then the door behind Tiffany Shattuck's desk opened. As always, Julianne Corbett seemed to Gregor to be less a person than an advertisement for Max Factor. She was wearing enormous gold earrings made of nesting circles of hammered metal. Her eyes had been made up to look like wings. "Mr. Demarkian," she said. "Mr. Jackman." She turned to Tiffany Shattuck. "Do you think you could get me a printout of that health care thing from Holland and send a copy to Mort Elstain in Bethlehem? I promised him I'd do it last week and I just haven't gotten around to it."

"Okay," Tiffany said.

Julianne Corbett made a face at *Modern Bride* magazine. "Why don't the two of you come in here," she said, looking straight at Gregor Demarkian. "Tiffany can get us all some coffee and we can be comfortable."

Gregor followed John around Tiffany Shattuck's desk to the door Julianne Corbett was holding open. He went through into her private office expecting some kind of revelation of the woman's character, or at least a significant change from the faceless blandness of the waiting room. He got neither. Julianne Corbett's private office was eerily reminiscent of a bad room in a second-rate motel. Even the carpet looked like the kind of thing that belonged outside near a wading pool, installed instead of tiles because it was less likely that someone could slip on it.

Gregor sat down in one of the Danish modern chairs. Julianne Corbett's desk was empty except for a single photograph in a frame. Gregor leaned forward and turned the photograph around. It was the picture of six young women arranged in a living-room-like setting that looked like it might be the common room of a college dormitory. Most of the young women were unrecognizable. One of them was definitely Karla Parrish.

"Are you in this photograph?" Gregor asked Julianne Corbett.

Ms. Corbett shrugged. "I suppose that depends on the sense you mean that. Sometimes I think I didn't really come into existence until I was practically forty. Until then I was nothing but a bundle of neuroses. Karla's in that picture though. Did you recognize her?"

"Yes," Gregor said. "I did. She seems remarkably unchanged from a picture that must be—how many years old?"

"Oh, more than twenty-five. I hate counting these days, but that was taken at Jewett House at Vassar College in 1967, I think. We were all juniors then."

"Then you are in this picture?" Gregor asked.

Julianne Corbett waved it away. "I haven't kept up with those people the way I should have. We all just sort of drifted apart after graduation. Karla too, of course. It had been years since I'd seen her."

"You'll be glad to hear that the word from the hospital is better than expected," John Jackman said. "She is expected to come out of it. Eventually."

"But 'eventually' could be years from now," Julianne Corbett said.

"I'm afraid so." Jackman shrugged. "The doctor I talked to

kept saying he was getting very good signs. Whatever that means."

Gregor picked up the photograph again. "You must have been in some kind of contact with her," he said. "You arranged this reception in her honor. You knew she was coming to Philadelphia."

"Actually, it was Tiffany who found out that Karla was coming to Philadelphia," the congresswoman said. "She keeps up with things like that. She's a very good assistant, really, in spite of the hair and the name and the brides' magazines. Not that Tiffany is in any danger of becoming a bride anytime soon. I hadn't even known that Karla was famous for being a photographer."

"She had a bunch of pictures in the Sunday *Times Magazine*," Jackman put in helpfully. "And she had lots and lots in *Vanity Fair*. Don't ask me why *Vanity Fair* wanted to publish a lot of photographs of starving Rwandans."

"It's compassion as a consumption item," Julianne Corbett said wryly. "You have to bleed for the wretched of the earth or your new Ralph Laurens won't be the right color red."

"When did you decide to give this reception for Karla Parrish?" Gregor asked.

"Oh, immediately after I knew she was coming," Julianne Corbett replied, "except, it was like I told you, it was all Tiffany's idea. Karla was asked to speak at Penn, did you know that?"

"Yes," John Jackman said.

"Well," Julianne Corbett said, "we thought it would be a good idea, you know, good for me in terms of the publicity, good for me because I'd get a chance to see an old friend, and good for Karla too, because it would introduce her to some important people locally. I don't care what kind of famous photographer Karla turned into. She's still the same old Karla. Socially awkward. Not a thing to say for herself."

"From what I recall," Gregor Demarkian said, "she wasn't standing in the receiving line the night of the reception—"

"Well, that isn't entirely fair," Julianne told him. "There really wasn't much of a receiving line. Karla was standing next to the punch bowl in the main room. It was much the best place for her. Everybody had to pass by the punch bowl. And as soon as the arrival crowds died down, I was going to stand there too. That was the plan."

"So everybody knew in advance that Ms. Parrish would be standing at that table," Gregor Demarkian said.

"Everybody who had any part in the planning of the reception," Julianne Corbett agreed. "Tiffany. And the other assistants. And the caterers and those people."

"What about this plan to have you stand there yourself? Was that generally known?"

Julianne Corbett looked honestly bewildered. "I don't know what you mean by 'generally known.' This wasn't a secret, you know, Mr. Demarkian. This wasn't as if we were planning campaign strategy or something like that. This was a party."

"You weren't worried about security?" John Jackman asked.

Julianne Corbett snorted. "In spite of the things you see in Clint Eastwood movies, most members of the United States Congress are not followed everywhere by Secret Service officers and have no need to be. Really. I'm just me. A middle-aged, middle-of-the-road woman who is going up to Washington to do her best. I'm not even on a committee yet."

"You're pro-choice, aren't you?" John Jackman asked. "This is a pretty pro-life state. And there has been violence against pro-choice advocates in other places."

"In the first place, what violence there has been on that score has been almost universally against abortion providers," Julianne Corbett said, "and pro-choice or not, I couldn't provide anybody anywhere with any kind of medical procedure. I can't even look at the blood when I cut my legs shaving. In the second place, there is a lot of pro-life sentiment in this state, but it runs to the bleeding-heart let's-get-down-and-pray-for-everybody variety. We don't have a lot of radicals in Pennsylvania. Not of that stripe."

"But pipe bombs do suggest radicals," Gregor Demarkian put in. "In fact, pipe bombs were first used in this country in an anarchist bombing in New York City. I think in the popular imagination, radicals is exactly what it looks like we have here."

"Maybe." Julianne Corbett was skeptical. "But what about that woman last week or whenever it was? The one who blew her car up in a parking garage? She wasn't a radical, was she?"

"Patricia Willis," John Jackman said. "She was a middle-aged housewife from a place called Fox Run Hill. It's—"

"I know what it is," Julianne Corbett interrupted. "It's one of those gated communities. Let's all huddle together and put a fence up to keep the barbarians out." She grimaced.

"Did you know that Mrs. Willis made several significant contributions to your campaign?" Gregor asked her.

Julianne Corbett bobbed her head vigorously. "Oh, yes. Tiffany found that out. It's like I said. Tiffany's a very good assistant in spite of the addiction to bimbo style. It was because of that that I asked Bennis Hannaford to make sure to bring you to the reception. I really am very sorry about Bennis, Mr. Demarkian, I didn't mean to get her caught up in some sort of mess."

"I don't understand why finding out that Mrs. Willis had contributed to your campaign would lead you to ask Bennis Hannaford to bring me along to a party," Gregor Demarkian said.

Julianne Corbett shrugged. "It's because of the exposure. Everybody's very worried about exposure. Anything at all, no matter how small, can sink you in politics these days. God only knows what I thought. That Mrs. Willis was stealing the money from her husband to contribute to my campaign. That she killed her husband when he found out about it. There's a scenario for you. How can I tell how people are going to behave?"

"Fair enough," Gregor said. He pointed at the picture on the desk. "You said that was taken at Vassar College. Did you graduate from there?"

"Yes, I did. Years and years ago."

"Did you know that Mrs. Willis graduated from there?"

"Did she? No, I hadn't heard that. What class was she in?"

"Class of 1969," John Jackman said.

Julianne Corbett looked bewildered. "Are you sure? I was in the class of '69. I saw her picture in the paper. She didn't look like anybody I had ever met."

"Would you have met every woman in your class?" Gregor asked.

"No, of course not. I wouldn't necessarily know all of them by sight either. It's just . . . odd."

"Maybe you knew her by her maiden name," Gregor said, "MacLaren."

"What?" Julianne Corbett said.

"MacLaren," Gregor repeated. "Her full name was Patricia MacLaren Willis. She was usually known as Patsy."

"Patsy," Julianne Corbett repeated.

"Is something wrong?" John Jackman asked.

"Let me get this straight," Julianne Corbett said. "What you're trying to tell me is that this woman who murdered her husband out in Fox Run Hill and then blew her car up with a pipe bomb in a municipal parking garage, this woman was the same Patsy MacLaren who graduated from Vassar College in 1969?"

"That's right," Gregor said.

"That's wrong," Julianne Corbett said. "Mr. Demarkian, I knew Patsy MacLaren. I knew her quite well. She was my closest friend. We were so close, in fact, that I was with her on the night she died—in New Delhi, India, four months after we graduated."

# FIVE

## 1.

SARAH LOCKWOOD KNEW SHE HAD to be careful. At this stage in things—the almost-but-not-quite, the just-next-to-done—anything could happen to screw it all up, and the last thing she wanted was for something she did or said to bring the whole thing crashing down on her head. Because of that, she was even grateful to Patsy Willis for killing her husband and bringing a pack of detectives down on their heads. The detectives made Kevin nervous, but Sarah saw them as a distraction. Joey Bracken was so fascinated by the things that were going on in the Tudor across the street, he was barely looking at the papers Kevin had spread out in front of him on the breakfast room table. The papers were the most impressive Sarah had ever seen. God only knew where Kevin had gotten them. They went on for pages and pages of utter incomprehensibility. There were maps too, but Sarah knew where Kevin had gotten those. They had been copied out of an ancient edition of the *World Book Encyclopedia* they had in the basement and then run through the computer so that they would look official. Now one of them had a "lot" outlined in red highlighter and marked with an X. Joey's cashier's check was paper-clipped to the page just above the X's top left tip. Joey was leaning sideways in his chair, trying to see if something was happening at the Tudor, although nothing was. It was too late in the day for policemen and too late in the week for anybody to be much interested in Patsy Willis. The explosion in Philadelphia at Julianne Corbett's party had taken everybody's mind off spousal murder.

"Do you think she did it?" Joey Bracken was saying, his pen poised above the paper he was supposed to sign like a safe poised to fall on Daffy Duck's head in an old cartoon. "Tried to blow up Julianne Corbett, I mean. They all say she probably did it."

"I don't see why Patsy would want to blow up Julianne Corbett," Sarah said. "From everything I've heard, she worshiped the woman."

"Yeah, I'd heard that too," Joey said. He sounded eager. Sarah thought he looked awful being eager. His eyes bugged out. The fat line across his stomach seemed to pulse. It made Sarah crazy to think that Joey and Molly had more money than she and Kevin did. Joey looked like he ought to try out for the starring role in a movie about a guy who spends his whole life in a diner and Molly—

—but Molly wasn't there. Sarah got up from her chair at the table and went into the kitchen, looking for Perrier water, looking for a way to calm down. She also took some nuts out of a cabinet near the stove, because unlike most of the people she knew, Joey Bracken ate most of the time. He had been in her kitchen for half an hour now and he had already gone through an entire bowl of potato chips and half a cheese roll.

"The way I see it," Joey was saying, "is that she's not quite right in the head. Patsy, I mean."

"That's the way we all see it," Kevin said. "Jesus Christ. We wouldn't want to think she was right in the head. We wouldn't be able to go to sleep next to our wives."

"What?" Joey Bracken said. "Oh. Oh, yeah. I never thought about it like that."

Joey Bracken's cashier's check was for thirty thousand

dollars. It was made out to himself, as if he had asked a lawyer for advice about it—but Sarah didn't think he had. She thought he had just asked somebody he worked with at his bank. She wondered what Joey really did there. She couldn't believe he had a serious job. He was just too stupid. She wondered what Molly's father did too. Maybe it was Molly's father who had the money, and he was with the mob, which was the kind of organization Sarah could imagine Joey succeeding in.

"The thing is," Joey said, "if you look at it this way, then she's likely going to try to strike again, right? The question is, where?"

"You mean Patsy Willis is going to try to blow somebody else up?" Kevin looked shocked.

"It stands to reason," Joey Bracken said.

"I don't think it stands to reason at all," Kevin said. "You don't even know she blew that party up. That's just speculation."

"It was the same kind of bomb," Joey said.

"It's a really simple kind of bomb," Kevin told him. "I could show you how to make one myself. I have made one myself. Back when I thought I was going to be a revolutionary."

"I never knew you thought you were going to be a revolutionary." Sarah brought the nuts to the table. Joey Bracken grunted when he saw them and reached out for a handful of cashews and Brazils. The peanuts were oiled and salted. Joey got a wash of grease across his palm.

"Are you just going to buy Molly the lot for a birthday surprise," Sarah asked him, "or are you going to get a builder and put the house up and present the whole thing to her as a kind of big package?"

Joey looked down at the paper he was supposed to sign. "Oh, I couldn't build the whole house without telling her. She'd know there was money missing. This is about as big a surprise as I'm going to be able to get. And I'm not going to be able to keep it a surprise at all."

"I keep a private checking account for things like that,"

Kevin said. "You ought to think about it. Otherwise, you can't buy them anything serious, and they like to have things bought for them. Wives, I mean."

"Yeah, I know. But Molly says she doesn't trust me with money. I work in a bank, she ought to trust me with money."

"I know just what she means," Sarah said. "I have the same problem with Kevin all the time. Men just don't have the same priorities women do."

"Molly wants to have a baby," Joey said. "It just doesn't seem to happen for us. I was thinking that maybe this would cheer her up."

"Well, it certainly is a cheerful place," Kevin said. "Sarah and I can attest to that. We get cheered up every time we think about it."

"And it's still so reasonable," Sarah said. "Oh, I know it doesn't sound like it when you're used to land prices in Pennsylvania, but in Florida these prices are ridiculously low. Especially for waterfront. Friends of ours just bought a waterfront lot in Boca Raton and it cost them three quarters of a million dollars. For the lot."

"Oh, I know. I know," Joey said. "And Molly wants a vacation place. She's said so over and over again. Did the Willises have a vacation place?"

"I don't know," Sarah said. "We didn't know the Willises all that well. They were—well, you know. Older people. Set in their ways."

"Stuffy," Kevin contributed solemnly.

"I was just thinking that if the Willises had a vacation house, Patsy could have gone there." Joey reached into the little bowl and took the rest of the nuts out of it. His whole hand looked salted. "She has to be somewhere. She can't just have disappeared. And yet she has disappeared. Just listen to the newspapers."

"Listen to the newspapers?" Sarah said.

Joey waved his greasy hand in the air. "To the television news. You know what I mean."

"The television news doesn't know everything," Sarah said. "I'll bet the police know where Patsy is right this minute. They're just biding their time."

"Biding their time for what?" Kevin asked.

"To have all the evidence they need before they go to trial," Sarah said. "To make sure they can lock her up. All those things. They don't like to make arrests and then later have the person go free at the trial. You know how it is."

"You watch too much television," Kevin said.

"I'd better sign this thing," Joey told them. He leaned over the paper and signed, which Sarah and Kevin didn't pay any attention to. Then he took the cashier's check out from under its paper clip and signed the back of that over to Kevin Lockwood. Sarah and Kevin did pay attention to that. That was what really mattered here. That was what was going to get the bills paid for the next couple of weeks.

"Well," Kevin said as Joey handed the check over.

"I got to thank you for doing this," Joey said. "I couldn't ever have done it on my own. I don't know enough about this kind of thing."

"There's nothing much to know," Kevin said. "And it's going to be old-home week down there next year. Evelyn and Henry are doing this too. It's going to be Fox Run Hill all over again."

"Molly doesn't like Evelyn and Henry," Joey said. "She thinks Evelyn is too fat. And she thinks Henry is a prick."

"Does she?" Sarah said.

Kevin put the check in the chest pocket of his shirt, folded up, out of sight. "Well," he said. "I'm glad you're doing it. It will be good to see you and Molly down there next year. Or this year. Whenever you decide to build."

"I still think somebody ought to check into whether or not the Willises had a vacation house," Joey said. "You don't want a person like that wandering around in the open, do you know what I mean? Even if it is a woman. It isn't safe."

"I'm really sure she isn't after you," Sarah said.

"The next thing you know, she's going to try to blow up the president of the United States, and then there are going to be days and days and days of Dan Rather moaning about how we never do things right and get them settled beforehand. You just wait. And don't forget: If she was gunning for Julianne Corbett, she didn't get her."

"What does that mean?" Sarah asked.

"She didn't get her," Joey insisted. "Corbett is still alive. Which means maybe they ought to have a guard on Corbett."

"Maybe she was gunning for that photographer who took the awful pictures of starving people," Sarah said, "or maybe she was gunning for that woman from the animal rights movement who got blown up. Or maybe it wasn't Patsy Willis at all. Really, the way people go on about this, you'd think space aliens had landed on the ninth fairway at the Fox Run Hill Country Club."

Joey Bracken got out of his chair and went to stand at the sliding glass doors that led out to the patio, and that also looked around the back toward the Willises' mock-Tudor.

"Maybe that's what happened," he said solemnly. "Maybe aliens landed at the country club. It sure as hell feels odd enough around here since Patsy offed Steve."

## 2.

There was a newsstand in the hospital lobby with its entire top front rack covered in copies of *Bride's* magazine. The picture on the cover showed a young woman with a long train swirling out from behind her to make a mountain of lace at her feet. She was holding a bouquet of flowers that was bigger than her head, and she looked scared to death. Julianne Corbett forced herself to look away from the display and smile at the nurse at the visitors' desk. In this day and age, she probably wasn't really a nurse, but she was dressed like one, and Julianne was too old to adapt. It didn't matter that she intended to go to Washington to work on health care reform. In her mind, hospitals were still what they were when she was small, staffed by nurses and nothing but nurses, except for a few aides in candy-stripe pink and white. These days, even the real nurses didn't wear caps anymore. Everybody's uniform had been streamlined. Nobody wanted to be what they were.

The woman, nurse or otherwise, behind the visitors' desk was leaning forward. "Here comes Dr. Alvarez," she was saying. "Dr. Alvarez can tell you everything you want to know. I don't know if you can bring all those—people—with you upstairs though."

All "those people," as the woman referred to them, were Julianne's regular contingent when she was on any kind of official expedition. Besides Tiffany, who was indispensable at any time except during a sexual tryst, Julianne had three stenographers, a photographer, a bodyguard, and an aide. They were supposed to provide a buffer between her and the public, and they were also supposed to act as witnesses. If some nut came up and started hitting her with an umbrella, she wanted to make sure that when they all landed in court she wouldn't be the one who was blamed. In the old days, this sort of caution would have been absurd, but nothing was absurd anymore. Nothing was unthinkable anymore either.

Dr. Alvarez was a young woman with very dark hair wrapped into a knot at the back of her neck. She had glasses with thick black frames and thin lenses. Julianne thought that she could never have been pretty, even as a child, and that now she didn't seem to care. As she came across the carpet of the lounge, she held out her hand and said, "Congresswoman Corbett? I'm Dr. Teresa Alvarez."

"Dr. Alvarez." Julianne took the hand. She had always hated shaking hands, but she had learned to do it. She gave this one a sharp, hard pull and then dropped it. "I'm glad to meet you."

"I'm glad to meet you too." Dr. Alvarez looked around.

"I'm afraid Mrs. Morrissey is correct. This many people, on an ICU ward . . ."

"That's quite all right," Julianne said. "We can leave most of them down here. I do have to take Ms. Shattuck though."

"Which one is Miss Shattuck?"

Tiffany stepped forward. "That's me," she said. "I'm Tiffany Shattuck."

"All right." Teresa Alvarez inclined her head. "We'll be going up to the fifth floor, to a ward called Five West. You understand that Miss Parrish will not be able to speak to you?"

"I understand that she's totally unconscious," Julianne Corbett said.

Teresa Alvarez shook her head emphatically. "Coma is not that simple. It's true that Miss Parrish does not at this point respond to stimuli. She makes no indication that she can hear or see us at any time. That does not necessarily mean that she cannot do either. Her brain wave patterns are good. She is not in a vegetative state. As far as we can determine, her mind is in good working order."

"But if her mind is in good working order, why isn't she awake?" Tiffany Shattuck asked. "If everything is okay, why isn't she sitting up drinking Coca-Cola?"

"I didn't say everything was okay," Teresa Alvarez said. "I said her mind was in good working order. And we have no way of knowing at this point whether or not she is awake, as you put it. We know only that she is making no visible response to stimuli."

"I don't think this makes any sense," Tiffany Shattuck said.

"It makes sense," Julianne said. "What I think I'm getting here, Doctor, is that as far as you know, it's perfectly possible that Karla sees and registers the existence of where she is and what's around her and that she can hear when people talk about her."

"It's possible. It's also possible that she knows when she has visitors. Which is why our visit has to be limited. If Miss

Parrish is aware of the people in her room, then too many visitors over too long a period of time could tire her, and we don't want that. No matter what is or is not going on here, Miss Parrish is still a very sick woman."

"I understand that," Julianne Corbett said.

Teresa Alvarez turned her back to them and walked rapidly away. "Come with me," she said, heading toward the elevators. "After we look in on Miss Parrish, I have to do rounds. There isn't very much time. I have to thank you for being prompt."

"I am always prompt," Julianne said. They got to the elevators and stopped. The elevator doors bounced open and let out what seemed to be a hundred people in various states of cheap dress, old brown nubby coats raveling at the hems, stocking caps and knitted gloves grimy around the seams, heavy lace-up shoes and battered socks. Teresa Alvarez waited until the elevator car was entirely empty and then led the way inside.

"Of course," she said as the elevator doors closed, "Miss Parrish has a constant visitor. She has a twenty-four-hour duty nurse and that young man friend of hers, Evan Walsh."

"A twenty-four-hour duty nurse?" Julianne asked. "Is that normal for ICU?"

"Mr. Walsh hired her. The hospital certainly doesn't mind, as long as she's a trained ICU nurse, which this one is. The way things are, we aren't in the business of turning down competent extra help when we can get it, especially for free. Actually, I think Mr. Walsh hired three nurses on three shifts. They seem to be working out."

The fifth floor was cleaner than the lobby. There was a polished metal hospitality cart parked in the foyer when they got out of the elevator with a stack of *Modern Bride* magazines weighing down one end of it. The aide who was supposed to be pushing the cart was reading one of the magazines instead, flipping through a full-color fashion section on miniskirted wedding gowns. Julianne had always looked awful in miniskirts and had no interest in wearing a wedding gown at all. She made a face at the aide and tried to keep up with Teresa Alvarez.

Teresa Alvarez took them through a set of fire doors, down a corridor, through another set of fire doors. In these corridors the hospital seemed quiet and empty, inhabited only by nurses huddled around nursing stations. Most of the rooms had their doors closed. The rooms that didn't had no people in them. Julianne saw charts and carts and trays and wheelchairs folded up. It wasn't even all that late in the day. Where had all the people gone? On the coffee table in a waiting room just outside the fire doors marked FIVE WEST, Julianne saw another copy of *Modern Bride* magazine, wrinkled and used this time, out of date.

"This is the ICU," Teresa Alvarez said, holding the latest set of fire doors open. "From here on in, we're under the direction of the head ICU nurse. If she wants to get rid of us, we go."

"Of course," Julianne said.

The head ICU nurse was a tall black woman in a uniform so white, it could have been the Virgin Mary's soul. She came forward as soon as Dr. Alvarez brought Julianne and Tiffany through.

"It's all right to go back," she told them. "I've informed Mr. Walsh that you'll be coming. And Mrs. Hiller."

"Mrs. Hiller is the nurse," Teresa Alvarez explained.

"I've been trying to hire her away from her temporary agency." The large black woman sighed. "She's very good at her work. But we don't pay enough."

"We never pay enough," Teresa Alvarez said.

Down at the end of an antiseptic-looking corridor—of course the corridor looked antiseptic, Julianne told herself, it was supposed to look antiseptic; this was a hospital—a small figure in wire-rimmed glasses came out of a room. Teresa Alvarez waved her hand to greet him.

"That's Mr. Walsh," she said. "We should go in now. But not for long. You do understand that?"

"Yes," Julianne said.

Suddenly, however, all Julianne wanted to do was to leave. Karla wouldn't be able to recognize her. Even if everything Teresa Alvarez said was true and Karla was conscious in there under all the blankness, there would still be nothing for Julianne to see but blankness. And then what? It was as if this were some kind of official visit, the kind Julianne hated most, like when the president of the United States took *Air Force One* out to some disaster area and stood among the wreckage, looking concerned.

"Miss Corbett?" Dr. Alvarez asked, polite.

Evan Walsh was shuffling along like an old man. His clothes looked wrong somehow, like the clothes Ozzie Nelson used to wear on that old television program, which Evan Walsh was probably too young ever to have seen. Julianne suddenly wished she had a good stiff drink.

Evan Walsh held out his hand. "Miss Corbett," he said. "Miss——?"

"Shattuck," Tiffany said.

"She's talking," Evan Walsh said. "She talks nearly all the time now. I wish I understood what she said."

"She mumbles in her sleep," Dr. Alvarez explained. "This isn't unusual in relatively mild cases of this kind."

"Relatively mild cases of this kind can go on for months," Evan Walsh said. "There was one a couple of years ago in England. Girl in a car accident. Didn't even know she was pregnant. And by the time she woke up, she'd had the baby. They say she was happy about the baby."

"That kind of case is *very* unusual," Teresa Alvarez said firmly. "Miss Corbett would like to see Miss Parrish, Mr. Walsh. She'll be only a minute."

"Oh, I know. I know. It's all right. Maybe she'll be able to understand what Karla is trying to say."

"I doubt it," Dr. Alvarez said.

"I think she's singing," Evan Walsh said. "Do any of you know a song about Marrakech?"

"No,"Tiffany Shattuck said. "What's Marrakech?"

"Karla was in Marrakech once," Evan Walsh said.

Then he turned and walked away from them. Julianne watched him go, feeling sick to her stomach. It was just the hospital, really, the smells and the tension. She didn't usually get sick in the middle of tragedy. She was used to dealing with trouble. Evan Walsh's back was bent over so far, he looked like he had a dowager's hump.

"Well,"Teresa Alvarez said. "Shall we go?"

## 3.

Halfway across town, Liza Verity, having gotten home from work, put her groceries down on her kitchen table and then sat down herself, as if getting off her feet for a moment would mean more to her than just relieving the pain in her feet. She had been thinking and thinking about things for days now. She had been reading the newspaper accounts of the explosion at Julianne Corbett's reception. She had been reading and rereading all the articles about the murder at Fox Run Hill and the explosion in the parking garage. She had been looking and looking and looking at the pictures they kept printing of the woman they kept calling Patsy MacLaren Willis. She didn't know what she was waiting for, or what she wanted or from whom, or what she thought was supposed to happen next to make it possible for her to move.

"I'm just being ridiculous," she said to herself now, out loud, so that her voice bounced off the walls of her apartment and the soft pile of her carpet. Everything in this apartment sounded muffled. It was that kind of place.

"I'll bet he isn't even in the phone book," Liza said.

The phone book was on a little stand with the phone next to the couch in the living room. The living room and the dining room and the kitchen were really just one big room arranged in a U. Liza got the phone book out and looked up

Demarkian, Gregor. There was a phone number there, but no address. She wondered why he had bothered to have his address left out. Everybody knew what his address was. It was in the papers all the time that he lived on Cavanaugh Street.

"I'm just being ridiculous," Liza said out loud again. "He probably wouldn't pay any attention to me. He probably has hundreds of people trying to give him information every day."

She should stop talking to herself, Liza decided. She should have called Gregor Demarkian the other day, after she talked to Shirley at the hospital. It was just that she got to a phone, and then the whole thing seemed ridiculous, and then—

"Jerk," Liza said.

She picked up the phone, punched in the number next to Gregor Demarkian's name in the book, and listened to the ring. The next thing she knew, a tape machine was bleeding its message into her ear. She hated tape machines. She hung up on tape machines. She almost hung up on this one, but then she decided she shouldn't.

"My name is Liza Verity," Liza said into the phone after she heard the beep. Then she heard another beep and realized she was going to have to start again. She hated answering machines. She hated everything to do with answering machines. She even hated her own answering machine.

"My name is Liza Verity," she said, starting again.

And then she crossed her fingers and told herself she wasn't going to give up this time, no matter what, because this whole thing was beginning to get bizarre beyond belief.

# SIX

## 1.

GREGOR FOUND THE MESSAGE ON his answering machine when he came in after having dinner with Tibor, but it was so garbled, he couldn't make out what it said. Gregor didn't work well with answering machines, or machines of any kind. He could make the VCR go on the blink just by looking at it. In the Behavioral Science Department at the Federal Bureau of Investigation, everything had depended on computers, but he'd never used one. He'd found someone who was good with machines to do all that and bring him the raw data on long folding sheets of paper so that he could read it overnight and be ready for briefings in the morning. The man who had taken over from him when he retired was supposed to be very good with computers. It was one of the requirements the Bureau had made for any new person seeking the job. Gregor was sitting in his old neighborhood in Philadelphia, doing terrible things to a phone answering machine.

The one thing that did come through loud and clear was the name and address. Gregor wrote those down, listened to the tape again, and decided that the message had something to do with the case of Patsy MacLaren Willis. Everything in his life these days had something to do with the case of Patsy

MacLaren Willis. Even Tibor had been talking about it, although that might have been a ploy to stay off the subject of Donna Moradanyan. Tibor was all ready to have a wedding, and this new business with Donna's old friend Peter had thrown him off. Tibor certainly didn't want to have a wedding for Donna and Peter. Tibor hadn't liked Peter even in the days when Peter was living in Philadelphia and seeing Donna on a regular basis.

"In the old days, a priest would have hoped for the normalization of relations," Tibor had said at dinner. "Donna and Peter have had a child together. Donna and Peter should recognize their responsibilities before God together. Donna and Peter should end up married. Now I think I would cut my own throat before I could officiate at the ceremony. Do you think he will come to Philadelphia himself to bother us?"

"I don't know," Gregor said.

"You'll have to do something about it if he does. We really can't have him here, Krekor. It just isn't right. Russell is such a very nice man."

"I know Russell is a nice man."

"And a lawyer, Krekor. It will be good for Donna. And for Tommy. What does Peter do for a living?"

"I don't know," Gregor said again.

"I will bet anything that he is still in school. That boy is the kind to be in school forever. One degree here. One degree there. Never getting anywhere."

"I thought you approved of education for education's sake."

"We are not talking here about education for education's sake, Krekor. We are talking about a boy who does not want to grow up. We are talking here about a boy who does not know how to live outside a fraternity house, where nobody ever cleans."

Gregor had no idea where Tibor had gotten the idea that nobody ever cleaned fraternity houses. From *Animal House*, maybe. Bennis and Donna were always renting movies to watch in Tibor's living room, although most of those were big-bug horror films from the fifties. Gregor picked up his plate and Tibor's and took them into the kitchen to put them in the sink. They had been eating on folding tables in Tibor's living room, a quieter place than the Ararat restaurant's dining room and an easier place to talk without being overheard. All the furniture in Tibor's apartment was stacked with books. Tibor read at least seven languages, including Latin and ancient Greek. He had copies of Plato and Aristotle in the original, copies of Erasmus and Clausewitz in translation, copies of Harlequin romances in Hebrew. He even had the latest modern Greek edition of *Cosmopolitan* magazine, which seemed to have something on the cover about rating your marriage for its "satisfaction factor." The words "satisfaction factor" were printed in the Roman alphabet, as if there were no Greek equivalent, as if there were no translation. Considering what "satisfaction factor" probably meant, there probably wasn't.

Tibor's kitchen was full of books too, but the table there was covered over with samples of wedding favors. There were little knots of Jordan almonds wrapped in white net and tied with white ribbons. There were silver and white matchbooks that spelled out DONNA AND RUSS in overelaborate script, in spite of the fact that neither Donna nor Russ smoked. Bennis smoked, Gregor thought, and Lida and Hannah and Helen and Sheila could use the matches to light the gas burners that went out after things boiled over on the stove. There was a stack of small white napkins with silver script on them too, that ubiquitous DONNA AND RUSS.

"She's going to have to marry Russ," Gregor said, making sure Lida Arkmanian's best blue serving platter didn't get chipped in the mess in Tibor's sink. All the food they had eaten tonight had come from Lida or Hannah or one of the others. Tibor couldn't cook anything that would not be responsible for food poisoning, and Gregor made only steaks in the summers on an outdoor grill. Gregor pushed Hannah

Krekorian's rose china soup bowl to the side—what had Tibor had for lunch?—and made sure that Lida's serving platter was lying flat along the bottom of the sink. Then he picked up one of the matchbooks and tossed it in the air.

"If they don't get married, they're going to feel pretty silly," he said. "They're going to be tripping over this stuff for the rest of their lives."

"If they don't get married, they're both going to feel miserable," Tibor said. "And what is worse, Tommy is going to feel miserable too. Bennis is making excuses to Russell."

"About Donna? Shouldn't Donna make her own excuses?"

"Donna would tell the truth. This is not a girl with a wonderful sense of self-preservation, Krekor. I should say 'woman,' except I shouldn't, because a full-grown woman would have more sense."

"Donna is over twenty-one," Gregor pointed out. "And she has a child."

"I wouldn't care if she had thirty children," Tibor said. "She is a child. She is especially a child about men. How is it that American girls can grow up with men all over the place, boys in their school classes, dates by the time they're fourteen, and know so little about men?"

"Maybe if they knew a lot about men, they'd give up the dates and demand to have duennas," Gregor said.

Tibor waved this away. "Don't be ridiculous, Krekor. When you are in the teenage, the whole world is about sex. You don't want to have anything to do with a duenna. But Donna should know better about Peter. He is not an unknown quantity. Even in the biblical sense."

"Well, she got Tommy out of that, Tibor. Good things come out of messes sometimes."

"No good thing is going to come out of this mess," Tibor said. "I have a plan."

"What kind of plan? A plan about what?"

"About Peter. About what we do just in case he shows up to spoil the wedding. Bennis and I have talked about it."

"Peter isn't going to show up to spoil the wedding. Don't be silly. Peter's irresponsible, Tibor, but he's not a complete fool."

"Even you don't know very much about men." Tibor said this disapprovingly. "He is a spoiler, that one. He does not like to see other people happy."

"You're making him sound like a psychopath."

"If he comes here to stop the wedding, I want you to arrest him," Tibor said.

Gregor nearly dropped the silver soup spoon he was holding. It was engraved in curving script *HVK*. Gregor was careful not to let it go where it might fall down the garbage disposal.

"I can't arrest anybody," he told Tibor. "I'm not even with the Bureau anymore. I'm a private citizen. And what would I arrest Peter for? Being a prime bastard? It isn't a crime."

"You could think of something to arrest him for. It wouldn't have to stick. It would be only to get him out of the way."

"You're out of your mind."

"Bennis says that if it is necessary, she could possibly find some marijuana and put that on him and then he could be arrested for that. She says her brother Christopher—"

"You're worse than insane," Gregor interrupted. "Tibor, this is the United States of America. There's something called the Bill of Rights here. There are also dozens of laws against the kind of thing you're talking about. Entrapment. False witness. I don't know. There are laws that apply though, trust me. You're going to get yourselves into a lot more trouble than you're going to get Peter into."

"I don't want to get Peter into trouble," Tibor said patiently. "I just want to get him out of the way."

"The next thing I know, you're going to be talking about cement overcoats," Gregor said. "You can't do this."

"We can do something," Tibor said stubbornly. "Listen, Krekor, it is a matter of only one week. At the end of the week Donna and Russ will be married, they will take Tommy off to Disneyland, everything will be all right."

"Right," Gregor said.

"The important thing is to get through the wedding." Tibor was adamant. "You do not believe me, Krekor, but it is true. He will come here. I will bet you anything you want."

"And I'll bet you anything you want that he won't. He isn't stupid, Tibor. I've met him."

"Stupidity has nothing to do with it. Could you promise me this? If he does show up, will you keep him away from Donna?"

"I don't know if I could do that. Peter is Tommy's father, no matter what kind of idiot he is. Don't you think Donna's old enough to handle these things for herself?"

"No."

Gregor took a piece of *loukoumia* off a plate of the things in the middle of Tibor's kitchen table. Even through the powdered sugar he could see that it was one of the pink ones, flavored with rosewater. Since it had come from Ohanian's Middle Eastern Food Store right down the street, it was also the size of a small brick.

"If Peter shows up, I promise you that I will do something to make sure that he does not stop this wedding. Not that I think anything can stop this wedding. Donna is just being Donna. When the time comes, she'll do the right thing."

"When the time comes, I will hit Peter over the head with the long staff. I will take the cross off it first, so as not to be sacrilegious. Take some of that *loukoumia* home, Krekor. I don't need so much for myself."

"I don't need any more than I've got," Gregor said. "I have a plate in my kitchen just like this one. Don't worry about Donna so much, Tibor. It will work out."

Tibor made a noise, which meant that he didn't think it would necessarily work out. In his life, things very often had not worked out. Gregor supposed he didn't blame him, but it made things complicated. Tibor always seemed to make things complicated.

## 2.

The message on his answering machine made things complicated too, Gregor decided. He played the message again when he got up the next morning, but it was just as garbled as ever. He wrote the name "Liza Verity" down on a Post-It note and took it back to the bedroom to check against his notes. He found the name in the list of people who were supposed to be at the reception but had not actually been there. The specific notation was short and unilluminating:

> LIZA VERITY—*friend J.C. and K.P. Vassar College—Nurse—Phila.———Did Not Attend*

Gregor took his notes back into the kitchen and put them down on the table. He couldn't remember when a case had called forth this much ink from him. He seemed to have spent all his time since John Jackman first called him in making lists of things. Lists of Patsy MacLaren Willis's friends and neighbors at Fox Run Hill. Lists of people who had attended the reception for Karla Parrish. Lists of people who had been in or near the parking garage at the moment when the Volvo blew up.

Gregor called John Jackman at homicide. When Jackman finally picked up, Gregor announced his name and said, "Well?"

Jackman blew an exasperated raspberry into his ear. "Well what? We're checking on it. We've been checking on it since yesterday. I can't find that trustee. He's off in the Bahamas or someplace. Not that I think that's going to matter. I don't think he ever met her."

"Did you talk to New Delhi?" Gregor asked. "Was Patsy MacLaren reported dead there in 1969? Did you talk to the U.S. State Department?"

"We're working on it, Gregor. For Christ's sake. We're not the FBI. We're working on it. Don't you have anything to do?"

"I got a message on my machine. From a Liza Verity. Does that name ring a bell with you?"

"No."

"She was one of the people on the invitations list for the Karla Parrish reception. She never showed up."

"Lucky her."

"She left a message on my machine, as I said. It's a little garbled. She seems to want to talk to me."

"So talk to her."

"I thought you might want to come," Gregor said. "She was at Vassar with Julianne Corbett and Karla Parrish. And, I suppose, with Patsy MacLaren."

"Hundreds of people were at college with Corbett and Parrish and MacLaren. It's probably nothing."

"Didn't they teach you always to check everything out?"

"Sure. They also taught me to have priorities. I've got a woman who put three bullets into at least one person and apparently blew up a whole bunch of others into varying states of distress and who now seems not to have existed for over twenty-five years. I've got as much to worry about as I want to."

"Meaning, I take it, that you don't want to come with me."

"If you mean to see Liza Verity," John Jackman said, "then no. Not today. I've got to straighten this other mess out to-day. Or at least make some headway with it."

"Will you mind if I go out there alone?"

"No, of course not. You're authorized. You're an official consultant. The woman called you. She could have called us, but she didn't. She called you. Go to it. Maybe you'll even find out something interesting."

"Thanks," Gregor said dryly.

"Give me a break, Gregor. I'm trying to find a dead woman here this morning. I'm up to my ass in communications in Sanskrit. Or something. I'll see you later, all right?"

Gregor hung up. He went back to his kitchen table and picked at the pastry he had left there on a plate before he'd gone back to the bedroom for his notes. Bennis was supposed to be sleeping late. In spite of the things she liked to say about how tough and unstoppable she was, she had to be exhausted by the traumas of the last few days. Tibor would be up to his neck in church business. There was a wedding coming up. There were also all the usual day-to-day things that had to be done in an Armenian church, especially now that there were so many immigrant Armenians in the neighborhood. Donna would be with her mother, going over wedding arrangements or making sure her dress fit. Either that, or she would be bothering Bennis with one more round of hand-wringing about the Peter situation. Gregor was fairly sure that Donna would not be telling her mother about the reemergence of Peter, because if Donna did that, her mother was likely to walk all the way to Boston just to kill the man. Obviously, there was nothing for Gregor to do on Cavanaugh Street, and there wouldn't be for most of the day.

Gregor went back to the bedroom, got into a good pair of light pants and a cotton shirt and a jacket. He had spent all his life wearing suits and he wasn't about to stop now. Then he made sure he had his wallet and that his wallet had money in it. Then he went out his front door and carefully locked it behind him. Nobody else on Cavanaugh Street locked their doors, but Gregor had been with law enforcement agencies for too much of his life to feel safe about doing that.

Gregor went down a flight, stopped at Bennis's door, and listened. No sound at all was coming from in there, not even the rhythmic ritual cursing of Bennis at work at her computer. He went down another flight of stairs and knocked on the door of the first floor apartment. Like many of the people

Gregor had known over the age of eighty, old George Tekemanian never seemed to do any sleeping at all.

Old George called "come in" from someplace inside his
apartment. Gregor opened the door—unlocked again; always unlocked—and stuck his head in. Old George was sitting in his wing chair in front of a television set the size of an
old CinemaScope screen, watching *Blazing Saddles*.

"I'm going downtown," Gregor said. "You want something
from the great world of Philadelphia boutiques?"

"Not a thing," old George said. "My grandson Martin has
brought me some videotapes. He thinks I will be shocked by
them."

"And are you?"

"No. I am embarrassed by the ones with the sex scenes,
Krekor, but Martin doesn't bring those anymore. I like this
one. Did you know Peter Desarian wants Donna to give up
Russ and marry him instead?"

"I know. You know. *People* magazine probably knows by
now."

"It is a very delicate situation, Krekor. I try to talk to Donna
about it, but I can tell she isn't listening. She thinks I am nothing but an old fart."

"Right," Gregor said.

"Of course she's right," old George said. "I've been an old
fart for years. But that doesn't mean I don't have anything to
say worth listening to. Especially about conceited little boys
like Peter Desarian."

"I'll get you a box of Ring-Dings," Gregor said. "You can
put a bow on them and give them to Martin and Angela for a
present."

"If I gave Angela Ring-Dings, she would put wheat germ
on them," old George said. "Take care of yourself, Krekor.
You're looking very tired these days."

Gregor left old George sitting in the wing chair and went
through the main foyer and out the building onto Cavanaugh
Street. The sun was hot and bright even this early in the

morning. The sidewalks were wet with the residue of a late night rain. Gregor walked out into the street and raised his hand to hail a taxi.

### 3.

Twenty minutes later Gregor Demarkian found himself counting out change on a street corner that looked less like the setting for an apartment building than like the sort of place where factories used to be back when big cities had factories. It was a blank, grimy neighborhood that had been going to seed for so long, it had nearly sprouted. It had none of the usual conveniences of city life. There were no dry cleaners or Chinese laundries—maybe they were Korean laundries these days. There were no delis or coffee shops. There were no newsstands. The only way Gregor knew that he was in the right place was that the building just in front of him had a sign that said BEAUDELIEU ARMS APARTMENTS. The building looked like it might be the perfect place to make hubcaps or sun reflectors. God only knew, it didn't have enough windows to qualify as housing.

Gregor saw several people on the street, none of them reassuring figures. There was a classic wino complete with ragged clothes and clear glass bottle in a brown paper bag. There was a young girl nodding out in a doorway, her eyes blank and her mouth slack. From the sateen short shorts she was wearing, Gregor assumed she was meant to be hooking, but somewhere along the way she had scored some dope, and now she didn't have the energy. There was a bag lady rooting around in the garbage too, but the garbage wasn't promising. It consisted of newspapers and empty bottles. The glass bottles were broken and the plastic ones were punctured. The bag lady was talking to herself in a language that was not English and not anything Gregor recognized either. It sounded vaguely Slavic.

Gregor went up to the front door of the Beaudelieu Arms and pulled on the handle. Nothing happened. He saw a buzzer next to the door and pressed it. Nothing happened then either. There didn't seem to be any other way to get in. He pressed the buzzer again. The day was heating up. Gregor could feel a faint line of sweat along his collar. He had a terrible feeling that the Beaudelieu Arms did not have central air-conditioning.

Gregor pushed the buzzer again. Nothing happened again. He pushed the buzzer one more time, leaning against it long and hard this time. He could hear the sound of it going off inside, the angry whine. He stepped away from the door and tried to see through the tiny window in the top half of it.

What seemed like an eternity later, there were sounds of shuffling and cursing inside the building. Gregor tried the grimy window again and got nothing. The door shuddered under his hand and he stepped back. Then the door swung in, open to blackness, and a man appeared who looked every bit as derelict as the wino Gregor had just decided was much too out of it to talk to.

Gregor cleared his throat. "Excuse me," he said. "I'm looking for a Ms. Liza Verity?"

The man shifted from one foot to the other, blank. Everything about him was blank. Even his clothes were blank.

"Liza Verity," Gregor repeated. "I believe she lives here. I would like to speak to her, please."

He might as well have been talking to Hal the Computer— except that it was worse, because Hal the Computer would at least have registered the fact that he was saying *something*. This man registered nothing. Gregor wondered if he was deaf, or if it was just that he didn't speak English or had had so much to drink or smoke that he didn't speak anything. Did he really want to look for explanations in a situation like this?

He pushed the man aside as gently as possible and walked into the building. Once he was off the street, it wasn't so bad. The lobby was clean and surprisingly lobbylike. There were a couple of small sofas placed on either side of a low coffee table. It didn't look as if they had ever been sat in, or as if the coffee table had ever held a cup of coffee. There was some generic modern art on the walls too.

"Is there a call-up board?" Gregor asked the man. "You know, someplace where I might be able to intercom up to Miss Verity?"

Blank. Blank, blank, blank. Gregor checked the piece of paper in his pocket with Liza Verity's address on it. It indicated an apartment on the fourth floor.

"I'm going upstairs now," Gregor told the blank man. "To see Miss Verity."

Movement toward the elevators did what nothing else had been able to do. The blank man not only moved, he actually spoke.

"No, no," he said. "No up."

The accent was thick and difficult to understand. Fine, Gregor thought. He wasn't dealing with a zombie here, only a man who spoke English badly and probably understood it worse.

"I have to see Miss Verity," he said again. "In Apartment 4C. Can you call up to her?"

"No up," the man said again, much more insistent this time.

Gregor was sorry he hadn't called first. Maybe he should leave now and try calling from a pay phone down the street, to have Liza Verity meet him in the foyer. The problem was, he hadn't seen a pay phone down the street. Like diners and laundries, pay phones were extinct in this neighborhood.

"I'm sure you must have a call board," Gregor said, trying once again. "I'm here to see Miss Verity."

The blank man was looking mulish. "You leave," he said. "No up. I call police."

Oh, fine, Gregor thought. That was all he needed. "I want to see Miss Verity," he said again, feeling a little desperate this time. "I was invited." What was he talking about?

"You leave," the no-longer-blank man said again. By now

he had begun to look menacing, hulking, and stupid. Gregor had never trusted stupid people. They got violent much too easily.

"You leave now," the man insisted. "I throw you out. I call police. You leave now."

Gregor didn't know what he would have tried next if he had had to try something. He was just about to repeat himself yet again—as if that were going to do him any good—when the rumbling started.

Actually, the first thing Gregor heard wasn't a rumbling. It was a *ping,* the sound of metal against metal, ball bearings falling to the surface of a stainless steel table. The next thing he heard was a mechanical punch, and then he had sense enough to be scared.

"Get down," he said, grabbing the mulish man by the arm. "Get down *now!*"

The mulish man fought back, but he was in worse physical shape than Gregor was and it didn't matter as much to him what happened next.

A second after the two of them hit the lobby's carpet, the elevator doors exploded outward in an arc of cheap sheet metal and shards of glass.

# PART THREE

*First Comes Love, Then Comes Marriage, Then Comes the Marriage Counselor and Six Sessions of Psychotherapy at Least*

# ONE

## 1.

NOBODY HAD ACTUALLY PUT A bomb in the elevator. It took a while to figure that out—and a lot of help from firemen and ambulance drivers and police officers—but where and why the bomb had been was the first thing anyone wanted to know, and it was what they worked hardest at besides rescue. The rescue was, in Gregor's eyes, bizarre. There weren't many people in the building at that time of day. It was the sort of place that would have been inhabited exclusively by artists and writers in New York City. The apartments were big and the space was appealingly "alternative." In Philadelphia that just meant the place was not as expensive as it might have been, given the amount of care that had gone into outfitting the rooms and laying down the carpets. It was the middle of the day. Almost everybody was out at work. Wandering through the empty halls, watching out for the progress of the small fire that had started up on four, rescue workers went through one empty hall after the other. There was an old woman hiding in her closet in 3B, convinced that the street gangs of Philadelphia had armed themselves and started a war. There was a small child and her Peruvian nanny on six. The nanny thought they were in the middle of an earthquake and was trying to get away down the fire escape. There was Liza Verity.

"At least, we assume it was Liza Verity," John Jackman said disgustedly after the crews had been at it for at least half an hour. He was standing next to Gregor in the lobby, looking through the door at the crowds gathered outside. Gregor would never have imagined that so many people would be able to collect in this one place, considering how few people there had been before anything happened. The people weren't all derelicts and bag ladies either. There were two or three young men in suits, and several young women in the brightly colored clothes Gregor had come to think of as "secretary uniforms." There were people from the press out there too. Gregor kept catching sight of camcorders and portable mikes. God only knew what they were saying out there to explain this thing to the people watching the news.

"The important thing is that we get back up there as quickly as possible," Gregor said. "There were a couple of things—"

"The firemen are adamant that we don't do any such thing," Jackman said. "There's been structural damage to the building. The whole thing could collapse under our feet."

"No, it couldn't. It was a pipe bomb."

"It blew out the elevator."

"You said yourself that was an accident. One of the bombs rolled out Liza Verity's door—"

"It might not have been an accident, Gregor. It might have been on purpose. Have you considered that?"

"Yes."

"Have you considered that whoever did this might be wandering around here still?"

"I've considered it the same way you have and I've rejected it for the same reason you have. There would be no point to it. Why should she hang around?"

John Jackman went back to the door and peered out.
There was a judas window there, which is what the doorman
had been using when Gregor was trying to get in. Gregor had
tried to use it himself, but it distorted everything. The
woman from ABC looked like she had a head the size of a
watermelon.

"Do you still think it was a 'she' who did this, Gregor?"
John Jackman asked. "Do you still think it was Patsy Mac-
Laren Willis?"

"Oh, yes."

"I've been thinking lately that maybe Julianne Corbett
was right. Maybe the woman is dead. Maybe she never even
existed. If I hadn't seen the body out at Fox Run Hill with my
own eyes, I'd begin to wonder if I was making all this up."

"There's a body upstairs right this minute, John. There's
Karla Parrish in the hospital. There's that poor woman with
her antifur buttons—"

"I know, I know. But it would make more sense if we were
dealing with terrorists or something."

"We're dealing with a fairly clever woman with a fair
amount of acquaintance with amateur revolutionary publica-
tions, that's all. It's not so surprising if you think about it. She
went to college in the sixties."

"Bennis went to college in the sixties. I'll bet she doesn't
know how to make a pipe bomb."

"I'll bet she does. And a few things more serious too. Let's
go back upstairs, John."

John looked around. There were people going back and
forth across the lobby, but the body hadn't come down yet.
One of the firemen propped the front door open. The delivery doors at the back were already open and being used for
personnel going back and forth with axes and hoses and bits
of debris. There were at least two mobile crime units at
work. The place still looked deserted. It was as if it swallowed
people whole.

"Do you have any idea why Liza Verity would end up dead?" John Jackman asked.

"Of course," Gregor told him. "So do you. If you think about it."

"I have thought about it."

"It didn't have anything to do with me, if that's what you were trying to make fit," Gregor said. "I doubt if Mrs. Willis even knew that Ms. Verity had called me. Though I suspect she suspected that Ms. Verity would do something of the sort sooner or later."

"You mean Liza Verity died because Patricia MacLaren Willis was afraid she would talk?"

"Yes."

"Things don't happen like that, Gregor. You're the one who taught me that. Maybe in mobs and gangs things happen like that, but ordinary people don't go around offing their neighbors for fear that their neighbors are going to talk to the police. Ordinary people trust their defense attorneys. And they're right too."

"This is a special case," Gregor said. "Liza Verity knew Patsy MacLaren."

"A lot of people knew Patsy MacLaren. Julianne Corbett knew Patsy MacLaren. She's not dead."

"I could say she might have been dead," Gregor pointed out, "because of that bomb at that reception she threw, but I won't, because it would be deliberately misleading. The point is that Liza Verity had seen Patsy MacLaren very recently."

"So had all those biddies out in Fox Run Hill."

"I know. But they'd never seen her *before* that."

"Christ," John Jackman said. "You're impossible. Do you actually know what's going on here?"

"I think I do, yes."

"Then tell me, for God's sake."

Gregor smiled weakly. "Let's just say that a very cautious person was hedging her bets," he said, "and then let's go upstairs and look around. The nature of this thing is such that we can't just go charging in like the cavalry, making accusations. We have to be reasonably sure."

"Reasonably sure of what?" John Jackman sounded exasperated.

"Reasonably sure of just who Patsy MacLaren really is. She really is a very cautious person, you know. Careful to a fault."

"Right," John Jackman said. "Pipe bombs blowing up the landscape in all these public places. India, for God's sake. If Patsy MacLaren is running around blowing up everybody who'd seen her in the last ten days or whatever, who died in India with Julianne Corbett in attendance?"

"Patsy MacLaren."

"The next time I need a consultant, I'm not going to get you, Gregor. I'm going to hire a psychic. It'll be easier on my nerves."

Gregor stepped out into the lobby. The elevator shaft was open and two firemen were working over it, directed by a bald man in a white lab coat from the mobile crime unit. The bomb squad, having done the emergency work of making sure there was nothing else around to go off, was standing by. Just in case.

"Let's go up," Gregor said again, gesturing to the door at the side that led to the stairwell. They had already been up it once since the rescue teams started arriving.

John Jackman sighed. "If they don't have that body in the bag when we get there, I'm leaving right away. Stabbings I can deal with. Shootings I can deal with. People getting blown up make my stomach turn. I think it's a good thing I never got drafted."

"I got drafted," Gregor said. "I never saw anybody blown up until I joined the FBI. Let's go."

## 2.

Out of the lobby, the building got better and better: neater, cleaner, brighter, newer. It was really a very nice place, except that it was in this neighborhood and guarded by a rogue troll, or whatever that doorman was. The stairwell was well lit. The hallways were well kept and newly painted and well lit too. Every once in a while Gregor saw a door with a bit of decoration on it, bright plastic eggs left over from Easter, little wooden "Pennsylvania Dutch" welcome plaques. Teachers and nurses, second assistant bookkeepers and car insurance agents—most of them, Gregor was sure, living alone. If you got married, you moved out of a place like this, to a little house somewhere in one of the less important suburbs. You only went on and on about how convenient it was to be close to the museums and the theaters when you didn't have children to put through school.

They got up to the fourth floor and found the fire door shut. Gregor opened it and looked through, only to be confronted by the massive head of a fireman in a very bad mood.

"This entrance is not operative," the fireman said. "The staircase is not operative. I don't know where you came from, but—"

John Jackman pushed himself forward. "Jackman," he said, holding out his shield case. "Homicide."

"Oh," the fireman said. He stepped back.

If anything, the fourth floor was in even worse shape than it had been the last time Gregor had been there, right after John Jackman arrived, when they were looking through the debris trying to figure out what happened. Still, Gregor thought, it was obviously a pipe bomb that had gone off, and not something bigger. The door to 4C was off its hinges, but the firemen or the bomb squad had done that. There was a lot of mess on the hall carpet and a little singeing on the hall wallpaper. There was not much else, except in 4C itself, and that was a total mess.

"We cleaned it up some," the big fireman said. "And the cops from forensics, they've put a lot into plastic bags."

Gregor went to the door of 4C and looked inside. The corpse was in a bag, lying on the living room floor, blank under white canvas. A pair of orderlies in white fatigues was unfolding a stretcher next to it. A tall man in a black suit was standing next to the orderlies, taking off a pair of clear plastic gloves. The man in the suit looked up, saw John Jackman, and nodded.

"Mr. Jackman," he said. "We're all done here. I've got to do an autopsy. Pipe bomb, my ass."

"It was certainly a pipe bomb," Gregor pointed out. "One of the first things we found was the pipe."

"This is Dr. Halloran," John Jackman said formally. "From the medical examiner's office. This is—"

"Gregor Demarkian," Dr. Halloran said. "I know. Phil Borley's here from the bomb squad. You ask him. Pipe bomb. Bunch of Chinese fireworks, that's what it was."

"Now, now," John Jackman said. "Let's not get too politically incorrect here. We haven't even been drinking."

"Are you trying to tell me it wasn't a pipe bomb?" Gregor asked.

"Phil!" Dr. Halloran shouted. "Phil, come over here. Of course it was a pipe bomb. It was just a *little* pipe bomb."

"It blew out the elevator," Gregor pointed out.

"That was because it was stuck in an enclosed space," Dr. Halloran said, distracted. He was suddenly joined by a short, slight, middle-aged man who looked eerily like one of those economic advisers the Clinton administration was always trotting out to talk to television reporters about the economy. "This is Phil Borley," Dr. Halloran said. "He's with the bomb squad."

"Hi," Philip Borley said.

"Pipe bomb, my ass," Dr. Halloran said again.

"I think Dr. Halloran is trying to say this wasn't a bomb,"

John Jackman said. "Or that it wasn't much of a bomb. Or something—"

"It wasn't much of a bomb," Philip Borley confirmed. "I'm going to take it down and run it through a few tests next to the ones we've got already, the one from the garage and the one from the other night. I figure we've got a good chance of them all being the same thing, don't you?"

"We've been counting on it," Gregor Demarkian admitted.

Philip Borley nodded sagely. "I guess you would be. I can't see us having two mad bombers running around at once though. Not that this one is much of a mad bomber. Lots of noise. Lots of mess. Not much damage."

"How can you say there hasn't been much damage?" John Jackman was indignant. "There are at least two people dead, not including the one she shot, assuming it's the same person—"

"It's the same person," Gregor Demarkian said. "She should have stuck with guns."

"Why didn't she stick with guns?" John Jackman demanded.

"Because she didn't think she was going to kill anybody else," Gregor said patiently. "She thought she was going to kill her husband, blow up the car, and disappear. And that was going to be it."

"Well, she did disappear," Phil Borley said. "If it's this Mrs. Willis you're talking about. I've been reading the papers just like everybody else. She's gone."

"She's in the papers," Gregor pointed out. "I don't think she expected that to happen."

"She blows up her car in a municipal parking garage and she doesn't expect to get into the papers?" John Jackman was skeptical.

"Oh, she expected to get into the papers with that," Gregor said. "It's too bad she couldn't have picked her time better. I think she was probably in a bind, or she would have. As it turned out, she blew up her car during a slow news week, and it got more attention than she had expected. Although it was supposed to get some attention."

"He talks like this all the time," John Jackman said. "Sometimes I'm ready to kill him. God only knows what he wants up here now."

Gregor walked over to the body bag and looked down. "You said it was a small bomb, and yet she died anyway. She must have been sitting right on top of it."

"Almost literally, I think," Dr. Halloran said. "The wounds are consistent with that interpretation anyway. I think somebody put it under her like a whoopee cushion."

"Which would mean it would have to be somebody she knew," John Jackman said. "Except that according to you, Gregor, she was supposed to have known Patsy MacLaren. In college."

"The message on the phone was garbled," Gregor said, "but I'm fairly sure that's what she said. But I don't think she would have let Patsy MacLaren get into a position to plant a bomb underneath her, do you?"

"What do you mean?" John Jackman blinked.

"Well," Gregor said, "look at it this way. For a week or so now, the news has been full of stories about how Patsy MacLaren murdered her husband and blew up her car, and lately there have been even more stories about how she's a suspect in the bombing of the town house where Congresswoman Corbett was giving a reception. This isn't what I would call a wonderful person to let get behind your back, would you?"

John Jackman looked confused. "You mean it wasn't Patsy MacLaren who planted this bomb?"

"As far as Patsy MacLaren could do anything, she planted this bomb," Gregor said.

John Jackman looked disgusted. "Except she couldn't do even that, because she's dead. You know, Gregor, we do seem to have a situation here where bombs are going off left and right and people are dropping like flies and there's no end in sight, and when we get into a situation like that, I begin to feel that it's not really all right for us to—"

"There's an end in sight," Gregor said. "I don't think

anybody's going to end up dead again anytime soon. Unless Karla Parrish dies in the hospital, God forbid, and that isn't what you're talking about."

"How can you possibly know that nobody's going to end up dead?" Phil Borley was curious. "I don't like the MO here, Mr. Demarkian. It's nuts."

"No, it's not," Gregor said. "Really, you know, it's all absolutely simple. The only thing that got complicated, like I said, was the timing, because the timing meant that there was a great deal more publicity about it all than there would have been. Or maybe that was a miscalculation on her part. Maybe, what with Fox Run Hill in the picture, there would always have been a fair amount of publicity. I think it might have been much different if the city was in the middle of a gang war or if there was a crisis going on in Korea. As I said, maybe not."

"If the timing was so important to her, why didn't she just wait?" John Jackman asked. "Crises in Korea don't happen every day, but gang wars are frequent enough. She could have found any number of excuses in no time at all."

"She didn't have the time," Gregor said. "She was very close to being found out. If she hadn't already been found out."

"You mean by her husband," Phil Borley said. "Hadn't they been married for years? What was there new about her that he could possibly have found out?"

Gregor walked over to the wall next to the hallway and looked carefully at the paint and paper. There were no telltale signs of bright and dark, no indications that pictures had hung there for a long time that were now gone. He sighed.

"Everybody always talks about how wonderful the sixties were," he said, "but have you ever noticed? Nobody ever keeps pictures of it. Nobody has his coffee table full of snapshots of long-haired boys dancing in mud or people with signs marching on the Pentagon. They have posters of that kind of thing, but they don't have pictures of themselves."

"You're looking for pictures of long-haired guys in mud?" John Jackman asked.

"I'm looking for a picture of Patsy MacLaren. The Patsy MacLaren who died in India. Do you think we could get hold of a Vassar College yearbook?"

"Probably," John Jackman answered. "This doesn't answer the question of why she didn't wait. Why kill her husband right when she did? Why blow up her car instead of just leaving it in the airport parking lot with all the other missing cars?"

"Steve Willis was being reassigned to work in his head office," Gregor said. "Remember? That was practically the first thing you told me about this case. Usually he traveled a great deal, but he was home on the night he was killed because he was being taken off traveling. He was going to be living at home full-time and working in an office just like anybody else. And of course, under the circumstances, that had to be intolerable."

"To his wife," John Jackman said.

"Exactly," Gregor said. "Do me a favor, check a few other things, all right? You're looking into this degree Patsy MacLaren was supposed to have earned at the University of Pennsylvania—"

"We're checking into everything," John Jackman said. "Like I said, that trust officer is off in the Caribbean someplace, but we'll find him. And we'll check everything. You don't have to tell us that."

"I know I don't." Gregor looked into Liza Verity's bedroom. There was a photograph in there in a shiny aluminum frame, but it was only of Liza Verity herself in a nurse's cap, holding what looked like a diploma. Gregor went over to her closet and looked into that, but Liza Verity had not been heavily addicted to clothes. She had a couple of the kind of dresses Bennis Hannaford would call "nice," meaning suitable for semi-ceremonial occasions. Gregor got the impression that they were of a cheaper make than Bennis would have worn herself. She had a couple of pairs of jeans, pressed and draped over hangers. She had several cotton sweaters folded on the shelf over the hanger rod.

John Jackman and Phil Borley and Dr. Halloran were waiting for him in the hall, looking curious.

"So," John Jackman said. "Have you got it all figured out?"

"Yes," Gregor said. "I need pictures."

"I need Patsy MacLaren. Assuming that Patsy MacLaren exists," John Jackman said glumly. "*Does* Patsy MacLaren exist?"

"Yes," Gregor said.

"Then Julianne Corbett was lying," John Jackman said. "Patsy MacLaren didn't die in India."

"Julianne Corbett wasn't lying when she said Patsy MacLaren died in India," Gregor said.

"Crap," John Jackman said.

"I really do need pictures," Gregor said. He went back out into the living room. The orderlies had the stretcher assembled on the floor—or was it disassembled? or unfolded?—and they were levering Liza Verity's body onto it. It seemed to Gregor like a very small body, but he might have been wrong. He had never met the woman. He should have met her. He went into the kitchen. Liza Verity didn't seem to have been very committed to cooking.

"Well," John Jackman said, following him. "Tell me this. Am I supposed to feel guilty? Is there something I should have figured out sooner? Could we have kept this murder from happening?"

Gregor shook his head. "I couldn't have. It didn't click for me until after I got here, and by the time I got here—hell, John. Practically the first thing that happened to me downstairs was that I watched the elevator blow up."

"Right," John Jackman said.

Gregor nodded. "On second thought, I don't think that was an accident. I think she dropped that second pipe bomb into the elevator shaft on purpose. I think that was how she ensured that she was going to have time to get away."

"Who?" Phil Borley looked bewildered.

"Patsy MacLaren," Gregor said.

"Oh, don't start that again," John Jackman said.

"Why didn't she just go out and get another gun?" Dr. Halloran asked. "From everything I've heard about what happened to the husband, she was good with guns. A gun would at least be quicker and easier and less messy than this kind of thing."

"She doesn't have access to a gun," Gregor said. "It's like I said before, if she'd realized she was going to end up killing anyone besides her husband, she would have kept the gun she had. My guess is that she acquired it a few years ago. Knowing that something like this was going to come up eventually. Planning it out."

"For years," John Jackman said.

"That's right," Gregor told him. "She's good at that. Planning for years, I mean. It's what she's always done best. It's just unfortunate for her that in this sort of thing, you can't really plan."

John Jackman was looking mutinous. "Are we still talking about Patsy MacLaren here?" he demanded. "The woman Julianne Corbett was *not* lying about when she said she was dead? That one?"

"Yes."

"So what is she? A ghost? Does her spirit return to wreak revenge on the living? Was it an astral projection who was married to Stephen Willis? What the hell is going on here?"

"Patsy MacLaren," Gregor Demarkian said carefully, "is a perfectly ordinary middle-aged woman who would appear absolutely no different from any other perfectly ordinary middle-aged woman if you had ever met her, which you have, once or twice, although you didn't know it."

"*I've* met Patsy MacLaren," John Jackman said. "Right. When was this? Before she murdered her husband?"

"No. Since."

"Right. During this investigation."

"That's it, yes."

"So I didn't know I was meeting Patsy MacLaren."

Gregor Demarkian shook his head. "John, John," he said. "Really. You're doing just what I did up until a couple of hours ago. You're making it much too complicated."

"I'm going to complicate your head," John Jackman exploded. "You can't do this to me. Goddammit, Gregor. This is a murder investigation. We have three people dead."

"I know you do," Gregor said. "Get me pictures."

"Of what?"

"Of Patsy MacLaren. Get me the Vassar College yearbook for the year they all graduated. MacLaren. Verity. Parrish. Corbett—and two others. There were two others. Remember what Julianne Corbett told us. There were six people who used to hang out together in a group. Those are the ones I want to see."

John Jackman looked like he was going to explode again, but Gregor decided not to hang around for it. He went down to the stairwell. The big fireman was still there, but he was no longer interested in Gregor. Other firemen were there too, carting things back and forth, checking the walls and carpets. Gregor realized that he had no idea what firemen did besides put out fires, although in big city fire departments they had to do a lot more than that. At the very least, they had to inspect things.

Gregor went down the stairs, looked into the third floor hall onto emptiness, went down more stairs. In the second floor hall he saw a girl of ten or twelve sitting on the carpet in front of an open apartment door. She had a pile of magazines next to her and a pair of scissors. When she saw Gregor she held up one of the magazines and smiled.

"Brides," she said, indicating a tall young woman in a fantastical white dress that seemed to be made of tiers and tiers of lace. "Aren't they beautiful?"

"Beautiful," Gregor agreed.

The girl turned away and started to cut the picture out of the magazine.

Brides might be beautiful, Gregor thought as he headed for the lobby, but marriages were complicated, and after a week like this, he didn't want to think about it.

# TWO

## 1.

THERE WAS A SHOW ON one of the cable stations about brides. Dozens and dozens of tall young women with no hips and arms like toothpicks paraded down a runway one after the other, showing off creations in satin and silk. Evelyn Adder watched them move as her husband sat at the kitchen table with Sarah and Kevin Lockwood, looking over some papers they had brought. For most of the time Sarah and Kevin had been there, Evelyn had been starving. It was unheard-of for Henry to be home so long in the middle of the day. Evelyn had the window seat on the landing filled with Hershey's Kisses and bagel chips. She had two dozen bags of potato chips and six of those dips you could buy on the same shelf as the refried beans. She had a box of frozen White Castle hamburgers that just needed to be fried up. Sarah and Kevin and Henry were all ignoring her. Kevin kept reading bits and pieces of the papers he wanted Henry to sign. Sarah kept talking about their winter vacations in Boca wherever-it-was, making the place sound like an upper middle class street in Victorian England instead of like a piece of Florida real estate.

"Being able to get good help makes all the difference," Sarah would say. "It changes one's life completely."

"The appreciation of land values over the last ten years has been truly phenomenal," Kevin would say, "especially land directly on the waterfront."

One of the brides on the runway had a dress that was cut up to her thigh in the front and had a long train. Another one of them had a dress that looked like millions of puffy pastel-green mints held together with string. There was a picture of Evelyn in her wedding dress on the shelf above the television set. She was very thin, and her dress was a plain white thing that could have been a uniform. There used to be pictures of Henry in the house when he was fat, but now there weren't any. Only Henry's publisher had those.

"What I like best about Florida is the lack of people," Sarah Lockwood said. "You wouldn't think it the way it looks on the news, but really all the overcrowding is down in places like Miami. Up where we are it feels like there's nobody around at all, except that it's better than that, because there really is. I think you picked the prettiest piece of land we had."

Evelyn picked up the remote and went from channel to channel, from shopping to fixing up old houses to cooking in a wok. She felt leaden and gross, the way she always did these days—but for some reason right at that minute it wasn't so bad. She found another show about brides and one about marriages. If you weren't careful to keep a psychological reference book on your bedside table at all times, your marriage would surely be doomed. There was a show with Martha Stewart about weddings, explaining how to make favors from bits of net and gold foil. Evelyn chose a local station with a soap opera on it and sat back. The soap opera seemed to be about impossibly thin people who were miserable about almost everything in their lives, although it was hard to figure out why that was.

"Thirty-five thousand will be more than enough for now," Kevin told Henry. "It's when you choose what you really want to build that you have to throw some more in. When your architect has plans you want or when you decide on one of the stock plans the development company puts out. Our house here came from a stock plan."

"Ours did too," Henry said. "The guy showed us what he intended to build, we walked through a model on the other side of the city, and here we are."

"I preferred the Victorian myself," Evelyn said matter-of-factly, knowing nobody was listening. "There were things I liked about this house, but I liked the Victorian better."

"We bought a stock plan down in Florida too," Sarah said. "It just seemed so much easier. If you're really picky, I suppose it would be all right to fuss with architects and all that sort of thing, but I really can't see it."

"I just don't want to wake up tomorrow morning and find that, cashier's check or no cashier's check, I don't own this piece of property because the owner thought someone else had made a better offer."

"Nobody else is going to make a better offer," Kevin said. "I'm as near to the owner as you're going to get. I'm not talking to anybody else but you."

On the screen, the soap opera flickered and jumped and disappeared, replaced by the dull black-and-white signboard that meant a bulletin was coming. When Evelyn was a child, bulletins meant at least the Cuban missile crisis or a major political assassination. Now they meant any excuse at all, because the local news crews wanted to feel like they were living exciting lives.

"There has been another minor explosion in central Philadelphia," the talking head said. "Details right after this message."

Evelyn wondered if there were advertisers out there who stipulated having their ads aired during bulletins. Did the stations have to guarantee the bulletins? The talking head was back. She was a scrawny blonde with limp hair and a strange curve to her lip, wearing too much lipstick. She stared soulfully into the camera.

"Police have been called to the home of a Philadelphia nurse this afternoon and forced to bring everybody from the fire department to the bomb squad with them as the third pipe bombing in under two weeks rocks the city of Philadelphia to its foundations—"

"Horseshit," Evelyn said under her breath.

"Did you say something?" Henry asked.

"There's been another bomb." Evelyn pointed to the television. "In central Philly this time."

"You shouldn't watch so much television," Henry said. "God, it's bad for your mind and bad for your butt. You ought to get up and move sometimes."

"I think Patsy must have been one of those SDS Weathermen in hiding," Sarah Lockwood said. "I mean, what else would explain it. Steve must have been one of them too. And he wanted to turn himself in, so Patsy executed him."

"I think it would have come out by now if Patsy had that kind of background," Evelyn said. "The police have been on it for days."

"Oh, the police," Sarah said. "I don't see that they're much good. They never seem to be able to catch the criminal with the least amount of intelligence. And Patsy had at least that."

"I thought she was boring," Henry said. "A boring, pudgy, middle-aged woman. Why do so many women get so boring after they pass the age of forty?"

Sarah Lockwood cleared her throat. "Well," she said. "I think we've got everything done we meant to get done. Kevin and I have an engagement this evening. We have to get dressed."

"Some people we knew when we were living in London," Kevin said. "They have a house near us down in Florida too. Lovely people."

"We'd invite you two along, but you know what the British are like." Sarah shook her head. "Throw new people at them and they go right into a deep freeze."

"They'll be all right once you get to Florida," Kevin said. "We'll have a dinner party to introduce everybody to everybody and tell the Brits all about it in advance."

"Don't you think this will be fun?" Sarah said.

Another talking head—another scrawny blonde, this time with a hand mike and a bright red blazer—was interviewing that black police detective who had been out at Fox Run Hill just a little while ago. Next to him was Gregor Demarkian, looking tired.

Henry came back from seeing Sarah and Kevin out. His face was red and mottled. His knuckles were white.

"You could have been a little less rude," he told Evelyn. "You could have talked to people instead of sitting in front of the television table like a dinner roll waiting to be buttered."

"Nobody wanted to talk to me," Evelyn said. "Even you didn't want to talk to me. Nobody was the least interested in hearing what I had to say."

"Maybe that's true, Evelyn, but if it is, it's only because of your weight. People are put off by your weight."

"In this case, I think people would have been put off by my point of view."

"Oh, don't start that again," Henry said.

"I'm not starting anything, again or otherwise." Evelyn stood up, one fluid motion, a dancer's exercise she had learned as a young girl in a local children's ballet class. It had been years since the last time she had tried to do that. It was incredibly gratifying to find out that she still could.

"I'm not starting anything," she repeated. "I'm just telling you. There's something wrong with it. It's some kind of scam. They're cheating you."

"Sometimes your background really comes out," Henry said. "Do you know that? Sometimes you're really nothing more than one more fat housewife from the Pennsylvania steel country, parochial and suspicious and small-minded and petty."

"If it's being small-minded and petty to be able to *add*,

Henry, then I'm small-minded and petty. Come to your senses for a moment. This deal doesn't add up."

"It isn't supposed to 'add up,' as you put it. This is a handshake between friends. That's the way people do things where there's a willingness to trust and a commitment to mutual advantage."

"Kevin Lockwood didn't trust *you* for that money. He made you bring a cashier's check."

"That was to satisfy the legal requirements." Henry sounded infinitely patient. "You always have to have a cashier's check when you buy property. It's standard operating procedure."

"We didn't have to have a cashier's check when we bought this property. At least, we didn't for the down payment. I gave him an ordinary check out of my checkbook when we decided on this house. I remember."

"We had to have a cashier's check later," Henry said.

"Yes, we did." Evelyn nodded. "We had to have it when we closed. But we didn't close on that property this afternoon, Henry. We just put a deposit on it and promised to buy."

"I don't really see the point in this discussion, Evelyn. After all, it isn't your money. It isn't like you made it and brought it to the marriage. I made it. My books made it."

"I know you made it."

"If anything, you've made it more difficult for me to make it. You haven't helped. Don't you think this—this appearance problem of yours causes me a lot of stress? Don't you think it costs me sales?"

"I wouldn't know."

"I know, Evelyn. I know. It's my money. And unlike you, I don't just want to sit where I am forever. I want to move up and out. I want to meet people I have something in common with. There are reasons why successful people stick together, Evelyn."

"I don't think Sarah and Kevin are successful. I don't think they'd be hanging around with us if they were."

"They might not be hanging around with you," Henry said, "but they would be hanging around with me. You may not be doing anything with your life, but I've been on *The New York Times* best-seller list."

The talking head was gone from the television screen. The soap opera was back. Evelyn suddenly had a distinct vision of Patsy MacLaren Willis pulling out of her driveway in the Volvo, the back of the station wagon packed with clothes on hangers.

"That's funny," she said.

Henry looked furious. "I don't see anything funny in the situation we're in. I don't know what it is you think you're doing here, but I've had this about as far as I can take it. I want a divorce, Evelyn."

"All right," Evelyn said calmly. "I'll make you a deal."

"About a divorce? You're going to make me a deal about a divorce? How can you?"

"I can make a deal about not being a problem to you," Evelyn said. "I can promise not to call you up at all hours of the night to make your life a living hell. I can promise not to follow your girlfriend all over town with a camera and a tape recorder."

"I don't have a girlfriend," Henry said. "And if I did, and you did any of those things, I'd have you put in jail."

"I'll give you a divorce if that deal of Sarah and Kevin Lockwood's isn't some kind of scam," Evelyn said. "If they're really and truly okay, I'll just pack my bags and move into an apartment in Philly and that will be the last you ever hear of me. I'll even go back to my mother. I absolutely promise."

"Christ," Henry said. "You're worse than impossible. You're ridiculous. I don't have to listen to any of this."

"If it is a scam, I'll fight you all the way," Evelyn continued. "I'll hire lawyers. I'll hire private investigators. I'll do everything that can be done, and in Pennsylvania it's a lot of everything, Henry. I'm tired of listening to you tell me how stupid and fat and lower-class I am. I'm tired of listening to you tell me how you know everything in the world it's worthwhile to know."

"I don't have to listen to any of this," Henry repeated. Then he gave Evelyn his best glowering stare, the one from which she always recoiled, and turned his back on her. Evelyn hadn't recoiled, but she didn't know if he had noticed that. His back was stiff and hard. His head was cocked at an odd little angle.

"I'm really sick to death of your attitude," he said. "I'm really tired to death of your lower-middle-class pettiness. I'm getting out of here."

"So go," Evelyn said.

Henry went. He went more slowly than she could ever remember him going, but he went. He kept his back rigid and his head at that odd little angle. He seemed to be waiting for her to do something or say something she hadn't done or said yet, but Evelyn didn't know what it was.

As soon as he was gone, Evelyn stepped out onto her back patio and looked up at the afternoon sky. The sky was blue and cloudless and somehow threatening. The air was hot and heavy and thick with moisture. Fox Run Hill was much too quiet. From back there Evelyn couldn't see anything or anyone of importance. The backyards for all the houses were carefully designed for privacy, so that a couple could screw stark naked next to the built-in charcoal grill and nobody would be able to tell. Somebody could scream and scream and scream out there and no one in the whole community would know it was happening.

If I were going to kill my husband, that's how I'd do it, Evelyn thought. I'd bring him out here and leave him lying next to the hydrangea bushes. I'd bury him in the compost heap. I'd leave him for the lawn service. Except that I wouldn't kill my husband. It wouldn't make any sense.

Evelyn went back into the house. She stepped out of her own front door and looked down the curving road at the Tudor where Patsy and Steve had lived. She thought of that

Volvo backing down the drive and then gliding down the road, Patsy with her hand stuck out a window, waving at Molly Bracken. She thought of herself sitting in Patsy's breakfast room one morning, looking at a picture in a sterling silver Tiffany frame.

"Those are the people who mattered most to me," Patsy had said at the time, and then gone on to whatever it was she had had to say that was more important than that.

Evelyn gave a last long look at the mock-Tudor and then went back into her own house.

It was funny, she thought again. It really was. But it didn't seem as if it could mean anything.

Evelyn went back into the kitchen and put on the kettle for tea. She could hear Henry rattling around upstairs. He expected her to come up and try to placate him, but she didn't want to.

Funny, funny, funny, she thought to herself again, and then: I wonder if it means anything.

Evelyn did not wonder if her marriage to Henry meant anything, because she knew it didn't mean a thing.


# 2.

For Evan Walsh, the news of the explosion in Liza Verity's apartment meant everything and nothing. He noticed it on the television when the news bulletin came on, but he was in one of those periods where he was counting every breath Karla took, so he didn't notice it with his whole mind and attention. Pipe bomb in central Philly, he thought, and then he bent more closely down over Karla's chest and watched it rise and fall, rise and fall, rise and fall, perfectly rhythmic, perfectly serene. If there hadn't been any of those tubes and wires, if this had been any other kind of room but a hospital room, anyone who didn't know better would have thought that Karla was just ordinarily asleep. She looked no different from sleeping princesses anywhere. Evan walked around her bed and checked her covers. He put his hand on her newly short hair and stroked against the stubble. He wished for things that made no sense: that they had not cut her hair; that they had let him buy her something nice and frilly to wear instead of this plain cotton hospital gown that looked to him like a shroud. Karla would not have seen herself as the frilly sleepwear type, but Evan could see her in lace and latticework. He could see her in satin as well as flannel.

Karla was breathing, breathing, breathing. That was all. Evan went out of the room and down the hall to the nurses' station. There were all these stories in the newspapers about the overcrowding in Philadelphia's hospitals, but this ward seemed to be nearly empty. There was nobody standing at the counter at the nurses' station. Evan went around the back and looked through the window in the door to the office. Shelley Marie and Clare were sitting in there, looking at magazines and watching television. Evan knocked.

Shelley Marie looked up, nodded, and came to the door to let him in. It was against all kinds of regulations, but Evan was a known figure on the ward by then. Except for one real dragon of a head nurse, they all tried to take care of him. Shelley Marie opened up and shooed him inside. When he was in, she shut and locked the door again.

"There's been another bombing," she said, her tone half hushed and half excited. "Clare and I have been watching a news story about it. This time the victim was a nurse."

"It was a nurse from a different hospital," Clare said. "She wasn't anybody we knew."

"I'd at least met her," Shelley Marie said. "At one of those all-city in-service things or something. Anyway, she's familiar. She's another friend of Congresswoman Corbett's too."

"One of the newscasters is saying it looks like some kind of political plot," Clare said. "You know, a string of assassinations. Although why anybody would want to get to Julianne

Corbett that way is beyond me. I mean, she's not that kind of politician."

"She's not even one way or the other about abortion in particular," Shelley Marie said.

"Maybe it's something else altogether," Clare said. "They've got that Gregor Demarkian working on it. He was on television not two seconds ago. Isn't he a specialist in serial killers?"

"He used to be a specialist in serial killers," Shelley Marie said. "When he was with the FBI. He's retired now."

"He doesn't look like he's retired to me," Clare said. "He's all over the place. So maybe this is a case of a serial killer."

"Killing a series of what?" Shelley Marie asked. "I thought serial killers killed young women with long brown hair parted in the middle. Or old ladies who carry canvas shopping bags."

"They do," Clare said. "Maybe this one kills middle-aged women who—who what?"

"Middle-aged women who have gotten dumpy," Shelley Marie said positively. "They were all dumpy. The woman with the animal rights movement who died when Evan's friend got hurt. And this nurse they keep showing pictures of. And this Patricia Willis—"

"But she isn't dead," Evan put in. "She's the one everybody thinks is doing it. Isn't she?"

"I don't know," Shelley Marie said.

Clare sighed. "They say she blew up her own car, but I can't see it. I mean, every other time one of these bombs has gone off, somebody's been dead, haven't they? So it doesn't make any sense that that car just blew up and nobody died. Maybe she was in it but she got blown so much to pieces, they never found the body."

"Don't be silly," Shelley Marie said. "That can't happen. You know that can't happen. You see the messes they bring in here sometimes, and they always know they've got a body."

"Car wrecks," Clare said solemnly.

There was a coffeemaker on the corner of the desk, one of those drip-through electrical ones with the glass coffeepot that rested on a kind of hot plate. Evan poured himself a cup of coffee and looked at the television set. The news bulletin was long gone. Two middle-aged white people were wrapped in each other's arms instead, whispering things to each other about how they really shouldn't. Unlike the middle-aged women dead so far from bombs, these two were not heavy or out of shape. They were, however, very saggy. Their skin wrinkled and stretched and folded and shook when they pretended to passion.

Evan used one of the little plastic containers of non-dairy creamer the nurses kept in a basket next to the coffee machine—it was incredible how terrible their eating habits were; with all the health propaganda that got spewed out in a hospital, you'd think they would know better—and sat down in the one empty chair. The chair swiveled underneath him and made him feel dizzy.

"Well," he said.

Shelley Marie held up her magazine, a copy of *Glamour* with an article in it called "How to Keep Your Wedding from Ruining Your Honeymoon." It was incredible to Evan how stereotypically everyone behaved. According to the best minds on the faculty at Vassar, all that moon-June-spoon business went out of style years before, as soon as women began raising their authentic voices against the oppressive assumptions of consumer capitalism.

"She's breathing very well," Evan said stiffly.

Clare patted him gently on the knee. "She *is* breathing very well," she said, "and if it's any consolation, she seems to be doing much better than most people who end up in her condition. I heard one of the doctors say just the other day that there isn't a single sign of brain damage yet, and that probably means there won't be any. And that's very good news."

"A lot of people who end up in comas for a long time are

really disabled when they come out," Shelley Marie said. "But Miss Parrish seems just to have been knocked out in a particularly unlucky way. I mean, she doesn't seem to be out for any structural reason or whatever."

"Ms.," Clare said. "I think she likes to be called Ms."

"I just wish it weren't so uncertain," Evan said. "I wish we could say, well, in two weeks or four weeks or six months, something would happen. Anything would happen."

"Well," Clare said, "we can't say that."

"If I were you, I wouldn't listen to all those stories about people who are in comas for years and years and don't come out until their children have children," Shelley Marie said. "In cases like this, it almost never happens like that."

"And you're doing the best possible thing you can do," Clare said. "You're staying with her. You're talking to her. The theory is now that she can probably hear most of what you have to say. It keeps her mind from atrophying."

"Minds don't really atrophy," Shelley Marie said. "That's a myth, like alligators in the sewers."

"I was just trying to tell him to keep it up," Clare said. "He should go on talking to her the way he does, and visiting her. It's good for her. It's probably good for him too."

"I know it is. But her mind won't atrophy. It isn't a muscle or that kind of thing."

One of Evan's professors at college was always saying that the mind *was* a muscle, but he wasn't a professor of anatomy, so maybe it didn't count. Evan put his half-filled coffee cup down on the desk. He didn't want any more of it. He hated the taste of nondairy creamer. He hated the sight of the bride on the first page of the *Glamour* magazine article.

"I'd better get back to Karla," he said. "Maybe it's *my* mind that's in danger of atrophying."

"I'll bring you something to eat when dinner comes around," Shelley Marie said.

Evan let himself out of the nurses' station office. He walked past four empty rooms and one with a heart patient in it before he came to Karla's door. The policeman who had been put there to guard her in the hours after the explosion was gone now. Evan went in and sat down in the chair next to her bed.

Later, he would wonder how long it had taken him before he began to realize that everything had changed. It was hot in the room in spite of the air conditioners. He was looking at the windows that looked out on the grimness of this Philadelphia neighborhood, wondering if they could be opened at all, just to let in a little air. Then he began to feel a little strange and he looked down into Karla's face.

And her eyes were open.

Her eyes were wide open.

They weren't staring.

They weren't dead.

They were simply open, and while he watched, they blinked.

"Jesus Christ," he said.

"Shh," Karla told him, her voice so hoarse it was a croak, and barely audible. "Don't tell anyone."

# THREE

## 1.

THE PRINTOUTS ARRIVED BY MESSENGER at 6:45 A.M. John Jackman arrived at 7:02, just as Gregor was about to leave his apartment to go to the Ararat. The brownstone was already a mess of noise and confusion. With the wedding now no further away than Sunday, Gregor no longer had Donna's decorations to trip over. He now had the actual preparations for the actual wedding to trip over. Donna Moradanyan's mother had come in from the Main Line God only knew when. Gregor was only sure that she was there when the printouts arrived; she was standing on the fourth floor landing, calling out directions in a voice that was half Katharine Hepburn and half Willard Scott. Bolts of cloth and bits of netting were everywhere. As John Jackman stood on Gregor's doorstep ringing his bell, a long ribbon of ice green floated down out of nowhere onto his head. Moments later Bennis Hannaford rushed downstairs, grabbed it off him, and rushed back upstairs again.

"Good morning, Bennis," Jackman said.

Bennis didn't even look at him. "I don't have time to argue with you now," she said. "The flower girl lost all the trim off her dress at the dry cleaner's."

Gregor wanted to ask what the flower girl's dress was doing at the dry cleaner's when the flower girl shouldn't even have worn it yet, but instead he shifted his stack of computer printouts from one arm to the other and said, "Your material came. Are we going to breakfast?"

"What's going on up there?" Jackman backed into a stairwell so that he could look up. There was a big bolt of white lace draped over the banister. Donna Moradanyan's mother was talking through pins.

"The Jordan almonds," she was saying. "Somebody has to remember the Jordan almonds."

"Jesus Christ," Jackman said. "They're going to kill somebody."

Gregor stepped onto the landing himself and closed his front door behind him. "Ararat," he said firmly. "Work. If you get caught up in the kind of thing that goes on around here, you'll never get anything done at all. Let's move."

"You can't have had much of a chance to look over the material." John Jackman was looking back up the stairwell again. Gregor wondered if Bennis was standing there. "Don't you want to study it for a while?"

"If it comes to conclusions I haven't reached, I can study it for a while. You can tell me that at breakfast. Let's go."

"Gregor—"

Gregor took him by the arm and started to tug him downstairs. The sound of female voices was high and harsh and unmistakable in the air above them. Suddenly, the whole brownstone seemed female. Men got married too. Why were weddings a female thing? Gregor dragged John Jackman downstairs, past Bennis's apartment on the second floor and into the lobby next to old George Tekemanian's door. Bennis's door had one of those big white and gold bows on it and old George Tekemanian's had a bouquet of silk flowers that looked like they were growing little pieces of glitter on their stems.

"Jesus," John Jackman said.

Gregor pushed him out the front door onto the stoop—but the street was just as bad, really. They must have done it while he was out and around with John yesterday, he thought, and he just hadn't noticed when he got back. Maybe it had been this way for weeks, and he just hadn't noticed at all. The street was a mass of silver and gold and white. It was more decorated than Gregor had ever seen it decorated before, even for Christmas, and Christmas was Donna Moradanyan's holy calling. There were at least three bows on every lamppost. If whatever department it was that was responsible for the lampposts ever decided to lower the boom on Donna Moradanyan, God only knew what would happen. The fronts of the town houses and the brownstones were all covered with bows too. Lida Arkmanian's window had a huge display of candles in it, all white with electric flames, all dripping fake but glittery wax off their uneven tips. The candles made Gregor feel instantly better. He knew they hadn't been there yesterday. He would have noticed them even if he had noticed nothing else.

"They must have been at it all night," he told John Jackman. "They're incredible."

"It's not Bennis who's having the wedding," John Jackman said. "You're sure of that?"

"Of course I'm sure of that. Who would marry Bennis?"

"Mick Jagger," John Jackman said solemnly. "Harrison Ford. The next candidate for president for the Republican Party."

"Bennis wouldn't marry a Republican."

"In this case she ought to, Gregor. He's probably going to win."

Weddings were bad enough. The last thing Gregor wanted was to get dragged into a discussion of party politics, Tibor's favorite pastime. He'd had enough of politics during the elections. He was going to have more than enough of it during the next elections.

The gray metal garbage cans had been covered over with silver plastic bags and tied with silver and white bows. The concrete frames of the basement windows had been painted over with silver paint and dotted with tiny faux pearls. Down the street, at Holy Trinity Armenian Christian Church, it looked as if the façade had exploded in little, tiny oyster eggs. Gregor turned his eyes determinedly toward the Ararat, and got moving.

"Incredible," John Jackman said when he finally caught up. "It really is incredible. You think there's any way you can get me asked to this wedding?"

## 2.

The Ararat was not as bad as the street was, but it was edging in that direction. When Gregor brought John Jackman in that morning, he found not only the bows on the little candles on all the tables, but bows on Linda Melajian as well. She was carrying a big pot of coffee across the main dining room with a white and silver bow in her hair, making the bow sway and shudder against her skull every time she moved her feet. Linda Melajian had very short hair. Gregor led John Jackman to the front booth with its cushioned benches and ignored his protests about how hard the thing was going to be to get into and out of. Of course it was hard to get into and out of. Gregor had problems with it every morning of his life. It was also the best booth in the restaurant, and the biggest, and they needed the room.

Gregor pushed aside a little candle with a bow and a little pot of silk flowers with ribbons all over it—silver and white, always silver and white—and began to spread the printouts across it.

"Come and talk to me," he said to John.

John Jackman sat down. Linda Melajian brought over her pot of coffee, noticed that neither one of them had a cup, and disappeared in the direction of the kitchen. It was a good thing the food here was good, Gregor thought, because they certainly took their regular patrons for granted.

"So," Gregor said. "Tell me about it."

John Jackman took his attention off the door through which Linda Melajian had gone and applied himself to the printouts. "In the first place," he said, "Julianne Corbett was telling the truth, at least as far as we can find out. A young American woman named Patricia MacLaren did die in New Delhi in 1969. The death certificate is on file with the authorities there."

"Are you sure this was our Patsy MacLaren?"

"I'm as sure as I can be, Gregor. A young woman named Patricia MacLaren left the United States on a Pan American flight in the late spring of 1969 in the company of another young woman, who was definitely Julianne Corbett, as far as we can be definite about these things. This isn't the Soviet Union, Gregor. This isn't even England. People don't have to carry identity papers or tell the police where they are."

"I know. Keep going. They went Pan Am."

"Right. They did. They went around for a while, in Europe some but mostly in India and Nepal and Pakistan and places like that. Then they both came down with dysentery."

"Both?"

"Yeah," John Jackman said. "I spoke to a couple of very nice people, Gregor, and they all spoke English, but there were language barriers just the same. Still, I think I got this straightened out. Julianne Corbett came down with dysentery first. Patsy MacLaren—they kept calling her the redheaded one; did you know she had red hair?"

"She didn't by the time that we saw her. But she was middle-aged by then. And mostly gray."

"She had red hair in 1969," John Jackman said. "Anyway, she brought Julianne in and stuck with her all the time she was sick and then just as Julianne was getting better, Patsy got sick herself. They put her in a hospital bed and filled her full of rehydration therapy stuff, but it didn't do any good. She never got any better. And one day she just died."

"Of dysentery."

"Right. I don't think that was a well-hidden murder, Gregor. Dysentery is pretty distinctive stuff. I couldn't begin to imagine how someone would bring on a fake attack of it in someone else. And it takes time. It's not like poison. It goes on for weeks sometimes before people die of it."

"All right. What happened then?"

"Well, the next thing was, in arrived this other friend of theirs, who from the description sounds to me like Karla Parrish. She was at least well, which Julianne really wasn't at that point. Parrish looked into making some arrangements about bringing the body back to the States for burial, but it couldn't be done right then. There was a cholera outbreak at the time and the State Department was holding up the repatriation of bodies—isn't that bizarre, that you have to repatriate a body?—anyway, they were holding that up for a few months in cases like Patsy MacLaren's, cases where there had been disease, because they didn't want to risk causing a cholera outbreak here. So—"

"Did they repatriate the body at all?" Gregor asked. "Did they bury her in India?"

"Just relax, will you?" John Jackman said. "They buried the body there. They had to, I think. Refrigeration was expensive."

"Patsy MacLaren was rich."

"Patsy MacLaren was only sort of rich," John Jackman corrected Gregor. "Anyway, the person I think was Karla Parrish went off and got all the forms to fill out for the United States Embassy and all those people, reporting the death of an American citizen abroad, and she made a bunch of arrangements with the funeral parlors and the caretaker of a Christian cemetery and that kind of thing. And then she gave them all to Julianne Corbett."

"And then?"

"And then they had the funeral, a very small funeral with

just the two of them in attendance, and the person I think was Karla Parrish left for Africa."

"Did you talk to the person who conducted the funeral?"

"No," John said, "but I talked to the priest who's taken his place since and he went through his files and found me what I needed. He even faxed a copy of the death certificate and the paperwork they keep on Catholic burials. Somebody named Patricia MacLaren was definitely buried in a Catholic cemetery in New Delhi in that year."

"What about the consulate and the embassy and all those people?"

John Jackman smiled. "Well, there, Gregor, you've got a few problems. Remember all those papers I was telling you about? The ones Karla Parrish got?"

"I remember."

"Well, Gregor, not one of them was ever filed. Not one. There isn't any record in the embassy in New Delhi at all of there ever having been a Patsy MacLaren in India, never mind a Patsy MacLaren who *died* in India. Of course, the embassy doesn't always know all the Americans who are on hand in a foreign country."

"This isn't the Soviet Union," Gregor said mildly. "And in the event of it, even the Soviet Union seems not to have been the Soviet Union."

"But they do usually get record of a death. I thought I was really onto something, but the woman I talked to at the embassy shrugged the whole thing off. She said it wasn't unusual for deaths not to be formally reported to them, especially when the American in question was being buried abroad. And she pointed out that we were dealing with a bunch of wet-behind-the-ears college girls here. They might have thought they had reported the death to the embassy at the time that they inquired about shipping the body back to the States. If you see what I mean."

"I see what you mean. Patsy MacLaren was buried and nobody notified anybody back here."

"That's it."

"Karla Parrish went to Africa."

"If that's who that was, yes. If Karla Parrish ever wakes up, we can ask her."

"What happened to Julianne Corbett?"

"She came back to the States. She took another Pan Am flight. She went back to Bethlehem and stayed with her family for a while, but it didn't work out. It seldom does when a working-class girl like that has been off at a place like Vassar. She applied to graduate programs at Penn and came up to Philadelphia to enter one."

"And at the same time, Patsy MacLaren—who was supposed to be dead but who wasn't dead—Patsy MacLaren was also taking courses toward a degree at the University of Pennsylvania."

"No," John Jackman said.

Gregor raised his eyebrows. "No?"

"We checked all that with the university," John Jackman said. "The woman who ever afterward called herself Patsy MacLaren did tell people that she was in a graduate program at Penn at the time she met her husband. She certainly told her trust officers that. For all I know, she told Stephen Willis that. But she was never really registered."

"The money for her tuition was paid directly out of the trust to her?" Gregor asked.

"According to the lawyer, it was paid directly to the university when they submitted a tuition bill, but I checked that out, Gregor. That was easy. All whoever this was had to do was wait till the end of the first week of classes, formally withdraw, and pick up the money at the cashier's office. No questions asked."

"Which is what Patsy MacLaren did."

"That's right."

"Do you know what she did with the money?"

"No," John Jackman said. "I don't."

"Do you know what she did with herself?"

"No."

"Do you know where she might have lived?"

"I don't think she lived anywhere, Gregor. I don't think she existed except for the purpose of getting money out of that trust fund. It's too bad she wasn't just a little richer than she was."

"Why?"

"Because with really big estates, trusteeships are a personal thing. Trustees know the people they're handling the money for. I sent a guy over to that bank; there wasn't a person in it who had ever met Patsy MacLaren, dead or alive, ever. There were a couple of people who knew her father. That was it."

"Is there any money left?"

"No," John Jackman said. "There was never all that much money, just enough to get Patsy through college and graduate school and a couple of years of hacking around. She spent it and the bank stopped worrying about her."

"So the money Patsy MacLaren took out of her checking account on the day she blew up her car wasn't money from her trust fund," Gregor Demarkian said.

"It was Stephen Willis's money," John Jackman said emphatically. "I've got the paper on that stuff too, if you want to look at it. As far as I can tell, Patsy MacLaren had been bleeding her husband dry for years."

"And doing what with the money?" Gregor asked.

"I don't know that either," John Jackman said. "Spending it, I suppose. Maybe she's got it with her now, wherever she is. Maybe that was the whole point. Marry the man, bleed him dry, kill him, and take off. Shazam."

Gregor looked skeptical. "Most people don't wait twenty-five years before they kill him and take off. She must have decided it was worth it to stay married to him at least part of that time."

"I know. Why did she marry him at all? This can't be the

real Patsy MacLaren, can it? Somebody did die of dysentery in India."

"Somebody definitely did die," Gregor said. "No, no. You have to assume the obvious here. The point of keeping a fictional Patsy MacLaren alive, at least at that point, had to be to drain the rest of what was in her trust fund. The interesting point here is that this fictional Patsy MacLaren stayed alive. For twenty-odd years."

"Over twenty-five," John Jackman said.

"The question becomes, why be Patsy MacLaren at all, when you're married to Stephen Willis? Why not marry Stephen Willis as *yourself*? Why the deception?"

"Maybe we're talking about bigamy here. Maybe this lady was married to somebody else. Maybe she had a husband or a boyfriend who beat her up, and she was looking for a new identity and she got one. Just like that."

"No," Gregor Demarkian said.

John Jackman raised his eyebrows. Linda Melajian had come back to the table with a tray full of plates and cups and knives and forks and spoons and the full pot of coffee too. She set the crockery and stainless steel dinnerware out on the table, bustling a little too much around John Jackman as she did it.

"Gregor's going to have one of his awful cholesterol specials," Linda said to John. "Do you want something actually healthy? Fruit? Oat bran? I've got really wonderful whole wheat muffins."

"Pancakes," John Jackman said. "With butter and syrup and a side of breakfast sausage."

"Try the hash browns," Gregor said. "Linda's mother makes wonderful hash browns."

"Hash browns," John Jackman said. "That sounds wonderful. Get me some of those."

Linda Melajian poured them both cups of coffee and left, looking disgusted. John Jackman poured a stream of half-and-half into his and then doused it with sugar. This was one of the things he had in common with Bennis. Bennis liked a lot of sugar in her coffee too. It was really too bad that the two of them didn't get along better than they did, Gregor thought. It was really too bad that circumstances so often intervened between people in real life.

Gregor cleared his throat. "So," he said. "We've got work to do today. I want to go to the hospital."

"I know you do. So do I. I go to the hospital every day."

"I want to check a few more records."

"Check away. My people are already ready to kill you over what we've checked so far, Gregor. I lost a secretary over one of those printouts. She was threatening to go to work for one of those companies that's just had an oil spill."

"These are simpler records," Gregor promised. "You've got to remember: You don't, at this point, have to prove that Patsy MacLaren murdered Stephen Willis. You already know that."

"I know. If we couldn't get that one through court, we'd be even more incompetent than the mystery books make us out to be."

"What you don't realize is, you don't even have to prove who set those bombs. Although the bombs are an interesting point. They're the key to this whole thing. Why bother with the bombs?"

"I don't think I want to work through these puzzles anymore, Gregor. I just want to get on with it. Can you get on with it?"

"Sure. Make sure you've got a guard at Karla Parrish's room at all times for the foreseeable future, all right?"

"She's unconscious, Gregor."

"She could wake up at any time. It might be a good idea if you got somebody in there who looks like a nurse but isn't one. It might be a good idea if that person was on the job when we went in there this morning to visit. If you see what I mean."

"You're sure it's necessary?"

"No," Gregor said, "but I think it *might* be necessary. Although I have to admit it, I can't see Patsy MacLaren blowing the hell out of a hospital room. That just doesn't fit."

"I don't see why," John Jackman said gloomily. "She's blown the hell out of everything else."

"Well," Gregor told him, "there are limits. Just try to remember what it is we're doing at the moment. We're not trying to prove Patsy MacLaren guilty of murder. You can do that later. What we have to do right now is to prove that Patsy MacLaren exists. Period."

"That she didn't die in India," John Jackman said wearily. "That they didn't bury her in a Catholic cemetery in New Delhi. That not one but dozens of people are lying to us, from a congresswoman to the staff of the Indian hospital to the Catholic priest at the cemetery—"

"No, no," Gregor said. "Relax, will you please? If we had to prove all that, we'd be doomed. Eat your breakfast and then come with me. I want to go out to Fox Run Hill for a moment. Can you arrange that with Dan Exter?"

"Sure."

"Then I want to go into the hospital and see Karla Parrish. I want to talk to Evan Walsh. Then I want to go across town and talk to Julianne Corbett. Really. We're going to have a very full day. Eat your breakfast."

Breakfast was there to eat. Linda Melajian had arrived with it on her arm, the plates marching from wrist to shoulder like the discs of a Vegas warm-up artist's balancing act.

"Here we go," she said, putting the plates down in front of them. "Are you sure you want to eat this stuff? He looks sick already."

"He'll be fine," Gregor Demarkian said.

Then the door to the Ararat opened, and Gregor Demarkian was not so sure. Standing there, in one of those spaghetti-strap sundresses with the contrasting T-shirt underneath, was Bennis Hannaford, looking about as good as Bennis Hannaford

ever looked, which was like a combination of the young Gene
Tierney and the young Vivien Leigh. John Jackman saw her and
blushed. Bennis Hannaford saw John Jackman and turned away,
as if he didn't exist. She went to a table on the other side of the
dining room and sat down next to the wall. Then she picked up
a menu and studied it, as if she didn't already have it memo-
rized. Linda Melajian shook her head.

"Bennis still isn't talking to Mr. Jackman, I take it," she
said. "Well, I'd better go over and find out what she wants.
Ever since all this wedding stuff started with Donna, Bennis
has not generally been in a good mood."

Bennis's broken arm was sticking out from the side of her
body like a maypole with a tilt. It was held up by this con-
traption of tape and stretchy bandage that looked about as
comfortable as a pair of porcupine-skin underwear. Maybe
she would be in a better mood if she were allowed to wake
up with her arm healed, Gregor thought. He also thought he
might be wrong. Bennis was Bennis. Bennis was a law unto
herself.

"You know," John Jackman said. "I think I'm with Tibor
and all the rest of them. I think you should stop kidding yourself and just marry the woman. You're never going to find
anyone better."

Gregor was going to point out that he hadn't found
Bennis—Bennis wouldn't marry him if he asked her every
day for a month while getting down on bended knee—but
nobody ever listened to him about this anyway, so he decided
not to try.

He dug into his pile of scrambled eggs and closed his
eyes to blot out all signs of Donna's coming (or not coming)
wedding.

Then he thought about Patsy MacLaren.

# FOUR

## 1.

*I*T HAD BEEN ON MOLLY Bracken's mind for almost a week, and once she saw Evelyn Adder packing Henry's clothes into the tall garbage pails in the walled-in little utility area behind the brick Federalist, it didn't make any more sense to wait. It didn't make any sense to proceed either. Molly knew that. It wasn't a real crisis or an honest break in time. It was just the point beyond which she didn't want to go. The "papers" Joey had picked up from Sarah and Kevin Lockwood were sitting on the side table in the family room in Molly's big Victorian, right next to the photograph of Molly in her wedding dress in the silver Tiffany frame. All Molly could think about was the fact that she wasn't like these women, not at all. Her life did not depend on her husband's money. She wasn't stuck here, like Evelyn Adder. Except that Evelyn didn't look like she was stuck here. Maybe Evelyn didn't care if she had to leave. Whatever it was, Evelyn was outside, packing all of Henry's Ralph Lauren Polo and Armani down in among the table peelings, and she looked less heavy and ungainly and miserable than Molly had ever seen her.

"I tried calling them three times this morning," Molly had

told Joey before Joey had stomped out—presumably to go to work, but really, Molly thought, to go anywhere at all.

"Don't you know enough not to buy land unless you've actually seen it?" she had demanded of him.

He had gotten red in the face, as red as he ever got, and begun to throw pro-life pamphlets at her from the stack she had left on top of the refrigerator.

"You think you know everything," he yelled. "You think just because your father has built a few houses, you're the greatest real estate expert since, since—I don't know who. You think you picked it all up in your sleep."

"I didn't have to pick it up in my sleep," Molly said. "It's something they tell you about on public service programs on Sunday morning on PBS. For God's sake."

"It was supposed to be a birthday present," Joey shouted. "It was supposed to be a surprise. For you."

As if that was supposed to change things. Molly wanted to throw a dish at him, or even the heavy plastic-coated metal dish rack next to the sink. She wanted to scream.

"They're gone," she said instead. "There isn't a car in their driveway. They've disappeared in the middle of the night with your cashier's check and probably not only yours either."

"They'll be back," Joey said confidently. "They own that house. They own all that stuff."

"The house is mortgaged to the hilt. The stuff was probably bought on credit cards. They don't own *anything*, Joey. They're just as fly-by-night as any wino down in central Philadelphia."

"I know what happened to Stephen Willis," Joey said. "Patsy just couldn't stand it anymore. That's what happened to him. He was just like you."

Joey hadn't even known Stephen Willis. Stephen Willis wasn't home enough for anyone at Fox Run Hill to know him really well. And Patsy was Patsy.

Joey slammed out of the house. Molly listened to the sound of his car starting up in the drive. When she heard the car roll off the drive onto the street, she went to the back and began to look out at Evelyn Adder, lumbering away among the garbage cans. The day was starting out nasty. The sky was dark and full of clouds. The air was full of a rain that wouldn't quite start to fall. The joggers on the winding road had plastic jackets on over their T-shirts in spite of the fact that it must be hot.

Nylon, Molly thought absently. Those jackets are nylon, not plastic. I shouldn't be so stupid.

She was wearing jeans and a T-shirt herself. The T-shirt was a funny kind of blue called pool and had cost twenty-four dollars from the J. Crew catalogue. Molly went out to her mudroom, slipped on a pair of flip-flops in the same color, and went out through the garage and around to the back.

"Evelyn?" she said. "Evelyn, what are you doing?"

Evelyn looked up from her work around the garbage cans. Molly had never noticed it before, but Evelyn had a really striking face. It wasn't pretty, the way fat women's faces were supposed to be pretty. It was *unusual*. And her eyes were a very dark and metallic green.

"I," Evelyn said, "am trying to see how far I can make him go."

"You mean Henry," Molly said.

"That's right. I want to see what I'd have to do to make him leave me."

"Well, this should do it," Molly said. "I'd be furious if Joey did something like this."

"But Joey wouldn't do something like this. Joey doesn't have any money. I don't have any money," Evelyn said. "That's always been the point. Henry has the diet books."

"Diet books sell very well," Molly said. "I see them whenever I go into the bookstore. They sell very, very well."

"I know," Evelyn said. "But I'm beginning to think they don't sell well enough. I came from a steel town, you know."

"No," Molly said.

Evelyn looked up into the clouds. "This was the point of it

all, in the town I came from. Getting married. Getting a house. The boys I knew always talked about winning the lottery, but the girls I knew always talked about getting married. Meeting a rich boy. Moving out onto the Main Line. Henry wasn't rich when I met him, but I thought he was. He was my professor."

"Professors don't make any money," Molly said. "My father says so."

"Next to steel workers these days, they make a lot of money." Evelyn was matter-of-fact. "I couldn't go home now. Henry knows that. I've been thinking I'd move down to College Station."

"You mean you want to live next to Penn State? Why?"

"I thought I'd get another degree. In something practical. Of course, I'd have to lose the weight too. There's that. I'd have to join one of those diet programs or something. People don't like the idea of hiring women like me, and eventually I would have to get hired."

"I think you ought to take Henry to divorce court and really rip him apart," Molly said virtuously. "That's the least you should get out of being married to a man."

"I'd probably have to lose weight for that too," Evelyn said. "I can just see Henry and the judge right now. 'Just look at her, your honor. It was all her fault.'"

Molly cocked her head. "Were you always like this? Fat, I mean. Is it something hereditary?"

"I was skinny as a rail the day Henry and I got married. It was Henry who was fat."

"Then what happened? Did you just eat and eat? Were you hungry?"

"I have no idea if I was hungry. I'm not hungry now. The funny thing is, I haven't been hungry for a couple of days. Henry bought some land from Sarah and Kevin Lockwood."

"He did?" Molly straightened up.

"I've been trying to decide ever since he did it if the land is real and awful or if it just doesn't exist at all. I tend to think it's real and awful. That at least gives them a leg to stand on in case there are lawsuits, which there probably will be. Henry likes lawsuits. They give him something to occupy his time."

"Joey bought land from Sarah and Kevin Lockwood," Molly said. "I just found out about it this morning. He didn't even look at it. I take it Henry didn't look at it either."

"No, he didn't. I'm surprised about your Joey though. Isn't your family in real estate?"

"He didn't consult anyone. She really was a Main Line debutante, you know. Her family really is some kind of high society. She has cousins and things that are in the papers all the time."

"A lot of people are high society who don't have any money," Evelyn said. "I didn't know that before I went to college, but I do now. It's breeding that's supposed to matter to those people, whatever that means. I think it's like high school."

"It is? What is? College?"

"High society. I think it's like the clubs we had when I was in high school. The only point of them was to keep some people out. Like this place. Like Fox Run Hill."

"Well, of course we want to keep some people out of here," Molly said. "The muggers, for instance. And the rapists. All that street crime in Philadelphia."

"The clubs wanted to keep out the dorks and the nerds and the dogs," Evelyn said, "but that wasn't what it was really about. I mean, those people were out anyway. It was the borderline cases who mattered."

"I don't understand what you mean."

"I went to a meeting of the country club membership committee once where they were talking about this couple. She was a schoolteacher and he was at some community college, they had enough money to live here because they were careful with it, and it was like listening to the talk in the girls' bathroom when I was seventeen. Did you see her shoes? Artificial uppers. So tacky. And we're all—what? Forty-eight?"

"I'm twenty-eight," Molly said.

"Whatever." Evelyn raised a hand in the air. "It all goes together. Fox Run Hill. Getting married. It's all *positioning*. That's all it is."

"That doesn't sound very romantic."

Evelyn put the last lid back on the last garbage can and wiped her palms against the matte brown surface of her skirt. Her skirt looked like burlap, Molly thought. Where did fat women get clothes that looked like that? The fourth finger on her left hand was blank. Molly wondered if she had done that recently, on purpose, or if she had just had the ring taken off when she grew too fat to wear it.

"I'm not very romantic," Evelyn said. "The only reason I can't imagine myself doing what Patsy Willis did is that I can't imagine myself going through all that trouble afterward. If I had done what she'd done, I think I would have just stayed there in the house and let whatever came for me come."

"I think she must have been so angry, she could hardly stand it," Molly said. "I think she must have been blind with rage. How else would you do something like that?"

"I don't think people who are blind with rage buy silencers," Evelyn said. "That is what it is she was supposed to have done."

Molly went over to the edge of the utility area and leaned across the wall. She could just see the mock-Tudor house from there. It seemed to rise up out of the mist like a ghost mansion. The windows were dark and blank. All the other houses on this street were lit against the advent of the gathering storm.

"You know what I've been thinking? I've been thinking that I'd love to get into Patsy's house. I'd love to get in there and look around. Maybe I'd find something."

"What? You've been in there a dozen times. We all have. Fake beams. Too much furniture."

"Maybe there'd be an aura left over," Molly said. "Maybe we'd go in there and Stephen's ghost would come out and try to tell us something. It wouldn't hurt to try. You could come with me."

"To see Stephen's ghost?"

"To see whatever there is to see," Molly said.

Evelyn stopped fussing with the garbage cans and came to stand next to the wall too.

"Your timing is off," she said.

Molly looked at the driveway. A car had pulled to a stop in it. Now another car was coming up behind. As she watched, three tall men got out and began to stretch their legs.

"The police," Molly said with distaste. "What are they doing here?"

Evelyn Adder laughed. "Molly," she said. "At the moment, I think they're probably the only ones around with any right to be here."

## 2.

It was very difficult to do everything the way it was supposed to be done. Evan Walsh had known that as a general principle for years, but it applied with even more force to working with Karla Parrish, and especially to working with Karla Parrish now. By Evan's estimation, they had managed to keep up this deception that Karla was still in a coma for a little over fourteen hours. He didn't know how long they were going to be able to continue keeping it up. For one thing, Karla wasn't that good an actress. For another, she had to act harder and harder all the time, because the longer she stayed conscious, the more conscious she seemed to be. Then there was the little matter of food, which was what they were working on now. Karla had been fed through tubes the entire time she was out. The tubes were still in her arms, pumping glucose or whatever it was directly into her bloodstream. This did not seem to make any difference to the fact that she was very hungry, and that what she was hungry for was French fries.

"McDonald's French fries," she had told him first thing that morning, as soon as they had managed to get rid of the nurse. "Just like in Paris."

It was true. The only thing Karla had wanted to eat in Paris was McDonald's French fries. Evan would make reservations at fancy restaurants, even at the Brasserie Lipp, and Karla would pick at her food until she could get McDonald's French fries. If they had had McDonald's restaurants in war zones, Karla might never have come out to visit civilization. Still, Evan thought, it couldn't be right to feed her McDonald's French fries when she had just come out of a coma. He wished he knew more about comas. He wished he had spent the last few days at the library, reading up on comas, instead of sitting here doing—what? Worrying?

"McDonald's isn't even making French fries this early in the morning," Evan told her. "They don't start making lunch until eleven o'clock. Would you want one of those hash brown potato things?"

"No," Karla had said. "God no. French fries."

"Okay. But—"

"I know," Karla had said. "I'll wait. Do me another favor. Go out and get me some papers."

"And leave you alone?"

"Well, Evan, you can't very well run errands for me if you aren't willing to leave me alone."

"I know," Evan said. "But you were the one who said you were worried about, you know, a recurrence of what happened—"

"If anybody knew I was awake. Yes, Evan, I know. But nobody does know I'm awake. Except you. Unless you told somebody."

"Me? No. Of course I didn't tell anybody."

"Good. Then go out and get me the papers and come back with them and then do something about the French fries. God, but I'm hungry. I don't think I've ever been this hungry. Have you ever been to Morocco?"

"No," Evan said.

"I think that's where we're going to go when we get out of here," Karla said. "It's the only place in the world where they've got something I like as much as McDonald's French fries. You can go to these little places in the old city of Tangier and eat appetizers for hours. And drink wine. You don't know what I would give right now for an enormous bottle of wine."

"You don't drink," Evan said. "I've never seen you drink."

"You're right. I don't drink. But something like this calls for it. Do you know that I've been in six civil wars and never been hurt once?"

"Is it six?" Evan asked.

"And here I am, back in Philadelphia, and what happens? And all because of Patsy MacLaren, for God's sake. I think she's crazy, Evan."

"Who?" Evan said.

Karla lay down flat in the bed and closed her eyes. "I think I'm going to pretend to go to sleep now. I might even sleep. Go get me the papers."

"If you really do go to sleep and something startles you, you're going to get found out," Evan said.

But Karla was asleep again, already. It was one of the ways Evan could tell that she was still in very bad shape. One minute she would be sitting up, bright-eyed and energetic. The next minute her eyes would be closed and she would be out, just gone, lost to the world. There were big dark circles under her eyes too, and her skin was too white. Evan thought that as soon as she ate those French fries, she was going to heave them right back up again, but he also thought it was useless to argue with a woman who could fall fast asleep in the middle of your peroration.

Now it was eleven o'clock, hours later, and Evan was back. He had the *Philadelphia Inquirer* and the Philadelphia *Star* and all three New York papers spread out across the foot of Karla's bed. He had the door to Karla's room firmly shut, but not locked, because there was no way to lock the room doors on this floor from the inside. This was, after all, supposed to be an adjunct to the intensive care unit. Karla was sitting up in bed, sucking on long strands of French fries as she went through one paper after the other. Evan had gotten the French fries by pleading with a motherly-looking woman who served as day manager for the McDonald's in Liberty Square. He had had to give Karla an imaginary baby that he was the imaginary father of, but he had done what he set out to do, and that was the main thing. That, Evan Walsh thought, was the entire point of his life.

Outside, the promise of a storm had turned into a real one, thunder and lightning, wind and darkness. The hospital room was air-conditioned, so the window was shut, but the shade was up. It could have been the middle of the night out there. Evan wouldn't have believed that there were so many trees in the middle of Philadelphia. He'd never noticed them until they started blowing around like that.

Karla paged past a full-page department store ad featuring a bride in the world's most elaborate bridal train and settled on the continuance of a story she had started to read on page one.

"None of these is saying anything," she said. "There isn't any real news at all. I wish I'd been able to talk to Liza before she died."

Evan hadn't wanted to tell Karla about Liza. He had thought the news might traumatize her. That would be all he needed. Karla back in her coma. Karla sick unto death. Everything his fault. He had no idea if bad news could put a coma patient back into a coma. He had no idea it would be so hard to keep things from Karla. He hadn't realized how it would be with the nurses either. They talked a convincing line about how any coma patient might actually be conscious under the veil of unconsciousness, but they said things in the sickroom as if they were dealing with a deaf-mute. Karla seemed to have heard all about Liza Verity before she ever woke up.

"Is the television news any better?" she asked now. "This stuff is really awful. Nobody is saying anything about anything."

"I think that's deliberate," Evan told her. "I think the police don't want the public to know exactly what's going on. Because it might jeopardize their case, you know."

"You watch much too much American television. What about this Gregor Demarkian person? You met him."

"Oh, yes."

"And? What was he like? If you got him over here and I talked to him, would he insist on telling everybody on earth that I was awake?"

"Karla, I think you should tell everybody on earth that you're awake. You're not going to be able to keep this up much longer. You have to realize that. Every time a nurse comes in here and you play dead, I cringe. You're not any good at it."

"Every time a nurse comes in here and I've got my eyes closed, all I want to do is laugh." Karla sighed. "I wish these papers were more informative. I wish I knew what to do."

"Fess up," Evan said.

"I wish Liza were still around to talk to. Do you know, I was thinking about it. If I'd known Liza was available and I had gotten in touch with her before the reception, then the reception would never have happened, and—"

"Shh," Evan said.

Karla got immediately quiet. They could both hear sounds in the hallway, big booming voices, male and unmedical. Karla pushed the papers off the bed and lay down again. The little white bag of McDonald's French fries landed on the pillow next to her chin and she shoved it into the air in the direction of Evan, anything at all in order to get rid of it. Evan grabbed the bag of French fries and stuffed it into the pocket of his jacket. Then he bent over and started taking sections of newspapers off the floor.

By the time the door opened, seconds later, Karla Parrish was completely still. Evan tried to see signs of incipient laughter in her face, but he couldn't. She was made of stone. One of the nurses he knew well, a very young Latino girl named Carmencita Gonzalez, ushered Mr. John Jackman and Mr. Gregor Demarkian into the room.

"Hello, Evan," Carmencita said. "There, you see it," she told the two other men. "Just the way she's been for days now. As far as I know, her vital signs are good, and that tells us nothing at all. Unless Evan has seen something the staff of the hospital hasn't."

"Me?" Evan said. "No. I wouldn't know what to look for."

"Speech would be a good sign," Carmencita said.

Gregor Demarkian walked over to the bed and looked into Karla's face. Evan shifted nervously back and forth on the balls of his feet. Demarkian was supposed to be a great detective. Surely, at this close range, he would be able to tell that Karla was faking.

He wasn't able to tell. He backed away from the bed. Evan tried hard not to be too obvious about heaving a great big sigh of relief.

"I know I should know better," Gregor Demarkian said, "but I'm always looking for the Gordian knot solution."

"What's a Gordian knot solution?" Evan asked.

"Alexander the Great," Gregor said. "He's supposed to have gotten to the gates of this city nobody had ever been able to conquer because they were held shut by a thick rope tied in a knot so intricate nobody had ever been able to untie it. So Alexander got out his sword and hacked the thing to shreds."

"Smart man," Evan said.

"He was a boy, really," Gregor Demarkian said. "He was only twenty-six on the day that he died."

"Forget Alexander the Great," John Jackman said. "What are we going to do now?"

"We're going to go visit Julianne Corbett," Gregor said. "That's all we can do. She's the only link left."

"Maybe we ought to do something about putting guards

around her," John Jackman said. "We don't want somebody blowing her to kingdom come and doing God only knows what to the image of law enforcement in the city of Philadelphia."

"Well, we at least ought to go see her. Although I think she's told us all she really can, under the circumstances. It's worth one last try."

"And if it doesn't work? Then what?"

Karla's body shifted on the bed. Carmencita was instantly alert. She hurried to Karla's side and peered down into her face. Then she got out her tiny flashlight and started poking at Karla's eyes. Evan thought he was going to faint.

"That's interesting," Carmencita said.

"What?"

It was Gregor Demarkian who said "what," but Jackman got to the bedside before him. Evan backed away a little and winced. Karla wasn't perfectly still anymore. Something odd seemed to be happening to her chest. It was hitching and heaving at uncertain intervals, and the rest of her body seemed to shudder.

Carmencita leaned forward and hit the emergency light. "Get out of the way," she told Jackman and Demarkian. "This may be a seizure. I need room to work."

Seizure? Evan felt suddenly sick. It was his fault. Of course it was. He should never have gotten her those French fries.

At just that moment Karla's eyes flew open and she sat straight up in bed. She looked wild—and she definitely looked green—but she didn't look as if she was having a seizure.

"Oh, shit," she said in a perfectly clear voice.

Then she threw up all over Carmencita Gonzalez's bright white uniform.

# FIVE

## 1.

BY THE TIME GREGOR DEMARKIAN and John Jackman got downtown to Julianne Corbett's constituent office, the clouds were pasted across the sky as far as anybody could see, and they were dead black. The rain was thick and hot and heavy in the air. The lightning was random and sharp and the thunder was loud and deep and much too close. Gregor could remember only one other storm in his life that was anything like this, and that had been a full-scale hurricane, lashing at an island he hadn't wanted to be on in the first place. Somehow, in spite of the fact that there was nothing for the wind to blow against here but solid brick, this was worse. The taller buildings all looked blank and uninhabited, like the buildings on the eastern side of the old Berlin Wall. The few places where there were lights looked just plain wrong. This was a relatively old section of the city, although not old as the one around Independence Hall. The buildings here had metal fire escapes fastened into the backs of them and windows that opened so that people could get some air or jump. The cars parked against the curbs were either old or oddly tentative, as if they wished they were someplace else. Gregor saw at least six of those metal steering-wheel clamps, the suburbanites' vehicular protection against the big city. Gregor had no idea if it worked.

John Jackman got a couple of umbrellas out of the trunk of his car and handed one to Gregor. By the time he had gone through all the motions, he was already soaking wet.

"God only knows what these are going to do," he said. "The office is only over there."

Gregor looked "over there." The big plate-glass revolving doors were still and dark. On the floors above the street, almost all the windows were lit up. People were working.

"Does she know we're coming?" he asked.

"I called her up and told her this morning, just the way you told me to. Are you sure you know what you're doing?"

"Of course I know what I'm doing," Gregor said.

The street was empty of traffic and very wet. Gregor strode across it, jaywalking and not caring if he did, and went in through the revolving doors. John Jackman followed him and went to stand by the elevators. Gregor stood next to the small newsstand and looked at the magazines. Whoever was supposed to man the newsstand was missing. He and Jackman were the only people in the lobby. The magazines looked damp and wilted in spite of the fact that they had been safely out of the rain. The one *Bride's* magazine looked positively grim.

"It must be something psychological," Gregor said. "Every picture of every bride I see lately looks grim."

"Let's go," John Jackman said. "Here's the elevator."

Gregor made himself stop wondering what was going wrong with this poor bride's marriage—she wasn't even a real bride, for God's sake, she was just a model—and went to join John in the elevator. John pushed the button for Julianne Corbett's floor and looked up at the ceiling.

"You're sure you know what you're doing?" John Jackman said again. "You haven't lost it all somewhere along the line? You aren't about to get me in some kind of trouble I won't be able to get out of?"

"I'm taking the next logical step. We have to find Patsy MacLaren."

"Who doesn't exist."

"We have to find her anyway. And the best place to start is with the last person who saw her alive."

"Which Patsy MacLaren are we talking about here?"

"There's only one," Gregor Demarkian said.

The elevator opened at Julianne Corbett's floor. The hallway felt too cold and too wet. The carpet under Gregor's feet seemed to squeak when he moved, the way cheap carpets do when they've been saturated. John Jackman had his umbrella tucked under his arm, the way British bankers did in Walt Disney movies.

The hall smelled as if someone had just walked a very hairy and very wet dog through it. Gregor got to Julianne Corbett's door and went in without knocking. Tiffany Shattuck sat at her desk, reading another bridal magazine, chewing gum. Gregor was willing to bet anything that Tiffany did not chew gum when Julianne Corbett could see her.

John Jackman came into the office waiting room and closed the door behind him. Gregor cleared his throat. Tiffany Shattuck looked up and dropped the magazine.

"Oh," she said, pushing the gum around in her mouth and trying to pretend it wasn't there. "Mr. Demarkian. Ms. Corbett said you were coming."

"I believe we have some kind of an appointment," Gregor said politely.

Tiffany turned her back to them and made heaving motions that indicated she was getting rid of the gum. Her bridal magazine was open on the desk, to an article on the perfect champagne toast. Did people really read articles like that? Gregor wondered. He supposed they must. The magazines were everywhere. They seemed to be successful. Tiffany turned back to them and smiled, her gum gone.

"I'll go right in and tell her you're here," she said.

Tiffany could have announced them on the intercom. Gregor didn't say so. Instead, he pointed to the bridal magazine.

"Are you getting married?" he asked.

Tiffany looked confused. "You mean now? Am I getting married now? I mean, I'm not engaged to anybody at the moment or anything, but I hope to be someday. If I meet somebody. If you know what I mean."

"Of course," Gregor said.

Tiffany looked down at the bridal magazine. "I just like these magazines," she said. "They're always beautiful. And there's never anything in them to get you upset. If you know what I mean."

"No," Gregor said.

"Well," Tiffany said seriously. "You know. About poverty. And violence. That kind of thing. And AIDS. Even the fashion magazines talk about poverty and violence and AIDS these days. But the bridal magazines don't."

"Oh," Gregor said.

"I'll just go get Ms. Corbett," Tiffany said. "I'm sure she wouldn't want you to be kept waiting. She told me to tell her as soon as you got in. She's very concerned about what's happening to Ms. Parrish."

Tiffany Shattuck hurried off. Gregor began to pace back and forth across the waiting room. There were posters on the walls now that hadn't been there a couple of days earlier. Somebody, probably Tiffany Shattuck, was making an effort to make this place look permanent.

"What was all that talk about the bridal magazines?" John Jackman asked. "Don't tell me your Patsy MacLaren is getting married again."

"No, of course not," Gregor said. "It wasn't anything. Donna Moradanyan is getting married. Marriage is on my mind these days."

"I think if you told me that Patsy MacLaren was off someplace getting married right this minute, I'd go out and shoot myself," John Jackman said. "I like it better when I know what you're up to."

Tiffany Shattuck came back through the inner door and walked up to the open reception window, smiling.

"Ms. Corbett says you're to come right in," she told them. "She's all ready for you. Just step around that statue thing that's in the way. I haven't had a chance to move it yet."

The "statue thing" was a plaster copy of Justice, blind and with scales, almost half as tall as Gregor was. Gregor wondered where it was supposed to go. He also wondered who was supposed to move it. Tiffany didn't look strong enough. John Jackman stuck out a toe and kicked the thing, as if it were personally responsible for the mess the current criminal justice system was in.

Julianne Corbett was seated behind her big desk, papers spread out on the green felt blotter, pens and pencils strewn across the polished wood surface. When she saw them come in, she smiled, stood, and held out her hand.

"Mr. Demarkian," she said. "Mr. Jackman. Come and sit down."

"I'll get some coffee," Tiffany Shattuck said, dashing out again.

Julianne Corbett retracted her hand and reclaimed her seat. Gregor sat down in the larger of the two armchairs that faced the desk. John Jackman remained standing, looking uncertain of what he was supposed to do next.

"Well," Julianne Corbett said, trying on a great big smile again. "I hope you're bringing me good news. I hope Karla's condition is at least somewhat improved."

"Actually," Gregor Demarkian said, "I came to tell you that I finally know where Patsy MacLaren is."

"I know where Patsy MacLaren is," Julianne Corbett said, "because I put her there. She's in a grave in New Delhi."

"Yes, I know she is," Gregor said gently. "But just a week or so ago she killed her husband, and a little time after that she killed a harmless woman who cared too much about animals, and a little after that she killed an ICU specialist nurse named Liza Verity. For somebody who's buried in New Delhi, she's been very active."

Julianne Corbett's expression didn't change. "You don't know she killed Liza Verity. You don't know she set the pipe bomb off at my reception. You're just guessing because what happened did involve pipe bombs. Any number of people could know how to make a pipe bomb."

"That's true," Gregor said. "Any number of people do. What's more important, however, is that I know who was married to Stephen Willis."

"You mean the woman who was calling herself Patsy MacLaren," Julianne Corbett said. "That's not the same thing. Unless she really was called Patsy MacLaren but she wasn't the same Patsy MacLaren. My Patsy MacLaren is dead and buried and has been for longer than I care to remember."

"I know who was married to Stephen Willis," Gregor Demarkian repeated. "Do you want to know who that was?"

"All right," Julianne Corbett said. "Who was it?"

"You."

## 2.

Later, Gregor thought about how odd it was. He must have been in this situation a thousand times. He must have seen every different kind of person there was to see in the position Julianne Corbett was in now. It turned out not to matter much if he was dealing with a two-bit drifter or a United States congresswoman. There were only three or four ways for a perpetrator to react. They could run. They could fight. They could lie. Or they could just shut up.

"Remember," the old man who had trained him at Quantico had said. "They all think alike, no matter how much money they've managed to make. They all act alike. If they didn't, they wouldn't be perpetrators."

Behind the green felt blotter, Julianne Corbett had gone very still. The skin of her face under her makeup had gone dead white. The pallor made it suddenly obvious just how thick that makeup was. There had been picture after picture of Patsy MacLaren Willis in the Philadelphia papers, but nobody had connected any of them to Julianne Corbett— because they couldn't. There was no way to see under all that foundation and mascara and blusher. There was no way to tell what her eyes were like under the weight of those five pairs of false eyelashes. Gregor suddenly wondered how she could wear the stuff without scratching at it all day.

Gregor reached into his jacket and brought out a little stack of clipped photographs. He had gone at the Vassar College yearbooks with a pair of scissors for hours the night before. He put one photograph on the desk and tapped it with his index finger.

"This," he said, "is the real Patsy MacLaren. She was five feet eight inches tall. She had very red hair, very blue eyes, and very white skin. She also had freckles."

"I remember Patsy MacLaren," Julianne put in harshly. "I knew her for years. I buried her. I told you."

"Oh, yes," Gregor said. "You quite definitely buried her. In New Delhi. In 1969. I checked." He put another photograph down on the desk. "This is the Patsy MacLaren who murdered her husband a couple of weeks ago. The matron of Fox Run Hill. She was five feet four inches tall. She had slightly olive skin. She was on the sturdy and stocky side."

"I don't see why that has anything to do with me," Julianne Corbett said. "That doesn't look anything at all like me."

"It doesn't look anything at all like you look now," Gregor conceded, "but nothing looks like you now. You wear too much makeup."

"I've always worn this makeup. You can check. I wore it in graduate school. I wore it when I worked in state government." Julianne waved her hands at the newspaper photograph of Patsy MacLaren Willis. "I've never in my life gone around looking like that."

"You did at Vassar," Gregor said. He went through his photographs again and came out with one that was longer and taller than the others. It was the photograph of six girls standing in a too-formal, too-impersonal-looking living room, the common room for a dormitory somewhere. One of these girls was clearly the Patsy MacLaren of the first photograph. Her willowy delicacy was unmistakable. One of the others was what Gregor would have recognized anywhere as a younger version of Liza Verity. Liza Verity hadn't changed much in growing older except to get a little thicker and a little grayer. Karla Parrish hadn't changed at all. Gregor pointed at a fourth figure.

"There," he said, "is what Patsy MacLaren Willis looks like. That woman there."

"And you think that woman is me," Julianne Corbett said.

"I know that woman is you. I can check this picture against the official picture in the senior section of the yearbook, but I know it's you."

"You can't check it," Julianne said. "I didn't have a picture in the senior section of the yearbook. It cost money and I couldn't afford it."

"I'm surprised your friend Patsy MacLaren didn't offer to pay for one. From everything I've managed to dig up about her, it sounds like the kind of thing she would have done."

"It was the kind of thing she would have done," Julianne Corbett agreed. "But I wouldn't have let her. I wouldn't have let anybody. I wasn't built like that."

"All right."

Julianne Corbett shifted a little in her chair. "If you think you're going to make this one of your grand murder plots, give it up," she said. "I didn't kill Patsy MacLaren. I didn't even want Patsy MacLaren to die. She died of dysentery."

"I know."

"It was terrible, really." Julianne Corbett shook her head. "It was all Patsy's idea to go to India and Pakistan and places like that. I wanted to go to Europe. But Patsy had been to Europe. She thought it was too bourgeois. She wanted to seek enlightenment."

"Did she find it?" Gregor asked.

Julianne laughed. "She didn't find anything. Neither of us did. Practically the first thing that happened to us in Pakistan is that our packs got stolen, and Patsy had to wire home for money. Money for both of us, of course. I didn't have anyplace to get money. And it was all awful. Really awful. Everything was dirty and everyone was poor. And we had so little cash we kept eating from the stalls and the stalls weren't safe. Not for people like us. Not for people who had never been exposed to those kinds of germs."

"So Patsy got sick."

"We both got sick," Julianne corrected Gregor. "I got sicker."

"And Karla came to try to help out," Gregor said.

Julianne got up and walked to her office window. Rain was being blown in gusts against the glass.

"Karla was taking photographs," she said, "and she came to see us by a kind of prearrangement, except that instead of being in the hotel we were supposed to be in, we were at the hospital, and Patsy was dying. So Karla tried to do all the practical things. I'm usually very good at practical things, but I wasn't that time. I was sick."

"You didn't tell the embassy that Patsy had died."

Julianne turned away from the window. "Patsy MacLaren was a friend of mine," she said positively. "I didn't kill Patsy MacLaren."

"I never said you did."

"Then what did you say?"

"I said you became Patsy MacLaren," Gregor said gently. "Not all the time, not every minute of every day, but when you needed to. You called yourself Patsy MacLaren when you dealt with the trustees who handled Patsy's money, so that you could use that to put yourself through graduate school."

"I worked when I was in graduate school," Julianne Corbett said quickly. "I had two fellowships."

"I'm sure you did. It was probably a very good thing, because Patsy MacLaren didn't have all that much money, and what was being spent was the principal. You used the principal. And you used Patsy MacLaren's name when you started seeing Stephen Willis."

"But why would I? Why would I?"

"I don't know for certain," Gregor said, "but what I guess is, Stephen Willis was a kind of insurance policy. You were ambitious even then, but you weren't sure that you would be able to realize your ambitions. And you didn't want to go back to being what you had been before you went to Vassar. So you did what a lot of poor girls have done. You married a man on his way up."

"I could have done that under my own name," Julianne Corbett said. "I could just have married Stephen Willis and gone on being Julianne Corbett."

"I don't think it would have suited you. I don't think it would have given you enough latitude to do the things you wanted to do."

"I don't see how I could possibly have had any latitude, as you put it, at all," Julianne said. "Marriage is not usually a liberating institution, you know, Mr. Demarkian. Husbands tend to like to know where their wives are and what they're doing."

"Your husband was on the road," Gregor pointed out. "Stephen Willis traveled in great six-week blocks of time several times a year. In fact, he was away most of the time."

"And while he was away I was running around pretending to be myself," Julianne said.

"That, and siphoning off his money. It's expensive to get places in politics these days. It's expensive to get anyplace at all in any business at all. I think Stephen Willis's money came in very handy."

"And you think he just sat still for it."

"I think you were very good at hiding it, and would have gone on being very good at hiding it right up until the conditions of Stephen Willis's job changed. That's what had happened right before Stephen Willis died. He finally got something he was looking to get for a long time. He finally got assigned to a stationary job where he wouldn't have to travel. At that point you had to get rid of him. Practically everything you have now is dependent on nobody ever finding out that you have spent the last twenty-five years being two people."

"And so I killed him."

"That's right."

"And then I blew up a Volvo station wagon with a pipe bomb."

"That's right."

"Why?" Julianne Corbett demanded. "Why make all that fuss? Why call attention to myself?"

"But you weren't calling attention to yourself," Gregor said. "You were calling attention to Patsy MacLaren. And Patsy MacLaren was about to disappear. For good."

"But she didn't disappear for good," Julianne Corbett pointed out. "At least according to the papers, she's been all over everywhere, setting off pipe bombs, causing havoc. I'm disappointed, Mr. Demarkian. I'd think you'd know I was more intelligent than that. If I'd wanted to kill—who? That poor woman with her antifur slogan button?"

"Karla Parrish," Gregor said. "Also Liza Verity. The two people anywhere around who might be able to identify the photograph of Patsy MacLaren Willis for who it was. Karla Parrish was more of a danger to you than Liza Verity. You'd seen quite a bit of Liza Verity over the last few years. She was used to seeing you in a ton of makeup. She was used to thinking of you as a woman wearing a ton of makeup. That photograph of Patsy MacLaren Willis bothered her when she saw it, but she couldn't tell right away why. The last time Karla Parrish saw you, you didn't have a dab of foundation on your face. She knew who that photograph of Patsy MacLaren Willis reminded her of right off."

"And so I blew her up with a pipe bomb," Julianne said sarcastically. "I put the bomb under a table at a reception I was giving and just let it go off. I killed some woman I didn't even know. What I read in the papers was that Stephen Willis was killed with a gun. If I wanted to kill Karla Parrish, why didn't I just shoot her?"

"Because you couldn't get hold of a gun," Gregor said. "I think that if you'd realized what kind of trouble you were going to be in after the death of Stephen Willis, you would have kept the gun you had. Instead, you left it at the side of the bed where Stephen Willis died, wiped clean of prints. That way, nobody could trace it to you, nobody could see it on you, there was no way you could be caught trying to dispose of it. It was disposed of. The pipe bomb in the car made a big fuss that obscured the whole mess and made it look more mysterious than it necessarily was. And you were back in your office by midafternoon, with the last fifteen thousand dollars from Patsy MacLaren's bank account and your makeup in place. But you couldn't get another gun, Ms. Corbett. You're not just anybody anymore. You're a member of the United States Congress. It would have been much too risky."

Julianne Corbett walked away from the window and back to her desk. She sat down behind the green felt blotter and put the palms of her hands down flat against the wood on either side of it. Her skin color was back to something like normal again. At least, Gregor couldn't find any skin color under the mask of makeup. He couldn't find anything at all in Julianne Corbett's eyes.

"I think," she said, "that this is all extremely interesting. I think you could probably sell it as a novel. But I don't think I have to take it seriously."

"I have to take it seriously," John Jackman said, suddenly reminding them both of his presence. "Gregor, for Christ's sake. Have you got any proof of any of this?"

"Of course he hasn't," Julianne Corbett said. "He couldn't possibly have. All of this is nonsense."

"It sounds like nonsense," John Jackman said.

Gregor Demarkian was nodding his head slowly, slowly. Outside, the storm was growing stronger and nastier. The wind had begun to whistle and howl and rattle the windows. The sky was absolutely black.

"There are a number of ways to prove what I've been saying," Gregor said, "starting with a very simple trace of the amounts of money Patsy MacLaren Willis contributed to your political campaigns."

"We already know she contributed to my political campaigns," Julianne said coldly. "We knew that even before Karla got hurt in that blast."

"We could also look into the days and times when Stephen Willis was home from his traveling and correlate them with the days and times when you were unavailable for work or meetings."

"I'm always available for work and meetings," Julianne said. "I have to be. I don't know how it is you think people get into the position I'm in, Mr. Demarkian, but it isn't by taking out great whacking blocks of time to mollify phantom husbands."

"And then there's the trump card," Gregor said. "There's the simple fact that Karla Parrish is now very much awake and very eager to talk. And her friend Evan Walsh has a few things he wants to say too."

Gregor didn't know what he expected Julianne Corbett to do then, but it wasn't what she did do, which was essentially nothing. Everything in Gregor's body had gone tense, expecting trouble. Julianne Corbett not only gave no trouble, she seemed to resign from existence.

She sat behind her desk with her hands still flat against the wood, looking as if she had been turned to stone.

# EPILOGUE

## *Here Comes the Bride . . .*
## *There Goes the Neighborhood*

### 1.

VERY EARLY ON THE MORNING of Donna Moradanyan's wedding, Bennis Hannaford came up to Gregor Demarkian's apartment, dressed in six yards of lace, smoking a cigarette, and ready to kill somebody. She used her key to get in. Gregor was really only half out of bed, with his thick red terry-cloth robe wrapped around his thin navy blue cotton pajamas and his slippers lost somewhere he couldn't begin to guess. He was standing at the counter in the kitchen, trying to remember how to work the coffee machine. Bennis found him with a coffee filter in his hand, looking confused. She took it away from him and started to make coffee.

"He came in at twenty after ten last night," she said, dumping black stuff into the filter. Gregor hated the way coffee looked when it was being made. The grounds. The black swampy slime. He turned away and took a seat at the kitchen table.

"I take it you're talking about Peter," he said.

"Of course I'm talking about Peter." Bennis did something with water. It didn't look to Gregor like the same thing he did with water when he tried to run that machine. "Anyway, Donna's mother had gone home for the night or I don't think there would have been a problem because really, Gregor, I think she would just have killed him, but she was gone, and it was just me and Donna, and Donna was acting like Donna, so here we are."

"Where are we?" Gregor asked.

"What? Oh. I don't know. Peter is sleeping on my couch. I have to give Donna that much. And Russ doesn't know anything about this yet. But Tommy does. Tommy woke up last night."

"And?"

Bennis stopped fiddling with the coffee machine and gave a little smile of satisfaction.

"And," she said, "he didn't even know who Peter was. It's been that long. He didn't know who Peter was and he didn't like him much either. Which ought to have brought Donna to her senses if nothing else did."

"Did it?"

Bennis sat down at the table. "I don't know, Gregor. The best thing right now would be if Peter would just disappear, but I don't think he will. He's down there on my couch, sleeping away, and he wants to talk to Donna before the wedding. Which is bad news, Gregor, because I don't know what Donna will do."

"Donna is in love with Russ," Gregor said.

"Of course she is."

"And she's not in love with Peter," Gregor said. "In fact, the last I heard, she didn't even like Peter much."

"I know all that, Gregor."

"Well then," Gregor said. "I don't see what the problem is. Donna is in love with Russ. Donna is not in love with Peter. Donna will not jeopardize her marriage to Russ in order to accommodate Peter."

"Honestly." Bennis stood up to go look at the coffee machine. "I don't know how you got a reputation for being such a great detective. You don't know a thing about human nature."

## 2.

Bennis made coffee. Gregor drank it. Then Bennis went up-stairs to see what was going on in Donna Moradanyan's apartment, and Gregor sat at his kitchen table, thinking it through. Really, he thought, it was much easier to understand why people killed each other than to figure out why they did what they did for love. Or even sex. Gregor had settled the love and sex questions for himself by marrying Elizabeth and staying married to her. He had settled those same questions for himself since Elizabeth's death mostly by staying out of the game entirely. He much preferred working on the mo-tives of somebody like Julianne Corbett, who could at least be counted on to be logical.

Peter, Gregor assumed, was still downstairs in Bennis Hannaford's apartment. Gregor got out of his kitchen chair and went out onto the landing. Above him, he could hear Bennis and Donna and Donna's mother talking about lace and trains. The landing was strewn with silk flowers and satin rib-bons. Gregor didn't know if they were accidental overflow from the fourth floor or Donna's latest attempts at decora-tion. He went down the stairs to the second floor and stood in front of Bennis's door. He was going to knock, but it oc-curred to him that Bennis usually left her door unlocked, and there was no reason to let Peter Desarian know he was com-ing. He tried the doorknob and found that it turned. He pushed the door open and went inside.

Peter was in Bennis's living room, stretched out on Ben-nis's black leather couch, drinking coffee from a delicate china cup he had placed without a saucer on Bennis's glass-topped coffee table. The china cup was from the set Bennis never used, the one that had belonged to her mother. Getting moisture rings on the glass-topped coffee table was one of the few sins Bennis wouldn't allow in her house. Gregor had forgotten how startlingly handsome a man Peter Desarian was. It was not a handsomeness that photographed well. In photographs, Peter looked like just one more prep school boy who wasn't ever going to be able to grow up.

One more prep school boy was all he was, Gregor reminded himself. One more prep school boy was all he was ever going to be. Gregor closed Bennis's front door firmly and walked into the living room, determined to do he wasn't sure what.

Peter Desarian looked up when Gregor came in and smiled. "Gregor," he said. "I was wondering where everybody had gone to. Isn't this Bennis Hannaford's apartment?"

"I live upstairs," Gregor said.

"Donna lives upstairs," Peter said. "God. Everybody lives on top of everybody else around here. How can Donna stand it?"

"The last I heard, Donna was having a fairly good time."

"It's Tommy we have to think about." Peter picked up his coffee cup and took a sip. He made a face and put the cup down again. "You know, before all this happened, I never thought about it. But environment matters. It matters a lot. Environment can make all the difference."

Heredity can make all the difference, Gregor wanted to say. Saying something like this was the intellectual equivalent of saying that grass was green.

"Is there something about Cavanaugh Street you suddenly don't like as an environment for Tommy?" Gregor asked.

Peter Desarian sat up very straight. "I haven't been taking my responsibilities seriously up to now," he said solemnly. "I realize that. I should have been much more careful. But I was very young when, you know, when Donna and I—"

"I know how young you were," Gregor said. "I was living in this building when Tommy was born."

"I was afraid of responsibility," Peter Desarian said. "I admit that now. I was afraid of responsibility. But it never occurred to me that Donna didn't know."

"Didn't know what?"

"Didn't know that it wasn't permanent," Peter said. "Didn't know that I'd come back for her someday. I mean, it was only a matter of time."

"When Donna got pregnant with Tommy, you disappeared. When you were found, you wanted her to have an abortion."

"I was panicking," Peter said. "I haven't said I wasn't panicking."

"So what are you doing now?" Gregor asked. "Donna is just hours away from getting married, and here you are. What do you want?"

Peter looked confused. "I want to stop it, of course. Didn't Donna tell you? I thought she told everyone."

"You want to stop the wedding."

"Yes. Right. Of course."

"Why?"

"Because Donna doesn't love him, that's why," Peter said. "She couldn't possibly. He's a policeman."

"He's a lawyer. He used to be a homicide detective. He is not now, nor has he ever been, Clancy on the beat."

"I don't care," Peter said. "She doesn't love him. And it wouldn't be good for Tommy, growing up with a man like that. After all, Tommy is my son."

"How do you know?"

"Oh, don't be stupid," Peter said. "Donna was a virgin when I met her. I could tell."

It figures, Gregor thought.

Peter stood up. He wasn't wearing pajamas or a robe, just a pair of Ralph Lauren bikini briefs. He seemed to think it was perfectly natural to stand there like that, half naked.

"I have to tell you, Gregor," he said, "I'm not going to sit still and let this happen. Donna doesn't want to marry this man. If she did, nothing could stop her. But I can stop her. And I will."

"For Tommy's sake," Gregor said.

"I've got to get dressed," Peter said. "I've got to go up and talk to Donna. I don't want to leave it to the last minute."

"I wouldn't go up and talk to Donna now," Gregor said. "Her mother's up there. You'll get thrown out."

Peter Desarian broke out in a big grin. "Thanks for the advice. Donna's mother is a gorgon. I'm glad somebody around here can see reason. God, the way Bennis has been going on, you'd think she wanted Donna to marry some low-rent cop and spend the rest of her life making corned beef and cabbage for Wednesday night dinner. What's wrong with you people anyway?"

## 3.

There was nothing wrong with anyone on Cavanaugh Street, Gregor decided ten minutes later, that a little prudent homicide wouldn't cure. After he had left Peter in Bennis's apartment, he had gone up to his own and thrown on some clothes. These were not the clothes he was supposed to wear to the wedding, only a few hours away, but hack-around things he almost never wore, that were easy to put on. They allowed him to get to the street before he would ordinarily have been able to get out of his bedroom. He walked up the sidewalk toward Holy Trinity Church humming softly to himself. In the three days since the arrest of Julianne Corbett, Donna (or somebody) had gone all-out. Now everything in sight was wrapped in white and silver satin. The windows all had bows in them, even his own. The trash cans were concealed under silver plastic bags.

The front of Holy Trinity Armenian Christian Church looked like a big white cake, two inches thick with icing. Gregor passed it by and went around the back through the little courtyard that led to Tibor's apartment. Donna didn't usually bother to decorate back there, except for Christmas. The courtyard couldn't be seen from the street. This time she had wrapped every tree branch in ribbons and even made a big papier-mâché display of candles for the courtyard's unused little birdbath. Tibor didn't fill the birdbath because, as he put it, "I do not like providing appetizers for cats."

Tibor's door opened immediately, as if Tibor had been sitting right behind it, waiting for Gregor to turn up.

"Krekor," Tibor said, ushering him into the realm of darkness and books. "I am glad to see you. It has been a very bad morning. Did Bennis tell you? Peter Desarian is here."

"Bennis told me. I just came from talking to him. He was sleeping in Bennis's apartment."

Tibor frowned. "Bennis didn't do something stupid? To make sure, you understand, that Donna got the point?"

It took Gregor a few moments to understand what Tibor was getting at. Then he blushed. "For goodness sake," he said. "Don't be ridiculous."

"I'm not being ridiculous, Krekor. I know Bennis. I also know Russ. He has been in the church since six o'clock this morning."

"Six o'clock? Why?"

"He says he does not want to be late."

"Oh, boy," Gregor said. He marched into Tibor's living room and threw a stack of books off Tibor's club chair. The stack of books was topped by Kant's *Critique of Pure Reason*, in German. There was another stack of books on the chair, topped with *Diana: The Untold Story*.

"Since when have you been interested in the British royals?" Gregor asked.

"I am interested in fairy-tale weddings. Krekor, please. You must listen to me. We must do something about Peter."

"I know."

"You know? You are giving me no argument?"

"I am giving you no argument," Gregor said. "The man is a first-class bastard. It's about the only thing he's first class at."

"You will take my suggestion, then? You will arrest him?"

"No," Gregor said. "I can't arrest him. I couldn't even arrest Julianne Corbett, and she'd actually done something to be arrested for."

"There is such a thing as a citizen's arrest," Tibor said. "I have seen this on television, Krekor."

"I know. Let me think. We need Bennis."

"Bennis will be glad to help."

"Let me think," Gregor repeated. Out in the courtyard there was the sound of bells. Church bells, Gregor realized, and then it hit him. It was later than he'd thought. It was getting very close to the wedding. He wasn't even dressed.

"Maybe that's a good thing," he said aloud.

"Excuse me, Krekor?"

"Never mind," Gregor said. "Listen. You have to do a few things for me, all right?"

"If I can. I have to get dressed. To officiate. I have to do it soon, because—"

"I know, I know. Now, listen. You give me about five minutes after I leave here. Then you call Donna Moradanyan. Insist on speaking to Donna herself, not her mother."

"Krekor, I do not speak to Donna's mother unless I am required to. Especially not with the wedding as it has gotten so close."

"Okay. So talk to Donna. If you get Bennis herself, tell her to go to my apartment immediately. If you get Donna, tell her to tell Bennis to go to my apartment immediately, and then tell her to meet you here, in your apartment, right away."

"But why?"

"How am I supposed to know why? Make something up. I just want to get her out of Peter's way. She can bring her mother here."

"Thank you very much, Krekor."

"Do you want a wedding to go off in this church today, or what?"

"I want a wedding between Donna and Russell. I do not want a wedding between Donna and Peter."

"You can't have a wedding between Donna and Peter, Tibor. They'd have to have blood tests. It takes two weeks."

"Krekor—"

"Just do what I told you to do," Gregor said. "I'll see you at the church. For the wedding."

## 4.

Less than three minutes later, Bennis Hannaford walked into her own apartment, lit her fourteenth cigarette of the morning, and looked Peter Desarian over like a side of prime beef. He was dressed to look like a male model on the cover of the J. Crew catalogue, and it suited him. As far as anything suited him. Bennis was of the opinion that what she ought to do about the Peter Situation, as it presently stood, was to burn the hell out of his face with one of her cigarettes. That would keep him out of circulation until the plastic surgery had healed.

Peter was not smoking. He didn't smoke. He was afraid it would stain his teeth.

"I hope you haven't come to try to talk me out of it again," he said. "I know your opinion of my position, Bennis, and I don't want to hear it again."

"I haven't come to try to talk you out of it. I came because Donna sent me. She wants to talk to you."

"She does? She's at the church, isn't she? I heard her come downstairs a little while ago. With her mother." Peter made a face.

"Donna's mother is at the church," Bennis said. "Donna is downstairs in old George Tekemanian's apartment. It's like I said. She wants to talk to you."

"Alone," Peter said.

"Why don't you ask her, Peter? I really haven't spent my

time this morning wondering what it is that Donna is going to do about you."

"Really?" Peter asked nastily. "Funny, I'd have thought that was exactly what you'd spent your time wondering about."

"She's downstairs in old George's apartment," Bennis said. "Come or not. Take your pick. In case you haven't been looking at the clock, there isn't very much more time."

"There's all the time in the world," Peter said firmly. "There isn't going to be any wedding."

Bennis walked out of her own living room, across her own foyer, out her own front door. She stood on the second floor landing and listened to the silence above her. Donna was gone. Donna's mother was gone. Donna's father was over at the church, trying to get Russell Donahue to stop pacing. Bennis went down the stairs to old George Tekemanian's apartment. Old George was sitting in the middle of his living room in his yellow wing chair, dressed in white tie and tails and helping Gregor Demarkian on with his black bow tie.

"Well?" Gregor asked.

"I don't know," Bennis said.

"It will be fine," old George said. "You will see."

"I hope it will be fine," Bennis said. "You saw how Donna was. We can't let him get near her."

There was a sound outside on the landing. The three of them looked at one another. Old George got out of his chair faster than he had in twenty years and headed for the bedroom.

"Quick," he said. "Get out of sight. Here he comes."

Old George disappeared into the bedroom. Gregor disappeared into the kitchen. There was a knock on the door, and Bennis Hannaford answered it. She had to take a deep breath to keep herself from screaming.

"Here I am," Peter Desarian said, leaning against the doorjamb. "Where's the lovely Donna?"

"She's in the kitchen."

"Which way is the kitchen?"

Bennis motioned right. The kitchen was mostly dark. There was only one small light burning above the stove. Peter stuck his hands into his fashionably wrinkled jeans and went on in.

Gregor Demarkian was standing just behind the swinging kitchen door, barely breathing. When Peter came through, looking left and right and up and down for a tall blond girl in a wedding dress, Gregor swung out from behind the door, grabbed Peter by the shoulders, and spun him around.

"What the hell?" Peter said.

Peter was younger than Gregor, and stronger, and more athletic, but Gregor had surprise and training on his side. He got Peter pivoted around in front of the open pantry door. Then he raised his foot, planted it on Peter's rear end, and kicked.

"What the *hell*," Peter said again.

When he stumbled forward, he fell. Bennis leapt into the kitchen and slammed the pantry door shut. Then she threw the bolt.

"Goodness," Bennis said. "And old George thought Martin and Angela were so stupid, building him this pantry."

Old George stuck his head through the kitchen door. "It was because Angela was watching PBS," he said. "She saw a program about old people who die of starvation because they imagine that their food is being poisoned. It is impossible to explain to Angela that old age and Alzheimer's disease are not one and the same thing."

Bennis tried the door. "It doesn't feel too solid," she said.

"Let me the hell out of here," Peter said on the other side of the door.

"It will hold as long as it has to," Gregor told Bennis and old George. "Let's get out of here. We have to go to a wedding."

"Your tie is not yet tied," old George Tekemanian said.

"Let me out of here or I'll sue somebody," Peter said. "Goddammit. I mean it. I'll sue somebody."

"He can sue me," old George Tekemanian said. "By the time the case comes to court, I will be so old, I will have all the sympathy vote."

Gregor took a stab at finishing off his bow tie, and ruined the thing altogether.

## 5.

Cavanaugh Street had been blocked off to traffic by order of the Philadelphia Police Department, but it was full of people. Gregor didn't think he had ever seen so many women in pastel silk dresses. Donna's many bridesmaids—there seemed to be hundreds of them, but Gregor knew that wasn't possible— were milling around at the front of the church, waiting to march in. Lida Arkmanian was walking around in a straw cart- wheel hat that Gregor thought ought to have been piled with plastic fruit. It was a beautiful June day, bright and warm with- out being too hot. It would have been terrible if it had turned out to be rainy and wretched the way it was that last afternoon with Julianne Corbett.

Gregor made himself stop thinking about Julianne Cor- bett and went up the church steps into the vestibule. Russ Donahue was waiting there, looking pale. The only good thing to have come out of the Julianne Corbett mess was the way Karla Parrish and Evan Walsh were getting along. A lot more good could come out of this wedding. Gregor put a hand on Russ Donahue's shoulder.

"Relax," he told him. "You'll be fine."

"Have you seen Donna?" Russ asked. "Is she all right? Is she really going to go through with this?"

"Of course she's going to go through with this," Gregor said.

"All week I've been thinking she was on the verge of changing her mind," Russ said. "It's been making me crazy. And here we are. Here I am. You know what I mean."

"We've been here all morning," the young man who was

serving as Russ's best man said. "He got me out of a sound sleep at four. *Four.*"

"Oh, God," Russ groaned. "Who cares what time it was?"

Gregor would have cared what time it was if somebody had woken him up at four o'clock in the morning. He didn't say so. Bennis was running up the church steps into the vestibule, trying to hold the train of her dress high enough up off the ground to keep it from getting dirty.

"They're going to start ringing the last church bells any minute now," she said. "Come, you two. Get up to the front of the church. And, Gregor. Do something about that tie."

"I'm supposed to go up to the front of the church?" Gregor asked.

Bennis shook her head impatiently. "The two of them are. That tie is unraveling or something. I've got to go."

She went. Gregor went too, into the church and the second pew from the front on the bride's side, where old George Tekemanian was already waiting. The church was nearly full. On Russ's side there seemed to be the entire population of the Homicide Division. They all wore the same navy blue suit, like a wedding uniform.

Up at the front, Gregor suddenly spied a glimpse of Donna Moradanyan herself, adjusting her veil. It was impossible to see her face, the veil covered it, but the set of her shoulders was very reassuring: not panicked anymore, not hesitant, not unsure. In the Armenian church the bride and the groom came up the aisle together. Donna would have to go around the church's side or through Tibor's apartment to get where she was supposed to be.

But it was where she was supposed to be, Gregor thought.

And finally, for the first time since the decorating had started for this wedding, he was no longer depressed at the idea of Donna Moradanyan, or anybody else, getting married.

Elizabeth would have loved to be present at a wedding like this.

# About the Author

JANE HADDAM is the author of fourteen Gregor Demarkian Holiday Mysteries. *Not a Creature Was Stirring,* the first in the series, was nominated for both an Anthony and the Mystery Writers of America's Edgar Awards. Other titles in the bestselling series include *A Stillness in Bethlehem, And One to Die On, Bleeding Hearts,* and *Quoth the Raven.* She lives with her two sons in Litchfield County, Connecticut, where she is at work on her next Gregor Demarkian mystery.

# SUE GRAFTON

"*Once again, the finest practitioner of the 'female sleuth' genre is in great form....*"
—Cosmopolitan

"*Ms. Grafton writes a smart story and wraps it up with a wry twist.*"
—The New York Times Book Review

| | | |
|---|---|---|
| ___27991-2 | **"A" IS FOR ALIBI** | $6.99/$8.99 in Canada |
| ___28034-1 | **"B" IS FOR BURGLAR** | $6.99/$8.99 |
| ___28036-8 | **"C" IS FOR CORPSE** | $6.99/$8.99 |
| ___27163-6 | **"D" IS FOR DEADBEAT** | $6.99/$8.99 |
| ___27955-6 | **"E" IS FOR EVIDENCE** | $6.99/$8.99 |
| ___28478-9 | **"F" IS FOR FUGITIVE** | $6.99/$8.99 |

"*The best first-person-singular storytelling in detective novels.*"
—Entertainment Weekly

Ask for these books at your local bookstore or use this page to order.

Please send me the books I have checked above. I am enclosing $_____ (add $2.50 to cover postage and handling). Send check or money order, no cash or C.O.D.'s please.

Name _____

Address _____

City/State/Zip _____

Send order to: Bantam Books, Dept. BD 26, 2451 S. Wolf Rd., Des Plaines, IL 60018
Allow four to six weeks for delivery.
Prices and availability subject to change without notice.          BD 26 9/96

*For everyone who loves Jane Austen...*

# STEPHANIE BARRON'S
## ~ *Jane Austen Mysteries* ~

## Jane and the Unpleasantness at Scargrave Manor

*Being the First Jane Austen Mystery...* Jane is called upon to save the reputation of her friend, the newly wed Isobel Payne, from the scandal looming over the suspicious death of her husband—the Count of Scargrave. ___57593-7 $5.99/$7.99

## Jane and the Man of the Cloth

*Being the Second Jane Austen Mystery...* On a family holiday, Jane investigates a captivating new acquaintance, Mr. Geoffrey Sidmouth. He may be responsible for a recent murder. Worse yet, he may be the notorious criminal known only as "the Reverend."
___57489-2 $5.99/$7.99

## Jane and the Wandering Eye

*Being the Third Jane Austen Mystery...* While on holiday in Bath, Jane alleviates her ennui by shadowing the fugitive Lady Desdemona. But this harmless snooping leads to a grave investigation, when the Lady's brother is alleged a murderer. ___57489-2 $5.99/$7.99